peel. . . As an incorrigibl

human in my deviance. I also worry about time and how it might scar me, unless it's watched closely, taken into my confidence, made love to. Writers of fiction want badly to make metaphors of the lines that time makes in us all.

I think the complicity required to do this is the same for writer and reader alike. We want to see the whole body of what in historical writing must necessarily be limited to a leg up or a shoulder to the wheel. I must sound as if I am impugning historians, Your Honour, but my intention is really to argue the case for the integrity of fiction by analogy. Imagination is the ability to see what we have never seen, by particularizing and generalizing from what we *have* seen, and may only dimly remember. To write successful imaginative literature, I suspect, one must see more vividly with the eyes shut than one ever does with them open. This is why the very best stories possess a dream-like essence, and why the finest novels possess irrefutable memory.

In a way, though not necessarily, the short story mediates—meditates even—between the denser texture of the lyric poem and the attenuated narrative of the novel. It is a meeting ground for another use of language, though not a different kind. This kind of language is moral to its bones in opposing "evil"—defined by Sartre as "the systematic substitution of abstraction for the concrete." I think of the story and novella as spiritually restorative forms, in the way a summer cabin is, where solitude winnows worry, and where the first deep breath puts us in touch again with the natural world. Meanwhile, a house in the city may be filling up with refugees, whose stories demand attention in the novel, with no less urgency, no fewer skeletons.

The windows of the world are innumerable. Which to trust our luck at, which to choose? I became an impostor to see into character, enter worlds not my own, entice others with the illicit I would make moral. But I can only write about home, no matter where I may set my stories. "Here" is the exotic location of every narrative, grounded in those senses. Or so I believe. Home is nowhere but the imagination, a world you finally re-enter, this house my father built with *his* father, crowned with chimney bricks from the old Hotel Vancouver, that year I learned to read, 1950. How can we know anything worth knowing until the anonymous soul of our home meets history? Here, as I imagine, will it still stand as fiction when all the hotels have fallen down.

If the skeleton of fiction is narrative, then fiction's flesh is a complex of nerves, brain cells, muscles, features, and senses. The interdependency of all these is taken for granted until the backbone, say, is dislocated, and the mortality of the human condition becomes increasingly apparent, important. The figures of fiction, both fat and starving, stand in awe of the brooding face of death. The resulting juxtaposition is what transfixes us.

IT MUST BE WONDERFUL. By what in fiction are we redeemed if it isn't the writer's love of life, growing out of his awareness of death? No fiction will be supreme unless it is haunted by Death. This is another way of saying it must be haunted by Time. We do not, as Julian Huxley argues, have memory because we are aware of civilization. We have it because we are always facing death.

Death in many forms. The kind of death affecting us least often is the death of people. Even for Charlotte Brontë, whose brother, sisters, and mother all died off like broom blossom, the fact of human death was only one death among many. She, like us, faced deaths of far less dramatic kinds: the death of holidays, the death of years, the death of seasons, the death of meals, the death

DAMAGES

ALSO BY KEATH FRASER

FICTION

Taking Cover
Foreign Affairs
Popular Anatomy
Telling My Love Lies
13 Ways of Listening to a Stranger
Charity

NON-FICTION

As for Me and My Body: A Memoir of Sinclair Ross
The Voice Gallery: Travels with a Glass Throat

ANTHOLOGIES

Bad Trips
Worst Journeys: The Picador Book of Travel

Damages

KEATH FRASER

SELECTED STORIES
1982–2012

WITH AN INTRODUCTION
BY JOHN METCALF

BIBLIOASIS
WINDSOR, ONTARIO

FIRST EDITION

Library and Archives Canada Cataloguing in Publication

Title: Damages : selected stories, 1982–2012 / Keath Fraser.
Other titles: Short stories. Selections
Names: Fraser, Keath, author.
Description: Series statement: ReSet series
Identifiers: Canadiana (print) 20189044306 | Canadiana (ebook) 20189044314
ISBN 9781771962933 (softcover) | ISBN 9781771962940 (ebook)
Classification: LCC PS8561.R297 A6 2020 | DDC C813/.54—dc23

Edited by John Metcalf
Copy-edited by Allana Amlin
Text and cover designed by Gordon Robertson

Published with the generous assistance of the Canada Council for the Arts, which last year invested $153 million to bring the arts to Canadians throughout the country, and the financial support of the Government of Canada. Biblioasis also acknowledges the support of the Ontario Arts Council (OAC), an agency of the Government of Ontario, which last year funded 1,709 individual artists and 1,078 organizations in 204 communities across Ontario, for a total of $52.1 million, and the contribution of the Government of Ontario through the Ontario Book Publishing Tax Credit and the Ontario Media Development Corporation.

These stories have previously appeared in *Taking Cover* (1982); *Foreign Affairs* (1985); *Popular Anatomy* (1995); *Telling My Love Lies* (1996); *13 Ways of Listening to a Stranger* (2005); *Best Canadian Stories* (2007); *Best Canadian Stories* (2012).

PRINTED AND BOUND IN CANADA

MIX
Paper from
responsible sources
FSC® C004071

He had often wondered what difference it would make.
But the emptiness in place of her was astounding.

– Alice Munro, "Leaving Maverley"

The artist's job, I think, is to be a conduit for mystery. To intuit it, and recognize that the story-germ has some inherent mystery in it, and sort of midwife that mystery into the story in such a way that it isn't damaged in the process, and may even get heightened or refined.

– George Saunders, *The Paris Review*

I assessed the damage. Save for a bit of a mess all was as it was.

– Patti Smith, *Year of the Monkey*

CONTENTS

THE BRIGHTEST
HEAVEN
OF INVENTION

The Oxford Companion to Canadian Literature says of Keath
Fraser:

> He is one of the most gifted of the new generation of
> fiction writers; his startling imagery, rich ideas, tex-
> tured language, and astonishing range of characters are
> remarkable ... 'Foreign Affairs' ... is one of the master-
> pieces of Canadian short fiction ...

Constance Rooke wrote of him in *The Malahat Review*:
"Keath Fraser is one of the most intelligent writers working
in Canada."

Antanas Sileika reviewing in the *Globe and Mail* wrote:
"Fraser's remarkable facility with language and images gives
many of the stories the density of poetry."

Why then, in light of these glowing tributes, is an introduction to his work considered desirable? Simply because
our society has failed to rise to meet his brilliance, failed to
involve itself with his quiddities.

In *The Canadian Short Story* I detailed my first encounter
with Keath, a story he sent me entitled "Le Mal de l'Air," a

submission for the 1982 volume of *Best Canadian Stories;* I spent pages in my book grappling with that story's first paragraph. It was an electrifying encounter.

During a panel discussion at the Wild Writers conference on the short story in Stratford in 2000, Keath said:

> I think writing is an extremely physical activity. Which sounds paradoxical, especially when I, as a writer, have for years envied the plastic arts, the visual arts, the painter who gets his hands dirty with paint, the sculptor who can feel that hammer striking stone. One of the regrets I have for the passing of the typewriter is that I no longer get to get my fingers dirty with the ribbon, the pages that smear you with wet ink. Everything seems now to be one level removed from where it used to be. But having said that, the physicality in writing is really in the concreteness of language.
>
> The thing that inspires us to write is often, I think, a reaction against the kind of language that we're assaulted with daily, the kind of words—the kind of buzz words—that drives us up walls as we watch television and read newspapers. And our desks are the last refuge for us as writers, where we can see how physical and concrete language can be. As writers, we're trying to inspire other people—readers—with examples, with illustrations, of how else language can act, in a way that doesn't have anything to do with the received language or the issues of the day.

I concluded my entry on Keath in *The Canadian Short Story* with an example of "how language can act."

What could I do but love the man who wrote this sentence: "His dinner lay in him like hooves"?

Hooves!

There's a simile to savour.

Keath published *Taking Cover* in 1982. This was followed in 1985 by the magnificent story collection *Foreign Affairs*. In 1995, he published the 582-page novel, *Popular Anatomy* which won the Chapters/*Books in Canada* First Novel Award causing consternation among the assembled booksellers. This was followed by *Telling My Love Lies* (1996) and a Selected Stories, *13 Ways of Listening to a Stranger* (2005).

In non-fiction, he published in 1997 *As for Me and My Body: A Memoir of Sinclair Ross*, followed in 2002 by *The Voice Gallery: Travels with a Glass Throat*. As editor, he published an anthology of travel pieces entitled *Bad Trips* (1991); in England the book was entitled *Worst Journeys*, an amusing example of the differences between North American and British English.

Since *Taking Cover* in 1982, then, he has been in Canada's literary world for nearly forty years, admired ... *this side idolatry* ... by a few of his peers but unknown to Best Seller lists and to the amorphous reading public. That academe has ignored him or, just as likely, has remained unaware of his existence, is no surprise; professors with a dogged interest still in CanLit remain bogged in the late-Victorian orotundities of Robertson Davies while their post-modern juniors, possessed by subfusc and nihilistic theories, cannot hear him as they scourge their betters "interrogating" and "deconstructing" suspect "texts." Their sad fervour conjures *Bartholomew Fair* and Ben Jonson's drab Puritan, Zeal-of-the-Land Busy.

Reticence with Keath is not an eccentricity; his innate reserve in a society sadly unbuttoned has contributed to his muted presence. It is all the more important, then, that we pay close attention to the two passionate and revelatory essays that he did commit, "Becoming Complicit" (first published in *Brick: A Journal of Reviews* No. 40, 1991) and "Notes Toward a Supreme Fiction" (first published in *Canadian Literature* No. 100, 1984). I have cobbled together from both, insights, necessarily abbreviated, into his ways of looking and thinking, into the depths of his feeling.

(The complete essays should be found in *How Stories Mean* edited by Metcalf and Struthers, The Porcupine's Quill.)

When I was growing up I was refused the world by class, religion, and penury. Or so I believed. In what I was encouraged to think a happy childhood, I felt enjoined by loyalty, Catholicism, and debt to make the best of what I had. What I had was a not unperky time, scarred by doubt and a deep yearning to be of the world. I wanted to travel, be loved, afford new shoes. The size and diversity of my family, just as much as its tenderness for outsiders, held little significance in what to me was my narrow and dutiful place. The heresy that imagination was shaped in such contradictions I would have called traitorous. I was certainly safe from the scoop that I might be cultivating an impostor's talents. Like every other child I could fly in my dreams; wish and I could peer down on earth. It was only natural that I read to escape.

Reflecting on how much felt forbidden to me then, I can see how climbing a neighbour's cedar tree and raising my eyes above the power lines must first have tempted me into voyeurism upon the world. I could gaze all the way to the Sea Island airport. Books themselves, my earliest windows, were few, until I discovered the new neighbourhood library. But even this well-lighted place had its moment of denial, when my father seemed on the cusp of having to refuse my admittance, until I could assure him a card would cost only 15 cents. My poor well-meaning father. My poor comprehensive catechism. 'Catholic,' as drummed into children of the fifties, meant 'universal,' and we parroted answers to encompass the world, anatomizing it from every angle judged necessary to defend the fort. Yet fiction was a way of wandering out through the gates into forbidden territory, preferably of a frontier variety, where tents, lean-tos, and longhouses contained even less furniture than we had. This incited my yearning to understand how the past, my city, the larger world could possibly be articulated, in that anatomical sense, to satisfy the child's wonder about everything outside him.

Believe me, everything was outside him. Or so I felt. Magazines, television, lessons, vacations ... I was forbidden to read Dick Tracy in the funnies. I have the feeling yet that the pearly world remains beyond, that a perpetual yearning preys upon my life. It seemed life had prepared me to look at the world with the eyes of someone plagued by an imagination bound in childhood like the feet of a Chinese daughter in pre-revolutionary Nanking. When it began to uncurl, I sensed an invincible need to plant myself firmly upon the earth and, God knows, wander. At university I would sometimes roam the campus at night, peering into buildings, curious about the many paths to the western sea, if only I knew which to choose. It soon dawned that not only would I never know or study what went on in these rooms of that particular faculty, *I would never even enter the building.* This appalled me. How could one learn to live within the limits of one's life, when the frontier instinct, from my grandparents to the first novel I can remember reading with utter absorption, about Pierre Radisson as I entered grade four, had uncovered in me the instinct opposite to limitations, confinement, stricture? The free enterprise of imagination, indeed the entrepreneurial spirit of a family of janitors and carpenters, cabbies and fishermen, shepherds and bus drivers, seemed to disavow the notion of inheriting the earth through doctrinal impoverishment.

I was fortunate in the way I imagine most writers are whose family lives have been too rigorous to turn out well-adjusted members of the body politic. Such an alien body, who could understand it?

In London, where I later went to study for three years, I began to realize that the voyeurism I'd practised as a child was becoming a problem. Now an outsider and foreigner both, still peering into rooms and wondering what went on in these, I began to surmise I was a chronic outsider, either too aloof or too shy to knock and enter the world I was already in. Besides, like a voyeur, I took my pleasure in solitude and imbibed it as I might lady jane (The Stones' drug of choice, and inspiration for that wonderful song of theirs). A mistake if one were preparing, as I was, to offer anatomy lessons to the body politic back home. I'd need to brush up on home, even as I continued to travel farther from my country.

To see ... is the voyeur's first and abiding desire.

I am not suggesting that something like the shape of my family, as recalled in these fragments as accurately as I can, wasn't responsible for my becoming a writer. An articulated quilt may have shape. But we like to know what's under the covers. Ideas are blankets with certain imaginative contours; but imaginative truth requires the voyeurism of wrinkles and those dyed red lines wrapped around flannelette sheets like ribbons. Metaphorical language isn't the blanket language of expository prose. It requires the illicit every line of the way. Absence of the illicit is probably a more accurate reason for my quitting teaching than was any growing up of mine to reject authority out of hand.

I've long had this thing about touching and smelling the world. It's no more possible for me to read a book without habitually raising it to my nose than it would be to make love to my wife without smelling her hair. I set aside the more obvious analogies of roses, roast pork, orange of days, the death of dreams, the death of visits, the death of books, the death of flowers, the death of altruism, the death of smells, the death of enthusiasms, the death of silences. In fiction as in life an awareness of death is the measure of perspective. Maturity is having learned to appreciate the didactic nature of memory. Growing up in Death's brooding face, our imaginations are educated. This leads to compassion. It offers redemption. The more experiences we have, by which I mean simply the more we *notice* of the world, the more deaths we live through. It was patently wrong of Wittgenstein to say death is the experience we do not live through. Auto-biographical (unlike Harlequin) fiction is full of death, death that is lived through, and it's in this way the novelist distinguishes himself from the historian. How to remember what he is looking at is the novelist's obsession. How to look at what he can't remember is the historian's. The perspective we value more, the perspective we *must* value more is the novelist's. His memories are created in the face of their deaths.

In *Taking Cover*, the opening story, included in this volume, was "Roget's Thesaurus," a story imagining Roget's career and told as in his voice at the age of 91.

As the story is brief, I am going to work my way through it, paragraph by paragraph, tussling with its movements and meanings.

I had begun my lists. Mother was always saying, "Peter, why not play outside like other boys?" Her patience with collectors was not prodigal; she didn't understand my obsession. I wanted to polish words like shells, before I let them in. Sometimes I tied on bits of string to watch them sway, bump maybe, like chestnuts. They were treasures these words. I could have eaten them had the idiom not existed, even then, to mean remorse. I loved the way they smelled, their inky scent of coal. Sniffing their penny notebook made me think of fire. (See FERVOUR.)

The story starts, then, with Mother urging him "to play outside like other boys," the capitalized Mother perhaps already suggesting something of what would seem to have been a close but testy relationship. But Peter wants to stay inside capturing words in his penny notebook. He wanted to "polish words like shells"; sometimes he played with words, "tied on bits of string to watch them sway, bump maybe, like chestnuts."

A curious line. First the comparison of words with chestnuts. Fraser is invoking the ravishing rich colours of chestnuts fresh from the spiky case, what Hopkins was to describe as "Fresh-firecoal chestnut-falls" capturing not the colours themselves but rather their glowing intensity. Secondly, and obviously, the line refers to the game of conkers. In this game, the child bores a hole through the chestnut, top to bottom, makes a big knot at one end of an 18-inch length of string onto which the nut is threaded until it sits on the knot. The game is to strike the opponent's conker as hard as possible, turn and turn about, until one of the conkers breaks. The word "conker" is associated with "conquer."

(When I was an evil child in the little world we soaked the conkers in vinegar—why I have no idea now—and then baked them in the oven until they were dull and wrinkled and brutal as cast iron.)

But Peter does not play this game outside with other children; he imagines the words held up in the air where they sway and "bump maybe, like chestnuts." He imagines himself playing conkers with words but shrinks from the physicality of the other children's play.

The words "bump maybe" are awkward rhythmically and suggest the child as rather timid and withdrawn. "They were treasures these words," says the narrator, too precious to smash together. The very word Thesaurus, the dictionary informs us, comes from Greek through Latin, meaning "treasure" and in English, "a treasury."

When he goes on to say he could have "eaten" the words, that he loved their smell, "their inky scent of coal," that sniffing his notebook made him think of fire, it is being suggested that the words have, for him, an almost physical existence.

> I fiddled with sounds and significations. No words could exist even in their thousands, until I made them objects on paper: hairpins, lapis lazuli, teeth, fish hooks, dead bees. . . Later on my study became a museum for the old weapons poets had used. Mother would have died. By then, of course, she had; pleased I had grown up to become what she approved, a doctor.

11

What is being described here is the exact *opposite* of conventional thinking, which is that words are an abstraction, that words are mere noises that betray the *thingness* of the thing described. For Peter "No words could exist . . . until I made them objects on paper: hairpins, lapis lazuli, teeth, fish hooks, dead bees . . ." For Peter these verbal abstractions are abstractions *until he "made them objects on paper"*; even as a child, then, he sees himself as a creator, a maker, an artist. He "fiddled with sounds and significations."

The adult Roget's study "became a museum for the old weapons poets had used." What does Fraser mean by "the old weapons"? Perhaps, simply, old books. Archaic usages? Perhaps "weapons"—the things they fought with—similes and metaphors? The word "weapons" is a curious use and must have purpose within the story. With a quicksilver mind like Keath's, "weapons" may be playing around again with the fight between conkers.

But hold on: didn't T.S. Eliot contend that while immature poets imitate, mature ones steal—this thievery no more dishonest, it seems, than a confident author's homage to his predecessors? In this instance Fraser has pickpocketed a line from the pre-Imagist poet T.E. Hulme: "Prose is a museum, where all the old weapons of poetry are kept." The anachronism here is that the historical Roget died before Hulme was born. Undaunted, Fraser's Roget is a decidedly post-modern narrator.

There is wry humour in the transition from the vernacular of "Mother would have died" to the flat actuality of "By then, of course, she had," a humour that possibly reflects resentment at his having become a doctor to please her.

The death of his mother and his profession as a doctor lead into the next paragraph about the death of his wife. This paragraph seems to me the core of the story.

> My young wife died of tumours the size of apples.
> That I was a practitioner of healing seemed absurd. It
> smothered me like fog, her dying, her breath in the end
> so moist. When *his* wife died my uncle took a razor to
> his throat. (See DESPAIR, see INSANITY, see OMEGA.)
> He died disbelieving in the antidote of language. Oh, my
> wife, I have only words to play with.

I approach anything Keath writes gingerly. As we all should. We must read and re-read and in Seamus Heaney's words we "must not submit to the intellect's eagerness to foreclose … but wait for a music to occur, an image to discover itself …"

(Heaney is using "discover" here in the sense of "reveal.")

The basic question to ask of this paragraph is: what is its *mood?* How is it meant to make us feel? Is Roget dismissing or diminishing the importance to him of her death, he having taken the antidote of language, of words? Or is he mourning her death and saying that fiddling with words, paltry playing, is all that is left to him? Desolate, then, or inoculated against grief? The answer would seem to me to lie, very possibly ambiguously, in the words "apples" and "moist." The yoking of "tumours" and "apples" is peculiar; "apples" summons pleasing associations, suggests his wife's youth, beauty, sweetness. "Apples" increases the horrors of "tumours." And "moist" works on more than one level. On a physical level, we might expect dying breath to be dry and scant. "Moist" seems to summon again the youth and beauty in "apples." Roget's physical (and emotional) closeness to the dying woman is also suggested in "moist"; he is bent over her close enough to feel her breath on his face. "Moist" also links back to "smothering fog," that thick, wet "pea-soup" fog for which London was notorious, a fog so dense that one was unable "to see one's hand in front of one's face," becoming directionless, disoriented.

"That I was a practitioner of healing seemed absurd."

This line, too, suggests emotional devastation. It might also hint at continuing resentment over his Mother's pressuring him into the profession. But the next line, "When *his* wife died my uncle took a razor to his throat," with its prompt that we should consult in his Thesaurus DESPAIR, INSANITY, and OMEGA, might seem rather heartless given the reality, the gore, of his uncle's suicide.

"He died disbelieving in the antidote of language."

"Disbelieving" means "not believing in" but it also means "not having faith in"; Roget implies that he *did* have faith in the antidote, that his faith in language counteracted the despair felt at his wife's death. The address in the vocative to his wife's spirit, however—"Oh, my wife, I have only words to play with"—seems to be saying to her shade that with her death his world has narrowed to trivial word play.

How to deal with what seems to be illogicality? "Apples" and "moist" seem obviously to carry emotion yet "antidote" seems to move in the opposite direction. Unless we see that early emotion as once-felt, but now are reading an old man's reminiscences?

I've often wondered how we'd understand the paragraph had Keath described the size of the tumours differently. Surely, "apples" and "moist" are emotionally load-bearing, "moist" intensified by its "so," the wet sibilancy. How would we read if Keath had described the tumours as being not the size of "apples" but as something else of roughly the same size, say, "the size of tennis balls"?

I remain rather puzzled.

Am I meant to be?

Or could it be "apples" connotes the kind of death he will go on at the end to suggest "refurbishes" him?

Meanwhile:

When I retired it was because of deafness. My passion for travel spent, my sense of duty to the poor used up, I remembered listening for words everywhere. At the Athenaeum, among the dying in Millbank Penitentiary, after concerts, at the Royal Society, during sermons in St. Pancras. I started to consolidate. At last I could describe— not prescribe. After fifty years I concluded synonyms were reductive, did not exist, were only analogous words. Unlike Dr. Johnson I was no poet. My book would be a philosopher's tool, my sobriquet a thesaurus.

This paragraph moves us many years forward. He represents himself as "My passion for travel spent, my sense of duty to the poor used up, I remembered listening for words everywhere," that is, remembered words gathered in the time before he became deaf. His task now would be their organization. How neatly that is put, "At last I could describe—not prescribe." That is to say, he no longer had to write prescriptions for patients, another instance of his dislike of doctoring.

"My passion for travel spent" ... is a deliberate echo of the line in Milton's *Samson Agonistes,* "And calm of mind, all passion spent . . ." Such an allusion, echo, would obviously be in the mind of a lexicographer and so adds texture to this auto-biographical account.

Keath often slips in such allusions. These allusions are often bravura flourishes, part of his exuberant, fizzing invention. There is nothing pretentious, affected, or eru-dite in these allusions and echoes; they are simply with him inevitably and constantly, the loose pocket change of an education in literature. In some stories, however, quotations and allusions are structural. In the story "Flight," for example, the section headed *Father,* his incorporation of quotations and references to Gerard Manley Hopkins' "The Windhover" are extensive and absolutely structural in that as the hot air balloon is blowing off-course and descending, running out of fuel, far out now over the ocean, the old couple in its wicker basket are reliving their lives in memories; as the balloon falls, the references are to the kestrel that rises, soars, and hovers. The quotations and allusions, by implication, set the couple's lives against the life of Christ and against the lives of those whose seemingly dull existence of service is, at its end, revealed as glory.

"Aren't we overdue?" wonders the wife.

"I wonder," says the husband (like Roget, also a retired doctor), "if we *are* heading a bit more off course?"

The Windhover:
to Christ our Lord

I caught this morning morning's minion king-
　　dom of daylight's dauphin, dapple-dawn-drawn Falcon, in his riding
　　Of the rolling level underneath him steady air, and striding
High there, how he rung upon the rein of a wimpling wing
In his ecstasy! then off, off forth on swing,
As a skate's heel sweeps smooth on a bow-bend: the hurl
　　and gliding

Rebuffed the big wind. My heart in hiding
Stirred for a bird,—the achieve of, the mastery of the thing!

Brute beauty and valour and act, oh, air, pride, plume, here
Buckle! AND the fire that breaks from thee then, a billion
Times told lovelier, more dangerous, O my chevalier!

No wonder of it: shéer plód makes plough down sillion
Shine, and blue-bleak embers, ah my dear,
Fall, gall themselves, and gash gold-vermilion.

Go back now into the story and read again in its final pages:

He rebuffs the big wind—
A billion times lovelier—
The mastery of the thing!
… this hot air's brutish
Their hearts in hiding, stirred …
sheer trudging …
When things seemed bleakest
ah my dear, fall

Against Hopkins' linguistically ravishing devotions are set the details of commercial tourism, the corny jokes: "D'you hear the one," asks the sandy-haired gondolier, "about the sailor in the desert who thinks he sees an albatross drinking lion piss?"

The story does not allude to the poem's final line that includes the words "Fall," "gall," and "gash," but those words hover, their absence a presence, a suggestion of the nature of the possible finale.

My contribution was to relationships. I created families out of ideas like Space and Matter and Affections. I grouped words in precisely a thousand ways: reacquainted siblings, introduced cousins, befriended black sheep, mediated

between enemies. I printed place names and organized
a banquet.

London had never seen anything quite like it.
Recalcitrant louts, my words, they scented taxonomy and
grew inebrious. Mother was well out of it.

These paragraphs describe the organization of the Thesaurus
as the discovering, recording, and bringing together of family members. The stress is on Roget's control, his fathering;
he sees himself as a paterfamilias. He imagines that London
(by which he means Fashionable London, Society) had never
seen such an occasion as this gathering-in, this banquet. He
imagines some of his words, the "black sheep" in the family, as
"recalcitrant louts" who have "scented" (suspected, got wind
of) "taxonomy" (classification) and became drunkenly riotous and rebellious. Mother was well out of this quarrelsome
gathering; she wouldn't have regarded it as at all proper.

This imagining of his words as people underlines Roget's
remoteness from actual people.

He is asserting himself in these paragraphs, imagining
himself as an enforcer, an officer perhaps, disciplining the
recruited rabble, a man necessarily hard, the sort of man his
Mother had never seen in him, the boy who didn't want to go
out and play with the other children.

With his Thesaurus he is asserting himself, perhaps essentially for the first time.

She knew me for my polite accomplishments, my papers
on optics, comparative anatomy, the poor, zoology,
human aging, mathematics, the deaf and dumb. I was a
Renaissance man for I chewed what I bit off. Still, I was
no more satisfied with my Bridgewater Treatise on the
design of all natural history than with my report for the
Water Commission on pollution in the Thames. Only
less pessimistic. By the time Asiatic cholera broke out,

and people were vomiting and diarrhoetic, my work
had been forgotten. Not until I fathered my *Thesaurus*
did I dream of prinking. Who knew, perhaps crazy poets
would become Roget's trollops, when they discovered his
interest in truth not eloquence.

Here again Roget reverts to resentment of Mother and his
lifetime's "polite achievements" dutifully carried out in part
to please her, all now forgotten by the public. Interesting,
too, that he comments on the outbreak of Asiatic cholera
against which he was ineffective, just as he had been unable
to cure his wife's tumours. Doctoring, then, had achieved
little. But there is a bass line running through this recital of
setbacks—"I was a Renaissance man . . ."; this music sounds
loudly at the paragraph's end to lead us into the clarion sound
of trumpets in the seventh paragraph. With the publication of
his Thesaurus, which he had "fathered," what a change we see
in the good and heretofore dutiful doctor.

The sexual implications of "fathered" now appear in his
dreams, dreams of "prinking," that is, dressing fashionably,
and consorting with promiscuous poets who would become
his lollipop trollops. (I seem to recall from a journal of hers
the poet Sylvia Plath once actually alluding to her flashier,
younger self as "Roget's trollop," not quite so enamoured
now, by what the hopeful Roget here imagines is to become
her "discovery" of "his interest in truth not eloquence.") The
loveliest touch in this sentence is that Roget for the first time
talks about himself in the third person—usually a sign of
delusions of grandeur as evidenced by what follows.

My book appeared the same year as volumes by Dickens,
Hawthorne, Melville—fabulators, all of us. (See FIC-
TION.) I too dreamed of the unity of man's existence,
and offered a tool for attacking false logic, truisms, jargon, sophism. Though any fretless voice can sing if words

are as precise as notes, men in power often sound discordant. Music isn't accident, nor memory history. Language (like the violin) so long to learn.

That third-person Roget has led us into this paragraph wherein he is claiming to be an artist, the equal of Dickens, Hawthorne, and Melville, "fabulators, all of us." His assertion should probably incline us towards the "delusional" reading in the previous paragraph—except that his belief, as expressed here, in the strength of words used precisely, musically, seems to incline us towards reading his Thesaurus as at least a handbook to the novel, a sort of score for the more famous works.

The words "(like the violin)," emphasized by the brackets, take us back into the story, quite deliberately I'm sure, to the second paragraph, "I fiddled with sounds and significations," and assert once again that what he has achieved isn't "fiddling" but a work of art as demanding as mastery of the violin. This vision of himself is confirmed by "Language . . . so long to learn," as "so long to learn" is another of Keath's quotations, this time from Chaucer's *The Parliament of Fowls*:

> That lyf so short,
> the craft so long to lerne,
> Th'assay so hard, so sharp the conquerynge.

There is no language, I used to say to Mother, like our own. Look how nations that we oppress trust it. It's the bridge we use to bring back silks and spices, tobacco leaves and cinnamon. Yet all one reviewer wrote of my work was it "made eloquence too easy for the lazy and ignorant." Eloquence I have always distrusted. Maybe this is why my *Thesaurus* has gone through twenty-eight editions.

Men are odd animals. I have never felt as at home around *them* as around their words; without these they're monkeys. (see TRUISM.) The other day I was going through my book and it struck me I have more words for Disapprobation than Approbation. Why is this?

Again, Roget reverts to his long-ago struggles with Mother for respect, his suggesting to her that words, far from being playthings, are actually keys to dominion and empire. He mentioned "silks and spices, tobacco leaves and cinnamon," benefits she could easily grasp, to justify his work with words, seeking still to coax from her long-sought approval.

Perhaps his book has more words for Disapprobation than Approbation because he has been coloured by Mother's lifelong disappointment in him. Or perhaps because, for him, "Men" (the word meaning the then-universally understood "Mankind") are sadly marked by simian characteristics?

So I spend my last days at West Malvern in my ninety-first year. I no longer walk in parks. I'm pleased I fear death, it makes me feel younger. Death is a poet's idiom to take the mind off complacency. (see SWAN SONG, see CROSSING THE BAR, see THE GREAT ADVENTURE.) I have never thought of death but that it has refurbished me.

"I'm pleased I fear death," says the ninety-one-year-old Roget, "it makes me feel younger." Makes him feel younger, presumably, by giving greater intensity to the days left to him. The oddest sentence in the story for me is the final one:

"I have never thought of death but that it has refurbished me." What a peculiar word, in this context, is "refurbished." The dictionary gives us as meanings:

       1. brighten up, redecorate
       2. restore, repair

The word is undeniably cheerful. The sentence echoes the earlier sentence about feeling younger and here would seem to mean that the thought of death spurs him on to greater efforts, encourages him to return to the fray but I cannot read the sentence without being looped back immediately and emotionally to:

"Oh, my wife …"

I'm left with the unresolved possibility that the final line calls into question the reliability of much of Roget's account.

Since the 1920s, stories in the modernist mode have reached towards endings beyond the end-mechanisms of plot; they have typically led us towards characters reaching some new understanding of themselves, towards characters moving in the direction of change—the "epiphany" story as we now call them. "Roget's Thesaurus" does not offer the comfort of that now-familiar ending; its ending pushes us back into the story with questions, questions such as—Is Roget quite the person he makes himself out to be? Can we believe everything he says about himself? If we believe in his feeling "refurbished," what were his feelings about his young wife?

"tumours the size of apples"
"her breath in the end so moist"

None of this is resolved. Rather, we are left gnawing on the story… Unless—could it be—somehow the word "apples," as Roget chooses to remember his wife's fatal tumours, serve to refurbish him via an Edenic memory of freshness? "The perspective we value more, the perspective we must value more"—as Keath wrote in his essay "Notes Toward a Supreme Fiction"—"is the novelist's. His memories are created in the face of their deaths."

Roget has indeed "only words to play with." By now one realizes that this infamous yet playful line from *Lolita*, which Roget steals retroactively from Nabokov, belongs to that other unreliable narrator Humbert Humbert, and that in apotheosizing his young wife, the "apple" of his eye, Roget is recalling a memory of loss he can't and does not wish to let go because it continues to refurbish him.

"Roget's Thesaurus" seems to work rather in the way that poems do, revealing more of themselves only as they lose their initial strangeness through repeated readings. The compression of the sentences, the weight that individual words and phrases and allusions carry, should tilt us towards approaching the story as a kind of poem. And meaning? A line of Archibald MacLeish comes to mind: "A poem should not mean but be," and that lovely aphorism of I.A. Richards' hovers: "A poem is an activity, seeking to become itself."

Keath's story acts rather like that for me.

Difficulty and strangeness diminish with the simple passing of time. When T.S. Eliot's *The Waste Land* was published in 1922, it was met by many with bewilderment and derision. One contemporary review described it as the ravings of "a drunken helot," the allusion being to the Spartan practice of making a slave (helot) babbling drunk in front of their sons as an object lesson in the wisdom of watering one's wine.

Nowadays, *The Waste Land*, while not easy to read—and why should it be?—is not seen as so fearsomely strange as it once was. That contemporary reviewer, by the way, was Arthur Waugh, managing director of the prestigious publishing house Chapman and Hall, a flabby old duffer who was intellectually scuppered by surging sentimentality, the father of Evelyn Waugh—who wasn't.

My first encounter with "Roget's Thesaurus" reminded me of my first encounter with Gerard Manley Hopkins, of reading "The Windhover" when I was fifteen.

No wonder of it: sheer plod makes plough down sillion
Shine, and blue-black embers, ah my dear,
Fall, gall themselves, and gash gold-vermillion.

To my young self it might as well have been written in Ugric but Robert Bridges' Notes tell us that sillion means a "furrow" and when we pay attention to the poem's dedication: *To Christ our Lord,* and when we stop connecting "plough" with Massey Harris/Massey Ferguson and *see* and *hear* what Hopkins is describing, the poem starts to become itself.

Not all Keath's stories are as densely packed as "Roget's Thesaurus." Chatting with him years ago, he said that some of the earlier stories in this first book, *Taking Cover,* were so deliberately wrought because he was "trying to make an impression," trying to storm the portals of the literary journals; on my portal he didn't even need to knock.

Most of Keath's stories are actually easy to enter; the voices that tell them draw us swiftly, almost helplessly, into each new world he makes, worlds never abstract, always concrete, intensely realized. The title of an earlier Selected stories, *13 Ways of Listening to a Stranger,* directs us simply *to listen.*

———————

Listen to Rajam, waiter and tennis whizz, as he talks at the opening of "Waiting."

This is a calling like any other, except I was not called. I was not chosen. I was born to it, as some bird to flight. People ask me, what is the secret of waiting? People ask me, do you like waiting? Okay, no one asks me, but I have a mind to tell them. The best service is given on an empty stomach. This is the secret. Hey, I am happy to work up high and have the gratuities of the high rollers. I am pleased to look down over this beautiful city and out to sea where the world comes from. Men on court would lose matches for a chance to wait where I wait. "Rajam," they say to me. "How do you rate a job at Le Soleil Couchant?"

"Give service," I answer. "Superb service."

"Oh, yeah? What's a raghead like you know about a French restaurant, hey?"

They are only teasing, and I thrash them according to my temper. I serve to their backhand and wrong-foot them. It is my laugh then. At the net I cut off their volleys to spite their noses. They pay up. They call me the Sick Sikh and the White Man's Burden, their burden. I laugh. I am the wild Indian with as many arms as Shiva.

"Hey, who's she?"

Stupid, stupid.

"Forest Hills Champ?"

These tennis bums make me laugh. I am lucky to be nimble and vanquish them soundly. I have my dignity and eat it too. Not like my mother and my grandmother in the countryside who pick blueberries all summer and stain their fingers with the blue globes. Their dignity is twenty cents a pound.

"Where's your turban, R.J.? You trash it?"

"I have no turban. I am Hindu."

"Yeah? Well. That's real fine."

They think I am a new-fashioned Sikh who cuts his hair and goes bareheaded.

How subtly Keath suggests Indian-English speech, an occasional omission of articles, awkwardness, a certain pomposity of diction stemming from what now seems to us an old-fashioned vocabulary, English proverbs and sayings not *exactly* understood.

> I was born to it, as some bird to flight.
> I thrash them according to my temper.

… I cut off their volleys to spite their noses.
I am lucky to be nimble and vanquish them soundly.
I have my dignity and eat it too.
I am an erstwhile Hindu.

The whole punctuated by Rajam's repeated mental commentary on the condescending and ignorant insults of his tennis opponents and the vapidities of restaurant critics: stupid, stupid.

Listen to the way we are introduced to the boarding house and its inmates in "13 Ways of Listening to a Stranger."

> *So who CARES if he's a recidivist* says Howard *so long as he respects the TV news hour and isn't responsible for the SMELL in the house.* Howard won't lock his door. He says Kerby's a shoplifter, not a thief.
>
> *What's the diff?* Andrew asks him.
>
> *Lots* says Howard. *Thievery is anti-social.*
>
> *Here comes the whale you guys so can it.* Old Gerry asking for quiet so we can find out more about whales landing dead on beaches in White Rock. Yesterday we got only part of the story and a full twelve seconds of footage. *Lookit* says Gerry. *Goddamn WHALE.*
>
> Around here we're conditioned to lifting words above TV.
>
> Gerry's divorced and a laid-off sawmill worker in his fifties *too one-stroke* he says *to do anything else.* He's never had a holiday, outings hardly. The beach, he confided once, he remembers for a memory of his son as an infant. Gerry was tending him in the sand at a picnic like a small fire in the wind. He cupped his hands around the cheeks, banked up the blankets, he didn't know what all he didn't do to keep his son warm in the ocean breeze. He's the only man I've heard admit nursing mothers aren't the

only ones who feel sexual twinges breast-feeding babies. *Nursing fathers feel it too, bottle-feeding. Boy, I don't want to sound like a PERVERT* said Gerry. *Just a fact. You feel twinges in your organ.* He guessed his son would be somewhere in his twenties now. Could barely remember the little boy. Gerry could hardly veil the sorrow coming back to him from a distance, when he listened.

The mildly looney logic of Howard's opening assertions, old Gerry calling for quiet because the whale is coming on, we can easily imagine this uproar at the supper table as a daily occurrence, the news always on the TV, always being shouted over.

Gerry, a sawmill worker in his fifties, divorced and laid-off, *too one-stroke* he says *to do anything else,* he's never had a holiday, outings hardly. Gerry is swiftly sketched in his speech—"he didn't know what all else he didn't do"—and by his implicitly identifying himself with a simple one-purpose machine—*too one-stroke.* He stands out, however, in his claim that bottle-feeding a baby can cause twinges in one's "organ." Though not old, he's referred to as "Old Gerry" because the other men feel affectionate towards him.

Later in the story, Gerry refers to his son, whom he says he hasn't seen in more than twenty years, an image so strange yet simultaneously so real that we understand from it the depth of his connection with the baby. The image is also strategic as it sets up the story's ending.

Gerry says he remembers Saturday mornings because his son resembled a dolphin. Gerry climbed the stairs to his crib. He'd find his son rocking on his stomach, making little squeals, fat, white-skinned cheeks shining and his mouth turned up in a gummy grin. *He had this bulgy forehead* says Gerry *and this bald head.*

On a rereading, one will probably make a connection between the dolphin and the dead whale on TV.

The play with italics and capitals throughout captures the yelling and uproar of the eight male boarders and is an unconventional and quietly brilliant way of describing scene and character.

Maurice Ringspear's confessional voice pulls us immediately into the story "Healing," a title we understand at story's end to be grotesquely outrageous:

> That summer my countrymen were in the news abroad. A violinist was found nude, gagged, dead at the bottom of an airshaft at the Metropolitan Opera House in New York City. In August, the Playmate of the Year died in a West Los Angeles house when a shotgun blew away her face; she was from the West Coast too. We all were. Even the one-legged cancer victim, the most famous of us, hopping across Canada on an aluminum hinge. Only I survived.
>
> My wife's disappearance revealed in me a stoicism the newspapers mistook for valour until the discovery of her body uncovered my cowardice. Declining to return to Lisbon, I turned down the chance to claim her remains after she was identified by the teeth as belonging to me. I couldn't face the emptiness. In Portugal I became a suspect open to questions and even trial.
>
> To recover from her death I left everything: position, car, house, city: and for the summer decided like a vagabond fruit-picker to migrate to the Interior. The lake here irrigated the desert. My clothes mouldered, my tongue soured, my hair grew. My stomach shrank. I became a fruit-picker.

Maurice fled holiday Portugal because he "couldn't face the emptiness" and because he became a suspect in his wife's death, "open to questions and even trial." The way in which he recounts this matter suggests that he, too, like the two women and the doomed man hopping his way across Canada, is a victim, a victim of Portuguese bumbling and wrong-headedness about his wife's disappearance and the discovery of her teeth and ashes in a plastic garbage bag.

As the story progresses, however, an undertone, an uneasiness builds. We begin to pick up that Maurice (he speaks of dropping his "identity" and of his "alias") is—well, there's something odd about him. Not easy to pin down the way he sees things . . .

We may begin to wonder if the Interior is more psychological than geographic.

"Smaller orchards . . . full of Winnebagos, Play-Mates, Centurions, Aristocrats, all hooked up to plugs and hoses like terminal cases." "Terminal cases," a strange association that flicks us back for a second to the shotgunned Play-Mate of the Year. Maurice's erotic dreams about Sr. Brabanto's daughter, little Maria, whispering to him in the dark . . . "Lick me, you bad doggie . . ."

Maurice brooding: "The right in any culture should be freedom from antagonism in the absence of accusation. Freedom of this sort has its ways. Institutionalized practices to divorce a husband; ritualized plots to get rid of a chief; ceremonial feasts to relieve anxiety . . ."

By what, exactly, is Maurice hagridden?

"Culture," he insists, "is a *tissue* of anxieties."

The insistence on *tissue* seems to conjure flesh rather than fabric and suggests, perhaps, the remains of his dismembered wife.

When I read "wanderings in the desert" and "Iconoclast Mt." there immediately, obviously came to mind Matthew 4: I-II, Jesus' forty days in the desert and his temptation by Satan.

Jesus was taken by the Devil to the top of a high mountain from which he could see "all the kingdoms of the world." He was tempted with dominion over all if he would bow down to Satan.

Maurice, on the other hand, is taken up Iconoclast Mt. by Monica who holds his hand. Jesse looks down on the tiny waterskiers and exclaims, "Holy Smoke . . ." Maurice smells real smoke and ash.

("Ash," significantly.)

There are no one-for-one correspondences with the biblical account but the smell of evil incarnate begins to taint the story's air like a whiff from distant burning.

("Iconoclast Mt." is really a touch too much, the suspicion of Grand Guignol a tad too early introduced. Except, perhaps, it's a caricature stand-in for Anarchist Mt. near the Okanagan town where this story would appear to be set.)

Maurice takes a dislike towards Sr. Brabanto's young daughter Maria, and to her large lab Othello. When Othello pisses on Maurice's pant leg, Maurice "accidentally shifted [his] boot onto Othello's paw." The child kicks Maurice in the shin. Her father reprimands her but she "sidled up until he patted her and said she looked good enough to eat. Spoiled children like that sicken me, frankly. Afterwards, Othello's yelp of pain was a pleasurable memory."

This skirmishing between Maurice and Maria continues; she throws a stick for Othello that "accidentally" hits Maurice, hard, in his ear, deafening him for days. The story unfolds with further antagonisms until the picking season is coming to its end and Maurice plans a farewell dinner for his fellow workers, Monica and Jesse. He tries to keep his preparations secret. "I had to coordinate my attack. . . From conception to execution dinner took a week. Thickening my sauce was really the last and simplest task of all."

Meanwhile Othello has disappeared but is found later tied to a bush in the hills, his jaws taped shut, still alive but flank-savaged by coyotes. Maria, too, seems to have gone missing. Sr. Brabanto drops by the bunkhouse with their paycheques and accepts Maurice's invitation to dine upon what we now will have understood to be his daughter.

On the morning of the following day a Mountie comes enquiring.

"Othello growled at the policeman. Jesse was sure she'd turn up, and Monica patted the father's hand. Sweet Marie. Maria, I mean. We said our farewells."

Sweet Marie being the brand name of a yellow-wrapped chocolate bar.

This tale told by a sociopath must surely be a by-blow of Evelyn Waugh's *Black Mischief* (1932), stemming from the scene where Basil Seal, upon the Emperor Seth's death, delivers the funeral oration at the burning of the body on a huge pyre. This oratory concluded, the feast begins.

> The company split up into groups, each round a cook pot. Basil and Joab sat with the chiefs. They ate flatbread and meat, stewed to a pulp among peppers and aromatic roots. Each dipped into the pot in rotation, plunging with his hands for the best scraps. A bowl of toddy circulated from lap to lap and great drops of sweat broke out on the brows of the mourners.

Later, sitting on the earth and staring into the flames, Basil is startled to see the drunken old man beside him pulling out from his cloth a bright red beret and fixing it on his pate. It was unmistakably his girlfriend Prudence's and he'd seen it last as she'd so recently boarded an emergency aeroplane in the grounds of the British Legation escaping the escalating revolt, destined for Aden.

> "Where did you get it?"

"Pretty hat. It came in the big bird. The white woman wore it."

"But the white woman. Where is she?"

But the headman was lapsing into coma . . .

"Speak, you old fool, Where is the white woman?"

"The white woman? Why, here," he patted his distended paunch.

Both novel and story are delicious verbal inventions and performances. There is probably little need to stress that both are *comic* in spirit and performance.

The story "Bones" opens with Bartlett's breakfast.

> In the wake of war and French colonial cooking, Bartlett's omelette tasted of shell, his butter refused to spread, the milk substitute clotted in his coffee. Nothing dissolved.

The country Bartlett is breakfasting in must be Cambodia and the city he finds himself in must be Phnom Penh. Cambodia was a French protectorate until 1953; hence the omelette. The Khmer Rouge led by Pol Pot took power in 1975. It is generally accepted that the regime murdered about two million people for demented ideological reasons in massive "re-education" programs reminiscent of the Maoist *Great Leap Forward* and the Red Book *Cultural Revolution*. The wearing of spectacles was a death warrant. Among the murdered were 250 thousand Vietnamese residents. The Vietnamese invaded in 1978 defeating the Pol Pot regime.

Bartlett, a chiropractor, attending a Southeast Asian conference on Alternative Healing, has been persuaded by Mr. Strajik of the Red Cross to visit the unnamed city . . . *why not? All expenses paid* . . . for urgent but unexplained reasons. His breakfast is an image that prefigures what is to come; "clotted milk substitute" is bad enough but "clotted" carries the inevitable connotation of "blood." This note is picked up again in the succeeding paragraph with "littered arteries" and with cars that had "lain down" in the streets, as if human, and died and decomposed. Slightly later, Bartlett's group drives to the city's "dead heart."

In other words, there are two currents flowing in the story, one denotative, and one connotative. The first gives us information, "tells us the facts of the story," while the second tells us the same story in imagery, in emotional terms. We should understand this approach to language and construction as essentially poetic; it applies to all Keath's work and to the work of many of the most accomplished writers of short fiction.

(In my book *The Canadian Short Story* I called this connotative current the *underlay* or *shadow-narrative*; it is explored in some detail in the entry on Alice Munro.)

Bartlett's task, it is reported, is to advise on the construction of ossuaries.

The story ends bleakly.

> The white dust of bones left out in the air would start falling years hence over this jungle, this country, this people. But no one would feel it, see it, know it. The dust would be falling over the ruins too. He heard the little spools of his diary dissolving in silence.
> *It'll never sink in anywhere,* he added, killing the mike.
> Against the wooden shutters the rain fell harder.

The "white dust of bones" should return us to the Romanian's "bad moult of dandruff or else psoriasis" at the story's opening, dead white flakes of skin drifting onto Bartlett's flesh; he, too, has been in some way defiled by the white dust, that particular

Cambodian dust a metaphor for a dust universal and diseased. What he calls "*the driven snow of history.*"

History, Bartlett's realizing, teaches no lessons.

He says to his tape-recorded diary, *It'll never sink in anywhere.* The words "sink in" also carry the colloquial sense of "be understood," "be learned." And the word "anywhere" extends beyond Cambodia. Bartlett's recording diary "dissolving into silence" should take us back to his breakfast: "Nothing dissolved."

But all does dissolve and all will.

We can hear the whisper of the tape running spool-to-spool.

"The dust would be falling over the ruins too."

The depths of this elegiac passage deepens if we know that the great civilization represented by Angkor Wat was entirely lost for centuries, was not rediscovered until French archeologists rescued the ruins from the fetid jungle as recently as 1860.

The shadow narrative gives us "killing the mike" and even the hard rain against the wooden shutters, given the context of the story, takes on more than meteorological significance. Indeed, in echoing the magnificent wintry conclusion of Joyce's story "The Dead," the ending of "Bones" returns us to that abiding credo of Keath's to do with the artist's "memories [being] created in the face of their deaths."

If Keath's stories resist you or seem to be leaving you without a compass, take heart from his remarks at the Kingston Conference on the short story in 1986:

> For me pleasure is the ability to "bury" a reader in a story even if we don't understand it at all. Have respect for the mystery. A fiction is more than understanding, it's perception and delight.

Much of my delight in Keath Fraser's work is being ambushed and shot; his sniper's eye is fatal. Few writers are as deadly. His hearing, too, is supranormal, his recording of what he hears and imagines pitch-perfect.

The kettle in the kitchen puckers, whistles, screams.

Who more accurately than Keath Fraser can pin the quotidian architectural ghastliness of "renewal" with the words, "the pink townhouse with brass numbers"!

The afternoon sun is hot. Ash trees are growing out of the garage, the lawn is knee high. A rhododendron has gone berserk, maybe ten years ago, and morning glory snakes through blackberry vines that've suffered the back fence to disappear in their clinging. A cherry tree drapes the whole small yard in shade.

To pretend he doesn't spy on bikinis from the sunroom, he goes outside this Sunday and sits figuring at the swaying picnic table. He's trying to balance numbers and survive. He can still see bare backs through the pickets. They lie in long grass basking, baking, in the fallen seed. Renters proliferate through these houses that landlords decline to keep up, in exchange for moderate rents. But the word is out. *Buzzword.* For in a diminishing world of rented houses, rainforested lots, impoverished tenants, it's this word "renewal" that's become the euphemism for demolition, clear-cutting and eviction. Grass grows in gutters, suites carve up rooms, and pigeons land on roofs as often as pizza flyers on porches. Renewal is no longer an option, but policy. In time their own house will also become the pink townhouse with brass numbers across the alley.

Oh, those bikini girls! Such *fecundity!*

And is the italicized *Buzzword* doing double duty as the sound of chainsaws?

> *... brass numbers!*

And then the Palace Hot Springs Hotel centenary celebration in "Memoir"—at a sort of heritage Harrison Hot Springs—for guests, municipal worthies, celebrities, and ex-employees:

> The dance was earlier tonight. There were six or seven hundred of us, swinging the night away to the Freddy Simms Orchestra, reminiscing among ourselves in swirling figures and seated at tables set up around the ballroom's sprung floor. There were balloons and streamers. There were corsages and boutonnières. There was boogie-woogie. Della wore a blue chiffon semi-formal. We noticed Frank across the room, the centre of attention at a table for the manager of the Palace, two Japanese couples, assorted dignitaries who looked like boiled beets, and Freddy Simms himself, whenever the orchestra took a break and he came off stage for a drink of something in a yellow Thermos.

Nice solid descriptive work, deftly done, cinematic, though nothing startling *until* . . . "assorted dignitaries who looked like boiled beets . . ."

I would give a body part to have written "boiled beets." Or this glimpse of married life in "Le Mal de l'Air":

> His wife, while not turning away from him, had started looking over his shoulder.
>
> Maybe this was normal for any marriage after sixteen years.
>
> Parking the Volvo he stepped out of the garage into a

pile of empty plant pots she'd left on the sidewalk.

Manslaughter was the disease of inattention.

Or this fast, deadly sketch of the Stay-A-While motel and its proprietor, Mr. Delmore, though he's more "owner" than "proprietor." From "Damages":

When I reported the record settlement for negligence against Howard Johnson, in the millions, to Mr. Delmore, he only stared out the window at passing traffic and said lawyers were so many farts in a closet. I think he said ten. He should know, he wrote the book on fustiness. Darkness. Not that litigation has ever threatened Mr. Delmore, he's too wary. I help Mr. Delmore to manage Stay-A-While outside Lacey. We're the last resort for travellers who, because of indifference or just bad timing, are unable to reach the coast before nightfall. They come out of the Interior, over passes, down the Canyon, before making their mistake. Our highway isn't the Trans-Canada but a secondary route down the north bank of the Fraser, veering off at Hope. "Typical," mutters Mr. Delmore. He's been trying to sell out for years. Power lines buzz overhead and remind him of electric chairs.

He's an aging man with gas-station sideburns and a need of blunt pencils. He'd rather go to jail than mark anything, a cheque or crossword puzzles, with a pen. The nearness of an eraser encourages in him the conceit of retraction and the second chance.

"... gas-station sideburns"

Or from "Libretto" these seemingly effortless sentences in satiric mode:

Physical choices had compounded. Coupled to a Walkman you could jog in special shoes; pump your sissy-shorted legs from the bony saddle of a ten-speed racing bike; stand rubberized on a sailboard slicing through the salt chuck. Beaches awaited summer. Volleyballs awaited nets. The sand awaited women who pumped iron and men who'd gone the impressive anabolic route to find themselves a perfect partner in the mirror. Surgery, available for chin tucks, was moving up from California.

I assume the "impressive anabolic route" implies what amounts to chemical castration. I note "*Coupled* to a Walkman"; to what sadness has the sexual world descended.

And as for Keath Fraser's ear, an American tourist in Athens from "Le Mal de l'Air":

From under the Cinzano umbrella in Constitution Square a woman's voice:

"This heat's worse than politics in Chicago. The bad smells make you wonder why we didn't fly right to Crete. No wonder the Caryatids are crumbling. The air's full of plague. Fumes, corrosion. All night it's bee bee beep. Sometimes I just wanna hold up a bank and run away with the loot to Palm Springs permanently. There's no percentage in exotica. This ouzo tastes like iodine."

In "Bones," I admired the deft handling of group-talk, its non sequiturs.

The guide and Mr. Strajik led him up steps and through a lavish vestibule into a ballroom of spectacular sunlight pouring in through open French doors.

Mr. Strajik paused.

"This is where you come in," he said.

Bartlett's eyes adjusted to the ballroom's unnatural brightness and saw one, then three million bones.

Fathoms of bones: hip, thigh, breast, collar, shin, jaw, rib, you name it. The piles seemed indiscriminate.

Mr. Strajik's "This is where you come in," given his stilted English, is mildly ambiguous, possibly meaning, plonkingly, the threshold, or the task Bartlett is to perform. Dazzled in the sunlight, Bartlett sees, I imagine, one bone at his feet, white against the dark teakwood floorboards or parquet, and then, looking up, fathoms of bones.

I'm sure that the DNA of the following dialogue would reveal traces of Evelyn Waugh and the elegant inventions of Ronald Firbank.

> "Me?" said Bartlett. "What is this place?"
>
> "Your advice," said the Swede.
>
> "The Grief House," said the guide.
>
> "Where victims," said Mr. Strajik, "of the government were debased and buried."
>
> "*N'est-ce pas?*" asked Dananga.

It is a kind of perfect Baroque music.

Although Keath has not expressed an opinion, I regard *Foreign Affairs*, the crowning glory of this book, not as a long story but as a novella. Readers often ask how one makes that distinction. There are no rules that make much sense; the *Canadian Oxford Dictionary* offers: "a short novel or narrative story." This definition is both tautologous and flatly wrong. My judgements about literary matters are very much a matter of hefting the thing, feeling its weight, experiencing the scope of it, experiencing the density of its texture, the chew of it. If most novels are supermarket sliced white, then novellas tend to be

DAMAGES

dark German Rye Wholebread, denser than Christmas cake. Novels are nearly always written in prose; novellas tend often to a heightened form of prose which moves forward in images and emotionally charged scenes that are edging towards a kind of poetry. *What* kind of poetry depends, of course, on the author's sensibility.

Obvious examples, *The Heart of Darkness, Death in Venice,* and closer to our time, V.S. Naipaul's shattering *In a Free State.* I'd also venture the heterodox view that Flannery O'Connor's *The Violent Bear It Away* is a novella as are Nathanael West's *Miss Lonelyhearts* and *The Day of the Locust.*

Foreign Affairs isn't difficult to follow in terms of events but its compression and strangeness demand rereadings, demand that we live deeper and deeper inside the confines of the world it creates. Again, Keath employs a poem, structur- ally this time, to parallel his story and prompt us in our experiencing of it. The poem he alludes to is W.H. Auden's "Musée des Beaux Arts." The poem's final lines record our passivity and evasion in the face of suffering, even death, we who have no time to pause or care, having "somewhere to get to."

Musée des Beaux Arts

About suffering they were never wrong,
The Old Masters: how well they understood
Its human position; how it takes place
While someone else is eating or opening a window or just
    walking dully along;
How, when the aged are reverently, passionately waiting
For the miraculous birth, there always must be
Children who did not specially want it to happen, skating
On a pond at the edge of the wood:
They never forgot
That even the dreadful martyrdom must run its course
Anyhow in a corner, some untidy spot

Where the dogs go on with their doggy life and the torturer's
    horse
Scratches its innocent behind on a tree.

In Brueghel's *Icarus,* for instance: how everything turns away
Quite leisurely from the disaster; the ploughman may
Have heard the splash, the forsaken cry,
But for him it was not an important failure; the sun shone
As it had to on the white legs disappearing into the green
Water; and the expensive delicate ship that must have seen
Something amazing, a boy falling out of the sky,
Had somewhere to get to and sailed calmly on.

What follows is the novella's opening page.

He's never wrong about suffering, this ex-diplomat. He
understands its spasms in his muscles and clonus in his
knees. How it can take place, as somebody said, while
you're eating or looking out a window or just dully rolling
along. Every year he has had at least one good attack,
lately two, when he's flat out in bed for months. Fatigue,
tremors, dizziness . . . forgetfulness, jigsaw-puzzle vision,
a tangled tongue. He has long since lost his intimacy,
or so Silas remembers hearing was his wide-open way,
with the far side of earth. Still, he's plotting once more.
Not to rebuild his ruined career, nor to have some say
in the world, but to pack the saddlebag on this chair he's
in and get outside. Eat his lunch rolling along a seaside
promenade, smell the salt, feel voluptuous again. Any
spontaneous remission of his disease (he paws himself
for signs) takes longer and longer every year to recur.
Already June and he hasn't been outside in five months.
Whimpering for it now, his zest come back, he even
dreams himself inside a woman's body, where he hasn't
been in years.

whim   purrrrr   ing   g

"You okay?" she asks.

As Nadine administers to his improving torso, he recalls the P & O ships that don't call this far north anymore, and haven't for years. San Francisco's their limit now.

He says to her, " The da   ay I sailed back from ab   road I could see men on the docks baiting their hoo   ks with shrimp. Pulling in shiners as fast as they threw in their li   ines." Speaking better and more coherently than he has in months, he can afford to reminisce. "W   ho ate these fish, I wondered, the Chin   ese? Were they carted over to Chinatown and peddled up alleys to Chinese re   estaurants where you used to get a ga   ame of mah-jong with the cook, if you happened to be Chinese whi   ich these fellows weren't? Must have been a dozen men, fishing. The market behi   ind was where I once got an apple for a d   ime. Chinese women all over pic   king up broccoli and buying sprouts. For what part icular holiday I had no ide   a."

"Like it when I do this?" asks the frizzy-haired girl.

He looks down at his chest to see what she means. "I don't fe   el a thing."

"You serious?"

"They whee   led me down the gangplank in a cha   air like this one. Only the tires were f   lat."

"How 'bout this, you feel that?"

The second quotation is one of Silas' rare expeditions outside his apartment. Nadine is wheeling him along as he gulps in all the marvellous sights that have been denied him for months. Krish is Silas' dog; both are drooling; there is little sentimentality in Keath's worlds. The intensity of the writing in this passage, each detail magnified in Keath's crosshairs, creates Silas' excitement and joy in this rare exposure to the world's wonders.

These three paragraphs are one of the great pleasures in the body of Canadian writing.

That evening she takes him strolling along English Bay to the bathhouse, where they park to watch the sea festival. His aroused vision of the world dilates. Like Krish he drools. His gaze is determined to covet everything. The filmy blouses of thin-strapped, heavy-breasted girls in white jeans and black heels. Helium balloons shaped like silver salmon tied to the wrists of oriental infants. Bowling pins in the air around a juggler's head. Krish, too, is agog at the drama. The mincing steps of male couples in pressed jeans and white sneakers. Sloops and yawls of drinking revellers anchored offshore in the twilight. An apricot sky turning tomato, and the mountains of Vancouver Island standing up to a pink apocalypse.

Ranks and ranks of bodies are walking in both directions past Silas, as in a film by Satyajit Ray. The traffic has backed up Altamira, all the way over to the harbour. Clumps of cops are searching out rowdy behaviour to deal with swiftly.

Past the bathhouse a rock band sings on a pipe-and-plywood stage. Nadine jerks to the time. Krish howls. World War Two Hurricanes roll acrobatically overhead, trailing smoke, followed by skydivers plummeting through the fruity sky. Who will hear the splash, see the white jump-suited legs disappearing into the green water?

The final page of *Foreign Affairs* defies comment. Except . . . except that it's difficult not to draw attention to Keath's reference to Nell and the pooped-out Silas as a *pietà* . . . that is, as a version of Mary holding the body of her son, the Christ, after it has been taken down from the Cross. The reference, like the reference to the Temptation of Christ in the story

"Healing," is not a one-on-one correspondence but more a suggestion, deliberately nebulous, I feel, but it sounds a resonance...

The story fades out with Silas' failing efforts to speak.

It tickles her to look down fondly at the top of Silas' head in her arms, to spot dandruff in his thinning scalp. This pietà of old Nell and pooped-out Silas. "You never know," she says, "when you might need a friend like old Nell. When you get on, you need more than your own company. Don't you, Silas? Say good night to your old friend, Silas."

                                        goo

                    goo

                                hee

                                he

                                nose

                a thin

                                g   or two

She has him   the shoulders now, big mus   cular Nell
fro   th   prairies dragg   in   him off   to b   lik   e
a   sac   of   whea

Harold Bloom wrote: "... when you read a canonical work for a first time you encounter a stranger, an uncanny startlement rather than a fulfillment of expectations."

Goethe wrote:

All great excellencies in life or art, at its first recognition, brings with it a certain pain arising from the strongly felt inferiority of the spectator; only at a later period, when we take it into our own culture, and appropriate as much of it as our own capacities allow, do we learn to love and esteem it.

In *13 Ways of Listening to a Stranger* Fraser used as an epigraph:

> *The burglar Time tiptoes away with our names.*

With *Damages*, Keath has caught that old tiptoe flat-footed. Unhouseled, disappointed, unaneled, Keath Fraser stands with Alice Munro and Mavis Gallant, one of the grandees of Canadian fiction.

– John Metcalf
Ottawa, 2019

THE ANTHOLOGIST
TAKES A HOLIDAY

N O SOONER had he uttered an oath about roving rich people than he heard Natasha rejoin: "If a man is alone in a forest talking, and no woman hears him, is he still wrong?"

Her response elicited chortles from other work-stations and he noticed above the duckboard maze someone's wrist shoot up in a brief triumphant twirl. He took in the mutinous arm and fine silver chain. His witty intern would soon be gone to another job, to an air-conditioned tower where she knew from fundraising forays that a controlled uptown environment discouraged blustering in the heat. Working in corporate comfort would only ask her to respect stock yield and understand why the windows never needed opening.

Eddy allowed himself another outburst.

"Oh, cork it," said Mrs. Petti. "Who wants coffee? Not you."

He welcomed their resistance. His first rule of organized non-profit stated that elementary zeal suffered without banter in a hot brick building. This from his periodic table of the perks required for toiling in a sweatshop. With no prospect of savings, or even a decent salary, Eddy recognized the need to be part of a droll alliance. After moving on to better jobs, his interns often reported back on missing the repartee in this one. Eddy hoped to keep them prudent while they weighed the alternative of going mildly crazy in real careers. Not Mrs. P., of course, who had run out of options and seemed content to go crazy here ... whether from summer heat or menopausal flare-ups, he couldn't say. The interns he adored for their willingness to sweat, albeit temporarily, for peanuts.

An hour later, not finished with rebuking the rich in a letter to the *Sun*, he paused. His impromptu e-mail meant putting aside an application to an American foundation he and Mark were compiling in support of a grant for apprentices in Uganda. Summer's arrival had left him vulnerable to such asides, to on-line flight specials, even to self-memos bearing eccentric empathies scribbled on a Century 21 pad. *Ask Mrs. P. get in touch Tom condolences.* And ... more recently, *If a woman is alone in a forest talking, and no man hears her, is she still wrong?*

I beg your pardon?

He'd miscopied Natasha's line.

He noticed, rereading it, how the riddle had abruptly lost its humour.

Its reversal caused him to wonder if the more sober line didn't explain a decline of the American "jokers" his dada had sometimes watched on an oval screen the size of a melon. Didn't today's comics deliver niche products to target audiences? Eddy couldn't imagine a joker from his father's era amusing women in a lesbian club for under-30s. He could remember grainy American video of western civ at its showboating zenith, the swanning car fins, before an Arab oil embargo had turned greed post-modern.

You could now outdo your neighbour with a Hybrid.

He wrote out Natasha's original line as some wiseacre probably first spoke it aboard Noah's barge. When she got off the telephone, he asked Mrs. Petti who her favourite comedian was. She paused a moment to wonder aloud whether he was still practising. "The bald fellow," she finally said. "Wrinkles. Riccles. Riccles Somebody. Dick ... no, *Don* Riccles."

"Did he play Las Vegas?"

"He probably roasted the Rat Packers."

"Was he funny?"

She tried to remember. "My husband liked to watch him on *Dean Martin.*"

If a man is alone in a forest talking, and no woman hears him, is he still wrong?

Doodling with his Parker, Eddy noticed he'd implanted hair follicles in the head of the punctuation mark. He could hear this Riccles fellow dispensing his bread-and-butter banter, just as Natasha had, for a laugh. But didn't the laugh depend on which of them was telling the joke—who the butt of it was? Out of Riccles' mouth the bushed man—the late Mr. Petti, say—was a henpecked victim and not, as Natasha dealt him, a bad-mouth like her boss to whom no independent woman ever listened.

No one in this office, anyway.

He popped a breath mint.

. . . Of *course* the man is still wrong: he was wrong before he left home.

In either scenario Eddy conceded that the man in question sounded pathetic. But this was just a convention. For Don Wrinkles the butt is really the woman—the present Mrs. Petti, say—she's the *real* talker, and, at home, an overbearing one. For Natasha the overbearing figure is the man ... well, not exactly: he *used* to be overbearing ... his long-suffering wife has since overcome her domestic deference and persuaded him to go hunting, or maybe golfing, where he's lost his stupid ball in thick timber off the eighth fairway. And now deserves whatever bosky indifference enshrouds him, the dickhead.

Eddy enjoyed the sight of charcoal skin from a leaky pen. He stuck his nib into the pocket-sized fan next to his keyboard. Freezing the plastic propeller made little difference to the small office's general clamminess. Natasha had donated this prank gift a week ago when summer kicked uncharacteristically in and their decrepit space became a Swahili kitchen. Causing her boss to announce: "Ideal weather for CASA interns. Inure the pack of you to field work for years."

"I bet you don't last long after your next jungle trip," said Mrs. Petti, fanning herself with documents. "Some like it hot. Not me."

Having forgotten to make coffee she now decided on tea, a more refreshing drink in tropical weather. Something grassy and organic from a hillside in Kenya. They lacked a fridge, so for milk she dropped small paper udders onto every desk. She didn't appear to notice that no one had yet learned to discharge these without collateral damage to important papers.

Eddy was not unhappy to recognize in his hairy doodle a default habit in himself. He felt sympathy for his fragile stickman; for the woman, too, just outside his frame somewhere in the kitchen. Eddy had come of age feeling sympathy for women in a way his father hadn't. If you *had* reversed Natasha's question and asked, *If a woman is alone in a forest talking, and no man hears her, is she still wrong?* his old-school dada would have chuckled. Wasn't the man always right? Any suggestion of sympathy for a delinquent woman would have mystified him. The notion of a nobler enigma, of a victim, would have stumped him. Dada wouldn't have understood what you meant by the shady presence of a bully.

He re-examined the original line, this time with Riccles asking if his monologuing man is still wrong. Wiseacre answer: this henpecked guy is not only *not* wrong, he's also *free*, now that he has done the right thing in finally leaving home. He's just too shocked to realize it yet.

Eddy capped his pen and unpeeled the nipple on his pouch of milk. He did his best to aim and squeeze, before turning back to his e-mail, standing to wipe the screen dry with his shirt-tail.

Re: "Ultra high-end deluxe vacations on the increase"
July 5:
Am I the only reader who found the subject of your wire item on a soaring demand for luxury tourism rebarbative? Baby boomers spending huge sums on private jet travel, luxury cruise liners, African safaris?

He was answering an odious Bloomberg article, read earlier today in the train.

We are told by a hospitality director in New York that elite vacations suffered a decline after the attacks of 9/11 and the invasion of Iraq. "To spend $3,000, $5,000, $10,000 on travel per day seemed inappropriate to many people."

Really? Well, apparently no longer. These folks now feel free to get out of the house with a clear conscience. In London, another elite travel agency has experienced a 40% jump in revenue with clients scuba diving off Easter Island, sailing around Cape Horn, cavorting at Four Seasons hotels. The empire has struck back and everywhere high-end inns are doubling their profits. A Florida agent claims deluxe travel has returned "with a vengeance."

Vengeance? What is it avenging? The limits on bad taste? The commandment against greed and manifest consumption? No one wants to miss out, but paying $60,000 US to look at African animals must set some kind of record for not seeing the jungle for the trees.

Eddy stopped reading to drink his tea. He then sent the cursor rabbiting down to his file's compost heap to retrieve a paragraph deleted after Natasha's chiding him. And pasted it back:

As the editor of *God Awful Abroad: The Penguin Book of Adventure and Regret* (whose three dozen international correspondents donated all their royalties to the poor in Mozambique), I foresee a new category of wretched travel but not the arduous kind portrayed in that book. Frankly, one is amazed by how many coupon-clippers and their enablers are evidently unashamed to indulge in this growing brand of seedy tourism. Are rich tourists so lacking in awareness (let alone imagination) they only think to spend obscene incomes romping the globe like caffeinated Pekingese?

Yours etc.

Ed Atwal did not include his non-profit affiliation; otherwise he'd have signed off as Edward. He wasn't writing to curry favour with potential donors but to demand on behalf of good citizens a more equitable planet. Less greed etc. More forbearing thrift. An absence of desire, really, to set them free.

On the train this morning Eddy decided the worst journey wasn't one you paid the price of anguish for at the time, but the one whose cost you began to understand only after it was over. Could you still hold up your head? If not, what had you lost? After his profitable moonlighting as importunate editor, he now thought a follow-up volume might take advantage of the theme of guilt.

The welcome wish to live without guilt was the driving force of philanthropy.

Excess ensured the survival of charity.

Emerging from the station, for his walk along Cordova, Edward Atwal found himself introducing in epigrammatic style a select omnibus of CEO-types who, jetting over violet horizons, had finally seen the light, and who their next time abroad had decided to go backpacking for whales or else tithing to combat infanticide. The reader's interest would lie in the force of their epiphanies. He might even float his fundraising idea when invited to lunch again at the Vancouver Club, asking around for contributors willing to confess their debaucheries in print before donning sackcloth in a final paragraph.

Eddy would cheerfully explain to them how such laudable turncoats were already on record, having done their one-eighties after killing off all the bivalve life in whatever fiord their company had once leached chemicals into: after contracting out running-shoe jobs to children's sweat holes in slummy Pakistan: after raking in obscene corporate profits so CEOs like themselves could be handed obscene stock options on their way to a Balinese five-star.

Renunciation, abandonment. Anyone listening? Departure.

Eddy was confident the confessions of company directors could open up a new market for non-profit. He could deploy Natasha, if she stayed, as managing editor of the project, with her growing array of connections in the netherworld of West Hastings. There over mahogany tables Eddy had learned how to banter with the shadiest venture capitalist: "Speaking of the opera, Rab, street people outside the QE are *begging* to get in. They hear the new heroine promises amazing highs." Ingratiating Eddy believed he could make friends with anyone, including the dead. His habit of including people with whom he didn't necessarily agree meant toleration by those willing to forgive his genial outspokenness.

They would ride him, of course, when he showed up in the *Sun*. His letter was about them after all, and who needed the publicity? Still, what were friends for? He called them friends, congenial men from the oak-inlay head offices he'd cultivated over two decades. Their bantering was just part of getting across his own message, quietly suggesting that while socialism might have the lock on public good, capitalism recognized philanthropy was in everyone's best interests. Not much disagreement here from the clubbies, who took this not-so-grim message as a compliment to themselves, especially

Eddy's ancillary concession that nothing much happened in the public arena without the generosity of capital. Smiling, he would then pounce, arguing the standoff between his and their two cultures continued to divide justice from its constituency.

This caused his friends to laugh in relief. He was an unsound commie do-gooder after all. "Ed, amigo. The milk of human blindness has infected you. Have another Heineken."

He would bob and beam, still hoping to solicit them to the cause.

Growing up Eddy to his family, he had always encouraged friends to call him Ed, saving Edward for the strangers who he hoped would soon call him Ed, if only to make it easier for these pending pals to indulge him in what he wanted—which, of course, when it turned up, he inevitably accepted as Eddy.

"We run an escort service," his interns learned. "No element should surprise us."

His own roles varied and with them his ID. Edward petitioned the American foundations and uptown head offices; Ed took care of basic schmoozing at luncheons and cocktail dos; Eddy was left to act as the breezy protege for staff and friends. He enjoyed every performance of himself and devoted his time to speaking, popping olives, bantering. It seemed Edward Atwal was almost as respected as Eddy Atwal was liked—and as middleman Ed was both liked and valued in the same package. This medley ensured an expanding welcome of CASA in assorted circles—concentric circles, since its director played the main role in each. Naturally, his point of view shifted according to whom he was with, unless he found himself alone, in which case, with no one to respond to, he missed his blocking and could no longer sight-read. He was no soliloquist, nor did he wish to be. At home, now that his wife had left him, he spent as little time as he could. Eddy found it hard to relax and be himself there.

The surprise of growing up in a large family, in a mouldering, mother-run house catering to his dada's whims, was that having also spoiled Eddy, making his child's reactions the centre of attention, this home had also managed to impart in him a sense of many rooms. He must have taken his prompt from a lot of relatives drifting in and out of these—eventually marvelling at how one roof could accommodate so many players as needy as he.

Sukki came visiting and placed beside his empty mug a proof for their next newsletter. "The cover shot will be a B & W photo of our well-boring project in Kenya. . . Small Girl, Jug on Noggin."

"I like the simplicity," said Eddy.

"I was trying to remember," said Sukki. "Earth, air, fire, or water . . . I chose water."

"Everybody loves a good drought," said Eddy.

"So you've told us. You should be ashamed of yourself."

Sukki hadn't been especially interested in Africa before she applied to him four months ago, and it was Eddy's genius to have parlayed her love of pop music into her agreeing to accept an internship on condition she be given the modest file on philanthropic rockers who'd agreed to support CASA's non-profit work in Africa.

Well, one of them had.

Sukki was fascinated to learn Geldof had once lived in the city, before she was born here, even before Eddy himself arrived and figured out how non-profit might prove a satisfying career. Africa had been hot for a while—now it was heating up again.

"Did you see the concerts?" she asked.

On the weekend, ten concerts around the world had aired in support of Africa. Sukki's newsletter and donation card were planned to coincide with the fallout of much goodwill and billions in debt relief from G-8 pledges.

"Confess I missed them. Saturday I was here at my desk."

She looked incredulous.

"Well," he said, "I didn't have you groupies pestering me."

These groupies usually played U2 tracks on a boom box at the window. The racket was not much worse than a labouring air-conditioner's, and besides, no non-profit founded on slave labour could expect or demand a serene workplace from entry-level workers. Nor, alas, a similar taste in music. Eddy would slip inside his earbuds, to listen to Ben Heppner sing Tosti; songs like "I should like to die" and "I love you no more" would keep him sane for his remaining days on earth. Bono, he once rashly suggested, could only dream his Italian-sounding name would outlive Tosti's.

His interns snorted at the idea. Mocked his callow innocence. Mimicked his Italian accent when he burst out singing... *Ma che dal sangue mio nasca l'aurora, E dal sogno mio breve il sole eterno!* Did his vibrato ever *suck*. They rubbished every Roman yodeller they could think of including the blind Bocelli. Teddy-boy should think twice before giving up his day job.

Eddy couldn't win. He enjoyed the inbred advantage of forbearance. Less so they, used to the disadvantages of privilege in young, well-educated lives. To be the butt of a joke, without its diminishing him, is what Eddy's charm included. He must have been charming as far back as childhood . . . could remember smiling in schoolyards.

Mrs. P. never smiled, not while wearing earplugs.

When she offered them all refills, Eddy asked if she would remember to look for a sympathy card over the lunch hour. "What?" she said, removing one plug. Tom and Benson's lab Tina had passed on, he explained, letting go her bowels on a worn old carpet after fourteen years, a period of loyalty equivalent to the partnership of his friends.

"Well, I could see them being sad all right. But wouldn't a new rug help?"

"Dogs are the new children, Mrs. Petti. The new grandchildren."

"Why?"

His manager enjoyed reproaching him, and as the only full-paid staff she felt more entitled than the cast of interns to comment on her boss's scattered routine. On most days he seemed all over the map, apparently needing to have his compass balanced. Or, as he could hear Natasha telling him, "Getting you to see the forest for the trees."

This was what the younger woman called him: "you." "D'you know where Tokyo Lounge is?" Once, after starting her job eight months ago, she'd unthinkingly called him "Ted"—then, ever since, a pronoun. His irreducible unit. He did wonder if he would manage to make a friend of Natasha before she decided to leave. She was in love, claimed Mrs. P., who seemed to think Eddy was answerable for this unpredictable state, with all his fancy-fellow connections he had encouraged her to hit on beyond this slum of an office. Eddy guessed a Ricky-Martin type, but possibly a captain in one of the glass towers she might have met on a tub-thumping round for CASA, a sailorly CEO with reassuring gunmetal streaks over tan ears.

This was unfair. Natasha had every right to a real job. He was surprised she was still at this one and could only suppose as a lucid advocate of economic empowerment for sub-Saharan women she'd found a role she still liked here.

Eddy praised her meticulous records of meetings with discretionary cash officers in resource companies, animation studios, computer software hubs, coastal fish farms, even the Stock Exchange. Thanks to big-cheese donors in the States, and possibly the odd generous rock star, CASA enjoyed a reputation interns such as Natasha took advantage of in their pursuit of funding. Eddy had to admit she was his all-time fundraiser, his crackerjack, and could easily have her pick of managerial positions just by wearing smart linen suits. Where did the cash come from for these—family? He thought her father either owned a paper business or else was a high-up socialist. So she was basically biding her time as well as donating it, bestowing wit when it amused her, and as soon as it pleased her, leveraging from an obliging non-profit Edward Atwal, Executive Director, Canada Africa Strategic Aid, his rave letter of recommendation.

———————

Lunching on cheese and crisp bread, the executive director pulled his letter to the newspaper back up—deleting Pekingese for a different breed, subbing "squalid" for "seedy"—then switching "squalid" back to "seedy"—and pressed Send. Afterwards he wondered if "compounding" might have worked better than "caffeinated"...especially with "chows."

He then discussed with Marlene, his newest intern and thus not shy yet of obduracy, her strategy for petitioning CIDA on behalf of a sustainable silviculture project for Ibo mothers outside Enugu. "Go for it!" he urged her. He also wrote his condolences on a sympathy card Mrs. P. found in Gastown; and then proceeded, in case the American institute they were counting on proved averse, to rank other foundations in order of their particular riches available to non-profits like his.

Before leaving to catch the afternoon train, he noticed an arm wearing a silver bracelet place beside him on his desk a manila folder.

"The numbers come in fine," said Mark. "No problem on that score."

The young man had completed his statistical portion of the proposal for their two-year grant in support of training three dozen apprentice electricians in Kampala. He had done a degree in Commerce, and was taking an unforeseen breather with Eddy's non-profit to think about the larger picture abroad, before venturing himself into the larger picture where he hoped to teach business and, incidentally, keep his hair plaited.

He said, "The problem, I think, is our apprentices are supposed to be HIV-infected."

"I forgot about the health component," said Eddy, gazing at the numbers.

"Well, isn't that *why* we're supporting the proposal? The HIV factor?"

"It is. Yes. Indeed."

"Totally," said Mark.

Eddy decided he would have to refine the narrative portion of their sponsorship request, in order to implant more guilt inside this foundation, cherry-picked for the HIV application because it had been established on coffee plantation money from East Africa. He quickly scribbled himself a memo to get to work on *their chance to lead productive lives, during any evolving resistance to antiretroviral therapy*—

Mark interrupted.

"The problem, I guess, is we need to talk about a flaw in our African partner's proposal. With hundreds of potential apprentices desperate for an education, you could argue staff 'll be flooded with applications from people just *claiming* to be HIV-positive. I bet most applicants won't know if they are or not. That's one dilemma. But if we ask our partnering NGO to require a certificate of proof-positive, from each candidate, that could lead to a black market in forgeries. Don't forgeries cost money? And so we end up with forged certificates, from poor people who can't afford them in the first place, claiming a disability that may or may not exist. Where do we draw the line? Do we want to draw a line? And what does it mean, by the way, to call a training program for people with HIV 'self-sustaining'? Is the eligibility for participation ill-conceived?"

Eddy listened. Sometimes, like now, he felt naive. Too trusting and therefore complacent, he could only think to poke the fan until its waspish little propeller jammed and finally expired. And then he told this young man with the chic bracelet that he was, in no uncertain terms, an unwelcome bloody analyst with sodding developmental genius and an infinite capacity for close discrimination.

Eddy promised to get to work right away on a narrative proposal that spoke frankly, and he hoped persuasively, to doubts they were now having about the thrust of their original intention.

"Now get lost."

Mark grinned, quite pleased with himself.

Eddy missed his train.

Each morning that week, and into the next, he parked his Echo to board the West Coast Express and claim his usual seat beside Micki Something-berg, an oncologist's receptionist at St. Paul's with whom he chatted, although he barely knew her. He checked up on the progress of his letter in the *Sun*. There was no progress. After a week, when no letter had appeared, he realized the world was not going to hear from adventure-and-regret anthologist Ed Atwal; worldly events had drowned out his rant.

Within hours of bombs exploding in the London Underground, the letter columns filled up with other cries for justice. Among these, in the interest of local balance, were printed the ongoing howls over unscooped pet mess in the city's on-leash parks. The coverage of free-range pets reminded Eddy of skirmishes fought in the commons and on the beaches of the West End, by Tom and Benson. His friends' support of Tina's rights had been fierce and tender. To Eddy, the world seemed increasingly divided between right and wrong at a time when it was growing more difficult to distinguish between the just and the aggrieved. This facile deduction made him feel better.

An inlet appeared beyond the alder copses, before it widened under the bridge and the silent engine pulled them west past grain silos, cranes and cargo containers, Angel-dockers escaping graveyard, and onward to shoebox ferry traffic shuffling through the chopless harbour.

A gull kept up easily with the coach.

The Sleeping Beauty appeared in the slanting sun out of deep divisive ravines. He loved how sun could complicate the world, floating up from the night.

The only person to have read his letter was Eddy's wife. It was characteristically loyal of her to have offered him feedback after his e-mailing it to her:

> Ted–: The international Rotarians still mention you as the on-going force behind their proud centre for amputees in Luanda. You might have got <u>that</u> into your squib, which is nevertheless most effective as it stands. I deal with these industrial tycoons all the time via MRI / PET scanners and other big tickets... Their holidays to the unimaginable go unmentioned by me, and quite understandably by them. Love, Brat

Her job was selling expensive machinery to provincial health authorities here and in Alberta. An executive Rotarian, she enjoyed giving back to others, and to Eddy, dividends from her estimable attainments. She and he had done nothing to interfere with the legal nature of their marriage, retaining the same address while living in separate residences. He'd continued on at the acreage in Pitt Meadows when she moved into her condo in Port Moody. Both properties belonged to Brat, although she allowed Ed to cover taxes on the land in exchange for living there. In return, he allowed her to keep claiming him against her income tax, his low non-profit income designed not to discourage donors, matching grants from CIDA, or interns. Without equity of his own, naturally, Eddy couldn't afford to sell out and move into town. Lost on acreage, he couldn't wait to catch the train every morning.

Couldn't wait to disembark downtown and head east with the sun in his eyes. He had died, after all, and come to work. The sun blotted him up. These streets had nothing in common with fields he'd left floating in mist over an hour earlier. No smells of the natural world could make him feel so not alone as city smells. The oily plume of a berthing cruise ship, hydrant water on old cobblestone, hopper-roasted coffee beans cheaply afloat in the morning air, leftover traces of last night's fried cod, faint grass pollen of Victory Square commemorating the wrongful dead.

A tramp in the alley was administering intravenously to an exposed arm.

Entering his office, via an Edwardian pile, Eddy departed the sunlight for two northern windows overlooking the tracks and a fractional view of mountains from the fourth floor.

He paused. "Oh!"

The presence of someone sitting at her desk startled him. "*You're* early! You … all right?" She looked … different.

"I came straight from clubbing," she said. "I decided to beat the heat and leave early today. If," she added, "I don't fall asleep." Wearing something like a leopard-skin dress, not her usual blouse and skirt, she lacked a firewall. Having ramped up the vamp factor last night, for her evening on the town, she now acted like her appeal had faded in the tired dawn. The performance didn't work. Something about it appealed to the offstage Ted.

"Good thinking," he said, hoping to encourage her spontaneous initiative.

"I think," she said, "therefore I am single."

He couldn't tell if she was mocking herself. Or, somehow, him.

It was seven a.m.

Natasha arose and moved to the window, which she proceeded to open, lifting it by hooking her forefingers into the frame's ancient tabs and jimmying ropes and pulleys.

"Yourself," she asked, struggling. "When are you leaving?"

"Me?" Was it silk, her dress? It moved less soberly than linen, clinging to her curvy rear. "Per usual, I guess, when the cows come home. Sometimes I miss the last train and have to bus back to paradise."

"Next week, I mean."

He paused a moment. "Mrs. P. will remind me. I think Thursday." He added: "I've started my malaria pills."

"Are the fans coming, before you go?"

Eddy had forgotten the fans, not feeling humidity as others did, and thought they must be due any day. Mrs. P. had ordered a pair of windmills the size of sunflowers and these promised, she said, to lighten dispositions.

Natasha excused herself and wandered past the frosted door into the hallway. They shared a water closet with the Art of Dying people next door. Awaiting conversion to lofts, probably in the not far-off future, the building remained a godsend to Eddy's budget. His landlord was donating back in return for a tax receipt the rent he charged CASA for its poky space. Eddy was the only tenant to receive such a rebate, and didn't know where they would relocate when the plug was pulled. He couldn't afford to stay downtown unless Natasha, on his instructions, happened to hear of a developer willing to give them a new home in exchange for rezoning concessions from City Hall.

His hope was to become the NGO equivalent of more acceptable non-profits such as theatres or low-cost dance studios benefiting from subsidized footage and decent washrooms. His thinking was always novel.

For instance, after Brat left him, Eddy refused to sweep the plank floor under his desk. This was not difficult to arrange, as the building enjoyed no janitorial service and no intern would consider stooping to pick up a broom. No danger Mrs. Petti would either. He checked periodically beneath his sandals. Accumulated dust bunnies now approximated the same number his wife would need to dispatch from under the table in her new kitchen, not having Ted around any longer to do jobs she hated. He supposed she now dined out on her way home from the dry cleaner's.

Eddy thought of himself as a New Man, but at 43 his interns considered him a museum piece. He had two decades on them, and several worlds, and while they professed to share his infatuation with this old structure and its bullet-nicked beam above their desks, its history of selling dogsleds downstairs to wannabe Klondikers, he was not deceived. He recognized their sense of time, like Africa's, had more to do with having survived the last bad drought—in their case, having gone a month before entertaining their next big career plan. Life was clearly ahead, one reason they found Africa so interesting, the expectancy of so many poor souls having already used up most of their own time on earth.

He wished he could afford to take each along on a monitoring trip, for them to see how important his or her contribution was to CASA. Eddy was scheduled to look at bore-wells in the Kenyan countryside, and to hand over a cheque to the project manager in Nairobi. Then he was flying to Kampala to sort out the apprentice electricians' program, afterwards to Dar for preliminary talks about treating tuberculosis in Tanzania, on the expectation of an endowment Natasha still hoped to wrestle from a major Canadian bank.

He heard the toilet flush down the hall.

Then she came back, sat down, and barefooted her chair around the duckboard into his cubicle. Sleeplessness seemed not to have creased her youthful skin, not around the eyes. But the voice felt smaller. Sleepy, or troubled, he couldn't tell. She had brought along their Tanzanian file and alluded to the bank's response.

"They said no yesterday. I didn't tell you."

"Ah, well. You're used to rejection by now."

She studied his short-sleeve cotton shirt. She was near enough for him to smell the early sun, the warming city, in her hair. He noticed how big it was, her hair, still piled in evening style with pale tendrils tangled at her neck. Or had these uncoiled at dawn?

He said, "We haven't promised anything in Dar. We'll turn up another sponsor. Have you tried Carotene Resources?"

Natasha rested her head in her palm and looked sideways into his eyes. "Getting money out of those folks would be like trying to fuck a bulldog."

Of course, he looked at her. Surprised. Her whisper was unmistakably empathetic, but, unless she had a headache, he had no idea who her empathy might include. Or what the change in tone had signalled. Not humour. She wasn't trying to mock him. Formerly, he hadn't noticed the diffidence, the whiff of inexperience, or was it consternation?

She then said, "You are an extraordinarily patient man."

She *was* mocking him. Her tone of inflated intimacy.

"Natasha!" he exclaimed. He hoped to exude forbearance, but also stamina, in case she happened to be right about his extraordinary patience.

Self-conscious, he began to prattle. It wasn't long before he was feeling a little like the man in her joke. He asked, apropos of nothing but his place in the forest, "You ever heard of The Ink Spots?" Eddy's father had once made a fuss of this group, listening to their black vinyl records on a crank-up gramophone when the electricity went spotty in the heat.

He supposed it was a way of keeping her amused until the other interns showed up.

"I wouldn't say no to toast," said Natasha.

"That café on Carrall never closes."

"No, your songwriter."

He had to think. "Tosti?"

She sighed. "I've been listening all night to Asian fusion. My limbs have left me." She dropped the arm propping her head, and straightened her shoulders. The forbearing tone made it sound as if she had left behind, overnight, her youth ... every element she once held bracing.

Whether she would still be here when he returned from Africa, or whether her funky bank remark was really her exit line, a campy reminder that she required a very personal letter of recommendation, he gained no inkling. Her tenure was informally up next week. He hadn't even discussed with her his over-the-top plot for another fundraising anthology, something he now regretted, as it might have amused her to hang on for another term soliciting company bosses for shamefaced contributions.

Eddy's own contribution to the anthology was unforeseen.

A month on, after boarding the catamaran back to the coast, he thought over his sun-struck week on the island. *I become vulgar woman. We should never met. Don't remember me with evil, Ted. You leave soon. But I have you in heart for long time.*

Her musical voice had enamoured him the more. And now traces of her shampoo set free from the fabric of Eddy's shirt in the gathering salt-shot breeze. Plus this envelope with its clovish scent, a letter she'd bid him carry unopened until sailing into Dar. He held it to his nose, sealed.

Stone Town began to recede under the calm island sky. A green Indian Ocean whitened furiously with the sudden roar, then lift, of the flagpole stern. Soon he would disembark back in Dar and in the morning fly home, sad, but with a restored sense of an offstage role to bounce off in the uncertain year ahead.

Maybe. First he would have to account big-time to Mrs. Petti for an unplanned week in Zanzibar, for having paid a large premium on his rescheduled flight back to Canada, and for having charged up a pile of shameful debt to CASA. If donors found out, his monitoring trip could become a minor scandal.

He would accept a smaller salary. Credit was redeemable.

Eddy hadn't dreamed of coming to Zanzibar as his father had, who'd long wished as a younger man to visit but never made it down from Mombassa. This abiding desire to escape offshore had followed dada into senility.

Onshore, after landing in Nairobi two weeks ago, Eddy had struggled with a severe bout of nostalgia. Of loneliness, really, from too much countryside in the absence of cities, and in the cities from too much timidity induced by the common threat of muggers. He felt timid.

In order to compose his reports on the thirsty, ill and dispossessed he preferred somewhere safer, saner, than Dar. He required more perspective to keep alive the grand but unmarketable truth of injustice. Figures, too, helped sell the illusion of the equity possible abroad. His donors needed to hear that for the cost of a cashew nut at the Vancouver Club, a pair of flip-flops worn as thin as lettuce wraps always returned more than its money's worth against the arid soil of Africa.

When he first saw Anna, a small dog was tracking her along the seafront. Eddy felt similarly attracted—perhaps to her detachment, or else to her air of hesitation. Later when he saw her walk by again in a long-sleeved T-shirt, flaunting a Disney mouse, he dropped his pen and headed down from his room. He removed his earbuds, before politely commenting to her outside in the sun about—well . . . he *loved* the sun, didn't she? . . . listen, he was just on his way to the dining room, did she feel like joining him for lunch while he rattled on about the native songs of Tosti?

Words, especially solicitous words, came easily to Eddy. Already feeling less alone, he felt more himself. He felt generous.

"From where he come your zinger? Tanzania?"

She sounded east European.

"Ortona."

"Never heard it."

"In Italy?"

He learned she was not staying at the Tembo, but at some other hotel away from the ocean. She was helping her husband collect Swahili folksongs. "Kodály guy," she said sweetly. "Good Hungarian." Her husband had yet to arrive on the island. She seemed uncertain where he was, but told Eddy she did not expect him for a week.

"I hope not arrive till after. I need some bad time to my own."

Her locution educed a frank and humorous response from Eddy about his own need for some bad time. She nodded, unsmiling. Nevertheless, he introduced himself as Ted. Her name was Anna Dridirits. Her trip had been the last minute.

After lunch at a table in the Bahari room they walked together through the streets of Old Stone Town. She was happy he carried a map because she usually got lost just searching for paw paws.

The streets enclosed and included them in unplanned confusion. Eddy was no longer feeling homesick. He even managed to find the cathedral whose steeple he'd glimpsed from the harbour on disembarkation.

"You holy?" she asked.

No, but he had been a cradle Christian and liked reading stones in the floor of any large church. They entered this one and Anna crossed herself with water. The nave reminded Eddy of St. Paul's, in Calcutta, where his pubescent soprano voice had lasted longer than those of other boys, and his father had called him an Ink Spot. Had Anna ever heard an Ink Spot sing? No, she did not think. So Eddy chatted to her about the lead tenor with a voice like a castrato's.

She snorted, covering her mouth. She whispered at the altar, "I not know. Is same with making some bass guy zing, what you would say, falsetto?"

"Totally." She sounded a bit like Don Wrinkles.

"Ted," she said. "In English is one letter from 'Dead.'"

"It is. Yes. Indeed."

She was keeping him on his toes.

"You a married?"

He told her it was difficult to say. "Let's continue this outside."

She took his bare arm. She kept her own arms encased in sleeves and Eddy believed it was to protect her skin from the African sun.

He talked inconsequentially at first, about hydrocarbons and crumbling stonewalls, the lichen on weathered mosques, about a rundown mansion similar to one he used to threaten with his father's Bunsen burner—and then about his arranged marriage.

Neither he nor Bharati had objected when they were her age, he told Anna, to their parents' wishes.

"No kidding?" Amazed, she hoisted her sunglasses. "I do check," she warned.

He must have passed inspection, because she squeezed his arm. Eddy sensed he had become exotic, a prince in a fairy tale deserving undivided attention. He told her that he and this young woman, his bride, soon realized her dowry might facilitate immigration abroad. They could both go abroad. He rashly promised to replace what the servants had performed in her parents' house …

"Washing?" asked Anna.

"And dust bunnies."

"Your babies?"

No, no children, said Eddy. Brat had blossomed as an engineer, and he was proud of her. He and she were surprised at how unconventional abroad they turned out to be. Maybe too unconventional. He evoked for Anna the acreage where he now lived, alone, a nightmare of sod and brambles.

He also evoked his dream for Africa.

She asked if he'd seen Live 8. She'd watched in Hungary last month on a rabbit ear. "Without some words."

Eddy told her he had cable at the Tembo, and if she agreed to come back and stay with him she could watch weather in the Arctic. "Your country is snow?" she asked. And so he loitered while she collected her bag from a small hotel she was too ashamed to show him, and could hardly find again in a back street.

Late that night she whispered shyly, "I become vulgar woman. We should never met." Only serving to convince Eddy they were right to have met, and they watched the weather from Dakar to Christchurch. Uncertainty, the angularity of her posture, was a large positive in Anna's favour.

The humidity soaked them, in spite of a whirling punkah. It didn't bother Eddy, this humidity, reminding him of home.

In the morning she asked, "You know if swim water has clean?" Charmed, he watched her change into a bikini beneath her mouse and head down to the pool.

That day he hired a driver and car to take them south on a spice tour, to visit plantations and Persian baths, then Jozani Forest. They followed a nature trail searching trees for the red colobus monkey. Their guide confided to them about the presence here of the leopard: *it is not true* he said. *No other guide would tell them this truth.* Eddy happened to turn and glimpse Anna, standing alone, beautiful without some words. He thought of whispering grass in an Ink Spot song, not telling its secret to the trees.

She had blonde hair, underneath which he suspected a colour closer to gypsy chestnut to match her eyes. He learned the cloves in her hands would keep him healthy, if he did a wolf thing with them.

"Wolf them down?"

"Yup. Wolf them."

It wasn't banter, exactly. She was too earnest. She borrowed aromatic properties to convey a more complex character than she seemed to possess.

They returned to Stone Town and moved to an even more exclusive hotel on the seafront. The Serena promised to put them in the lap dance of luxury she said. Eddy did not know how she knew about the larger rooms, the air-con, or the better pool. She worked the mini bar, the channel hopper, the hair dryer, and wrapped herself in yards of mosquito netting like a market slave at Christmas. She ordered room service.

She wore the silver-studded sandals he had bought her at a stall.

He awoke in the morning to hear her trying out a song, but when he looked at the sheet music over their breakfast in bed he saw only an Italian glam mag.

From what Eddy could piece together, it seemed she and her husband had visited the Balkan states, even Turkey, hoping for a UNESCO grant. Looking for ways to bump up their collection of rural rhythms, to mingle European and African folksongs in a crossover CD like Paul Simon's ...

"Paul I love. 'Diamonds on Soles of Feet.'"

"'Shoes,' I think. I used to hear it sung several times a day."

On this third morning she suggested they try northwards. So Eddy hired another car. They found themselves lunching on seafood at a small but pricey beach resort, and here, instead of returning to Stone Town for the night, they decided to stay on in order to visit turtles tomorrow and watch local boatmen build dhows.

Eddy found he was now paying for two concurrent hotels; and a waiting car he couldn't figure out how to get rid of without forfeiting their ride back to town.

And then he paid for Anna's scuba lessons.

He might never get back to composing his reports of the less fortunate world.

A day later she asked him to charter a dhow and sail her to a tiny island off Zanzibar, where she dove down with her instructor to the most beautiful coral reef in the world.

Out of his depth, probably also his head, Eddy, or was it Ted now, began to feel he was losing something like his freedom in succumbing to desire. In less than a week he found himself in hock for two or three million Tanzanian shillings—five- or six-thousand dollars' worth of these flashy bills charged to his credit card at the official rate of exchange.

His new friend repeated how she did not wish to fall in love because she was unworthy for this. Instead, she listed in him all the good stuff she would vote for to keep him on the island: his diet hips, his sunshining words, his friendness to her, how he listened. *And he let her boss him.* Plus, she said. He looked too young to be a real boss, more like Euro zinger from France. She forgot the best. She liked him in helping the poor people. She was a poor people. She and Karl had to crush their euros. "Pinch them?" said Eddy. All of which, for Anna, was why this blow-the-mind week would always be in her memory as the saddest one.

He must hate her, she said, hopping to the Sky channel.

Opening up further, she claimed her bad feeling arose from playing the fields when both were married to the other people.

This surprised Eddy, who wondered about her bad feeling even while he found its illicitness captivating. She wouldn't allow him to remove her T-shirt, but did let him use his slim-jim hands underneath and all over—however he wanted to do it. Neither would she allow him to remove her silver-studded sandals, as these went with the slave net.

He felt they had become complicit in the way lovers do. If she remained doubtful, he was doing his best to allay her fear by remaining up-front, assuring her he hadn't had intimate relations since before diseases were launched to tickle the Pharaohs. She smiled weakly, and still asked him sometimes to wear the safe.

He told her he would always remember the way she allowed him to enclose and *be* enclosed. It was a role he didn't find a lot of chances to play these days. Such admissions did not entirely purge her bad feeling.

"Don't remember me with evil, Ted. You leave soon. But I have you in heart for long time."

Te ne ricordi ancor? Te ne ricordi ancor?

Listening to Tosti, letting the sun blot him up aboard the flying catamaran, Eddy remembered nothing of his birth in Kenya. His parents had returned home to India when he was two. East Africa soon reverted to a mythical place for his father, driven out he claimed by the avarice of lawyers, back to his maternal Bengali family. Eddy seemed to have inherited, as just another unfortunate area of the continent to heed, the local geography of his birth, after immigrating himself into the North American Diaspora in pursuit of a chemist's career that he later renounced for the do-gooder's.

With the low-slung harbour of Dar now in view, the craft cut its hydrofoils and their lift off the sea settled rapidly along with Tanzania's black-striped flag. Eddy reduced the volume in his earbuds. He removed Anna's letter from his shirt pocket, the scent of cloves filling his nostrils as he unsealed it. It was written on letterhead from the Serena Inn. *Hi Ted* spoke the childish hand:

> You in my hart alot.
>
> I might have pick up –, how do say in English, blood thing from going so much with Karl in loud places. Better do check. I do check. I feel better since one test at Napples.
>
> I said lie when Karl is husband. We only travel for companions. And to some countries for maybe CD album.
>
> Better do check. Do me Hotmail. You all ways in my hart.
>
> Anna

I beg your pardon? He tried rereading the lines.

Oily rainbows were dissolving in their small bow wake, and for a moment Eddy forgot what port he'd entered. His geographical sense had fractured, gone back to school, mutated. For a guy seldom surprised by corporate johns, he was not a little shaken to read in her letter how he'd become eligible for his own intended record of confessions and disavowals.

Had he?

Jesus Christ.

She had somehow managed to include him within an even larger copy of the unfortunate world than his own. And you, Edward Atwal, didn't have a clue.

He hadn't any idea.

I had no glimmering.

We didn't, any of us, understand at all.

Ted insisted on sharing his naive blunder with his other non-profit selves. Was he standing in the right spot?

He looked out past the mooring lines, beyond Dar, to the vast hinterland where for decades he had heard the cry of Africa, a sound he soon realized he had never really understood. Eddy supposed his heart was no island anymore, cut off from this expanse, but now a continent joined to it.

This facile deduction made him feel better.

He looked down again at the letter. He would e-mail his test results to her promptly, but noticed she'd neglected to include her Hotmail.

A familiar babble of hawking voices arose from the tar-smelling dock.

If he wished it to be, his future was predictable. Why not?

Once home he might learn that Sukki, expecting to renew her internship, had taken a job in Calgary doing voice-overs for oil.

Natasha, to his surprise, could well have decided to stick with non-profit a while longer and make herself available for more plunder of the corporate sector.

And so preparing to disembark, trying to look on the bright side, Eddy smiled.

Just thirteen killed on the entire Tanzanian coast in last December's tsunami. Off Somalia's coast, reports since spring had lessened of pirate hijackings and bungled seizures.

He could still imagine leaving Africa a better place.

Eddy turned the volume of his vibrato louder for the unshakeable consolation of the great tenor's voice. The gang-plank rattled, but he did not hear it.

ROGET'S THESAURUS

HAD BEGUN my lists. Mother was always saying, "Peter, why not play outside like other boys?" Her patience with collectors was not prodigal; she didn't understand my obsession. I wanted to polish words like shells, before I let them in. Sometimes I tied on bits of string to watch them sway, bump maybe, like chestnuts. They were treasures these words. I could have eaten them had the idiom not existed, even then, to mean remorse. I loved the way they smelled, their inky scent of coal. Sniffing their penny notebook made me think of fire. (See FERVOUR.)

I fiddled with sounds and significations. No words could exist even in their thousands, until I made them objects on paper: hairpins, lapis lazuli, teeth, fish hooks, dead bees... Later on my study became a museum for the old weapons poets had used. Mother would have died. By then, of course, she had; pleased I had grown up to become what she approved, a doctor.

My young wife died of tumours the size of apples. That I was a practitioner of healing seemed absurd. It smothered me like fog, her dying, her breath in the end so moist. When *his* wife died my uncle took a razor to his throat. (See DESPAIR, see INSANITY, see OMEGA.) He died disbelieving in the antidote of language. Oh, my wife, I have only words to play with.

When I retired it was because of deafness. My passion for travel spent, my sense of duty to the poor used up, I remembered listening for words everywhere. At the Athenaeum, among the dying in Millbank Penitentiary, after concerts, at the Royal Society, during sermons in St. Pancras. I started to consolidate. At last I could describe—not prescribe. After fifty years I concluded synonyms were reductive, did not exist, were only analogous words. Unlike Dr. Johnson I was no poet. My book would be a philosopher's tool, my sobriquet a thesaurus.

My contribution was to relationships. I created families out of ideas like Space and Matter and Affections. I grouped words in precisely a thousand ways: reacquainted siblings, introduced cousins, befriended black sheep, mediated between enemies. I printed place names and organized a banquet.

London had never seen anything quite like it. Recalcitrant louts, my words, they scented taxonomy and grew inebrious. Mother was well out of it.

She knew me for my polite accomplishments, my papers on optics, comparative anatomy, the poor, zoology, human aging, mathematics, the deaf and dumb. I was a Renaissance man for I chewed what I bit off. Still, I was no more satisfied with my Bridgewater Treatise on the design of all natural history than with my report for the Water Commission on pollution in the Thames. Only less pessimistic. By the time Asiatic cholera broke out, and people were vomiting and diarrhoetic, my work had been forgotten. Not until I fathered my *Thesaurus* did I dream of prinking. Who knew, perhaps crazy poets would become Roget's trollops, when they discovered his interest in truth not eloquence.

My book appeared the same year as volumes by Dickens, Hawthorne, Melville—fabulators, all of us. (See FICTION.) I too dreamed of the unity of man's existence, and offered a tool for attacking false logic, truisms, jargon, sophism. Though any fretless voice can sing if words are as precise as notes, men in power often sound discordant. Music isn't accident, nor memory history. Language (like the violin) so long to learn.

There is no language, I used to say to Mother, like our own. Look how nations that we oppress trust it. It's the bridge we use to bring back silks and spices, tobacco leaves and cinnamon. Yet all one reviewer wrote of my work was it "made eloquence too easy for the lazy and ignorant." Eloquence I have always distrusted. Maybe this is why my *Thesaurus* has gone through twenty-eight editions.

Men are odd animals. I have never felt as at home around *them* as around their words; without these they're monkeys. (See TRUISM.) The other day I was going through my book and it struck me I have more words for Disapprobation than Approbation. Why is this?

So I spend my last days at West Malvern in my ninety-first year. I no longer walk in parks. I'm pleased I fear death, it makes me feel younger. Death is a poet's idiom to take the mind off complacency. (See SWAN SONG, see CROSSING THE BAR, see THE GREAT ADVENTURE.) I have never thought of death but that it has refurbished me.

BONES

*Telling myself things in the dark because the light's
rationed. And at home I worry after a storm if I have to
reset an electric clock? We're all grateful about landing.
The Belgian said an Ilyushin doesn't land, it gropes
for earth like a shipwrecked sailor. This place really is
something else. In the morning for sure I want a bath.*

N THE WAKE of war and French colonial cooking, Bartlett's
omelette tasted of shell, his butter refused to spread, the
milk substitute clotted in his coffee. Nothing dissolved.

After breakfast a soldier led away the terse Swiss adviser
and this left their party at five, not counting the pretty guide
who welcomed each of them with a handshake into the black
limousine.

"Good morning, Dr. Bartlett."

Her holster rode high like a Mountie's under the right
breast of her uniform. Asian, her breasts tripped demurely in
bondage of their own.

"Just Bartlett, Miss. We all set?"

If you asked her to disco he bet she'd find out what it was
and come back ready to shoot you for the frivolous invitation.

Something voyeuristic about his own profession made him feel slightly exposed here, like standing at a London Drugs' scanner with the name and price of his last purchase frozen above in bright green light—Sheik Condom—while the cashier takes her time wiping down the last litre of Ivory Snow, spilled and unwanted by other shoppers, with a bottle of Windex and a rag.

He still thought of the world in terms of home.

Along littered arteries of the capital no other traffic flowed and the passengers sat peering into deserted streets. Grass had taken over: grew in potholes, out of sidewalks, along curbs. Cars had lain down in the middle of roads and rusted through. Locks and shutters of shops bore the spreading rust of more than one monsoon season. Their limo's unexpected appearance startled a tattered trespasser into hiding down a side street. The Malaysian grunted. In response to the Romanian adviser, the pretty guide assured her the citizens would be permitted to return to their city soon. Rockets or angry elephants appeared to have gnawed away at entire buildings.

"Mortar eggs," explained the guide in an alien locution.

The Romanian looked fifty and sensitive over a bad moult of dandruff or else psoriasis she kept ruffling from her blazer onto Bartlett's bare arms. He tried coughing to blow it off.

His arms had a flush of winter tan. A golden beach, bar girls, the fragrant frangipani nights. Agreeing to come here, cutting short his stay in Pattaya—Bartlett now wondered if his elevator went all the way to the top.

Walls around suburban mansions mouldered under lichen, not a stray dog could be seen. No one's woof or word broke the serenity until far out on the decaying highway a roadblock suddenly loomed. "Trouble?" asked the Belgian. Soldiers stood around a cordoned-off patch of the cratered road. An armoured truck was the first vehicle they had encountered since Jeeps at the airport.

Mr. Strajik, the lanky Swede, spoke to the Malaysian first, who stepped out of the car with the Swedish official clapping his shoulder and returning his black suitcase. This Malaysian adviser they left behind in gesticulating conference with an officer.

Two decades ago their limousine was fit for a prince. Today it bumped and swayed with the grinding of age and a will to be liked. Bartlett put it down to shot shocks. He enjoyed the wily movement of this lover past her prime, a fine perversity. The air conditioner rattled on loyally, stubbornly, trying to be cool. For January the sun was getting hot.

The Belgian, who spoke excellent English, was telling everyone about his infant daughter. "I like the way my wife can plunk her in front of an old Shirley Temple movie and be certain sooner or later the little actress will belt forth a song that nips crankiness in the whaa!" Like Mr. Strajik he was a man used to addressing himself to the spaces between people. He knew about travelling.

The village on stilts they came to next looked lifeless and its rice fields parched. Dusty bicycles stood abandoned, not a hen clucked.

"I will see you later, please?" chirped the Romanian, opening her door reluctantly.

"Right," said Bartlett, unfolding his arms. He smiled warmly. "Break a leg."

"No, never," she replied, misunderstanding.

After introducing her to several peasants, emaciated and fervent, who emerged from a shed to shake her hand, Mr. Strajik climbed back into his jump seat. He gave the woman his thumbs-up sign but she was busy nodding attentively at her welcomers.

A secondary route of even worse surface led through scrubby jungle and in time to a bombed-out bridge. At the riverbank was a little camp of huts and an old woman turning a pig on a spit. It was the Belgian's turn. Mr. Strajik introduced him to a grim-looking soldier carrying large scrolls under either arm and a weariness that gave him a stoop. The Belgian walked him down to the river as he might a child whose walking stride was not his own. He listened carefully, thoughtfully, as the guide translated a summary of the project to hand—or something just as brief.

Alone now with his host and the pretty guide, Bartlett watched Mr. Strajik spread his elongated limbs out on an empty seat as the driver turned the limousine around. Over the decades the leather seats had cracked into dried-up tributaries with the wear and rub of privileged backs.

"Dananga and I were going to drop you in the countryside," said Mr. Strajik in his Swedish lilt. "Maybe, you know, to break in slowly?" Bartlett, curious about his role, knew nothing. He felt thirsty. "But she insists priority is in the capital. So we are returning you to the city."

"Okay by me," said Bartlett. He relaxed, getting used to this escort service, wondering if Dananga was as unassailable as she appeared.

They re-entered the capital, moving with black purposefulness to its dead heart, where the driver turned down a boulevard of large shade trees and stopped before a grand house—it looked to Bartlett like a reclaimed embassy.

The guide and Mr. Strajik led him up steps and through a lavish vestibule into a ballroom of spectacular sunlight pouring in through open French doors.

Mr. Strajik paused.

"This is where you come in," he said.

Bartlett's eyes adjusted to the ballroom's unnatural brightness and saw one, then three million bones.

Fathoms of bones: hip, thigh, breast, collar, shin, jaw, rib, you name it. The piles seemed indiscriminate.

"Me?" said Bartlett. "What is this place?"

"Your advice," said the Swede.

"The Grief House," said the guide.

"Where victims," said Mr. Strajik, "of the government were debased and buried."

"*N'est-ce pas?*" asked Dananga.

She introduced a civilian she called the curator, a short man with intense eyes in a moon face. She spoke French to him, moving her hands like budgies in distress. He might have been Bartlett's age, in his early thirties.

"He hopes you will show his workers all about skeletons," said Mr. Strajik.

"How to rebuild them," suggested Dananga.

"Where to begin," said Mr. Strajik.

They were constructing, it turned out, a bone repository.

Bartlett was floored. There were thousands: thousands of shattered skeletons, it looked, hundreds of thousands of bones.

"Listen," he said. "I'm a chiropractor, okay?"

Mr. Strajik studied his hot face closely. "Yes, exactly." To Bartlett he seemed to be saying, in a very concerned way, "You don't play ball, I'll close down your bingo hall."

Workers with wheelbarrows were circling in through the French doors with more and more bones. Their soiled booty already covered the dance floor. Women with rags were wiping earth from these bones in a slow, dispirited way. Flies buzzed them, buzzed the remains. The gardens outside had been heaved up by relentless digging and implacable fatigue.

"Imagine," said the Swede, "if these neighbours"—he nodded in Dananga's direction—"had not made their invasion and driven out the thugs …"

But Bartlett was having trouble imagining what he was looking at.

The pretty invader said to him, "The survivors of the Grief House wish to commemorate the Holocaust."

Mr. Strajik, wiping a hand through his thinning hair, glanced at his watch. "Our Swiss banker at the exchequer will be wondering, yes?" He touched Bartlett's arm, politely. "You will excuse me, Dr. Day. I must see if he has all the records he requires? Thank you."

"Hey," piped Bartlett. "What am I *doing* here? What am I *supposed* to be doing?"

Dananga pointed. "Follow, please."

She threaded a little path among the bones to a huge dining table around which the curator had gathered half a dozen assistants. "Please," she smiled, touching the table. "A lesson."

There were bones all over the once-gleaming surface. *Who'd eaten here?* he said later to his diary. *Who'd danced?*

"Listen," said Bartlett. "I manipulate backs."

"Politics," Dananga prodded him, a little curtly, "is only medicine, I think, on the big scale?"

In Bangkok, when Mr. Strajik had introduced himself at the International Congress of Alternative Healing, he'd said nothing of bones. "It was the way you handled yourself, yes? I felt I should come and talk to you."

Bartlett had beamed.

Mr. Strajik was with the International Committee of the Red Cross, though reluctant to mention that particular organization "at this congress," he'd said, his gaunt face smiling slyly. That evening over dinner he had asked Bartlett to delay his flight home in order to assist him with "something of a nightmare." Nightmare? Had invited him to a needy country, all expenses paid, a small delegation.

"What country?" asked Bartlett, painting his *gai yang* with a sharp Thai sauce. He was still all pumped up with the success of his lecture. "Sir?"

"It's a secret," replied Mr. Strajik.

Bartlett chuckled. "A secret?"

"Singapore. That's the first stop."

"That's south a ways."

"There we will meet up with the others at Raffles and wait for the Aeroflot flight."

"That's Russian," said Bartlett. When he swallowed, the chicken caught fire.

His new acquaintance said, "Unfortunately, no one else is allowed to fly there."

Bartlett drank off a glass of water. "I'm no politico, okay?"

"You won't get us into trouble then."

"Trouble's a possibility?"

"You're a man taken by history—I could tell that listening to you this morning. This is a chance to bear witness." He leaned across the table. "Dislocation?" He was reminding Bartlett of his speech to the congress. "Doesn't dislocation *require* adjustment?"

Unimpressed, Bartlett had quoted Strajik's compliment in his diary that night. Then added, giving in to the revolving little spools in a fit of enthusiasm, *Hey I should consider it. I should just take off.* He could cut short his scheduled holiday in Pattycakes—however you pronounced it.

Dananga translated the moon-faced curator's question into English.

"He wishes, Doctor, that you show how to know bones and what bones to lay out to tell the awful stories of this mass grave."

"Hey, listen," said Bartlett.

"On the floor," she said. "In the fields."

"I'm sorry. What?"

"You will please show these workers how to cope." She spoke smartly. "The driver will return for you in due time."

With this she retreated across the bony reach of femur and clavicle, radius and tibia and sternum, phalange, humerus, metacarpal, fibula. Rafts of bones. Bones by the ton.

Bartlett gazed at the table where someone had placed a skull in the middle as though to confirm that every skeleton required one. He wondered if bone assemblage qualified for foreign aid in Ottawa. The shovels seemed to have set asunder every bone they aspired to raise.

After a while he said to the curator, "Listen." He was trying to sound sensible. "I don't see any vertebrae here. Get me some vertebrae. All I see is ribs."

But the museum workers only stared at Bartlett Day's white coat.

"I don't believe this," he said. Turning, he heard a loud snap and discovered, looking down, his saddle shoe mashing a shoulder blade.

"Hey, listen," he exclaimed. "Where's Dananga?"

Their pretty translator appeared to have vanished in Mr. Strajik's jump seat.

———————

Perhaps it was his bluff way of complaining only about the workers and not also the grave that made Bartlett's news more shocking to his fellow advisers. His seeming lack of anxiety when he told his story impressed them. They set down their forks, their reserve, and self-importance.

Comparing notes over dinner in their empty hotel, they were lamenting the bridges down, mines planted, farms in ruin, currency worthless and—after Bartlett spoke—the bones interred.

A time of interregnum, pleaded Mr. Strajik. They must all please contribute what they could to national reconstruction. There were villages and towns to visit. To dally was immoral.

Mr. Strajik was a guy with both oars in the water.

Of course they now realized what country he'd brought them to, descending by turbo-prop over pagodas and temples, ushered by an alien guide into an empty city. The rumours were confirmed. The tragic little nation was still out of bounds to international correspondents—its fate only suspected—and Bartlett refrained from mentioning the country's name in his diary in case their hosts, the invaders, should resent his blabbing and confiscate the recorder.

Instead he mumbled quietly, *The driven snow of history...*
The water had come back on, he was lying in a dark tepid bath trying to soak away slime from his hands and body. In Bangkok, like a beggar, the humidity had at least stayed outside. The Kingdom Hotel was barely a memory.

"'Coordination is the principle of harmonious action of all parts of an organism, in fulfilling their offices and purposes...'"

Announcing this mothball text for his Bangkok speech, he'd patted his plastic skeleton on her backside, moving right into a joke by pretending his voice was hers, complaining about her spine.

"True," he'd told his audience. "Maybe you haven't heard about bipeds like ourselves, whose vertebrae were supposed to be flat, but whose brains tempted them to stand up on two legs instead of four. Right, so today our joints suffer. Our pelvic floors aren't what they used to be. Neither is anything else. Arteries bulge, sinuses clog. We get rickets and the runs, fallen arches and flat feet. That kind of stress isn't natural, it saps our energy. All because our brains told Mother Nature to buzz off."

He was warming up the conference to his profession although pedigree was not a trait particularly valued among alternative healers. There were holists from Cairo, nutritionists from Buenos Aires, hypnotists from Marseilles and Perth, psychic surgeons and herbalists from Shanghai—God, body therapists from Bombay, biofeedback practitioners from Singapore and Cologne, naturopaths and iridologists out of Dacca, Kuala Lumpur and Atlantic City, all kinds of Indonesian and Burmese reflexologists, plus Rolfers from Melbourne and a trichologist from Rhodes. Every country had its specialists. In one thing alone were they all united. They resented the worldwide clique of the drug and medical profession, with its germ-centred theory of disease.

"Know what I mean?" Bartlett had asked them from the podium. He sipped water from a glass. The conference room was large and panelled in expensive-looking tropical wood along the top of which ran, in a hidden runnel, diffuse golden light. "Whenever it's a matter of deep pain I work hand in hand with Mother Nature. That's why I'm a chiropractor and not some vivisecting doctor. Out to restore the natural balance." He looked at his audience. "Like you. One of you comes into my office, say. I ask you when was the last time you had a spinal examination? You could have a dislocated spine and not know it. Razor back, for instance. A deviation of the thoracic verte-brae, some sort of structural disturbance, short leg, for exam-ple, or spasms in the shoulder girdle. You should make a date with me if you've been doing any improper lifting. Any bumps, jars. You might've slipped a disc, I'd tell you, and be wondering what the pain in your backside is. Know what I mean?"

Ever practical he'd rattled Bea his skeleton out of her sleep. "Sometimes I just grab hold wherever I can. Right off the bat, by whatever hold I know. Bilateral transverse, the million-dollar roll, the shunt. If we had time, I could show you a full nelson, a knee chest drop, even a lower sacral thust."

Bartlett raised an eyebrow and it got a laugh.

"In case anybody's skeptical, ask the Workers' Compensa-tion Boards. I'm paid to get loggers and longshoremen back on the job. Ask the old ladies who come in, the athletes, the shoppers, I'm hand in glove with the whole population. Pop singers, cartoonists, boxers. Ask them."

Leaving home seemed to have loosened his instinctive rein on fabrication there. Reality was just different when you travelled: What your nose detected in the air determined what you could get away with. Entering other people's houses you tested the air as a matter of course. *You never do this entering your own house. It seems the same with countries.*

Entering the ornate ballroom next morning, Bartlett met a man cautiously plastering the wall with unsmiling photographs of men, women, sometimes children, posed before the same black curtain. Prisoners who had been processed and tortured in the Grief House—whose bones, said Dananga, Bartlett already knew. He stared at this luxation of time, breathing shallowly in his dirty white coat.

At the table the curator and his assistants awaited them mutely for the lugubrious lesson to commence.

In order not to feel queasy, Bartlett decided he would have to move, act, and be aggressive. Hollow in his eardrums he could detect the deep, repetitive sound elephants make with their teeth eating hay.

"Right," he said cheerfully. "Today we've got wire. Yesterday we named bones. Today we'll dangle this composite rascal from the chandelier. We'll wire her together."

Dananga's translation puzzled his clients. Answering, the little curator sounded self-righteous.

"They think you are making light of the dead," explained Dananga, deadpan.

"Pardon? Oh the chandelier, it's just a place to start, you know, to hang the specimen?" Bartlett was eager to please. To straighten up their stooping postures, charm, get a bearing on his situation.

He had a situation on his hands, no question. And he was thirsty.

Without a drill to thread an exact space between bones—ribs, for example—he set about wiring together yesterday's remains, lashing joint roughly to joint and sockets into place. Two and a half hours later he was ready, after tethering pelvis to torso, torso to eye orbits, to raise Rosemary to the chandelier and see if this makeshift method of knotting wire around bones could be used to suspend other approximations of skeletons in a similar manner. What did they want in this grief pit, boneracks on a thousand hooks? Stiff articulations for the sake of visitors? Bartlett asked his assistants to bear Rosemary—but on second thought he dropped his habit of naming every skeleton he met and referred simply to "the victim"—to bear the victim by table into the centre of the ballroom.

The curator walked on bones in his haste to clear a way wide enough through their tide. The case history lurched a bit in passage.

Bartlett studied as it moved this work of his upon a bier.

"Listen," he finally muttered. "It's buckshee."

"Please?" inquired Dananga.

He ran one end of copper through the cavity of the absent nose, stepping daintily, for a plump man, onto the table to loop the rest through a crook in the chandelier. Warning the others back, he proceeded slowly to raise the victim off the table, skull followed by bones in more or less correct sequence like a toy train with dangling boxcars, until what tarsal and metatarsal bones they'd managed to find left the table, and Bartlett stood there in a hangman's muffled pride, the wire cutting into his palms with the collective weight of who knew how many victims' bones.

"Look upon me," said the skeleton, protesting its hybrid composition. He pulled the wires.

Bartlett pulled the wires.

The curator and assistants applauded dutifully, as though saluting the winner of an Olympic contest whose flag they didn't recognize.

In the midst of this ceremony, misfortune struck. Somewhere in his construction a knot slipped, causing the victim to collapse with a rat-a-tat-tat on the table, leaving a few bones still hanging from the chandelier like fractured concrete at a demolition site. The squatting women with their rags glanced up at the racket.

"This is definitely dumb," he said, standing at attention on the table.

The wheelbarrow men, too, were watching the show. But the curator and his assistants chose to stare at their feet rather than embarrass a foreign expert.

"This really is definitely dumb!" repeated Bartlett with feeling. Throwing up his hands, he released the final remains and the skull plunged to the table, gouging the mahogany. It thudded like a cigar box.

"Jesus," he exclaimed. "The idea stank in the first place." He felt preposterous. A tubby Canadian in a lab coat jumping off his platform, a quack.

Dananga commiserated, but without much sympathy. She seemed to think his lack of persistence pretty childish.

Bartlett tramped up the curling rococo staircase to the second floor. From the balcony outside, a barren flagpole slanted towards the boulevard. He stood out here wanting water. Turning abruptly, he travelled through the vast colonial mansion, Dananga following him room to room pointing out where inquisition and torture had gone on. "*Murder,*" she stressed.

Trying to recall home he couldn't get through.

She indicated iron cots where corpses had lain abandoned by the retreating murderers as brute evidence of their genocide. Of their tragedy. Used for eliciting confessions, electric wires dangled from ceilings. Leg chains hung from springless bedsteads. She tried to shock him with shreds of fried flesh scored to the metal, strands of hair, blood and brown stuff staining mattresses. Mouldy clothes thrown into corners.

"Primary exhibits," warned Dananga. "Touch nothing. We leave everything."

Like any man in an awkward position, expected to deliver and unsure of the map, Bartlett could feel the shape of his jaw and set of his teeth. He detested the Grief House.

But she was on to something. He told her, "No. Mixing and matching isn't where it's at, you're right."

"Explain?"

He couldn't, not in so many words. But below in the ballroom he actually watched himself take the wirecutters to rescue his contorted victim from bondage. He was suddenly impatient. "Nix the skeletons. Piles are where it's at." Dananga did her best to translate. "Just piles and piles. Skulls. Let's quit being fancy."

He went at it bluntly, up to his elbows, pitching eagerly into bones. Bones that shed no clues of having danced inside bodies anywhere. He suggested to the curator that he order a halt to wheelbarrows dumping any more discoveries inside. The digging ceased.

Bartlett did not stop for lunch.

He was a willing pioneer.

Out of the crests and valleys he asked that all skulls be carried to the far wall. Here he coordinated their anchoring in rows, faces forward, one on top of another.

The humidity made everybody sweat like pigs. Bartlett longed for a glass of water. But the work's rhythm, the bending to salvage, the squatting to drop, felt good. The curator's intensity, instead of waxing in the turmoil, waned in phases. The mounting skulls spoke mutely without jawbones, in a chorus of death. Yet the clamouring silence dissolved none of their pain nor the house's grief. The walls wailed.

That night the bathwater spun slowly down his drain the colour of mud. The spools of his diary were spinning too. *Bones*, he spoke decisively, *are the driven snow of history.*

At dinner he avoided the Romanian agronomist keen to quiz him on the museum's infrastructure.

"Their goals, yes? Are the same as I describe in villages without tools and fertilizer?"

She dusted the tablecloth with anxious hands and tucked her elbows into the nest of her hips.

In the morning he fell mesmerically to work again. He avoided breakfast. When the workers had collected and stacked four thousand skulls plus, when no more skulls remained above-ground that were not piled to the ceiling opposite the wall of photographs—buttressed along the floor with a low wooden paling—he began to contemplate the tens, hundreds of thousands of other bones of which the human frame is composed in such a mass grave.

Outside, the heaved-up earth would have to be levelled and returned to gardens.

Singing birds.

From home he had a sudden strange feeling about his canary.

Inside, plotting his release, he wandered back and forth across the dance floor. He was coordinating a plan.

Starting with the kitchen, and working his way through other rooms on this floor, the curator could fill these up past the embassy's windows with undulating seas of bone, into which—as in rooms of a carefully preserved heritage house back home, where visitors are prevented from entering by a braided cord—future visitors might peer. Bewildered, they could also look in from the gardens. The little man under- stood and nodded at the unreality of it all.

"He says you are a shrewd adviser," said Dananga.

That evening, avoiding the Belgian who wanted to play cards, Bartlett told Strajik his work was done. "Ask Dananga," he added.

Mr. Strajik bridled. Had Bartlett not promised him two weeks? The Belgian agreed. Bartlett's claim to have completed his aid would single him out for the disapproval of his peers. Even envy. "Work beyond imagination," said Mr. Strajik. "There is no end of reconstruction, I'm afraid." The spirit of the time would teach him patience. *Patience, who has time for that?*

There followed discussions of roads, villages and disarray. Foreign workers were expected soon to follow up Mr. Strajik's advance guard with resident agencies of international rescue. In the meanwhile, stressed the Swede, cost of contribution was not a price you paid with ingenuity, but the value you offered in time. The others agreed. They seemed used to thinking of themselves as interdependent citizens in a very compressed state of being.

At dawn, as if dreaming, Dr. Bartlett Day found a message at his door to pack up and prepare to travel deeper into bones. A white Lada awaited him, driver and guide. He'd been all ready to go home.

His progress north was slow. The pilgrim ate dust as the sun rose in the sky bathing dispossessed nomads. It was no country for old men. People evidently requiring the chiropractor's expertise made his guide stop everywhere.

Villagers were blighted.

Starving, actually.

"Supposed to eat, yuh yuh," said the decrepit guide, probably no more than forty, making eating noises with hand and mouth. His English relied on semaphore and could no more uncover idiom than a flag could shuck an oyster. In this country, it was enough.

People mopped the fields for blades of forgotten rice. Their forced labour had produced only years of sterile fields and ransacked souls. Bags of rice appeared and disappeared, bicycled in from a border, selling and reselling for profit. Nobody without means to barter could afford free Red Cross gifts.

These sterile fields turned out to be Bartlett's goal. Their excavation was leading to spontaneous catharsis all over the country. Liberation, if it had removed fear of murder, was also renewing the grief. He drank greedily from his canteen.

Each village uncovered its proof. The educated and disobedient, the suspected and despised: Their bones were bleaching upon every one of his arrivals. Wrist bones still bound with wire, skulls still blindfolded. Even better as graves than the rice fields were B-52 craters, saucers in the earth now overgrown with vegetation.

The simplicity of his advice made Bartlett's transmigration nimble. He took a stick, he drew in the dust. Long, twoshelved sheds open to the air. *Look,* he pointed, upper shelf for skulls, lower shelf for all these other bones ...

Every village offered a variation of the same story. Five thousand, eight thousand, ten and more thousand in bigger towns, struck on the head with iron bars, pokers, rifle butts—anything to save bullets, said his guide—and buried by fellow villagers, after victims had dug their own graves.

And every night Bartlett the voyeur told this story to his diary. Record, tally, log of each pit's disclosure. It felt like a lie. Parched, he slept on dirt floors and ate infested rice. He was gnawed into lumps by mosquitoes. His quarters smelled. Dysentery touched him with the hand of hyperbole. Storing up memories deliberately for the first time in his life, he treated himself to new batteries and might've bartered dead ones for food.

News becomes news as it gets famous, he spoke sombrely into his machine. *I don't even recognize stuff I can't look at on a screen.*

These suddenly liberated people seemed to expect more of him than he could hope to deliver. They wanted hope for their lives, not advice about the dead. He was certainly hand in glove with the lot of them—or might've been had he any real relief to offer. They still felt enchained. They showed him trees where people had been tied and left for twisting hooks to extract their livers.

Back home, he recalled, his office was full of gadgets to keep suffering patients coming back. Technology soothed, so did tradition.

"'Look well to the spine,'" he'd told delegates at the Congress of Alternative Healing, quoting a potted Hippocrates, "'for many diseases have their origin in dislocations of the vertebral column.'"

He liked to tell the story of the human back, from ancient Egypt through the fall of the Roman Empire, the Dark Ages, the evolution of bonesetting in the Renaissance. This story of dislocation gave his profession a history.

By the time he got to the invention of chiropractic—and here he pressed home his facts—by a Canadian one September afternoon in 1895, who had to migrate south before he could overthrow the old ideas of taking care of bodies, Bartlett had quoted from ancient Chinese documents on tissue manipulation, cited examples of spinal adjustment by a number of cultures including the Inca, Toltec and Maya, plus the Sioux and Winnebago. Even today, he claimed, the Maori in New Zealand still walked across each other's backs to cure pain caused by non-aligned bones. Bone manipulation was a democratic phenomenon given international distinction by a Canadian.

He'd suggested this rather proudly, sipping water.

And concluded confidently, "Bones are character. Bones helped our forefathers get to my country. Bones helped them make sails, splice ropes, hook fish. I know their secrets by the bones they kept. In the old country they kept bones for shuttlecocks and chastity belts. In Canada they turned them into clappers and pastry crimpers. Bangles and snow goggles. Earplugs and dog whistles. Bones," he boasted, "keep me in touch."

He'd given his amanuensis another slap. Bea's slats shone as white as snow in the lights. Hubris made them both glow. He had hired an enterprising Thai to make a video of his address and planned to play it in the waiting room of his office at home. With Bea he even waltzed a bit and got a hand.

In this Bangkok hotel on the river, plied once by trading schooners and seafaring novelists, he was asked to dance that evening by the striking, pearl-necklaced hypnotist from Marseilles named Dr. Legatt, and Bartlett told her he was going to Pattycakes—Pattaya—in the morning and she should come too.

DAMAGES

"I feel," she replied, in very limber English, "your idea with me is the best thing since apple betty." His heart had skipped at this domestic little allusion that was confident of, indeed pleased with itself as idiom. "But my husband and I leave tomorrow for Rome."

"Not," she added, hands on his chiropractor's shoulders, "that my husband would mind."

Reported Bartlett, later, *We could learn a lot from the French*...

Now, on his last night in a fractured little country, he ended up in an abandoned luxury hotel, once a refuge for travellers from around the globe. Over the country's ancient ruins it had started to rain. The jungle smelled sour. Vast temple mountains, towers and courtyards, balustrades and moats, shrines and niches to ancestral kings of a dislocated future—a wonder of the world, claimed his guide, just beyond the window. Bartlett dutifully wondered.

He thought of home, the old house shared with friends, still standing between apartment buildings, and he imagined an empty city. The way a neighbour's rusted Pontiac no longer returned like a tired animal, tires scraping the curb, engine rumbling until kicked to charge it up for morning, then switched off, sounding like the last and unexpected breath of a buffalo.

In the morning a small plane would land at the unused airstrip and return him to the capital. He had no answer for the guide and driver who wanted to see the skyscrapers of Singapore.

Bones are the driven snow of history. Bones not stones were the real record, a nation's memory. The record of experience was bones.

And grief, he concluded.

Without it you were a quack.

Tuneless.

He got out of bed to close the shutters in the large, unelec-trified suite. He felt his way back again in darkness.

The white dust of bones left out in the air would start fall-ing years hence over this jungle, this country, this people. But no one would feel it, see it, know it. The dust would be falling over the ruins too. He heard the little spools of his diary dis-solving in silence.

It'll never sink in anywhere, he added, killing the mike.

Against the wooden shutters the rain fell harder.

LIBRETTO

"MIRROR, MIRROR in the sea, who's the fairest going to be?" There was a pause in her performance. The ice princess spread her wings and awaited an answer. The audience down at Uptakes strained to hear whose head she might lop next. Her city in review offered more pageantry than she could possibly stage in the year's last show.

She could recall in the spring of that year, on a clear day full of Oriental plum blossoms lining countless residential blocks, a V of geese had flown straight down Altamira Street between shops and walk-ups, above cars and trolley wires, the entire distance without deflection or ascent from harbour to bay. They pumped past dry cleaners and doctors' offices, corner groceries and barbershops, keeping a wary eye on a pair of sparking trolley poles. At a café called Carrots, cappuccino drinkers, alerted to something strange in the traffic—to a rhythmic squeaking, then a honking someone called quirky and another loathed—glanced up into an awning and witnessed nothing.

She remembered the Queen, the Prime Minister, an American aircraft carrier, and the Pope all happened to visit her city that year, the first of the decade. Citizens against the

Crown and western alienation, nuclear bombs and a male-dominated priesthood accosted each dignitary in turn. The right to protest was enjoying its heyday. As was, she reckoned, in its own cycle of bang and crunch, real estate—making this year unofficially, for scrambling boomers, professional flippers, even office secretaries taking out personal loans to get in on equity pools, the Year of the House.

The stand-up comic broke her silence.

"Boomers, flippers, secretaries . . . sounds like a hot-tub party for the nouveau fiche!" She wagged her fins. New Year's Eve was her final act in a year of one-night stands. "Mirror, mirror in the sea, who's the fairest going to be?" Her city, like Rio, known far and wide as the most beautiful in the world, was absorbed in having its legs and bikini line waxed. In making nonsense of the whole, she resented how this skinny-binniness reflected on them all. "Rio duz Ya'narrow," she muttered.

Sulking. Then quoting from memory, proceeded gravely to advise her assembled subjects: "'In the second century of the Christian Era the empire of Rome comprehended the fairest part of the earth, and the most civilized portion of mankind . . .'" Silence, though a polite, expectant silence, waiting loyally for her to resume rattling their local chains with gags or another riddle. Her accompanist *had* warned her. Was she crazy, she wondered, planning to go down and live in L.A. where the real empire would *catcall?*

The news here at home was ripe. Taxes and divorce rates up, jobs plentiful, despair and beggars scarce. She knew litigation and lawyers had flourished, as had hookers. Ditto speculating seniors in gold bars and coal. Fortunes routinely squandered and remade. The stock exchange—renowned abroad for raising venture capital in unregulated ways along with police inquiries, celebrity roasts, plus names of local promoters to legendary status—had replaced the familiar crapshoot with a roulette wheel. The bucketshop with a chandeliered casino. A cabinet of car dealers throwing at every citizen five free shares of a few bailed-out sawmills, encouraging voters to buy thousands more in a company sure to prosper as an election neared. Didn't you just love it? She loved it. Hatched to foil socialist rivals this big fat egg was going to drop. "Can't you *hear* it dropping?" As in other Pacific cities—Sydney, Lima, San Francisco—inflation had taken hold, and not always with the pleasurable bite of the teething babe's. . . Only if you listened—mothers could—did the whimpering infant sound on occasion like a brooding hen.

Bwok-bok-bok-bok-bok-bk-bk-bk-bk-bk-bk-bk—

"Enough!" she screamed, interrupting herself with a palm to the windpipe, wringing her own Chicken Little neck and flapping elbows. "*The sky is—!*" she cried. "*The sky is—!*" None would sleep tonight, if she could help it. The young laughed, waiters served, her personal piano player encouraged this ballooning madness with troubled chords. Comic city. Why then was she counting on the market in L.A. to discover her atonal act, bouncing off walls like a beach ball, worth booking in the new year?

The past year had gone by, *whiz*, citizens racing to keep up but also ahead. Her audit of it extolled the well-known for greed, climbers for envy, and ordinary folk—who'd begged from relatives, remortgaged themselves two and three times over, or cheated on tax returns—for hypocrisy. A sea change, clearly, in the way they looked at the world and who should rule. *Not* the spendthrift socialists. "It's not how much I have," noticed a retiring missionary doctor from Beijing, interviewed on *City, City.* "It's how much I have compared to the other guy." She mimicked his observation, as if mocking what she thought true might make it *un*true. Everybody's eggs in one basket, with a killing—killings—to be made. She brooded over this civic distemper. The more you guarded against risk by separating your eggs, *bwok-bok*, the more you fell behind. "Consider, friends, the *disease* we're risking when prudence cracks! Yours and mine, the body's shell . . ."

To the young in her audience, and all looked noisomely young, it felt like life had reached its zenith and disease was the only crime. Body factories had come into vogue that year, mirrors on walls, ballet barres, pulsing music in the ears of aerobic figures dressed in leg warmers and neon tights. "God," she asked, "aren't these busy-body shop stewards *embarrassing?*" Physical choices had compounded. Coupled to a Walkman you could jog in special shoes; pump your sissy-shorted legs from the bony saddle of a ten-speed racing bike; stand rubberized on a sailboard slicing through the salt chuck. Beaches awaited summer. Volleyballs awaited nets. The sand awaited women who pumped iron and men who'd gone the impressive anabolic route to find themselves a perfect partner in the mirror. Surgery, available for chin tucks, was moving up from California.

"What next, eh, coffins by IKEA?" She pulled the dumper chain and plugged her nose.

She held it closed. A go-to word had grown in popularity that year and would probably take many years to wear out. She confessed reverence for it herself. "*No, really . . . forget what it is?*" Journalists were now dishing it up once or twice a story on local chefs, corporate mergers, elkhound dogshows, and the chances of building a cyclotron to let university physicists put their city (and pions, for twenty-six billionths of a second) on the map. People liked *saying* this word, for it conferred a feeling of import and made a coming city feel orgasmic. Nose plugged, she enunciated its syllables with curling tongue: "*world-class.*" The word itself, like the voices that caressed it, the keyboards that knocked it out, was an urban favourite among bulimics and bankers, rakes and rollerskaters.

"Mirror, mirror, in the sea. who's the fairest going to be?"

With the sea change citizens seemed suckered by the future. And so did she, she admitted. Listen, the past was a crock, yes? Everybody now knew offshore money had replaced domestic money and that an eighty-cent dollar had begun to look very attractive to exporters of raw logs to Japan and penny stocks to Dublin. The buck also looked good to L.A. movie makers in white trucks who'd renamed her city for theirs. She said since the place always got shot to *disguise* it as L.A., hey, she was just as glad to be moving there.

". . . Join 'em to beat 'em, like an omelette. Why did the chicken cross the—?" And she made them wait for some improbable mating of bird and fish they'd come to expect from her adulterated civic rant. So whimsical she risked taking off from her stand-up position of fins, wings, and helicoptering tongue.

Her memory returned to the street last spring. "I walk heavy. My elbows jut. I kind of tip forward." When the golden geese flew by she wondered who could help *her* move with the same grace. Some fella maybe to adjust her spine, realign her wheels . . . caster, camber, toes.

"*Rem, rem, rem* . . ." cried Chicken Little, watching them pump west over traffic. What hosy necks! What grace! She resumed her walk, at a saunter now. This little brush with the extra-terrestrial had delivered her a glimpse of the sinuous line through nature, indeed through herself. Why would any woman miss being, or ever want to be, a *tomato?* She was learning to breathe all over.

The geese themselves, not about to squander their fame as egg factories, made landfall at the Planetarium on ponded lawns lapping to the sea. "*Bwok-bok-bok-bok-bo—*" She had to admit they were as bad as battery hens. In fact so plentiful this year, during our emergent boom of free enterprise, she insisted these welfare birds needed to be rounded up and trucked back to nature.

". . . And why not, folks? Step in this one you'll break your mother's back." And signalling her accompanist, the ice princess spread her wings on stage and sank down to sniff their brazen droppings on pricey urban ground.

"What is born each night and dies each dawn?"

She wondered, rising up like a ballerina, about love. A clumsy swan, too heavy for music, she plucked a chicken's egg from between her knees and tossed it neatly to her accompanist who caught it without missing a note. Deprived of body factory and chin tuck, she played hard on her own considerable heft. And on local crime. "Imagine my material," she half-lamented, "if I was to *forgo* L.A ...". Hadn't an oil tycoon been fined three thousand dollars this year for gross indecency with two underage hookers in what the prosecutor had called "a whip and harness session?" *He* was a faithful supporter of the cabinet minister—either Ping, Pang, or Pong: all the bloody same—who'd ordered four bottles of Pouilly-Fuissé at public expense at Le Soleil Couchant. "And speaking of restaurants, did you hear the one about. . . ?" A Chinese couple, kidnapped that year from their Szechuan restaurant, and found dead in sacks near an ore mine up the sound, was about as funny as ... Gibbon.

Maybe she had a death wish.

Or maybe just hated Shaughnessy, goose-proofed by poodles, where the May sun had brought out crescents full of cone blossoms standing up among leaves like tents in a meadow . . . chestnuts certain to be shelling German cars come fall ... unless parked in carriage sheds. She made herself sound like a schoolmistress with pickles up her nose.

"Carriage trade! Whence our sexier agents derive their nomenclature . . . from old stables! *Pee you* . . . and you and you ..." Her fans whooped, nuttier than eggnogs.

And so the year had gone by, warmer than usual.

That same May, not on the famous First when armies in Moscow marched for TV screens in the West, but on a little-known day of stasis, full to bursting with blossoms drunk on their own nectar, nothing in nature had seemed to move. She watched lawns going to seed in front of frame houses slated for destruction. Her city and its suburbs—blown full of salty gulf air the night before—had basked before her in sunshine, unmindful of a Russian sub prepared to cough short-range missiles into fire higher than encircling mountains.

Chicken Little clucked. ".. . On such a day, friends, who was going to *believe* it?"

Peace marchers, that's who, on their annual pilgrimage over a downtown bridge. *No Nukes* said their banners. *Ban Cold War. Ban Hot War. This City Is a Nuclear-Free Zone.* With apocalyptic fervour abroad, with everyone waiting for the much-reported volcano farther south to blow its top, whales had beached themselves for no reason at Boundary Bay, and she could recall guests at parties boasting how their city was on the edge of greatness. You could see how time had altered perspective, Hong Kong money now fuelling its sister city, *this* city, in the event China got greedy when a treaty with the British expired, still years down the road. "World-class" had become a *burden,* she told her audience. ". . . But can't you just feel the vibes?"

She could. The American volcano had blown its lid late that May, with an explosion two-and-a-half thousand times greater than the one over Hiroshima. Fifty-seven people killed, buried in dust that drifted as far north as this side of the border. She had a field day recounting an event she boldly linked to the woman's movement. Her accompanist again struck dark and ominous chords. That June a local girl had been named Bunny of the Year and two months later found nude in her L.A. bedroom . . . blown apart by gunfire. The comic lamented fate in L.A. including her own. "It's a crapshoot down there. It's a crapshoot up here."

Wished for or not, urban absurdity was *in.* All year the price of land had continued to rise and landlords, ardent to develop properties, had been serving notice on tenants as architects drew up plans for larger, more luxurious condos to house fewer and fewer people. This local news was just as senseless as the foreign news of street kids and death squads. Yet it was, she stressed, *world-class* news. Citizens *wanted* to be

mugged, raped in parks, shot at—be driven out of their own
city by uncollected garbage, declared bankrupt so they could
start in again on credit, and be given emphysema by tons of
carbon monoxide spewed forth from gridlock. Her audience
at Uptakes applauded these reminders of metro envy. Nothing sacred, except growth, was now safe. The past had gone
out of fashion and books of photographs, introduced by the
mayor, celebrated a glossy present.

"Mirror, mirror, on the wall, don't look now, here's the
wrecker's ball..." Or his dynamite, or the matches of a stranger
on commission. She doused them all with another riddle.

"What flames warm like a flame, yet is no flame?"

She thought she knew what it was. Her. You couldn't be
a comic princess unless you fumed. Over the future, say,
now looking much cleaner than the past. Shady newcomers
investing in the city were certainly safe from any past here.
Even newcomers, who couldn't afford the future, were beginning to arrive as boat people and refugees with big ideas. Thus
nobody's imagination rushing ahead was fired by the wish to
preserve memory. "Cells are dying, no? How do you preserve
brain cells? Freeze 'em? Baste 'em with formaldehyde? *Brrr*...
Anyway, it's *Newww* Year's!"

Beer whoops from her audience. Her propensity to piss
on the past while squatting on the future challenged her
piano player to something skitzy now, something scat. Instead
he played Puccini.

"Mirror, mirror, in the sea, who's the fairest going to be?"

At night in its lithe lit-up towers her city's figure was
reflected in the bay, where the USS *Ranger* had anchored at
a seductive angle, monumental in its power, so sailors could
go sprinkle cash in the streets and screw the whores. Citizens
had resisted this American brawn in the slippery protests of
scooting rubber rafts. Greenpeace stars had shackled themselves to the anchor chain for photo-ops and interviews. All
so incredibly world-class that she'd already forgotten, pre-

tending not to mourn, the name of the stranger who'd *proposed* to her this week of all the whoopee.

"Connubial bliss, I said to him. I'll pass. I'm dieting."

Summer had put a lot of tattoos on the arms of East End mattress workers, hope in the hearts of single comics, and the bounce in svelte heels downtown, such a *beautiful* summer the office towers disgorged workers in record mobs to bag-lunch it. Executives sat down with construction workers to shoot the breeze about financial security in gold bars and untested art. Funny, the workers were all ears.

". . . Cuz inflation's booming, right? Exploding, like we've been neutronically nuked." Civic vision, including hers, had expanded like sixty—though where in the world to? Into the future, she guessed, though you needed to *know* the future in order to get there, when economic prediction was everyone's favourite game.

Still, it had proved an *un*predictable summer for the young (like her niece) who'd lived in downtown apartments east of Altamira. By July's end toilets were sweating in a heat wave, a girl lay cold in red bathwater (slit wrists), and a gay couple, giving its first party, dumped a jar of coffee into the kitchen sink, adding a kettle of hot water and telling their friends (among them her, the comical chicken) to dip in their mugs. By that hour hosts were too tired to cater. Next day, instead of heat, a ferocious summer shower. The tanks dried off, the dead girl found, the stained sink sprinkled with Bon Ami.

"Another six years, folks, we uncork our centenary. Let's prink!"

Prink? Every morning and evening that summer the newspapers had published coliform counts for the beaches. High, she remembered, on account of the heat. Yet swimmers still swam, as they always had, since genesis and the raven. Shining city, emerald city. It'd stood up to the blue mountains as tides ebbed and the far shoreline sprouted high-rises. East-siders like herself, walking out on the sands, could see where they'd bussed over from. A factory fire had smudged the whole effing centrefold. Look, it was everybody's damn pollution.

"Mirror, mirror, in the sea, who's the fairest going to...No, seriously, ladies, you ever heard of a city having its bikini line waxed?"

Here was a line the comic had developed come fall, come inspiration, come up here on stage, handsome, and rescue me! Working her audience on improv, losing them sometimes to impenetrable riddles, dumb puns, and preparing herself like Chicken Little for a crash landing. "*The sky is—!*" they echoed her, they chanted after, "*The sky is—!*"

She would miss this Playmate. An uplifting city open to all kinds of cracks and cupboard skeletons. The last swimming beach still in use in October, as long as sunshine held, was the nudist beach hidden at the bottom of clefts and cliffs, secret ravines and bony logs, on a peninsula jutting into the gulf and accessible only to cultists, migrating swallows, and satellites. She began to muse. "What *was* that stranger's name?"

From her eye in the sky, like a traffic reporter for badmouth radio, she tracked the ardent stranger, telling her subjects how in that last fine month of the year this guy had wrenched his back on the cliff's clay face straining for a gander at the smut below. "*Wouldn't you love to behead this creep?*" Anyway, he couldn't move, his back throbbed, it was alien to him this lowdown place. Doubtless a prince, he lay lamenting the loss of pleasure by the now sunless sea. He wasn't into bourgeois values like whining. He traced his tattooed arm, dreaming of a miracle.

"A damsel with a dulcimer!" she cried. "Me!"

She made sure he wouldn't sleep. He was unable to move for pain. He found the trees like an icy cave beginning to overwhelm him. He yearned for space and the sound of geese. He spotted stars as light fell, early Spaniards on the beach below. A yacht from the gulf tacking home.

She wondered again about leaving hers. A wet November had all but pushed her into the arms of L.A. She'd come out of cinemas to rain and the sound of swishing tires. From the illusions of Milan and New York, Calcutta and Barcelona, she'd emerged into the wet reality of a shrunken city in its drabbest season. A comic city, but not one for claustrophobic comics. Posters of missing children had begun to appear on the sides of rented U-Hauls. Evidently a pattern was developing, like the recent bad weather, a westerly flow of moist unstable air, which is how the weather office put it though the police department refused to comment. Better the smog and bad water of California.

"Better a desert," she muttered.

By December the flight of the rich had begun. No shopping lineups for these citizens, already napping in Palm Springs, listening to tour guides atop Mt. Alban, toasting their hides in Kihei. Travel agents, in for higher product volumes than normal, had sent citizens junketing to Reno, playing tennis in Phoenix, skiing in the Rockies. All because a high-Arctic cold front had pushed far south, off its normal track, bringing temperatures cold enough to freeze ponds for the first time in a generation. "Cold enough," in the words of her landlord, "to freeze the stones in a steambath." People who didn't normally take a winter vacation, but who had credit lines to the sun, were lined up to fly out.

It was as if her city had tipped ten degrees of latitude—but instead of California warmth got a tundra shock instead. Within three days a deep freeze had penetrated the rainforest, shore birds had ruffled up, and the Automobile Association was running four hours late servicing batteries as dead as bricks. The geese now wondered if they shouldn't, like her, head south.

"It's all a plot by IKEA!" shouted the ice princess. "Hands up, heads off, anybody who can't imagine sun warm enough to melt my wings! *Bwok-bok-bok-bok-bk-bk-bk-*"

With this she swooped suddenly from her stage on spread arms and piano wire suspended from the flies. She was, she shrieked, L.A.-bound.

She had stuck a feather in her hair and ruffled up her jumpsuit into the costume of a bright bird of passage by flouncing her cape. Maybe she *would* crash. It was a crapshoot down there. It was a crapshoot up here. She was disappearing into darkness. She caught the big fat egg her pianist tossed back to her through smoke and operatic accompaniment. And then she dropped it, deliberately. Who cared if they hissed now? Fervent fans were supposed to hiss.

"The ice that turns to fire, what can it be?"

She hung there in darkness, dying for love. They were drifting from her, chattering now among themselves, as the waiters slung Kokanee. *They* would sleep, even if she didn't. She waited to be reeled off and unhooked. Her wax and feathers gathered up in a stranger's arms. Today, New Year's Eve, windows had flashed across the East End and longshoremen, pulling down toques under hard hats, indifferent to brain cells, had sipped Canadian Club from risky aluminum cups. She'd heard ships shudder at berth, observed their cranes ablaze in Christmas lights. She'd watched forecasters predict still more exotic weather—ridges to lock in smog and refract sunsets, wash white peaks in orange and the bay in indigo. If she couldn't make it as a big-city clown, for sure she wanted to come home to do local weather and other phenomena on TV.

With things so frozen, jailed by deepening frost, no forecaster, she predicted, including a migrant teacup reader who fluttered through hair salons for East Indian women on the south slope, even suspected the new year was going to sock them from below, of all directions, a rambunctious trounce on the Richter scale ... followed by aftershocks like something from the shaky substrata of an arid Third World capital.

Nothing was permanent, least of all the future. Her future. Like memory and a city, it too needed to be imagined.

MOTHER AND
FATHER TALK OF
GOING SOUTH

*Inflation gradually pushes the whole community toward
speculation, since ordinary life begins to require speculator's
skills.*

— William Rees-Mogg, *The Reigning Error*

1

S UN gives me the rapture, lying in it like. Days like this
I worked for all my life. *How come you're not lying in it
then?* I came in for some coconut oil. *You want to burn?*
Right now I'd settle for a burn. *Sam's gone.* Sam? Sam's a
professional. By lunchtime professionals have long gone.
You used to be gone by breakfast. Yeah, look where it got me.
Hammering and sawing my life away and not a buck to show
for it. *The cost of living ate you up.* Up! Being a carpenter was
no guarantee of amounting to a hill of beans.

2

What do you want for lunch? Coconut oil. *Your skin isn't
ready for coconut oil. Use your* PABA. PABA wouldn't tan dog

dirt. Look at me. I'm white. I've had it with that stuff. *So am I. I'm white. Coconut oil hasn't helped my skin.* I'm whiter than white. Albino. Besides, you're a woman. *No whiter than me.* I can *see* I'm whiter than you. Bleach I use screens out brown rays and lets in white ones. I'm white! *You're used to delayed gratification, it's in your blood.* If it is the chemo's killed it. *Not like Sammy. He wants something he wants it right away.* That's why Sam's an entrepreneur not a carpenter. Why you got Sam to thank for this penthouse, not me. *He's your son too.* Where's the coconut oil? *Sam never listens to me.* I can't figure it out.

3

I'm looking down on the beach and it's like Bombay. I'm using binoculars like. I can see bodies lying around the sand like candy bars. Same with the park. I'm looking down on the park and everybody's chocolate . . . picnickers, rollerskaters, men in earrings, children . . . chocolate-brown bodies. They're all using coconut oil. I can smell it on the wind. *Maybe it's me you smell.* You? You weren't such a piker you'd let me put that oil of yours on my legs. All over me. I look anemic. Look. Don't I look like I've been through chemotherapy? Skin shrinking? Brain bulging? Eyes popping? *Put your wig on.* I look like I need a tan. Head, chest, legs . . . *You want lunch outside?* I want my legs rubbed. I can't reach my shins or I'd rub them myself. Therapy did that. Pumping chemo into my whole body. Veins running through me like wires . . . red-hot wires. They stiffen you up. Therapy stiffens you up. Here. Use this to kneel on. *That's your hair.* Sam doesn't want oily knees on his broadloom. *How am I going to land on that little patch?*

4

Where do you want it? Feel any hair below my knees? *I wouldn't call it hair exactly . . .* Christ, I'm turning into an Inuit! Better start with the shins. Rub it in good. *Like sorrow? You're doing a good job rubbing that in yourself.* I don't take a cane.

5

Listen . . . there's that mouth-organ again. On the patio. I don't hear anything. *Your ears are worse than your posture.* The chemo ate away the stirrups in my ears. Which affected my balance. Which definitely affected my hearing. *You're standing on one leg.* You haven't oiled my foot. *I thought you were ticklish.* Tell me about it. Nothing tickles with chemo inside you.

6

Who is that kid anyway? Is Sam training him to be a houseboy or what? *It's lunchtime.* Past lunchtime. The sun's past zenith. You haven't done my thighs, my back neither. Tits and skull I can do myself. *That's a funny way to put it.* Talking's a funny language.

7

You still have a healthy pair of thighs. They're bald too. Bald head, bald legs, bald balls. I used to have hair. I used to hate the wind. It blew the kind of hair I had around like horsehair. My barber called it horsehair. It wasn't good hair but it was hair. I had a mane at one time resembling a stallion's. Now it feels like a beach ball. *You want your wig back?* A tan would give me some spunk. Look like I had spunk.

8

Living here next to the water drains you. The swelter. *You make it sound like a toilet.* Oceans *are* toilets. If you read the newspapers. *Not ours.* The Indian Ocean? Effluence is what they dump in that ocean. You could be swimming off Djakarta and see a lump float past you. The fish don't like it. They're clearing out. They're dying out. *Well, here we've got salmon and crab.* Oysters, yeah, ling cod … *And you want to go south?* Who said? *To the tropics. You did.* We can't stay here the winter. *How come? When you retired Sam said come and live here with him.* Here! There's not enough sun to keep a bug alive. Without sun I shrivel up. Already the days are getting shorter. Next thing it's fall. Falling all over you. Fall's no good for tanning. The fog takes half a day to burn off. The sun comes down on you at an angle, not from overhead like now. Right now's still summer. I can't understand how come I'm white. Might as well be lying in the freezer. Soon will be, if I don't go south. *The pension isn't enough to keep us in coconut oil let alone travel.* Retired couples always travel south. *Well, we travelled west. From the East Side to the West End.* People freeze to death without sun. *This isn't exactly a stable.*

9

The boy's got a yacht. *Who does?* Sam's got a yacht. Tied up in the tropics. *Turn around, I need the backs of your thighs.* I read it in the newspaper. Sam's famous now. A real saviour of free enterprise. *Sam never hears us anymore.* Works too hard, forgets to relax. He's going to have a breakdown. *He's got secretaries.* Secretaries? Sam doesn't dip his pen in the company inkwell. *What?* He's too busy to even go sailing. *How come he's got a yacht then?* Took it in down payment on a hockey team. Can you beat that? Paying a crew just to sit on his yacht. It's probably peeling in the sun right now. I could slap some paint on it for him. If he needed them, I could build him lockers. *No crew wants you barging in with your hammer.* Doesn't matter what the crew wants. They're crew. Just like we're crew here. You cook. I'm the handyman. *I don't take orders.* You anticipate orders. Because you know how to crew . . . instinctively. You enjoy crewing. You get a cranky crew and you get mutinies. *There's that boy's mouth-organ again . . .* I'll broach the matter with Sam. You and me could live aboard the winter taking out charters. We could take charge of his crew. Make sure no-one's cheating the absentee landlord. We'd get to lie on the foredeck and suntan. Make our son a return on his investment. *A pipe dream if you ask me.* Well, we can't stay here the winter. *Geese stay. The lagoon is full of geese. The ocean is full of whistlers. They migrate here on account of winter.* Winter would kill me. *Here's your wig.* You haven't oiled my head.

10

The little bugger likes to stare, doesn't he? *He's never seen you without your hair.* He doesn't have to gape. *Just wants his reward.* What for—that mouth-organ stuff? I gave him some change a week ago. *He's got his expenses.* Him? What's he need coconut oil for? He's got a suntan. It's in his genes. *He's got to eat. Look at him, he looks like a coat-hanger.* Look at me. I don't eat. In this heat who needs to? *I like his playing.* Sounds like a funeral parlour. *The trouble with you is death on the brain.* In case you missed it, I've got terminal cancer. That kind of music makes it *in*terminal . . . *I know . . . I'm sorry.* I don't want to talk about it.

11

Where's lunch? *You want lunch?* Get me a glass of tomato juice. *I'll bring you a glass, keep your shirt on.*

12

What good's generosity when he's lonely? Got no friends, doesn't speak the language. The tarbrush has definitely affected his social life. *Poor little beggar. All he wants is his reward.* Secret is to make do with what you've got. *Not when you've got nothing. Not even when you've got everything.* I haven't got anything. *And you want a trip to the tropics.* Are you going to oil my back so I can start tanning? *First I'm going to offer him a glass of tomato juice.* Mud in his eye ...

13

He was thirsty. Make sure you wash that glass out good. *You were nicer when you had hair.*

14

You want your handlebars oiled too? What? *You're still heavy around here.* That's where the chemo collects when it's through circulating in the blood. *Feels soft.* Softness incorporated. *I can make my brain move.* Make sure that oil's on even. *Exercising the hemispheres is good for you.* What are you talking about? *Keeping alive my mental fibre.* You're not a ghost or something. *I exercise.*

15

I dream a lot. At night. *That's healthy too.* I'm not bored. *You're up with the sun. How could you be bored—a man who gets up with the sun?* I'm not dead. *A good dream is good for you.* Last night's was a stinker.

16

I'll tell you ... maybe you won't believe this ... I had a dream I was fresh dead. That I went up to heaven in the rapture. I went up in the rapture, and when I got up there it was so real I could hardly believe it. Then it started to spoil. Right under my nose. Boats, junks, sampans, rafts started sailing in off the gulf, landing on the beaches below me. Scrambling out of these junks were families . . . Indian, Chinese, Indonesian . . . black families talking funny. The tanners in the sand, of course, they all stood up to watch. Couldn't believe their eyes. They thought they were dreaming. *I* thought they were dreaming. They got pushed back by the boats landing, people landing . . . dozens, then hundreds, thousands. Thousands of junks, thousands of people, thousands of rags, covering the sand. And fires! Burning all night, all over the beach. When the sun came up I couldn't see the shoreline for smoke, rags, bodies. . . You couldn't hear the gulls for the babble babble babble. For the screaming and crying. I could smell the garlic. I could see men tearing apart their rafts to build leantos in the sand. When it got too crowded for spitting they started walking into the forest. . . I was watching them from on high, a whole migration. Clogging the trails, tramping down ferns and salal to set up their hovels in the park. Boys in loincloths grabbed squirrels and wrung their necks. Acted like they'd skinned squirrels all their lives . . . cooked squirrels. Families spilled into the lagoon. Knotted the necks of the geese. Cooked the swans. All of a sudden a thousand acres of wilderness were real wilderness. The park looked like a jungle. The zoo looked like a slum. These folks opened up cages to let out monkeys they ate. Same with the parrots and penguins. I'm telling you, instead of peacocks crying and seals barking, nothing but a hullabaloo of sing-songing voices. Which people in the city must have heard. They got in their cars and drove down to see, locked their doors and wouldn't get out, crawled through the park peering out their windows, the rose gardens littered with defecating humanity. Trees kept falling for firewood. Smoke hung over the forest like a cloud. I could smell it. Spreading out across the city, up the coast. I could see it, day after day. No rain fell and the lagoon nearly dried up. Millions used what was left to wash in. Their laundry covered the rocks and rushes.

They squatted, fought, ate grass, crapped. They murdered the policemen's horses, cooked the timber wolves, ate the buffalo. At night their fires burned on the beaches and in the forest. I kept watching them with my binoculars. They were staring out of the forest, pointing up at the skyscrapers. You couldn't stop them. You didn't want to watch them. They were copulating like rabbits. No sir. I went up in the rapture and got stuck with a stinker.

17

You're done. We ought to put our money in gold bullion. *What money?* Our pension money. *The cost of living ate that alive.* Sam's then. He's got money to burn. It's *going* to burn unless he puts it in bullion. His stocks, his hotels, his shopping centres, his arenas. All his hedges up in smoke. *And your skin.* What? *Your skin is going to burn too.* My skin is goddamn asbestos.

18

Listen! He's playing a jig. Must think we're made of money. *I've got a little something in my bag here...* You've always got a little something, haven't you, in that bag. A little something, a little treat, a little nest egg... It's usually a big disappointment your littleness. *Five dollars?* What? *All I've got.* Exactly! Give him a quarter. *Look at him, Father. He's hungry.* Give him a Smartie. I can tell you he'd turn down a Smartie, a trained seal like him. He isn't hungry! *Don't shout.* He's trying to skin me!

19

He looks disappointed. He doesn't understand the language *...He can translate spectacles like yours.* Sam, when he started out, wasn't any older than him. I can tell you he didn't start with handouts. Sam will tell you. He worked for what he got. He wasn't a musician. Sam never asked for more money than the value he gave. *You can't put a price on music. Music isn't a commodity like pots.* Pots! Sam never sold a pot in his life. *Music is priceless. The Queen of the Arts.* I know it is. But it isn't worth five bucks. Not that music. For $5 you could buy the mouth-organ. Violins are different. *Listen! . . . Bravo!*

20

He can play all the tunes he knows, I'm not giving him $5. That beats the band, that does. *Go on, Father. Give it to him.* Nope. *He played his little heart out.* I appreciate his talent, believe me. I wish I could talk his language to tell him how much. Plus to explain why I can't give him this. *Nonsense. That bill's losing value anyway. Since you've been holding it, it's probably lost a nickel. Since I took it out of my purse it's dropped a dime.* It's the principle of the thing. He can stand there till his toes jam. *What principle? Times change. They're changing all the time.* If you don't stand on principle, where are you?

21

Suppose there's a special on cellulite where a woman can get rid of all her cellulite for $250. What's cellulite? *Fat. Only it looks like cottage cheese a woman gets on the thighs.* Suppose the woman's thighs look like holy hell. *That's why she'd need a salon . . . to tone them.* For two hundred and fifty bucks? She'd be a lunatic. *It wouldn't be just one treatment, it'd be a number, a whole series. If you look at the way prices are going up, it'd be a bargain.* Bull toot. *It's got to do with time. The price of time keeps going up. The salon's time, this boy's time. People's principles change. They've got to. They lose their value.* Not mine. You go to that salon don't bother coming home. *Me? I'm*

*using it as one example. Five dollars isn't what it was in the great
arc of time.* Huh? *We don't need it anymore.* What, time?

22

NO MONEY! NEXT TIME! I GIVE YOU MONEY NEXT
TIME! *Oh, brother.* NO CHANGE! SAVVY? NO MONEY!
You're making it worse. He doesn't talk English so I got to
talk pidgin. *You sound like a skinflint.* I know I sound like a
skinflint. *You look like some tourist.* I feel like one. In my own
country! *He's going to cry.* It won't wheedle anything out of *me*
if he bawls. *A principle is a principle.* That's right! ... At least he
isn't diseased. I'm diseased, I can't even tan. I'll talk to Sam. He
likes the kid. He'll give me some change. I might ask to borrow his kid for the yacht. In the tropics, he'd feel right at home.
Playing for the tourists. We could adopt him. If he keeps practising that mouthorgan, who knows what—

23

That—that is bloody disgusting. . . *I think it's the funniest
thing I've ever seen!* Shut up, Mother. *Look!* Gimme your bag.
My lighter . . . where's my lighter? *He thinks you're looking for
money.* This here's one language he'll understand. *Understand
what?* This . . .

24

*That's using your brain, that is. Sending it up in smoke instead
of giving* him *the money!* He's got to learn he can't go around
insulting people. *It was you who insulted him!* Not my fault he
can't understand English. *You've burned off your nose to spite
your face. What kind of a principle is that? A nice little boy who
loves music . . . and you go and insult him twice in a row.* Nice?
You call rubbing his bum in our faces nice? His asshole? Even

I could hear him. I could *smell* him. He was making smells. *He wasn't!* He was insulting us both very deliberately.

25

Mother, go into the kitchen, this isn't for a woman's ears. *It's you he's insulting.* Where'd he learn language like that? *Paying you back. You probably turned him into a delinquent.* This is Sam's doings. *You talk about adoption?* Who? Don't make me laugh.

26

It hasn't happened overnight. Things have a way of building up. Little things out on the patio. Like you acknowledging his presence. His music. He threatens you. Why? Just because he has a suntan and you don't? I don't know why. Maybe you think he's lazy. Why doesn't he go off and find himself a job you said. I don't know why he doesn't. Maybe he'd rather play his mouth-organ. Maybe he's too young. Maybe he thinks you're lazy. Maybe he thinks we're both senile. Oiling ourselves up to lie down in the sun. Trying to burn our skins. What he must think of your wig! What he must think of mine... We're kept people, Father. Hasbeens. Your son, my son ... he shares his penthouse with us ... food if we want it ... views. We can see the sea. Making harbours inside harbours. Sea, mountains. Those islands way out. Not a worry in the world up here. No struggle anymore. And we can't even adapt. We didn't need that money. We don't need any money. Our big shot son's got money to burn. And you end up burning the little bit we could've given the child! You talk about adoption? I'm ashamed, Father, I am ashamed...

121 appears in right margin

27

I don't take a cane. *That sounded like a foghorn.* May not have any hair on my head or my balls, but I don't take a cane. I can still walk. *What time is it?* There's still heat left in the sun. *Didn't you hear it?* Hear what? *The foghorn.* What are you saying, woman? *That foghorn is saying it. Can't you hear it? Winter is coming.* I know winter is coming. Before it comes I want to get a suntan. *Well, you'd better get a wiggle on.* What for? It's hot enough to cook eggs out there. *By the sound of it there's fog rolling in.* Fog? I just oiled myself. *Have a look.* What? What kind of holy smoke is this with fog rolling in? . . . It's white! . . . *Fog.* We've missed the goddamn summer. *Nothing ever changes.* I've got to talk to Sam. *What for, a miracle?* I'm not spending the winter here. Sam's got a yacht. *The sun is still shining.* Pretty soon it won't be shining. If you hadn't taken so long oiling my back . . .

28

Just think, Father, days like this you worked for all your life. I'm going to lay in what's left of it. When Sam comes home I'll ask him about his yacht. *Good Shepherd Sam.*

29

Sam, I'll say . . . I'm cold. My marrow's like ice. You can hear the goddamn foghorn, Sam. What we need, your mother and me, is to be standing around in the shade at a hundred and four. Under a flame tree. Having a mango, Sam. Coconut milk's the thing to keep us warm. We'd get a rascal to climb a palm tree. We know one we could take with us. He could help us anchor your yacht, Sam, in deserted coves. Over the winter. Rowing us in, rowing us out. Rowing around the tourists . . . the ones that rent your yacht that we'd be taking care of, Sam. At night he could build fires on the beach out of monkeypod wood. We could lie out under the stars. Tropical nights, your yacht at anchor, the smell of the fire. It's a lot to ask, Sam, I know. After what you've done here, setting us up in the sky, in your

own penthouse. This is paradise, Sam, believe me. But with
winter coming I can't breathe. Smell even. My wrinkles freeze
when I smile. My liver feels like iced cod. I want to wear my
sunglasses for a reason, Sam. If we were wealthy, son, like you
I'd climb into my Lear and whip it into the sun. I had a dream
your mother was making milk again in the grass.

30

I'm going outside. *So go.* I am going. *What's the matter?*
Nothing. Did you oil my neck? *From your neck to your toes.*
You're ready to be cooked alive. I'm going then. *So go. My love.*

WAITING

THIS is a calling like any other, except I was not called. I was not chosen. I was born to it, as some bird to flight. People ask me, what is the secret of waiting? People ask me, do you like waiting? Okay, no one asks me, but I have a mind to tell them. The best service is given on an empty stomach. This is the secret. Hey, I am happy to work up high and have the gratuities of the high rollers. I am pleased to look down over this beautiful city and out to sea where the world comes from. Men on court would lose matches for a chance to wait where I wait. "Rajam," they say to me. "How do you rate a job at Le Soleil Couchant?"

"Give service," I answer. "Superb service."

"Oh, yeah? What's a raghead like you know about a French restaurant, hey?"

They are only teasing, and I thrash them according to my temper. I serve to their backhand and wrong-foot them. It is my laugh then. At the net I cut off their volleys to spite their noses. They pay up. They call me the Sick Sikh and the White Man's Burden, their burden. I laugh. I am the wild Indian with as many arms as Shiva.

"Hey, who's she?"

Stupid, stupid.

"Forest Hills champ?"

These tennis bums make me laugh. I am lucky to be nimble and vanquish them soundly. I have my dignity and eat it too. Not like my mother and my grandmother in the countryside who pick blueberries all summer and stain their fingers with the blue globes. Their dignity is twenty cents a pound.

"Where's your turban, R.J.? You trash it?"

"I have no turban. I am Hindu."

"Yeah? Well. That's real fine."

They think I am a new-fashioned Sikh who cuts his hair and goes bareheaded.

"How 'bout a dagger? Maybe a dagger in your shorts, huh?"

They are teasing. I just tell them watch it or I will pull it out and cut off their dickies.

"Dickies!" They lie down laughing. "Me Dickey, you Janey! Dickey me, Janey you!"

So I show them how to carve lark. A make-believe lark in the air, above their heads, the way the chef shows me with his sharp knives.

"Hey, listen, Rajam. Only kidding."

I do not mean to frighten them.

"Okay, I am cool."

Who can play games and not take them seriously? I play to win, so I am a victor. I listen to a joke, thus I laugh. But what I am still having to learn is leisure. I will never tell them this is what I am learning. "Leisure? What's that, Rajam? Not getting enough?"

Hey, I am getting plenty, I could tell them. Mind your own beeswax. No, I want leisure so I am not all the time moving so fast to please and conquer. I want to win and not look like I am trying hard. Okay? When I am good with the ladies is when I look lazy-go-lucky lying here on the lawn and my dark legs are shining against the white cotton. I obtain the best gratuities when I pretend not to care so much what diners think of me. In the French way, like Maurice and Ted, those two. Maybe I will be arriving in the right direction someday soon.

My mother is happy when I send her a few earnings. She passes some on to our family in India, and tells them of Rajam in the city in his own apartment. Dialling his own telephone, painting his own bookshelves. They are all waiting to come and have their apartments too.

In the actual fact, I have told my friends a lie. I am not Hindu, I am an erstwhile Hindu. So there is no way I mind being called a Sikh. It is my friends' ignorance. The Sikhs get called Hindus. The Hindus are called ragheads. Indians all over creation answer to Paki. No way I mind some bad vibes like my father who cannot defend himself. My father has never played tennis in his life. He waits in fields for his place in the truck to bring him home. When you are good-looking like me, good things happen more than bad things. They balance through.

Hey, I get enough. All right?

Their silly insults. I look forward to thrashing them.

"You swing good, R.J. For a goddamn turban winder."

Their grammar is bad. They could not wait on a hot dog stand. Stupid, stupid.

"No way, R.J.!" They cannot believe I will beat them again. And I do.

What I want to know is where are the anonymous waiters of History? This is what I would like to know, where are the anonymous waiters of History in the world today? The past is upon us before we know there is a future. The burglar Time tiptoes away with our names. I think we too deserve some cognizance for our service.

Hey, no way, says History.

Hey, why not, I am asking.

The chef choreographs, the waiter dances. I am enjoying it, no question. In the sky like that, who would not? I go up early and water the figs and the pothos. I pinch the dead leaves. I drop the bamboo curtain until later, when the sun squats down in the gulf out of diners' eyes. I perk up the napkins like lighthouses, brush crumbs off seats, set out some breadsticks and butter patties on ice cubes. Welcome to Le Soleil Couchant, I am thinking. Some day for sure I will have my restaurant like this one. No way, R.J.

Down below in Altamira I could be buried in a little Vietnamese restaurant or a Greek one. I could be waiting in Taj Mahal with no expectations and many empty chairs. Or the noodle place, smoke and mirrors, glass tabletops instead of cloth. Not to mention Ned's Halibut full of smoke and fried grease. The takeout pullet restaurant or the Kosher Pancake House. How about the Italian ice-cream parlour? He or she who waits below ends up with the earnings of a bottle collector and lassitude. Not R.J. I am at the top already and heading up.

Still, I would rather be a tennis player.

Okay, I am not good enough to be a seed in tennis. If I practised one hundred hours per week, like some of them, no question. I already beat these welfare bums who practise a hundred hours a week plus. That tells you something. I have the reflexes for pro, and the looks of an actor, so I would be popular, definitely, for signing autographs. I could be good on the stage also.

Notwithstanding, my restaurant is a stage, no question. Especially if I do my gavotte around flambéed quail, fiery omelettes, our pepper steak soaked with cognac in a silver dish. I and the water boy do our ensemble when he is refilling the glasses and I am serving the vegetables and pouring the sauce. I am always bowing and keeping my tongue. Listening. A good supper makes people have memories of other good suppers. This is the only test. Sometimes not to put my oar into conversations, to question how their supper is, I bite my mouth. I could be looking pacific for all they notice.

"Slow down, Rajam," the chef says to me. "Take a smoke break," Louis says to me when my customers take too long over coffee, when I wish they would leave and give room for the second sitting. He says, "The customer is always right." No question, I am learning patience from Louis a little. His ancestors came to Canada in the last century to work in the gold fields and to open laundries. He has not learned leisure, but he knows patience.

What is a Chinese cook doing in a French restaurant? You could say what is Ivan Lendl up to playing in the French Open? To win, that's what. No way would I tell my friends Louis is a Chinese. They would lie down laughing. They would soon be thinking waiting is not so hot at Le Soleil Couchant, Le Soleil Couchant is going downward. This is a lie. Louis learned cooking in a logging camp. He taught himself cordon bleu in the long seasons up the coast. Loggers are not so fussy if they have enough to eat. "Tons to eat," says Louis. "Nobody held French food against Louis. They thought I was Number-One Cook."

Okay, but at Le Soleil Couchant we have critics infiltrating all the time to see us on our toes. Louis changed his name from Wing to St. Laurent so they will judge him for his food and not his copying. "Chefs all copy," say Louis. "Copy first. Create second." These critics disguise themselves and write nice things or bad things afterwards. "The noble kitchen of Louis St. Laurent," they write. "The dashing Louis St. Laurent," they begin. Louis shrugs his stooped shoulders. Not to care what they write, he takes off his mushroom hat and points to his brain upstairs. "Still Number-One Cook, okay?" He beams. His scalp is shiny in the cooking vapours.

The waiters are another business. We receive some stinging vibes like "The service was unfriendly." Or "The exuberance of the meal was not quite erased by the austerity of our waiter." We are lumped together when it is the mincers, Maurice and Ted, who turn up their noses at customers for snuffy purpose. No question, they should be criticized by their names. We should wear tags and receive our due for better or for worse.

Rajam Olivier. R.J. Brillat-Savarin. Hey, only kidding. The ones who went to Hotel Management think they know everything. Stupid, stupid.

"Hi my name is Ted and I am your waiter this evening. Our menu this evening features fresh . . ." It would serve him right to be made to stoop to the level of that lower-down-the-scale waiting. I would like to dropshot Ted and leave him flat-footed on his own baseline.

History bears no witness. I have looked into the history of food from a waiting standpoint. Nothing. I wish to know who served the first sheep's feet in white sauce at Boulanger's in 1765. I wish to know why the Revolution did not give the common waiter more honour after 1789, at Aux Troi Frères and Rocher de Canacle and Almanach des Gourmands and Café de Chartres and Café de Foy and Cadram Bleu, etcetera. Tout de suite the jealous guilds got trashed. The restaurant owners built up their own menus with pâtés and roasts and soups and stews. Very fast they built their monuments on the backs of anonymous waiters. Hey, the Revolution did not liberate the waiters. Is not one of the reasons for revolution food? "Let them eat cake," said Marie Antoinette. Okay, what I wish to know is who served it?

Garçon. The word in French is insulting.

In English it has more dignity. No question, there is some virtue yoked to the word. Waiter.

Waiting. We are still waiting for our cognizance. Gratuities will not buy us off forever. We will get angry someday at all the eating people paying no regard. We are like a family waiting, having our differences, without doubt. So wide are we scattered we have need of some movement as the women have in the world today. We would like some heed for our long service, for keeping our tongues and bowing down.

Peerless media people eat at Le Soleil Couchant. At lunch we serve businessmen in high favour. At supper we seat the retired, the middle-aged, the young. Tourists and couples and coupon-holders and gays and conference-goers and women. Women together are on the ascent and these are my favourites to serve. With a smile, I drag them under the tablecloth. No way, R.J.! But I give extra service when I please. I redispose the cherry tomatoes in their salad like parrot hearts.

For sure, people like to eat out at a good restaurant. It is the pleasure of our time. Even better than sex. Eating lasts longer, without doubt. Flirting is with the glasses of wine and breadsticks. Hors d'oeuvres like Assumption Day salad and goose-liver pâté and hot oysters in the shell are the foreplay. You know what is the canard aux pêches and saumon grillé au beurre blanc and filet mignon, only it lasts longer. No problem. Ask yourself, when is the reciprocity in life better than over a nice supper? Ask yourself, when is your own performance as an individual person better, when you are stuffed, or when you are looking forward to the taste of your dinner? It is why waiters are more eager on empty stomachs.

Between lunch and dinner at Le Soleil Couchant I like to come here in the park and play the girls with their skins as fair as bites in a McIntosh apple. Okay, they are tanned by the sun sometimes. Golden apples, freckled apples. I serve at forty love to them and volley.

"Harder, R.J.!"

"Show her some toe jam, Rajam!"

"Hey, R.J., go for it!"

Stupid, stupid. These tennis bums are surprised I have the advantage with these girls. Maybe they are a little jealous too. I never let a girl beat me on court and the girl respects me better. Not like Mike Boy. He pretends to lose so she will feel good. No girl wants a handout, but Mike Boy just looks over at us and wrinkles his brow like a rabbit's nose, and thinks he is on to it when he double faults. "On to it, R.J. Hey?" He never is. The girl is saying in her mind, "Take a hike, Mike." From the man she is wanting the clean pop of his serve against a tight-strung gut. Hey, really! I tell myself, go for the apples, R.J.

"French her, Mike. Like R.J. here!"

I am no connoisseur of the haute cuisine. I am no gastro-nomic. Sometimes I go to McDonald's for an apple turnover and chocolate shake to watch the waiters serve. And I think, think how high you are, R.J. Think of the level you serve at, how auspicious to be waiting at a place high up, compared to these poor counter hoppers. You are not so many years older than these waiters. But no, they will have their destiny too.

Here is the gist for argument. Who is thinking of what they are eating? Okay, except the critics, who comes to a res-taurant with a beautiful view to pay attention all the time to the crispness of her asparagus? To how much chopped tarra-gon Louis has placed in his Béarnaise sauce? Some critics, if I knew who they were, I would like to puncture with a fork. Talk about hot air, in the winter we could heat Le Soleil Couchant for free. Hey, I would like to rate them at their tables with lip-stick marks on the tablecloth. One balloon. Three balloons.

Stupid, stupid. They cannot taste anything except their own wind. How I hate their word "succulent." How I hate their words "fresh" and "delicious." Even their word "meal" irritates me. What they think is tough or not good to eat is limited to their tiny world and their language having no adjectives for poverty. And I have more annoyances. Their understanding of hunger is the four or five hours since their gourmet lunch. They do not understand Time or what is in the waiting to eat somebody's leftovers. That tells you something. They think Le Soleil Couchant is theirs. They bellyache how long our ser-vice takes when we who are trying not to hurry them bite our mouths. Not to make them feel unwelcome, who would skiver their balloons? Not us.

Sometimes I will think in my sunless thoughts, all din-ers are the same. At sunset I raise the bamboo curtain. Those people are surprised at what they see, even when they expect it. The blood-red sky, the grain ships, the ocean west. What did they expect, a storm blowing in out of the blue? Dhows and vallams off the Pacific? Some terrible deluge to overtake them? Why do they feel agitated when I touch them and say, "Look at our view!" André, the other waiter in my section, tells me, "They're not used to friendly service, n'est-ce pas?"

Hey, no problem. When they are finished worrying their entrées I tell them, "For our special dessert, please, we are having crêpes suzettes or flambéed bananas."

Poof.

I do my dance again, with rum in the chafing dish. For a moment all the eyes turn around on me until the flame dies and the voices begin again, the glasses clinking against the plates, the tinkling laughter.

Another word I hate is "tips." It sounds coarse like you know what. In a café I have seen a sign, "Please Don't Pinch Our Waitress's Tips!!" In the picture of her she has a pair of crazy ones. Ted knows I hate the word "tips." He sniffs, "How were your *gratuities* this evening, Rajam?" He too teases me.

August, my favourite month, is upon us. The blackberries have begun to surge in thickets along the seaside cliffs. They are blackening, no question. The public lawns have gone ochre for stint of rain, thistles cling to the ground like starfish to a jute mat. They becalm my soul. I am saying to myself, patience, everybody is waiting for a better time. For the food line at Mission Light to get moving, the beer strike to end, the chiropractor to tug harder when his office is teeming with patients. The present I am thinking is no laugh. There are multitudes that hunger in darkness.

"Okay, R.J.?"

My friends worry when I am not following their gambling and talking. We are lying on grass by the tennis courts, tanning. Only I am not tanning, I am learning leisure. The big plane trees shade us a little in their pleasure, the fleshy leaves of many hands, draping all over these welfare bums and pennystock players at the backgammon board.

"Hey, R.J.'s tugging his dickey! Cool."

These bums make me laugh. I lie back some more to listen to the rhythmic smacking of balls in the asphalt courts. Balls clink the fence. Girls fly squealing at our nets. A seaplane homes in from the sea to pass over this isthmus for the beautiful, safe harbour. Only the ruffling crow is silent in the scabby limbs.

Lob and smash. The coup de maître. My friends are betrayed by my thoughts.

The sun has swelled to its hottest and I am waiting its slow return from tropical to temperate heat. No question, I am a patient fellow, a handsome bird who is threatening no one with my shiny looks. After one more game of tennis I will walk home to my room and put on a white shirt and my black jacket. I will preen with the leisure of a scavenger. I will put the screws to this old Slazenger and step out to my vocation.

Hey, outta the way for R.J. He's got his eye on all the marbles.

This morning the moon was still up. I was walking in the park with my bicycle by the sea. A child asked his father, "Can a bird get to the moon?" The father answered the child, "The moon is far out in space."

This is how I feel some of the times. I feel like a bird, waiting for the moon to beckon me. "Waiter? May we have our check, please?" I don't want the moon. I am happy enough lots of days. I will pilfer from Time's leftovers and have my memories. Tomorrow I will go swimming and bob in the salt.

But tonight I will be sad after waiting. I will be a little lonely for some company. No way would I ever tell these friends here I am sad. "Hey. R.J.'s getting blue." They think I am in the eye of the hurricane at Le Soleil Couchant.

I am, too. Watching.

Waiting.

LE MAL DE L'AIR

SUPPOSE he had a three-day-old festering on the elbow, ate pork at his mother's on Sunday and got sick: his wife would rather blame his illness on bee stings than on worms in a good woman's meat. Bees she believed just as likely to cause nausea and the shakes as they were a slowly puffed-up arm. Her responses were intemperate, and increasingly persistent. She had been to the doctor who could find nothing wrong inside her long, splendid body. Once she took her cello to the Gulf Islands and played on the beach for a pair of misplaced whimbrels. She wasn't happy. You had to conclude that something had infected their marriage. "Or am I just getting bitter," wondered the discomfited Miles, "as the two of us grow alike?"

He marshalled particulars in no sense of a brief. For what he was catching from her couldn't be put into words, not yet, and certainly not in court. As a child he had formed the habit, witness in the box, of recounting events leading up to some imagined crime he'd witnessed. Over the years it got complicated. How much of what one observed was relevant to what one saw? How much indeed of what one saw justified even mentioning what one imagined? A tricky, indulgent business.

Like telling the jury about this man ahead of you in line, who ends up robbing the bank: do you bother saying you had a premonition he was a bandit, because the colour of his pants reminded you of a mole's belly? What kind of evidence was that? What sort of connection—unless you also explain that the smell of freshly turned earth never fails to remind you of a childhood friend named Anton Speke, sitting together long ago in a field plotting to shoplift a Meccano set from the hardware store one fall morning. Was that clear, Your Honour? Fields and theft? Moles and theft? No, the bridgework was defective. Besides, you didn't smell his pants, you were looking at them.

He could imagine crimes with the same mislocated fervour as Ruth courted birds. If he ran into an old girlfriend in Safeway, one he hasn't seen since high school, she might be coming down the aisle when suddenly shots ring out and a little bulldog of a man with oily hair dashes past and disappears into the stockroom, his pistol smelling. In your judicious reconstruction of events, do you mention you both had mop handles sticking out of your baskets? Both? Should you mention the woman at all? (Let alone mops.) What, precisely, was *irrelevant*? Her gaudy rings, maybe.

The surfeit of event and contingency was a potluck supper. All dishes welcome but eating them in the wrong combination made your stomach ache, possibly your head. The right equations—since Miles was a civil engineer with responsibilities for, if limited accomplishments in, the Third World—the right equations turned up sooner or later once he spotted the invalid ones.

That child on the curb. You watch her warily in case she springs into the road in front of your car. She does, you hit her—kill her—though your shoe on the brake was poised. Shoe, who cares? Not a jury. Certainly not for any of your compassion towards a ragged kid, seconds before impact, with you imagining what you might, as a man with money in the bank, do for her squalid life given the chance and inclination. (A life, Your Honour, that smelled of onions outside my window, desolation.) How far, in other words, did words go before they no longer conveyed the truth and became, well, icing on neurosis? Talk in search of straws? Irrelevance for the sake of survival? (Surely there were signs.) How exactly was Miles to account for what he was catching from Ruth?

Exactly?

Russians were outfoxing him in Indonesia. (Impossible.)

His wife, while not turning away from him, had started looking over his shoulder.

Maybe this was normal for any marriage after sixteen years.

Parking the Volvo he stepped out of the garage into a pile of empty plant pots she'd left on the sidewalk.

Manslaughter was the disease of inattention.

It really went back to dogs. Not that he was a big dog-lover, but lately when her fear of dogs returned it seemed to infect his own trust in them.

Trust was an innocence Ruth had long ago lost. Newly married she'd kept her fear under control; when they strolled she let Miles carry on talking whenever a dog came up for a sniff. She lowered her eyes, flushed, caught her breath. Cavalierly, Miles could snub a Doberman pinscher by paying it no more attention than seagulls or a clump of bamboo. Dog gone, her tall body loosened, her dark eyes resurfaced. She would make fun of her fear. They would kiss and talk about the future. He could remember whole days of walking; the smell of sun in her shampooed hair; a nick on his lip from shaving. He asked did he taste salty, and she, licking his nick said, if he did it was a sugary sort of salt. Those days the kinds of shoes he wore were inexpensive but jaunty pairs of Argentine imports never quite broken in. (Only in retrospect do your mistakes begin to press through the sides of your socks like hives.)

These days Ruth went out walking on her own. Miles sat in front of his drafting board neglecting her for cantilevers and plate girders. Perhaps she'd just had some particularly violent encounter to have rekindled her fear of dogs, she never said. Sweeping lawns and gentle dogwood, this neighbourhood was the most beautiful they'd ever lived in, unthreatening, quiet. The crickets only ripened the quiet, thought Miles. One evening when he insisted on accompanying her, a large spotted dog came off somebody's porch to give them a sniff. She bloodied his palm, she was squeezing so hard. Her nails went through his sweater just above the bicep.

"Jesus!" he told her. "R*elax!* It's a Dalmatian. Here boy!" He looked at his wife amazed. "You know, a fireman's dog? They're friendly, Dalmatians."

She was quietly sobbing. "If only Wing's dog hadn't savaged me."

Wing's dog, an Alsatian, had terrorized her one summer day, twenty-five years ago, when she was buying parsnips for her aunt. Springing from the Chinese kitchen like a panther, snarling, gnashing, knocking her down on a dirty wooden floor, this animal, trained to scare off burglars by night, had awoken suddenly at noon with its wires crossed. Ever after Ruth felt betrayed. She hated violence. She hated her aunt for not going back and tearing into the grocer for letting his dog tear into her! "We'll see about Mr. Wing," she promised. But with the greengrocer cheaper than Safeway, and without ever referring to the incident again, her aunt started going back to him for her potatoes and leeks.

Thereafter the complex that Ruth developed around dogs revealed itself in petrification and a purply complexion. This was her "dog-scare skin." To Miles it looked like roses in dark cheeks: making her even more beautiful. Garbage, she said, for in the mirror she saw veiny cheekbones and sodden eyes belonging to her father, who used to lunge her way muttering in Spanish, drunk. (How eyes, Your Honour.)

The roses lasted days. At two dinner parties in a row she brushed off questions from friends with pretty lies about skiing the sunburnt glacier on Baker. Rooted deep in her childhood, this complexion, this fear, was entirely credible. Miles could, if not like its recrudescence, understand its persistence. The trouble was him—what her fear had started doing to him.

The span between them began to crumble.

Take the Sunday afternoon they went walking after lunch, along a country road beyond his mother's farm. The second farm they passed had a big white dog with floppy lips and a tail that swished up the dust. When Ruth saw it—there was something about this dog—she felt safe. "It's a setter," she decided. "There's setter blood in it." Setters were even-tempered and trustworthy; around setters she felt no shame.

It trotted ahead to sniff slough grass and point at swimming mallards. It was like walking their own pet.

Miles, worried that stones were wearing through his expensive Italian loafers, pretended to look at the ducks while trying to clean off his soles by casually walking in the grass.

After half a mile their dog started to whine. "Look," said Ruth. "He wants us to go back."

Tugging their held hands gently with its mouth it signalled why: just ahead was a black Lab as big as a bear standing on the road outside a dilapidated tarpaper house. The setter, its tail hugging its haunches like wet hemp, was terrorized.

"I don't think we should go any farther, Miles. Let's go back."

"Don't be ridiculous," said Miles.

"I want to go back."

Miles refused and kept on, pretending an equilibrium neither Ruth nor the setter embodied. His wife changed sides and held on to both his hands, walking sideways. Humming like a witch doctor. The setter whined. They pushed on like a little safari.

At some line on the road they crossed with no more warning than Capricorn, the Lab charged, its shoulders swaying from too much food, chain collar clattering in the sunlight.

"I *told* you we should've gone back!" Ruth screamed.

Everything happened so fast, hackles up, lips curled—a dog fight seemed inevitable and the setter, cringing submissively, appeared ready to die climactically. Bristling, the Lab pulled up three feet away, eyes like foglights trained on their now-whimpering dependant. Ruth had closed her eyes and was squeezing Miles's hand like she meant to punish him for hubris. Wincing, he told her to grow up. *You* grow up, she said.

Afterwards in silence you sit down in the long marsh grass by the river. You discover you're trembling. Her fear seems to have passed across. (You too hate violence, the thought of being challenged physically after giving some van driver the high beams, say, for cutting you off, enough to make you lock your door at the next stoplight.) For a moment you hate her, hate yourself, since irrational fear's irritating fear. Debilitating. But is it irrational? A fly on your loafer makes you think of candy, the fudgy colour of your shoe, the shoe itself. Communication itself, its direction. The river ebbs, the log booms beach. Droning up the channel a cabin cruiser disappears into the sugarloaf mountains. September sunlight. Enchanting river. You have no idea if your setter's saved. There's a great blue heron standing on a log mired in mud. You watch her watching the bird.

Walking back along the dike, Miles said wouldn't it be nice to be on Cozumel now that fall was here? (Winter he meant was coming.) Holsteins grazing the dike, the grass gone to seed. Had she noticed, by the way, this far up the river there were no bridges? Her cheeks just bloomed.

This his mother put down to sitting too near the wood stove. "There now, Ruthie. You drink this fresh milk." She tempted her with dessert. You could tell, Miles could, his mother was hoping for darker, more maternal reasons for her daughter-in-law's exotic flush.

On the way home Ruth said she'd like to kill herself.

She had black reddish hair, shoulders of supple round bone, and breasts—breasts their male friends would lapse into staring at when their brains were awash in wine. They (her breasts) had the shape of large citrus fruits from Tobago, adding to the foreignness about her, for apart from her exotic skin and Haida jewellery, her eyes looked Ceylonese and her movements, at least in the stride of her long legs, African. She pushed shopping carts like unfamiliar toys, holding nothing craved since she herself ate little and indifferently. She gave the impression—had given Miles the impression the first time he ever saw her, hitchhiking—of exquisite laziness: something of the concubine with a hint of a self-reliant Amazon. This lazy look was a ruse, her energy northern not southern. At nineteen she'd quit university to go into hairdressing, which she soon built into the ten-chair business Crimpers decided it couldn't ignore, so made her an offer she chose not to refuse. When they returned to Vancouver after a year's travelling, and after living in London for two more years, she applied what she'd learned about carpentry and interior design at a polytechnic in Chelsea to revamping neglected houses. She got Miles into buying and selling houses at the right time ("moving up" their friends with the same passion called it), and after a decade they'd lived in more large and wonderful old westside homes than any other couple they knew. They liked to say he was with his third company, and she their seventh home.

A friend of theirs with hair like a veil was saying, as she parted it to peer, "We're all into second adolescence, right? Like when we were going around in high school and breaking up and going around again. That's what most of us are into all over in our thirties, metamorphosis. Political survival. New partners as negotiating weapons. Like when Bob and I were being worse for each other than tainted sockeye, okay, and decided to break up? Neither of us lost because each of us was dealing from a position of strength. He had this divorcée from Yakima who'd chew bullets for him." She went on. "You two are different, you travel a lot, you're not into parenting. You keep busy. Boredom's what killed Bob and me. Sheer fucking boredom. That was the product somehow."

No season more prone than another to the shufflings of friends, no particular smell a reminder, unless it was cigar smoke and (no, Your Honour) Miles hadn't tried, or thought, to understand the connection between that smell and divorce. The language varied. Bright colours, as in green pumps or scarlet ties, made a little more sense in this evolutionary perspective of expanding friends, when their old friends brought around new husbands, new wives, to parade like peacocks through meals and conversations. They were always eating rice. Or orange peels in yogurt. Ruth put little of herself into culinary fashion. (Though, as somebody put it soberly, she may have been setting the fashion.)

Friends agreed having children could be just as selfish as having none. You did it to fill a hole in your lives. Couples Miles knew with children lacked a certain edge, which made living, if safer, less challenging. Childless and underdeveloped (as he and Ruth) you had this space at the edge of things, a kind of fear, across which you built a relationship out of shared perspectives like the way burning leaves smelled in autumn or a wavering falsetto voice sounded on a Punjabi music program driving home. The danger was over-engineering. Divorce was seldom constructive—childlessness rarely without risk. Married to Ruth he felt the same uneasy excitement as being married to his career. He could snuggle up to Third World countries on behalf of his company, help prepare its bid for a contract coveted by other countries and financed by the World

Bank, hoping in the pit of his stomach to forge the necessary link, using greasy circumlocutions and a faulty lingua franca with cabinet ministers, corrupt company presidents, contractors, blackmarketeers. Always too many children on the streets, or living on pilings around jetties. Part of his job was to hang around riverbanks taking soil borings, planning abutments. The fear in Peru as at home with Ruth was this space you sat on the edge of—dangling your legs.

That winter, following her resurgence of dog-fright in the fall, Ruth began to smoke. As a student she'd smoked but stopped because Miles had asthma, which cigarette smoke triggered if he was tired. Also, later, women who came in and paid good money to have it cut hadn't appreciated smoky smells in their freshly washed hair. It was just as easy to give up smoking. Now it surprised him how far down into her lungs she persisted in dragging her smoke. This to soften attacks of what a friend told her was angst. Earwax she made it sound like.

Her first attack came on a beautiful day after Christmas, clear and cold. She just got up from her seat and walked away. They were riding the ferry across the Gulf of Georgia through great rafts of floating goldeneyes; in Active Pass an eagle had fallen like a star.

"Did you find some?" he asked.

"Only Camels. So I got Camels."

"They're filterless."

She said, "I need a sharp bite."

This was how she began again, by biting herself with Camels. Miles wheezed. She felt calmed down she said. He asked if she remembered the old man who used to walk around Jericho wearing a jacket with red letters on the back: Lung Cancer Cures Smoking. She smoked five in a row and the angst went away. Miles stepped out on deck. Pines leaned like palm trees off the ends of little islands. Proboscis monkeys moved like interlopers when you saw them on a road through the jungle. Among the islands a dead wind.

"I feel much better," she claimed.

But after their weekend at the Empress, on a luminous New Year's Day, she faced it again when they cleared the islands on their return voyage and encountered the bucking gulf.

"Oh," Miles was thinking, "how in love with light I feel. I'm in love with what light makes."

"My God," muttered Ruth. "I feel it coming back."

Taking a cigarette from her handbag she lit it with fearful fingers. (She had bought a whole carton in Victoria.) A fading afternoon. Viewing the American sunlight on Baker, the pink snow of nesting glaciers, gleaming ridges of smaller mountains at the volcano's knees, he felt sad.

"I don't know what's the matter," she said, inhaling. "I can't get it down fast enough."

The ferry pitched into darkness and he lost sight of the volcano—pink into violet into nothing. Pressed an instant too long a steam iron stained shirt collars (forever). He reached for her hand.

"Don't let me start smoking, Ruth, will you?"

"You? What do you mean?"

What did he? "It stains the teeth."

"Well, at least you can drop yours in a solution every night."

That night he dreamed his mind full of seedless apple pie. Sitting in a café in Algeciras where he'd just given a talk on lemon meringue to Brownies, none of whom understood his French, or had ever seen dental floss, he helped himself to a large piece of whipped brain, his own.

He woke up wheezing in a cloud of fumes blown south from a pulp mill up the coast. Crown Zellerbach, poisoning men without recourse at four in the morning. He felt sick. He had no desire to go in to work, his holidays were not until June.

Suppose you reach out for her in bed and she isn't there. Smoking, Your Honour, like a chimney.

———————

Delayed until his graduation, their honeymoon had been a year's journey around the world. Miles had grown a beard. He'd imagined crimes such as having their passports stolen out of hotel pigeonholes in countries with no Canadian consulates, and nomad shoe robbers leaving them barefoot on the Russian-built highway in the middle of the Afghani desert. Pickpockets were a worry, so in Barcelona where he had a suede jacket tailored he demanded a large inside pocket which, when he felt the depth of it two days later, travelled from nipple to hip. Starting in Morocco they zigzagged by boat and train between North Africa and Mediterranean Europe, before pushing across Asia in fly-blown buses. It seemed they'd taken each other for better or for worse in every country under the sun. Only a year older than he, but far wiser in the ways of making a living, she told him that despite his fresh engineering degree he couldn't expect to call himself educated till he learned to handle money. Thus, with their letter of credit in *his* name, he learned to buy and sell some of the world's most exotic and least significant currencies. (Thanks to her acumen and Crimpers' acquisitiveness.)

The farther east they went the more threatening the black eyes following their movements, hers in particular, in countries where women, if seen at all, were covered up in chadors like nocturnal birdcages or else secreted in bar-windowed rooms, usually up little lanes beyond bazaars. Once, in an empty lot outside Istanbul, coming across uncovered Muslim women weaving rope, they suddenly felt like intruders. The women laughed. "Only in their masters' absence," said Ruth. She blamed men for choking half the laughter in the world.

"Bastards."

Also in Istanbul (no enlightenment here) the conjunction of a stained toilet bowl in their hotel and a wintry, coal-smelling city full of sullen staring men, caused her to break down. The ostensible cause was a postal clerk who said she couldn't mail a parcel of clothes back to Canada without unwrapping the ends. Her response was out of all proportion to the man's smug indifference. She exploded. Then, trembling, cried. Miles was amazed. It dawned on him you couldn't gauge his new wife's happiness by her lazy look, for underneath were currents of considerable voltage. The real culprit he guessed was the toilet bowl over which they'd quarrelled the night before. It depressed her. All a dirty toilet made Miles do was think of shoe polish; that and his light, comfortable travelling shoes he hated because they were pointed. You could not, though he'd been trying for weeks, wear out a pair of outmoded Hush Puppies.

Ruth, worn out by the bizarre customs of unsympathetic cultures, found little to keep up her spirits. To her nothing anymore seemed unfamiliar. Nothing surprised. Miles, on the other hand, was taking notes like a lunatic, on bridges they were crossing, had crossed, hoped to cross. Accepted by the London School of Economics to study Political Economy the following October, he was already planning to write his thesis on Fixed and Moveable Connectives Spanning Selected Third-World Rivers. (Eventually published in a condensed version by a firm off Shaftesbury Avenue specializing in nutritional tracts for uneducated mothers in countries like Botswana. Certain diagrams that the printer found too elaborate he had to redraw.) This, naturally, slowed them down. The middle of nowhere, removing themselves and luggage from a bus that vanished down the highway, all because Miles decided he needed an hour or two's sketching. Then off again in some vehicle carting pullets to market, or forced to spend the night on the banks of the Euphrates, Indus, Ganges, Irrawaddy, Mekong. His hair was the length of the sixties and no matter what bank they ended up on people dismissed them as travelling freeloaders, especially women who came down to spread out laundry and found the sun rising on two lumps in sleeping bags. No wonder Ruth picked up a bug, drinking bad water. Travelling infected through Isfahan, Shiraz, Maashad, Herat and Kandahar—through the Khyber Pass to Peshawar—before falling so violently sick they had to spend ten days at Dean's Hotel, in an expensive garden bungalow, where she tried to be cheerful but felt as weak as a beggar. Miles fell sick too. He vomited his false tooth into the toilet bowl and fished out the plate with his hand. Her little joke was he should invest in a bridge. Throwing their budget to the wind they stayed on, sleeping till tea, listening to myna birds in the peepul trees. By that time, without having washed her hair since Kabul, Ruth discovered she had lice.

"I hate travel," she said. "There's nothing in it but bones."

They quarrelled. The intense heat replaced compassion with passion. It was all him him him and his stupid notebook and whimsy. *He* had infected her by making them travel in broken-down buses instead of planes. She didn't *have* a sense of adventure, no, and what was more, irrelevant field notes like his were only so many little egoprops. She cried; he went silent.

Taking the train to Karachi they booked a plane to Bombay. They travelled by plane to Trivandrum and Colombo, Delhi and Rangoon, Bangkok, Phnom Penh, Hong Kong. They took trains to Calcutta, Mandalay, Chiang Mai. The planes were worse. Yet inside the cool thick walls of some hotel of the Raj, in Jaipur, say, or Cochin, where splendid rooms and lavish meals cost little and punkahs diluted the humidity, they reaffirmed their love, laughed at themselves, palmed each other off like towels. You had to wonder why the starving didn't steal the hoarse peacocks and wring their necks in the golden morning air. Miles bought himself sandals that smelled dungy. Down south among the lagoons and coal-black fishermen you got this feeling the stirred-up cells of parading Marxists were incapable of reason. Ruth gave rupees to beggar children selling jasmine (one leper sold her limp hibiscus). Sometimes they discussed children of their own.

But never fear of flying. He held her hand taking off and landing, in a monsoon over Goa, during the rocky descent into Madras. He'd talk about candy, the Beatles, his preference for travellers' cheques—anything to take her mind off the vulnerability her trembling betrayed. Yet going on to discuss the black market, roller skates, Asian odours, he began to realize that it was his own mind he had actually leashed to the patient guide of relevant irrelevance. (Like pimps, dogs in India were cowards, skulkers, undersized pariahs, with a very low estimation of themselves. Tails between their legs was the way they ran away from Ruth. In Malaysia she was pleased to discover hardly any dogs because of the curious Oriental practice of eating them, fried.) Sometimes with the sky completely calm, and them suspended in it as in a vacuum, Miles would be gripped with an apprehension that she, reading a magazine or sipping a drink, quickly sensed. She flushed. Blamed him for the colour of her skin when they "de-planed." Any other bride she said wouldn't have come nearly as far—given the free associations of his particular habits as a traveller.

Only on their last leg, between Tokyo and Vancouver, when the plane bumped taking off, did Miles have to hand her the bag marked "Pour le mal de l'air." He felt so sorry for his beautiful bride his eyes moistened and he thought how much gnawing must have built up inside her during their peregrinations, to fill a bag like that. Hanging around the stink of excremental waters full of junks in Hong Kong harbour, she'd waited patiently for him to finish his notes on the proposed tunnel between Kowloon and the island. Because her shorn hair hadn't grown all the way back, Your Honour, the rickshaw coolies were hiding smiles. He imagined them kidnapping his wife, dumping her drugged into a closet, waiting for her hair to grow longer before selling her off to the boss of some secret society. Instead, one of the coolies with a pigtail, as if to put his booty on file, merely went over and marked her arm with a razor.

What he had studiously thought of as *her* irrational response to fear and the unknown had perhaps, after all, its root in him. Soon to be a scholar in London, he brushed the hair from his eyes. He could feel bluebottles on his toes, even though he was flying, martini in hand, higher than Everest.

"It's a bear or something," she was saying now, years later. "I keep seeing it coming for me out of the darkness."

"Your cankering angst?" he asked but the joke fell flat.

Towards spring she began to lose four and five hours of sleep. It was an odd feeling to wake up in the middle of the night, thinking of work, and find the bed beside you empty. He'd find her downstairs reading a novel, smoking.

"I couldn't sleep, Miles. Poor Oyster. You go back to bed."

He tried, wheezed heavily, got up and drank milk. Sometimes they made love, felt drowsy, dropped off. But she would wake up again, unable to sleep, fearful.

He arrived at his office anxious and tired.

Came home the same.

"Sleep is a habit," she told him. "Break the habit and you have to learn all over."

A remark that called for a shot of Teacher's instead of milk, so some mornings he had a headache besides. No matter how far away seemed the Third World he had to remind himself he was living, in Vancouver, on the edge of the same seawater. The same Pacific Rim. New language crept in, new directions, but whether we were West and they were East, or we North they South, his country should have been building more hydro dams and bridges, definitely more bridges.

On her birthday they ate a large meal of roast beef and scallops at a restaurant (Miles did, Ruth had salad), drank a bottle of Dao, saw a movie at a second-run cinema, and dragged themselves to bed where they dropped off like children. Neither slept long and she ended up on the sofa curled naked under the afghan, a gift from his mother. A position she'd had some luck with two nights earlier. He went back to bed and slept fitfully, dreaming of Susannah York's bare breasts; Alan Bates had reduced them to jelly, after annihilating her husband with an aboriginal shout of stupendous proportions on a North Devon sand dune. He woke up stunned. Ears buzzing. His dinner lay in him like hooves.

What we really need, Your Honour, is a duvet filled with white goose feathers.

In the morning Ruth went to her doctor who ran a cardiogram, a mammogram, and took a Pap smear. He prescribed tranquillizers.

"Just till I get back into the habit he said."

They worked. One Valium one half-hour before bed and she was out for eight hours the moment head touched pillow. Time just collapsed. She said it felt unbelievable to have got back her habit of sleep. She was thirty-eight. Her general cheerfulness made him realize how infrequent her spurts of it were, and how delightful. So rested did the nights now leave her she felt expansive. Not content with her house (at the moment re-tiling the upstairs bath) she started learning the Prokofiev cello sonata, reading Georg Lukás, even to torture herself wondering if her angst were merely away on vacation. She actually seemed hungry for symptoms to appease.

"Try one of these," she urged him. "It'll break a bad habit."

He took one and slept soundly flying through jungle in a winged lorry, while all around marched the empty boots of workers, even soldiers.

A month later he woke up short of breath. Feeling for her in the dark, he thought the sheet's space seemed vast, his fingers touched nothing.

She was downstairs smoking.

"What is it?" he asked.

"I've lost the habit. I've taken three, I don't want to take any more." She sounded sad.

But taking a fourth she fell asleep at five a.m. She might as well have passed away. Miles stayed up and read a paperback by Jacques Hébert. At breakfast she told him, "It's a sinking feeling I get. I start thinking I'm not going to sleep. And then ... who knows why ..."

Who knew anything about creeping uncertainty? Your wife decides to spend the weekend on Salt Spring Island. You've built up trust like a bank account and then this uncertainty about the balance looms, as if the man in charcoal slacks has a prior claim on it—on your wife who secretly withdraws a sizeable sum to bury in her garden near the birdbath. She has fantasies of flight, of nectarean air, especially of a country where dogs love her. You listen to her cello. You bring her coffee where she sits by roses complaining of languor. In the flowerbed a bulldog the colour of a mole is helping sniff out secluded places.

Well. Waking up to facts, Your Honour, is looking at hair on the back of your hand for the first time. It's as mysterious as muddy shoes on a dry afternoon: unlike a child you look for a car and puddle to blame. Mud and hair. Languor and angst. You learn to deduce, seduce, reduce signs so they come out equal to these, less equal to those. My wife's appetite improves. Why? Gradually your world becomes more unpredictable than predictable. More vulnerable to competition, failure. Suppose these drawings you are preparing for presentation this month on a causeway in Surabaja suddenly go up in smoke one night when the office sprinkling system has been turned off (for repairs, so it's claimed, to the main valve in the basement). Sabotage? Eyes eyes eyes ... how you need eyes growing older. Your own espionage. Seventeen years ago he could stare at a beautiful girl hitchhiking and trust his reflexes to be on the job—at the wheel, on the brake—raising warnings of their own. Now he couldn't even create on paper the interchanges he used to erect as a student in his head. The steel was colder, more real. You used to look over your shoulder changing lanes and trust the car in front not suddenly to brake and . . .

Now you wonder if the distance across spaces can be measured at all.

"Did you say something, Miles?"

"I remember seeing Soviet advisers in Cuba, when I flew there from London. They kept discreetly in the background. Wearing black trunks around hotel swimming pools. You could spot them by the way they flicked their cigars."

"What are they wearing these days? Jogging suits?"

He smoked, he got up and read, he took Valium. Her angst had infected him like a fishy affair she was having with one of their friends. The more his brain wandered with formal preoccupations the wider grew the zone around his body in need of protecting, the space a confident person instinctively guarded with tuned senses.

He sought to defend this zone methodically. He gave more car lengths between his car and the next; he walked around the block with glances behind him every twenty flagstones. He gave more space in line to the man at the bank.

He incorporated caution to arrest shrinkage.

Yet mistrust between them robbed him of a balance he used to take for granted. They began blaming one another for cranky good mornings, for not replacing the toilet roll. Not putting dirty dishes in the dishwasher. His ability to grab *any* carrot held out by the World Bank seemed diminished by his preoccupation with discovering professional answers through domestic equations. Accidental contacts were better than none, but a successful (initialled) agreement meant finding a way to communicate precisely. To talk of top chords, shoes, bottom lateral bracings was all very fine; far harder to agree on the kind of bridge in need of building.

With summer approaching, his boss acted relieved to see him preparing for a five-week vacation in Greece. Lately, at his drafting board, Miles had been working too hard to get anywhere.

Ruth went back to Salt Spring.

A week before they were to embark for Athens a bee stung him in the garden. He had stopped to smell a rose on his way in from the garage. That Sunday, visiting his mother to say goodbye, he started shivering so violently after dinner Ruth drove him home. He felt awful, like his insides were being sucked out of him, but when he tried vomiting, nothing came.

It wasn't his mother's pork, she said, *it was the stinger in his elbow.*

She hated the unexpected. Plans had been made. She managed to get him onto penicillin in a hurry. *She* felt very well, thank you.

Not a boast true for long, because two nights before their flight, walking Miles around the block to test his strength, she was attacked on the sidewalk by a hairy young man where the chestnut trees blotted out the streetlight.

Jogging past them one way, then their own way, he spun and dove, implanting his hand on her private parts, shouting wildly.

Vanishing, like an incubus.

Miles swept hysterical Ruth into his arms to cherish her. He felt hysterical himself. Tried to tell her it was nothing—a man high on drugs—no harm done.

"He could have had a knife!" she cried.

He put her to bed with Valium, with no improvement.

"I keep seeing him coming at me!"

Miles kept seeing him too: with the premonition he was up to something, passing and repassing them on the sidewalk. But the scent of honeysuckle from somebody's garden, the feeling of euphoria from his own medicine, prevented Miles from understanding someone else's sickness and thinking to protect his wife.

He sat up reading her the account of Mrs. Jellyby and they both smoked. Too drowsy to read anymore he lay down on their bed and remembered nothing. He never asked what time she came to bed; she was cutting tiles in the morning when he went in to shave. The glue smell reminded him of burnt cocoa at Scout camp. They agreed they were both still shaken.

At the barber's an effeminate voice addressed him from behind. "Ready, sir?" He jumped a foot. The young man stood there in his designer T-shirt surprised, and very neat. "I'm sorry," he kept repeating. "Really, I am. I didn't mean to be rude." Holding a white comb patiently in the fingers of both his hands, extracting pleasure.

At home Ruth was packing his Wallabees. Feeling diminished and languid he'd begun to fear her. Neither of them looked forward to connecting flights in Toronto and London; neither looked forward to Greece.

Grapes, heat, temples: these connected with nothing at all.

Two hours before leaving for the airport, he received a call to say that his rivals in Surabaja had been triumphant, with their proposal for an altogether different sort of bridge.

The impossible, it seemed, proving otherwise.

From under the Cinzano umbrella in Constitution Square a woman's voice:

"This heat's worse than politics in Chicago. The bad smells make you wonder why we didn't fly right to Crete. No wonder the Caryatids are crumbling. The air's full of plague. Fumes, corrosion. All night it's bee bee beep. Sometimes I just wanna hold up a bank and run away with the loot to Palm Springs permanently. There's no percentage in exotica. This ouzo tastes like iodine."

At their hotel on Mitropoleos the heat wave made sleep impossible (that and the man coming at them with a knife).

"I hate travel," said Ruth. "Why did I let you talk me into this? It's your fault. I was perfectly happy staying in Canada for the holidays. There's nothing unnatural about the way I feel. You just don't understand. It's all you you you. You don't care about *me*. All you care about is yourself. You haven't got any sympathy. You're a cold person, Miles. I hate you."

However, after a nap and shower she would say, "I'm sorry, Oyster. I'm a weakling, aren't I? I promise to do better."

Democracy, taken away since their last visit sixteen years ago, had been taken back. *Demokratía.* The traffic didn't care, its law was the jungle's. Too hot for more than sitting under pomegranate trees in the Agora, or drinking cups of Greek coffee in the Plakka, they waited to call back the car agency to hear if the doctor from São Paulo, Brazil, who'd "encountered emergency" in Thessalonika (transmission? run-over shepherd?) and was three days overdue, had yet returned the VW they'd booked two months ago.

No other vehicles were to be had.

Ruth kept insisting, "I *knew* we should have booked with Hertz."

Miles got sweat stains on his Wallabees before having the sense to put on sandals.

He roamed the *Blue Guide,* also his Greek dictionary.

In thick traffic their escape from Athens in a badly tuned Fiat took half the morning. Should he be involved in a *dystychema* he wanted to know who exactly no-fault insurance covered. Ruth smoked, but because of the pollution outside refused to open a window. Not till they got into the Peloponnesus did the heat moderate, in towns like Nauplia where they slept well for two nights in a hotel of bougainvillea,

roses and caged thrushes. In the walled garden Ruth sang
to the cages. Miles daydreamed his way through Tiryns. In
Githeion their hotel overlooked fish boats tied up like bulls to
heavy iron rings. Above Sparta, mountains were topped with
snow.

For nourishment he looked to the countryside's bright
light on olive leaves, stone fences, prickly pear. She found it in
more novel things (for her): souvlaki, tomato salads, mous-
saka, veal and roast potatoes, fruit, pastries, baklava. Of course
eating like the Greeks she got used to olive oil on everything.
It started in Kalamata where she just walked into the restaurant's kitchen pointing to dishes on the vast iron stove. Out
of this act of independence grew her appetite. She began eating like a horse. Depressed, Miles merely nibbled. Ruth ate
his share as well as her own. And eating made her sleep like
a child. Dreaming no more of attacks she grew unaccount-
ably jolly, she quit smoking. Miles, on the other hand, started
smoking Dutch cigars, drinking Demestica wine, and at night
dropping his front tooth and plate into a glass of water made
rabid by an extra Polident tablet.

He had trouble sleeping, not to mention catching his
breath. He said he would quit smoking when she stopped
eating. She needed a mad *skylos,* he said, to scare her onto a
diet. Cave Canem. She laughed, telling him to polish his shoes
instead of jiggling his plate in his mouth, it was disgusting.

In Pylos she navigated them to the Castle Hotel and its
little drawbridge she felt he'd admire. *Yéphira.* He hated it. He
hated her cheerfulness. The place felt grimy and harboured
mosquitoes. He felt lost travelling without a reason, and tried,
while she ate, to talk about it.

THIS RESTAURANT
IS UNDER THE PO-
LICE CONTROL PRICES

Like the sign, it seemed when you tried to talk a language you weren't easy in, the sign of it was stiffness, closure. His throat hurt.

Leaving Pylos for good they encountered another sign that imposed a frontier it hoped to dissolve.

CAME AGAIN

There was a fork in the road.

In the car, for Ruth, was a doggy bag (a doggy box).

Dropping in on the Palace of Nestor they purchased blue tickets with Solon sketched on each, precise in every respect, down to his fine nose and curly beard. Only his eyes were vague, pupil-less, pencil hatchings, his words therefore contingent on memory:

BY WINDS THE SEA IS LASHED TO STORM, BUT IF IT BE UNVEXED, IT IS OF ALL THINGS MOST AMENABLE

Driving back to Athens through Patras, Delphi and endless wheat of the hot, windy Boeotian Plain, Ruth sang till his ears hurt, before the seaside mosquitoes in Skala Oropou dined all night off his toes. Two days later, free of car, they sailed from Piraeus for the islands, Miles hoping to make sense of the suspicion—this space—between them. Aboard ship were Germans, cats and backslung infants. Inside a frescoed chapel an Algerian was eating watermelon drowned in honey; he offered a piece to Miles who got seeds under his plate.

They were in and out of islands all day. He brightened seeing the whitewashed face of Paros and Naxos, but not till sighting the snowiness of their own island in moonlight farther south did he actually toss his cigar overboard and breathe without choking. They had sailed all day and half the night. That night Ruth longed for her cello.

Next evening she ate like a refugee. Stuffed herself with food Miles only toyed with.

"Not hungry, Miles?"

"I was thinking about Indonesia."

"Guilelessly, no doubt."

"No. Well, maybe. I don't know."

"It wasn't your fault. Why don't you build North American bridges? It's a waste of time pandering to Oriental whims." She tongued her baklava redly. "You aren't corrupt enough. You need a felonious mind."

"I have one."

"In your imagination, maybe. The point is you mistake plain talk for straight. You take people at their word."

At least they were talking again. Yet with less commitment than in years past to the idea they should help one another, *could* help one another. They carried their own clothes to the little laundry; when he lent her his copy of *Poetics* she just laughed reading it; he refused the morsels of lamb she proffered. She said he wanted her to need him more than he needed her. He said it was help they each desired from the other. But she claimed there were not drachmas in the world to satisfy her growing need to eat after so long a diet.

On Sunday the Greeks dressed their children in sailor suits and pinafores. Shoes, too, of shining, absurd patent leather. (Whose patent?) Shoes, the sign of wealth parents everywhere—except maybe for the little old lady who lived in one—loved to pretend it was their children's inborn right to parade. Among the poor, thought Miles, this was the shoddy liability of having children in the first place. The world suffered because of children; too many millions needed shoes. (I should have gone to work for Mr. Bata, Your Honour.) Only the engineer responsible for the vast Howrah Bridge in Calcutta, E.P. Richards, could really say his structure made anything in the Third World happen, appealing night and day as it did to ox carts, beggars, rickshaws, cows, refugees, trucks, bicycles. Most bridges Miles worked on helped only the rich to travel from one side to another (in Mercedes); cap-teethed politicians to take credit for his designs; firms he'd worked for to prosper. Yet for even these kinds of bridges he'd begun to lose contracts. Lose faith. Unless he decided to change careers he might eventually find himself out of a job.

Very civil engineer would like to meet potential partner with foot fetish to establish a meaningful relationship. Some experience in leather desirable, though not necessary for a successful undertaking in exotic surroundings. Applicants should be fearless of travel and possess at least one foreign tongue, preferably unforked.

"I don't think we're communicating like adults, Ruth."

"I hear what you're saying, Miles." She may as *well* have added, "But I'm in a different space."

Perhaps she had.

Language curled around premonitions like slow water. Afterwards he couldn't be sure he was remembering what she had said to him, he to her, they to themselves. He wanted to escape the little lanes and mazes where he tried discussing the bonds of affection. Here they encountered no dogs of the size bred in Canada for guarding property, and so he put Ruth's blossoming skin down to her eating up everything in sight, like the rate of inflation in Bolivia. But for him to talk about "the middle crass," as he liked to, was, as Ruth put it in an equation of her own, like the pot calling the kettle black. They did not see eye to eye.

Wheezing, he dreamed his mother died. In the same dream Ruth's mother fell in with a travelling roadshow called Marty Buckerfield, who sold kitchen gadgets at fairs and home shows across the western provinces. Actually, she'd left

Ruth's father, later found with his chin in a beer-parlour urinal, dead, and was never heard from again. Ruth grew up with her aunt.

Rootless tourists, they peered past doors of meagre white-washed homes, glimpsed children singing, children chanting, children quarrelling. The Greeks tolerated their curiosity, depending as they did on tourists to live, on them and other creatures from the sea. (This was not Atlantis.)

Hanging along the quay like roots in the sun were octopus and squid. Who knew, Your Honour, how many days or weeks they hung drying before the harbourside restaurants bought them, chopped them into mouth-size pieces to serve as appe-tizers afloat in olive oil?

Suppose such arms against starvation had offered premo-nitions: Ruth would have called him schizophrenic. Would have blamed his not eating on some sort of malice he felt towards her for eating too much. Taking their customary waterfront table that evening at the restaurant called Diastáv-rose, they awaited the meal she went into the kitchen to order. He could see wealthy tourists drinking cocktails aboard rented yachts in the harbour. The island's crops were cherry tomatoes, figs, pistachio nuts. Depressed, Miles diddled his food and drank more than his share of Demestica. He fin-ished the Camels Ruth was now cured of.

He felt like killing himself.

———————

When he awoke in the morning, on the day of their intended departure, he gripped his pillow sadly. The sun was high and the room hot. His head ached, he went back to sleep. His dreams' patterns (for he dreamed with pinking shears in his paw) drifted apart like plates of the earth's crust. It was the smell that finally dragged him from sheets he might have swum through to her side. He woke up to reach out, refused to believe his fingers, rolled over and slept. It went on and on his sleep, eons.

When the policeman came by with the carpenter and lifted her into the box Miles thought of blame for the first time. If only, Your Honour, I could point the finger. There was, of course, an investigation. Yet the Cyclades were gangster-free, certainly free of feuding Sicilians, even free of metaphysical wrath with all these white churches standing as shrines to the god of sunshine.

No one else had caught her disease. No one else had suffered. Nobody else had died.

Writing out the restaurant's name the policeman would have closed the place down were there proof other stomachs besides Ruth's had bloated up with squid (or lamb or zucchini) and stopped digesting for good.

The owners had nothing with which to test for putrescence except their noses, but by then the squid had disappeared.

A few stomach aches, nai, officer, but nothing serious. We are poor, forgive us, and her eating so much, every night, all at once. Nai, yes, an accident. just a symptose is all (coincidence, explained Miles's hotel manager, concerned about his rent and so a willing translator). Miles couldn't believe his ears. Just so far was bad squid in your intestines like dogshit on your shoes; it could also kill you.

Should you mention the fat, black-robed priest at the next table, whose sweat had dripped in his food?

With no religion to save her, Ruth had simply died.

"Privacy! Privacy!" you shout when the sympathy has flowed like olive oil. Bereft, you decline to eat what's brought you, by this hotel manager and his family.

With the continuing investigation you miss your ship by three days.

Suppose instead you'd come with another woman who drank contaminated water, got hepatitis, died. The *reason* for her death would have been obvious: water infected by adultery equalled suffering. An event to clip words to, track the scent of, reconstructing . . .

Should you mention the young American couple who ordered the same dishes as Ruth? How was *her* health? Both from Arizona, where they owned nickel stock and a nursing home, claiming they never contended.

We contended, Your Honour. In Tiryns. Our whole lives! Imagine our case at the end of every voyage . . .

The pair of you sailing on the *Kydon,* second class, cabin 53. There on the floor beside you she's in a heavy, slender box. On the wall you read:

THE SIGNAL FOR ABANDONIG SHIP IS SHORT BLASTS OF THE SIREN OR RINGING OF BELLS AND 1 LONG

It gives you a headache, this sign, and you insert *sics* with a drafting pen, *sics* for spelling, *sics* for syntax.

In the passageway is the greasy little man who arranged to have the coffin brought into your cabin when the dockside officials ordered it into the cargo hold. Arranged, that is, after you slipped him pocketfuls of drachmas to confirm his suspicion the coffin was full of contraband, making him smirk knowingly, and hang around in case you needed any more assistance in lubricating a way into Piraeus. You open the door. He's passing time with the ship's whore, sharing comic books and Chiclets.

Miles crawls into the lower berth to dream his dream of Tiryns, or what had seemed a dream, about a lemon tree whose blossoms he'd started smelling like some drunkard would a still. Above him Ruth was still gliding over the vast stones in the ancient walls from which he'd just come down, irritated and wanting the guide book for himself. He was cooling off in the shade alongside an orchard.

"Selfish," she was shouting. "You you you!"

Bee stings, he was thinking, what a curious *sic*.

Heat irritated, tempers shorted, minds frayed—travelling. Anyway, who wanted to be an archeologist on a day like this, digging to uncover deadness, boning up on boredom. Let her have her guide.

It was then he heard in the lemon tree a sound like truck tires, pulsating softly on a distant highway. The sound never got closer or went away. Just a glowing roundness. Constant and pulsating. The country's heart.

He thought of working the fields as a boy with his long-dead father.

He had Ruth listen when she came down from antiquity.

"Bees," she said. "In the blossoms."

She was charmed, and they forgot to make up over the 163 *Blue Guide.*

"You get to the essence of things," she said.

And he took delight in her compliment, like a child its toy, his mood turning tuneful on the road to Mycenae. Because he saw men hammering ties in the sun, which reminded him of Cheez Whiz, of sandwiches he'd made himself as a student working summers on a green chain, he sang. (Droned, Your Honour.)

"*I've been workin' on the railroad, all the live-long day.*"

What was that smell in the car like fallen mangoes?

She went right into "Colonel Bogey's March," teaching him words she made up about impeachable Burmese bridges.

The oleander looked like it needed rain. Like rain the light fell drenching everything. And sound: schoolchildren in Epidaurus dropping coins for one another at centre stage; goat bells against mountains in Mycenae; nuns at Mistras singing wildly.

You wake up. Were you ever asleep?

On the wall in the dark is the other sign you know by heart:

THE FIRE-ALARM SIGNAL IS A CONTIOUS
BLASTS OF THE SIREN OR RINGING OF BELLS.

Sic sic. Why doesn't somebody just shout? You feel water in
your eyes. Do sirens blast? (Another *sic.*) You refuse to hurl
yourself upon her pyre, yet compassion blooms like cigarette
smoke and you cough back to sleep, a beggar.

In London soft rain is falling in Cartwright Gardens. You
look out on it from a large first-floor room with long French
windows and a little balcony stuck with flags to celebrate
the Queen. St. Pancras strikes four and two chestnut horses
ridden by policemen clipclop past. Plane trees drip onto
tennis courts, your feet swell inside your shoes.

Ruth is at the airport, yes, awaiting your connecting flight
back to Canada.

In Athens, because of the smell, you had to buy her an air-
tight box.

She used to sit in St. Pancras sniffing the furniture polish
wishing she could play the organ. Suppose you go to Woburn
Place, if the sun comes out, and light a candle.

The scent of wax.

The Thames running out, ebbing, uncovering old boots
old toilet seats stuck in mud. Heart of darkness holes of ink.
Soon the pubs will re-open, the stages light up, the primeval
shouting begin.

DEAD SLOW
WAY OUT
NO DOG NUISANCE

Signs of a settling culture, imitated in former colonies like
India and Ceylon, where all driving is also done on the wrong
side of progress, people queue, and complain about the times.
Everything falls.

Cakes, language, bridges.

Suppose the sun breaks through and you hear the *pock* of tennis balls.

The sun comes out, the trees steam greenly.

An arthritic dog by the garden fence, unwilling to be tempted farther by the soundless shaking of its lead in a pensioner's hand, cannot lift its leg.

Behave knave.

Beware, beget, be kind.

Suppose the river winds back to a land of milk and.

Bewitching river. Making combs of your boots.

HEALING

HAT SUMMER my countrymen were in the news abroad. A violinist was found nude, gagged, dead at the bottom of an airshaft at the Metropolitan Opera House in New York City. In August, the Playmate of the Year died in a West Los Angeles house when a shotgun blew away her face; she was from the West Coast, too. We all were. Even the one-legged cancer victim, the most famous of us, hopping across Canada on an aluminum hinge. Only I survived.

My wife's disappearance revealed in me a stoicism the newpapers mistook for valour until the discovery of her body uncovered my cowardice. Declining to return to Lisbon, I turned down the chance to claim her remains after she was identified by the teeth as belonging to me. I couldn't face the emptiness. In Portugal I became a suspect open to questions and even trial.

To recover from her death I left everything: position, car, house, city: and for the summer decided like a vagabond fruit-picker to migrate to the Interior. The lake here irrigated the desert. My clothes mouldered, my tongue soured, my hair grew. My stomach shrank. I became a fruit-picker.

Surrounded by mountains, Sr. Brabanto's orchard sat on a bench above the lake. Here I dropped my Gs, my culture, my identity. (And fruit, for I was still tentative.) My meekness was more than a mask, for I wore it well, like a dolorous old Lear. This was certainly the way to observe without being noticed. In the folds and creases of the hills were greasewood, sagebrush, cactus, rock cliffs, rabbit-bush, painted turtles, rattlesnakes. Higher up grew Ponderosa pines. When a dry wind swept down the lake setting poplars afire and the air on edge, the whole mood shifted, mountains moved.

In a heat like Portugal's, Monica picked Oxheart plums and at night made love to Jesse where the Rainbird sprinklers soaked them lying in the long orchard grass. The stars were a rash in the sky. Together they lay down in the drenched grass like horses and wriggled, writhed and snorted. Tsk-tsk-tsk . . . the sprinklers must have stung their backs like sandpaper. I could tell in the morning by the way she walked Monica had been wrapping her long legs around a peach trunk's bark, who knew, to scratch her thighs. I admire an imagination.

The place had an inescapable Mediterranean feel. The semi-arid sweep, the vineyards and cerulean sky, even the names on the highway fruit stalls: de Sousa, Agastinho, Fernandes, Patrochino, Diaz, Lazlo, Ferriera . . . like the Mexicans in California, the Portuguese here had refounded their culture. The French pickers who arrived every summer from Quebec, *that* summer made national news when western rednecks attacked them. To do what he could for these Québécois and other pickers, Jesse contacted a magazine writer and announced his willingness to talk about living conditions at Witches' Bowl.

At Sr. Brabanto's, not long after I moved in with him and Monica, Jesse asked me to join his union. For a dollar I received a card that read PICKERS ASSOCIATION. (He'd neglected the apostrophe because he wasn't into grammar—those days being over. He meant high school's good old ones.) *This is to certify that Maurice Ringspear is a member in good standing with the aforementioned association, liable to agreements as they are drawn up, and who consents to the laws* etc. My alias, I felt, carried the right note of authenticity. The three of us lived undisturbed in the bunkhouse where they tolerated me with amusement, even respect. "There's still a few years of picking left in *you*," said Jesse. Sharing work, trips with them into town, wanderings in the desert, helped my healing. When we climbed Iconoclast Mt., Monica even took my hand. "Holy smoke," said Jesse. "Look at *them* . . ." He meant tiny skiers in the lake making long upside-down Vs behind launches. In the air I caught whiffs of ash, forest fires, from beyond what Jesse called the bloody pale. He meant the mountains.

Accommodating but not nosy, here was an oasis into which tourists had followed fruit farmers. Smaller orchards than his had compromised their integrity, in Sr. Brabanto's view, by renting parts of themselves out as trailer camps. Lake View, Dalton's Hill Resort, The Oasis, Betty's Hideaway, Springvale—orchards full of Winnebagos, Play-Mates, Centurions, Aristocrats, all hooked up to plugs and hoses like terminal cases.

For these Anglo-Saxon orchards Brabanto had a proverb: "'*Se te fizeres mel, comer-te-hão as moscas*' . . . 'If you make yourselves honey, the flies will eat you.' Those orchards aren't farms," he said, "they're flytraps. You can't be a farmer and a campground councillor! Who's serious about coddling moths and leafhoppers when there's trailer sewage to shovel? Eh? No way!" He swept his tanned arm across his own orchard. "To grow peaches and apples you don't need tourists. Look at me. I done pretty good, eh?"

He had leaned back on his patio where he was interviewing me, to sip espresso. While the master spoke, his large black dog urinated on my pant leg. When I tried to cuff its ear it nipped my thumb, playfully. Brabanto said I looked like a man who'd knocked around, and hired me. I put away my soft inexperienced hands. The house was a long whitewashed rancher, with a red-tile roof, wrought-iron gates and an inner courtyard of naked cherubim holding jars that poured real water into flashy beds of petunias. There were lanterns in the plaster walls, arches over doors, barrels of roses and hanging cacti.

When I accidentally shifted my boot onto Othello's paw, a tall girl of nine or ten, who had been eating a carrot and staring from inside the patio door, opened it, came out and kicked me with her cowboy boot—very hard in the shin. I could feel a scab forming like peach peel over my wound. "What are you doing?" demanded her father. "Nothing," she complained. "Nothing will *come* of nothing if you keep that up!" He told her to apologize but she shook her head. "Then take your doggie for a walk," he ordered. Instead she sidled up until he patted her and said she looked good enough to eat. Spoiled children like that sicken me, frankly. Afterwards, Othello's yelp of pain was a pleasurable memory.

––––––––––

Brabanto never referred to his wife—if that's who lived inside his hacienda. He spent his time urging on his pickers, watching Monica like a lecher in her lime-coloured halter, hanging around trees she was up and sniffing her sneakers. I think he thought he could smell her. He was a middle-aged Latin who never dreamed his appeal to women could have faded.

Monica and I sometimes conversed in French. From Montreal, she was the daughter of an English-speaking anthropologist, and a graduate that spring from McGill—in theatre, which had disappointed her father. (He'd wanted an economist, she said, a bookkeeper to help him moonlight in his drafting business.) Coming west aboard a Greyhound she had discovered a country that was like nothing she'd dreamed. Middle of the cherry season she arrived, spent three nights in a room at the Sahara Motor Inn with lamps bolted to the night tables, before finding work with Brabanto, and a bunkhouse on his orchard that did not smell (like her motel) of cleaning fluid, but rather chemical sprays stored in drums. In the orchard her hands flew among the apricots like swallows, and I would have been ashamed at the rate my own bin wouldn't fill, if I hadn't felt (happily) more leering than competitive. Shaded by boughs her doe eyes moved sensuously in her head, across a dark face with its sickle scar fresh upon her cheek. She had breasts like peaches and I wished that Jesse had sometimes reminded her to wear the aluminum pail with its sackcloth bottom in a position that wouldn't bruise them.

Jesse, bleached and muscled, picked faster than anybody and had done so every summer since he was fifteen. Monica said his wanting so badly to organize pickers was because his father had once fallen from a defective ladder, onto a limb of dead pear wood that left him bouncing in air with the end poking through his neck. He had to be taken home in a Greyhound luggage compartment, dead. Picking conditions hadn't improved at all, said Jesse. No benefits, no insurance, little recourse . . . the hazards he could enumerate. Not until the demands of his Pickers Association started to heat up and threaten the growers, did Brabanto insinuate that Jesse's father was alive, languishing in the federal penitentiary for an unspecified crime committed back home in the Kootenays. The police (according to Brabanto) had found him in an indentured orchard near Melville picking pears. Brabanto— who always shouted when he spoke, because he couldn't hear himself any other way—whispered this in my ear one hot day by the peach bins.

Such heat. When the temperature in July went over a hundred, dark clouds would gather all afternoon until a hot wind blew them south across the border. This left the willows by the lake streaming hair. The water lost its blue, and whitecaps sprang up like rabbits. But it never rained, never stormed, and by dusk there were stars. At midnight once we watched a meteor shower from sleeping bags. In between dropping stars was conversation, dozing. I told my new friends I had children their age, if they could believe it, one of either sex and laid back like themselves. With them I felt very open, like the parachute that blossomed over the lake every afternoon behind a tow boat, reminiscent of fat Germans ascending from the beach in Albufeira.

Jesse was suffering disfigurement by mosquitoes. Monica offered him liniment her grandmother in Val-de-Bois sold to fishermen. It was meant to *prevent* stings, but applying it from her brown labelless bottle soothed him. Her hands, I could see in their starlit applications, stroked his bites like swallow bellies.

Keeping an eye peeled for indolence, the patrolling seigneur would call to his daughter, who went about her father's business less beset, more sneakily, than he: "'*A experiencia é o fructo, que se colhe dos erros.*'" From Maria in a dutiful child's voice came the punchline: "'Experience is the fruit picked from the tree of errors.'" His proverbs fell from her lips like overripe fruit. They were always about fruit.

Othello, the black amanuensis, preceded her arrival, invariably laying down a turd at my boot's criss-crossings in the long green grass. My boot stunk up the bunkhouse—worse than the drums of chemicals, said Monica.

She and Jesse slept in the corner where they'd pushed together their bunks. Following my little suppers that they ate full of praise, and if they didn't decide to raid the orchard, they were into bed and finished with love faster than it took to skin a weiner. Really, we had room for eight pickers, but the others—all Québécois—preferred to live in tents at Witches' Bowl. There they partied every night and hitchhiked to the orchard every morning, where, sometimes, they fell asleep in the limbs.

Witches' Bowl had become the rallying point for Jesse's political ambitions. Especially after the bat-swinging, head-cracking incident in June, when men in hard hats arrived with baseball bats to teach the frogs a lesson. "You should have been there," Monica said to me without thinking. She described the screaming that night, the sound of beaten glass, the cinder from a campfire that burned her face. She and Jesse had rolled under a log, listening to bats break windshields, heads, canvas, logs. People running in the dark, men shouting obscenities in two languages, women crying. At last their attackers had withdrawn in trucks up the lane, refusing to turn on their lights.

People who can't savour another culture without abusing it are very sick, in my opinion. It's like polygamy and people's narrow attitudes about that. One thing I can't stand is an ethnocentric attitude.

In time five local men stood trial, the charges of assault reduced to wilful damage because no one could identify their shadows with conviction. In court, the condition under which pickers lived began to receive publicity, thus allowing Jesse to consolidate his union. Monica translated his speeches, shouting in Witches' Bowl through a speaking-trumpet, about fundamental human needs like garbage pails. At sunset you could observe the detritus of neglect at the edge of the smoking peat bog this camp took its name from: butts, bottle caps, fish cans, used batteries, biscuit boxes, bean tins, cocoa lids. What filth. Whenever someone emerged from a clump of poplars by the beach carrying a toilet roll, Jesse would call for the installation of toilets. He finally went to the Fruit Growers' Association about lack of facilities in the orchards themselves—few growers provided any.

Brabanto, who did, laughed when he heard about Jesse's petition. A good idea. "So many growers don't have respect for their workers! Look at me. A bunkhouse if they want it. They don't want it!" He couldn't help it if pickers preferred to sleep in tents and their own filth. Jesse replied it was the chemicals in his bunkhouse that kept pickers away.

"Balls," said the farmer.

Jesse expanded his argument to include spraying. "Fruit in Eden wasn't sprayed," he announced.

Brabanto looked as if he might deny it. Instead he answered, "'*A homem farto as cerejas amargam*'... 'To a cloyed man cherries taste bitter.' Eh, Maria?"

Like an informer his daughter hopped innocently, deceptively among the trees in cowboy boots and a white dress. To him, I could tell, she looked delectable. To me she offered inklings of depravity. If she'd wanted anything badly enough I thought her capable of being very nice, say, to the place where she'd booted me in the leg. Even of kneading suntan lotion into my back, solicitously, down at the lake. Yes. But she pulled too many faces to trust—how her father, a fruit grower, could trust a daughter who preferred carrots to apples was a joke to me. I mean, whose daughter was she? I felt sorry for him.

We must have run into each other several times at the beach before I began to suspect her motives. Once we were swimming and she offered to "learn me," as she mockingly put it, the frog kick that her long legs were very good at. I could never escape the feeling that she was about the particular business of spying on her father's hands. She liked to tempt us. Not trusting her for a moment, I would try to disarm her with little confessions of heartache, even with the candy she loved.

But back in her father's orchard she left me feeling stiff and sorry for my pains. Once she spat back a chocolate I'd given her. She also laughed out loud at something I had mentioned to her in confidence (trying to make peace over her dog) and the other pickers snickered. Afterwards, I saw her whisper like a supplicant in her father's ear. Dog-hearted daughter. Brabanto chuckled. Othello barked and laid down his own business in my path.

The next day she sniffed in my direction. "'*Agosto tem a culpa, Setembro leva a fructa.*'"

"Bravo!" roared her father. August gets the blame (it seemed), September takes the fruit.

She turned up her little nose at my Tydemans and batted one coyly off a limb lower down. I wanted to swat her.

"Pick pick pick!" shouted Brabanto.

And so every day the sun shone like blazes.

My hands hardened. I could no longer swear they were mine.

"There's apple scab in the Goldens," complained Brabanto. "But the Reds look good, eh?" The apples would make up for the cherries. "A catastrophe," he claimed. "Wet weather, brown rot, wind-whip. We didn't spray enough." The apples might even make up for the peaches.

When Jesse persisted with his petition to the Fruit Growers' Association, Brabanto grew dissatisfied. The union was threatening to disrupt the apple harvest—which looked the heaviest in twentyfive years. The long-term effects of chemical sprays on anybody, declared Brabanto, were zilch. No amount of political agitation by a union could get farmers like him to stop spraying their orchards. *No way,* he said.

We printed posters.

He removed his chemicals from the bunkhouse.

We slept better, or thought we did, though I could still hear my children snuffling in the night.

Jesse pressed him further.

"Horseshit!" exploded Brabanto. He called Jesse a loudmouth, a troublemaker, whose fruit was often bruised because he tried to pick too fast, a showoff. He wanted to fire him. He said he knew what was going on between him and Monica because he had his spies. It was none of his business, he said, but he didn't like that kind of thing going on in any orchard of his, any bunkhouse. Turning to me he said he didn't know how

I could stomach it. Othello growled. Maria threw a stick—for Othello, but it struck me on the ear, accidentally.

I couldn't hear right for days. Numb in fact for a week I considered whether the life here wasn't starting to lose its gloss. I began to feel naked—and the sensation, as if I had eaten my clothes in public, was dyspeptic. Maria's little mouth worked at my chemical-free sleep with such a tongue—a feather, really—that at midnight I beheld her soliciting eye.

"Listen," she whispered. "Can't you hear them bruising an old man's apples? It's rotten what they're doing. Don't you care? Be nice to a blind girl and show me where they're making applesauce of my daddy's living. I'll find out anyhow. Daddy says it's poison. He's warned me. Those two make the apples fall off trees. Please, Mr. Suntan, in your clown's pyjamas, don't let me get a spanking. Help Daddy's little helper. Nice old boy—listen to your tummy growl. I'll feed your sweet teeth. Lick me, you bad doggie. Drown me in lotion to stop the stinging. Daddy spanks the daylights out...he hates me."

Of course, worries about losing my disguise were extravagant. I still looked feckless, not at all consequential. I had regained my composure as if the feral attacks on my reputation down on the coast were a distant memory. Here in exile I blended into the tyrannous day. I now knew what tourists meant when they said how brown summer lawns are by the sea. There we have little of the obsession for irrigation common everywhere in the hot Interior. Coastal people expect Nature to avoid extremes, to give green endlessly, and they just sprinkle. Watering is for farmers and the upper crust— like my wife and me who watered with Japanese gardeners. (We lived in a house I designed myself.) Any nostalgia I still feel for brown August lawns belongs to a time when I imagined them, accurately it turned out, the same colour as the Algarve.

With my improving appetite I grew strong enough to cherish hates. Certainly I hated Othello; he was a disobedient dog. The right in any culture should be freedom from antagonism in the absence of accusation. Freedom of this sort has its ways. Institutionalized practices to divorce a husband; ritualized plots to get rid of a chief; ceremonial feasts to relieve anxiety. Culture is a *tissue* of anxieties . . .

But enough. In a friend's truck Jesse drove the three of us to an outdoor movie. The white screen was a sail in the desert. The pair of them leaned up against one another sipping Coors— weak American beer, because our brewers were on strike that summer. When Jesse accidentally knocked the soundbox to the ground, Monica became a lip-reader. The smell of sagebrush deepened as night spread. Listening to the tinny voices from nearby cars we all had trouble with the story. This nettled me. On the way home no one could account convincingly for the doped-up stallion, the cowboy and the TV commentator.

The other irksome thing was going to the races where the pair of them ate impulsively: hot dogs, hamburgers, onions, chips, candy bars. Really, it was sickening to watch them poisoning their bodies. They wagered money with the same lack of self-control. Monica took her winnings from one race, $29.50, and bet $25 on the nose of Star Blaster in the next, ridden by a girl called Dorothy Wiffle. She won another $60. Jesse, not to be outdone, put $50 on the nose of Attica and Stormin' Helen, two horses for the price of one, and finished out of the money. (Was sport no more than this?) In the fourth they both bet heavily on Foxy Fergus, a quarter horse with big haunches and an imposing record—and lost everything. Monica said she should have gone with her hunch, Sassy Saint Luna, whose rear legs in the winner's circle were lathered sweetly.

Too small for bedlam crowds, Desert Track was a large dirt oval, bleachers and the nauseating smell of quarter horse and frying onions. When we escaped, Jesse had lost $96.60, not counting the cost of admission to the track, his program and enough junk food to sink a ski boat.

Food. It occurred to me, far from taking offence at any lapse in taste, that I might repay them for their companionship by cooking an elaborate farewell dinner, rather more impressive than my usual bunkhouse suppers. Not that they disliked these, or were unappreciative of the ambience I tried to create, for they inquired politely about my life and enjoyed hearing stories. To amuse them, I occasionally made some up.

Not about my wife, however, I told the truth about her. Her jabbering, for instance. I repeated things she used to say, imitating her smile and the way she described a dinner party, say, as if I hadn't been there.

"'When the kettle started whistling,' she said, 'I made up my mind to ignore it, like some Indian mother her baby crying in the night with a burning bottom. I sat there listening to this steamy little orifice crying to be taken off. Screaming to be. I was eating After Eights and refused to go into the kitchen. Sizzle sizzle. I wasn't going to lift another finger, Maurice. Burn, bunny, burn I said. Well. This excited my crotch and I even thought of treating it to a chocolate. I almost thought my brain'd burst a vessel. I can tell you there was pressure, steam pressure, making my head ache and it seemed to be coming from the kitchen where this pot of tea awaited its making. Guests wanted tea. *Coffee* was not what they wanted—they wanted tea so they wouldn't stay awake all night! They thought I couldn't *hear* it . . . this kettle! They decided I was tired or something from making dinner, conversation, *them happy*. Burn, bunny, burn I said just as softly as I am saying it to you, Maurice, and everybody sat there listening to the whistling, crying, angry kettle. When it stopped everybody went home. And *I* sat sniffing air for telltale smells of molten metal. Ten, twenty minutes I sat, smelling only the ashes of guests. Finally I spat a chocolate all over my dress. Because. In the kitchen I discovered some bastard, some vagina-virtuous guest of mine, had turned the element to zero. My element. *My stove.* If I'd had gas, Maurice, I would have turned on the oven and stuck in my head for a real sniff. I cried and cried, then fell asleep in my chocolatey dress on the kitchen floor.'"

I assured them my wife was not a well woman. Which was an absolutely true fact, even without the rider, about which I said nothing, that is about her being dead. It was no use telling them she had disappeared suddenly off the face of the earth in a flea market in Lisbon. They would have remembered the case. Or not believed me.

The police later found her teeth and ashes in a plastic garbage bag near Silves. This dismemberment was the most barbarous act I had ever heard of. *Who can begin to understand the rites death claims?* The fact that it happened among Portuguese never antagonized me towards Sr. Brabanto or his family, though a sophist might argue that prejudice, like junk food, is sometimes craved and therefore justified.

I will say this much: my going to jail for a sit-down strike against the fruit growers took more exasperation than courage. I speak of my part in the trial that followed. This during the middle of the apple harvest in September. Without warning I stood up in court and picked up my Gs. The prosecutor's glib and oily complacency angered me and I used my tongue to attack it. I mean, if you cannot count on a court of law to preserve a nation's language, where are you?

As a man from whose lips eloquence will sometimes spring unfertilized, I smothered his legal argot. For my contempt I was given two days behind bars to eat, as they say, humble pie. In the eyes of my children I had definitely taken a step up. I regretted this. Jesse thought the Pickers Association was beginning to command respect. I said I thought it was a sign of the times.

The court order allowing Brabanto to truck his produce to market left him without any discernible grudges. He was too sensible, or desperate, to retaliate against his pickers. Meanwhile the apple of his eye harried me with disappointed looks.

"'De tal arvore, tal fructo,'" crowed her father. "'Like tree, like fruit,'" she responded warily. As the fruit of her father's labour, however, she was definitely rotten. He had spoiled her rotten. I kept my distance, worried that if I had not already blown my cover in court, then Maria might discover some way to betray me for refusing to indulge in her little games of espionage. Indeed my children, as I now called them to their faces, had started calling me an impostor, and said in real life I was probably a brain surgeon or a physicist! (In fact I'm an architect with international credentials.) Anyhow, the union made gains, the equinox arrived and the apples ended.

I had read that apples ripen faster on the ground, closer to gravity. The infinitesimal speed of this difference bore no dwelling on. I just happen to believe life lived higher up lasts longer. Some mountain men in Ecuador live to an age of 140. I am certain, had I remained in the Interior, its relatively good effect on me would have continued. Unlike the effects lower down of coastal mists and refracted light, here there was no undergrowth, no lack of contrast between rock and shadow, black and white. Thus Maria, in no uncertain terms, seemed to feel she could get away with denouncing me to her father, for spending too much time in the orchard with Monica, and not enough picking. It was a lie, of course, and she knew it. Monica knew it, or so she said, and her sympathy fanned my dislike of Brabanto's little helpmeet. To the end her sympathy, and Jesse's, put me firmly in their debt.

My farewell dinner took on the dimension of an old West Coast feast. It required planning, of course. At first undecided what to serve, then making up my mind, I worried that the bunkhouse stove wasn't big enough to cook the meal I wanted.

Interest in the meal increased with my preparations, although I tried to keep them secret. I had to coordinate my attack, aware that my periodic absences from the orchard would go noticed. In town, on an errand for Sr. Brabanto, I shopped for marjoram, garlic, rice, sour cream, beefsteak tomatoes, chives, etc. I cultivated yeast. Punching, squeezing, rolling the dough, I practised baking bread. From conception to execution, dinner took a week. Thickening my sauce was really the last and simplest task of all.

On the evening of our farewell, the aroma of these steeping and rotating pots put the lid, so to speak, on our relationship. My guests regretted they had brought nothing—while I was offering a mountain of food.

To my surprise they dressed up. So I dug out a business suit that hung on me like another man's, left off the jacket, and rewound myself in the apron. I am afraid the silk tie looked suspicious and renewed their interest in guessing at my profession.

"A blue-eyed sheik?" asked Monica.

"Nope." (Like hers, my eyes were dark.)

Lighting the candles Jesse chuckled like a kid and said this was the life he should have grown up in to keep him out of politics.

When we were eating our soup, Brabanto came by looking for Othello and I invited him in. It was a mellow evening; you could smell the ripening pears. From the door he noticed our china and wondered where it had come from.

"Your wife," I said, "was kind enough to lend me an old set."

He looked at me. "I guess you mean my sister." His voice sounded subdued, not its usual pitch. "Not my wife, alas. My wife is gone. My wife's sister."

He wouldn't join us, he said, he was looking for his dog. The screen door banged shut and a fly buzzed against the mesh. The children snickered.

As dinner progressed, so did compliments for the chef. They toasted me with local wine and Jesse made a little speech. After that we gulped our wine and laughed, talked about Brabanto and next summer's union. It was me, finally, who suggested the old fellow really wasn't the bastard he seemed. Frankly, I felt sorry for him.

Of course who should return to our screen but the master with paycheques and ostentatious thanks for our weeks of work. As if he had overheard my defence of him, and appreciated it, he was back wishing he had more pears so we could all stay on picking through the rest of October. Avoiding any mention of the Pickers Association, he stepped inside.

I repeated my invitation to dinner. He accepted and Monica, surprised and a little reluctant, prepared the fourth plate. He studied her appreciatively. And told us about Othello. Had Jesse—any of us—ever noticed his tongue lolling out in the orchard? Black. Pink and black. This was because he was a husky. Part Lab, too. He told us how he'd bought him one summer from a romantic bronco buster named Tex Moore driving a dog team to California. Othello had been just a pup in this fellow's sleigh on wheels. (In fairness to the dog, I should confess this was my own name for him.) Brabanto admitted that he had probably paid too much, but didn't mind since the pup had turned into such a wonderful watchdog—which was how he'd come to notice him missing, two days ago, when his bark disappeared.

He stopped chewing. He leaned forward with a troubled look, before swallowing. A hiker, he confided, had just found Othello in a lair on the mountain—where someone had taped his jaws shut and left him tied to a bush, to be gnawed in the flank by coyotes. Right now the poor dog was eating like a beggar up at the house.

Brabanto laughed with relief. My pièce de résistance, he said, was delicious. We got along well; he kept staring at Monica, and winking at me.

———————

On the morning of the following day I was saying goodbye to my children—suitcases, packs, pillows at our feet—when the Portuguese owner came down the lane with a Mountie. He looked distraught and we found out why. Maria had not come home last night. Had any of us seen her? When was the last time we *had* seen her? To me it seemed like days ago and Jesse and Monica were no help at all.

Othello growled at the policeman. Jesse was sure she'd turn up, and Monica patted the father's hand. Sweet Marie. Maria, I mean. We said our farewells.

I got the Mountie to drop me at the Greyhound station in town. Jesse had decided to take Monica home for a visit to the Kootenays, where his sister now lived alone. Watching them stick out their thumbs I suddenly felt a loss.

Instead of travelling to the prairies, which was my original destination, I decided to return to the coast. Hardened though I was by labour, my hands like pads, the thought of a prairie winter appalled me. I preferred to face the real, if tasteless, pity of my colleagues. My fieldwork had released a smaller, more self-contained man. I sold my house. I bought a condominium in an unfriendly building and this suited me well.

NATION, NATION

*F*ROM THE BLUE *no conversion comes like a bolt ...*
From the blue no conversion ...
From the blue ...

Standing on the ferry's top deck speaking into Howe Sound, for some time now she had had a bad habit, when speaking formally, of fracturing syntax. Of

Yet how to begin? Already tangled up. She turned to watch the green spinnaker of a passing yacht.

Like a bolt ...

No conversion comes ...

Less than two days to sit down and compose herself, so when her moment of glory arrived Friday evening she could read out her speech in a clear, confident voice.

Wwaaahhkkk ...

She touched the oak rail, bemused. With an audience of gulls—gluttons who'd rather eat than listen—she required clean, curling syntax like fishhooks to snag *their* attention.

A bright, no, brilliant October afternoon. This at least was a beginning, coming to the island. She abandoned her podium by the lifeboat and began her descent. From mainland to island the ferry took twenty minutes and she needed five minutes to climb down two decks to her Citroën. A brisk, middle-aged woman who took a cane and smelled of L'Heure Bleue, she had a last look at the sunlit, sawback mountains and disappeared inside the vessel.

Waiting to disembark were a flatbed truck with building materials, mainly lumber, and a bakery van. She followed the van up the humped ramp, past the village coffee shop, to the grocery store where she bought an early edition of the midweek *Sun*. To the newspaper she added a bottle of Liebfraumilch, a package of cigarettes, a box of Peek Freans. In the car were enough groceries to last till her return to the mainland on Friday.

Although she liked to drive fast the absence of police on the island had the curious effect of slowing her down. Maybe it was the absence of other cars. Through the rainforest, at any rate, she had time to look around—at the broadleaf maples in gold, the vine maples in crimson. To her left she caught sight of a summit, the highest point on the island, covered in firs as thick as jungle. She passed the asbestos-shingled United Church, a farm, small tarpaper cabins perched on outcroppings as if wired to the rock. After a mile and a half she glimpsed the ferry re-entering the sound, gleaming white layers piled in diminishing size, one atop another like a cake.

A headache she was unaware of until it stopped, stopped.

High above her on the mainland she noticed the Himalayan-size peaks, a backdoor view of them, from the west. Like a tourist she pulled up on the road to gawk. Living at the foot of mountains, in Dundarave, she and her husband looked out on none. Their view was flat across the bay to the city. "Very nice," Warren said, fifteen years ago, when they were used to seeing more of their view, more of each other. Now because of her job it seemed they were always passing in the night. "For Pete's sake," he would tell her fondly. "Slow down why don't you?" So here she was, in need of a speech, the toast of her profession.

More winding brought her down to the flat, grassy driveway of her brother-in-law's beachfront house. Parked under an arbutus tree she studied the wide, white-pillared verandah looking out on the sound. This house recalled the large clapboard houses she knew as a girl growing up in Nova Scotia. It was built, she guessed, in the twenties. The kind of house she loved to list—traditional to the point of empathy, done over inside, smart. Waterfront property was sounder than gold. With money coming in from the east, the Middle East, the Far East, the market here was booming. The value of property had taken off the last two years, the last year, the last six months. Time merely accelerated it. She wondered if her brother-in-law wouldn't be wise to list his house for a whopping price and let the market meet it in time, since he never came over anymore, not since his wife's death two years ago. It wasn't as if there were grandchildren to look ahead for. Unlike her and Warren, whose son was killed in a plane crash in Toronto ten years ago, her husband's brother had never wanted a family.

"For the line you sign on the house."

"I beg your pardon?"

No, sometimes she failed to catch herself, words scrambled, and the buyer sat there bewildered, starting to twitch over the size of his Interim Agreement.

But appearance and charm pulled her through. Mercifully, she had learned to poke fun at herself. Warren encouraged her to take days off; together they occasionally came over to the island at his brother's standing offer. This was her first time alone.

Inside, things were as she remembered them from a weekend visit seven weeks ago. A little dusty, a few fat flies, but dry and spider-free. She ate cheese and crackers with a small glass of wine. Warm enough to leave open the latticed door, she sat listening to waves and gulls. Tide at its ebb, the waves made only lapping sounds. She arose and made her way outside. Standing on the verandah she breathed the smell of salt down to her knees. She could hear finches in the still-green alders. A great blue heron was fishing stick-legged along the foreshore.

Despite her own stick, or perhaps because of it, she had prospered. So much so that she was, for all her feminine and apparently lame appearance, to be honoured by the Western Realtors Association as "Man of the Year." Of course she had come to the profession late, just a decade ago, when her husband urged her to take up a career. Poor Warren, an insurance broker, today she was making more money than he.

Inside she cleared away the dishes and sat down again to compose her acceptance speech in a small notebook.

From the blue (she began) *no conversion comes like a bolt.*

Before crossing it out she wanted to see what the sentence looked like.

She read it aloud. The abrupt conclusion went against her intention. It required softer landing.

She tried again.

No conversion comes like a bolt from the blue.

Closer, yes. Wasn't that what she meant in the first place?

But the next sentence refused to come. She told herself, relax. Trying too hard to impress the gulls, she couldn't remember what she wanted to say. What *do* I want to say? She knew she wanted to raise the tone of the dinner with her speech. So she wondered, is the tone my message? Tone of renewal? Tone of rebirth?

Oh dear so fervent. Still, it was good to remember realtors also helped make the world go around, if only they could believe, as she did, in the real value of property. It was possible to keep from falling behind, falling apart, by owning a piece of the country. Secretly she wanted people to dissociate *real* estate from real estate. Naturally she never stopped to ask exactly what she meant, any more than she would of vague metaphysical beliefs she held, but it seemed like a worthwhile distinction because it enhanced the integrity of her pursuit, all their pursuits.

Trying to write this down she kept crossing out, juggling, rearranging. Time and again she found herself saying the same thing over. Why did words from other pens, other mouths, seem effortless and not hers? Knotted up ad nauseam—though not her advertisements, she could certainly write *ads* (stock phrases, abbreviations, scrappy sentences). These she would emboss with the name of her own modest company and box them inside solemn black ink. A photograph was the easiest syntax of all. Indeed, for her five percent commission on the initial hundred thousand, and two and a half percent on the rest, she was obliged to publish at least one picture with every listing.

She picked up the package of cigarettes, stripped off the cellophane, raised the lid and lit her first cigarette in weeks. The newspaper she had been reading over lunch was beside her on the table. Absently, she thumbed through it, settling on the lead editorial in order to examine the secret of its tone. It rambled on about resources, very dry. She turned the page.

The sub-headline of a long article caught her eye: *Sure, everyone says what an awful thing it is. But if it weren't pleasant, it wouldn't be happening...* It was an essay, she saw, on inflation. According to the brief bio, its author lived in Los Angeles and had written a book on Khrushchev. He opened with Freud.

When she had read the essay right through she felt cheated. He ended up, so help him, comparing inflation to alcoholism. The pleasure of inflation stopped any real desire for a cure. Inflation was a perverse, self-destructive pleasure. Old values like saving caused guilt. Self-sacrifice was worthless because not to spend money was to lose it. Not to owe money was to fall behind. Since she was one of the "haves," he was suggesting, she had a stake in inflation. Inflation was a collective disregard of reality.

One thing is certain (she read). Economists will never solve inflation or even make a dent in it. Poring over figures instead of looking into the human soul, they may be the last people to know what it is. But what *is* inflation? Ultimately, like any other vice, it is a dislocation in the soul—in this case, the collective national soul. How can this be cured or alleviated?

He didn't know. In his own country the writer foresaw reactionary backlash, racism, even totalitarianism if inflation continued. Trust an American, she thought, to overstate the problem.

By now the late-afternoon sun was pink on the mainland mountains. A thin strip of fog bluer than asters entered the sound along the coast. Carefully, she made her way over the rocky beach, and down the gangplank onto the bleached boards. There was guano drying on them everywhere. A sleeping mallard, startled by her approach, flopped off the float into the sea. Nailed along the float were old car tires for boats to rub against in summer. One whitewall tire said in worn-out rubber letters, TIGHT GRIP. Two miles away the big ferry to Nanaimo was drumming the sea. The sun had left the salal.

Usually she counted on the effects of light to erase an inky brain. Daylight, sunlight. She looked down into the water where the sun's slanting rays still held particles in the green like motes in air. Rowing out of Sheet Harbour as a girl she had often been invited by her vision of sun on a white jib to travel as fast as light, yes, so no one could ever tell her it was too dark to stay out in her skiff. Light permitted independence. It pacified. Only now—what was it?—she felt *un*pacified. Unsettled, momentarily, on the Pacific.

Walking back along the beach she thought of the Atlantic where she grew up. Her back was starting to ache. Pacific gulls seemed different. The West Coast felt foreign. Tropical? Greedy? Like magnolia blossoms the gulls were settling on the ocean without a ripple. What deceptive birds. Thousands of tiny snails and barnacles sucked the uncovered rocks.

By the time she reached the verandah she sensed a buzzing in her left buttock. Bending over to pick up a piece of firewood she felt her back slip an inch at the bottom of the spine. By dinner a pain as if on a wire stretched all the way from the middle of her buttock to the heel. She had to walk bent over, and the wire tugged painfully. Her buttock crawled like a dog's cringing rear end. Christ, she thought.

"Exercise, exercise," said her chiropractor the first time they met, as he held her in an unbecoming position, pressing. "Exorcise, exorcise," she thought she heard. His being young and chippy only made things worse. But she had to admit he helped her walk again: more than once, for her sciatic nerve would arrive squeezing, like a reminder on the road to Emmaus.

To distract herself she turned on the radio and listened to the prime minister deliver his eloquent speech on the Constitution. Now why can't *I* formulate thoughts as effortlessly? A very balanced speech, she felt, until afterwards, she heard the pundits criticize his speech for centre-leaning assumptions. Her trouble, she guessed, was that she listened too much to voice and not words. At times she even thought she heard in the minister of justice's voice an instrument like hers, scrambled and fractured, when it should have sounded steady and reassuring.

Restless with pain she went outside and thought she overheard her husband's brother talking about his dead wife. "She slept out here when the stars were bright. Sometimes a leaf fell on the porch and scratched. The ferries went by lit up like palaces, making waves that broke to bits on the beach." Two years ago, after the funeral, the three of them had come over for the night and felt very tender, close, loving.

After a painful night, she hobbled downstairs and opened her little notebook to work on her speech again. She made coffee and smoked, but it hurt to sit and nothing came out of her pen that satisfied. (Not even when she rearranged the syntax.) The sun flooded in, a cape of the distant city bobbed on a fog mattress. To the east a hot wind was skidding off the coastal mountains, making patterns on the sea, some whitecaps, a mirror of the light.

Around noon she decided to exercise her back by walking to the village, where she would buy a copy of the *Sun* and sit in the coffee shop reading the two ads she had placed in today's edition on Monday. Later, after dinner back here, she must pull herself together and write a speech straight off, since her banquet was tomorrow evening. Tomorrow afternoon she had an appointment to show a house in the British Properties.

The walk did her back good. The spine needed a rhythmical movement—which is what it got along the bright hilly road. Her cane's rubber tip bounced off the asphalt. There was a warm, pungent smell of earth, leaves and cedar sliding imperceptibly from island to sea. Beside a freshly cleared lot smelling of lumber piles, a mashed snake was imprinted on the road where a tire had flattened it.

Her two discreet ads appeared prominent in the Business section. Rereading them she was satisfied they would attract inquiries. One described a waterfront estate in Caulfeild, the other a Gaudi-like mansion in Point Grey, whose owner was wanted in Portugal for having murdered his wife.

Out of the ...

Looking for inspiration she turned again to the editorial page. How depressing, she thought, sipping her coffee. Better the sports page. Glancing through letters to the editor she noticed, at the bottom of the page, a letter titled "Equal Time."

Strongly as I object to Konrad Keller's excessive article on inflation (October 2), may I point respectfully out the danger in making assumptions about reality. His observations about America unfortunately will be picked up in Canada as time goes by quickly enough.

Prediction is a sport that involves climbing down cliffs backwards. Mr. Keller, it appears, is neglectful of the danger. Instead, he writes smugly, blissfully on.

It was signed Tabitha Page, Eagle Point, Elizabeth Island. It was a letter from herself.

She sat there shaken. Was she dreaming? She reread it. The syntactical quirks crippling its flow were immediately recognizable to her. But it was impossible. Even if she *had* written it, how could any letter have reached a newspaper downtown, slipped past a copy editor, and appeared in print in less than twenty hours? She read it again. Oddly, the letter seemed to express sentiments she wasn't aware of holding yesterday. Familiar, maybe, but words now sounding like people from an old neighbourhood she'd outgrown. She felt uncomfortable with them. *Queasy.* She kept thinking *This letter I can't so soon or actually have written...!*

Yet who to turn to for confirmation that she had not? The coffee shop was empty, and the shy owner, if she accosted him, would back right off. The newspaper didn't exist in the way it ... in the way she thought it did. Obviously her brain was headed the same way temporarily as her tongue.

Walking home her back was worse again. Flawed, thinking lacked accord. Modifiers dangled, ideas begged order, balance, clarity. The letter had spread like underbrush in her head. Sweet Jesus, would she get *any* speech written? Or would she, stooped over in pain, have to accept her award dumbly? Demoralized?

Exhausted from walking, in considerable pain and bewilderment, she arrived back at her brother-in-law's house to find it sacked. The windows and doors smashed out. Verandah torn up. The sink, tub, toilet, shattered by boulders.

Whaaa?

Standing inside, the—she—the only thing preventing her from collapse and believing all this possible was the damage looked like it had happened weeks, even months ago. Come

193

again? The damage? The electricity didn't work and the water had been turned off. Rusty beer caps, dozens, lay on bare wooden floors. Graffiti painted on the living room wall felt old and flaky; where someone had tried to set fire to a kitchen cupboard, the ash was cold. A stale smell of urine pervaded the empty house.

At the top of the narrow stairwell a light breeze was blowing through the broken dormer window. *Have I got this right?* Here it was bright and cool, with a smell of old plaster. In her slope-ceiling bedroom only a chair remained, and she sat down on its hard wood to collect herself, to gaze out over the sea to the pink mountains. Her brain was still flapping through rooms on a mangled wing downstairs. LANDLORDS TO DEATH said graffiti down there. She took the small notebook from her handbag and waited. *Bananas* she thought *I'm going bananas. No one is going to believe me. Ordinacy out the window, value up in smoke, property in ruins. Maybe that American was right. Maybe there is going to be a crash . . . has been a crash. What is it therefore I love I love I love?* Sitting there numb.

Downstairs she heard a noise.

Not quite, she thought.

She heard a noise downstairs, somebody walking over broken glass, room to room, crunching. The hair on her neck stood up and wailed. She wondered if an anarchist had returned with his paintbrush.

A dark, beardless young man with the stealth of a Sherpa appeared in the hallway outside her door. Unobserved, she sat watching him in his running shoes examine the walls, the ceiling, the floor.

"Oh!" he said. "Someone *is* here. I saw a car." He studied her a moment, unsure of himself, then asked, "Is this house yours?"

She hesitated. "No."

He looked suddenly cheerful, ingratiating. "Do you mind if I ask whose it is? Who owns this house?" He was very polite. Who was he, anyway? He looked well enough dressed not to be a squatter. He had a slight accent.

"The house is not for sale," she said automatically.

Well, explained the young man, he was just driving by and had been struck by this old Cape Cod house. He couldn't believe a beautiful old house like this had been smashed and splintered. "How did it happen?"

"Vandals. I was away."

"Quite a while, by the look of it," he offered.

"Four hours."

He looked at her. "Hours?"

She wished he would leave and let her, as best she might, get on with her speech. Yet she knew you didn't rush people, not when they were discussing property. Dealing with people and houses the problem. . . Dealing with people and houses she had learned instinctively you didn't wish them away, you listened, smiled, nodded sympathetically. Sooner or later came the closing, she had negotiated hundreds, they were all the same.

This young man would tell her he was out looking for property to fix up because he was thinking of coming west to live. He would tell her a lot of folks were moving west. He himself was visiting at the moment: the island, the coast, the west. From Ontario—would he be, this immigrant? And she would go on nodding.

Instead he said. "Want to know what I can't get used to? The light. Here in the west I mean. You're still up and the Chinese are ready to get up. When you get up the world's had all day to make news. To kill itself off, die of hunger, announce five-year plans. Suntan. Here you're just getting warmed up. There's still all day to avoid saying the wrong thing, making enemies, flying in the face of reason. In the west, when you think about it, you're younger than other people. You're ahead being behind. Time is different here, you're still alive."

In his sneakers, in his glory. What was he, a born-again hippie? What a preachy young man.

"I really want to live," he said. "In the west."

No, she would say goodbye and sit listening for him to drive away. Her leg would not be aching anymore.

Actually, her leg was not aching now.

By the remaining light she would open the little notebook in her lap and begin to write and write. *I must change my life* she thought. He would not still be standing here gaping at the beams.

TAKING COVER

Ladies and gentlemen, to kick off we'd like to welcome you officially. Children and singles too.

WHOOP WHOOP WHOOP WHOOP WHOOP...

This is the emergency distress call for anybody locked out of their rooms during a red alert. Knowing how to whoop may save your lives.

In a few minutes you will all be shown to rooms that are hermetically sealed. The different corridors have coloured handrails and you should remember the colour of yours. For your own protection it's imperative to stay inside your rooms as much as possible, because corridors are less well protected from the radiation outside—and incidentally more likely to harbour other people's germs. Visiting hours you'll find posted on the back of every door. But as the corridors are narrow you should make plans to visit other rooms well ahead of time to avoid congestion. If the contamination level in the corridors is high they may be closed for extended periods. Suddenly and without warning. It should be remembered this auditorium will be closed till further notice and no public meetings scheduled after you are admitted to your rooms. This space is contaminated.

The world is contaminated. It's a fate worse than death.

To pet owners apologies are due. Noah was kinder to pets but Noah had fewer people to accommodate. Since there's a limited supply of uncontaminated air, everybody here is in competition. Children shouldn't lose heart. Their pets may prove defiantly resilient outside and even survive this internecine war. Suffice to say the penalty for smuggling in an animal is the pet itself. So no dogs, cats, hamsters, crocs or cockatiels.

On the subject of breath you ought to be aware of the Tibetan Monk Chant. This consumes less oxygen than normal breathing, and has the additional advantage of exercising the lungs. It's also helpful in meditation and relaxation, and serves as a warning to others that introspection is in progress.

mmmmmmmmmmmmmmmmmmmmmmmmmmmmAAA AAAAAAHHHHHHHHHHHH...

This teaches you how to hold your breath for long periods at a stretch by exhaling slowly from the bottom of the spine.

As you will all be here for quite a while, learning how to pass the time is an important means of understanding how to survive. How to manage, how to cope, how to keep your heads above water. You're all in the same boat. So to weather the storm and tide you over, to keep you high and dry as well as steering clear of disaster, here are some rules:

No dumping on your neighbour, okay? No hogging hot water during the shower hour. No showers more than once a week. No loud tape decks. No flushing of toilets in the middle of the night unless absolutely necessary. No metal in the garburetor, olive pits, sanitary napkins, pencil stubs. No pissing in the shower. Otherwise we have a lot of happy-go-lucky refugees doing what they feel like with no regard for the community and the business to hand, i.e., survival through mutual cooperation.

Privacy is privilege. Social shame remains an ethical system. The ways of doing time are oriental.

No people whose word for "yesterday" is different from their word for "tomorrow" can be said to have a loose grip on time. 199

You are requested to make your beds wash your dishes flush your excrement mop off your tiles dust the furniture polish your mirrors vacuum the carpet recycle your water but remember:

This is no place for the morose. This is a clean well-lighted place. A place in need of your decorating ideas. The vigorous here are in one another's minds the sick in one another's arms the young in one another's dreams. Our theory of space is transformational. This is no place for the languid. No place for the worn-out and despairing, for the self-important the mean the small-talkers. This is no place for the unregenerative. This place is no place you thought would save you.

Nothing transfigures all that dread but you.

Breathe normally so as not to use up more than your share of oxygen. No jogging in the corridors, around rooms, on the spot. Light torso movements all right, likewise isometrics, toe-touching, but no push-ups or arm wrestling. And definitely no aerobics. Dancing's allowed in your own rooms during our hour of recorded dance music every evening, but don't expect heavy rock, Strauss or hoedown. Nor any mournful melodies. Count on foxtrots and the Bossa Nova. Discourage your thirst: the supply of uncontaminated water is strictly rationed.

Where you are going space is constricted and time capacious. Time makes everything happen but space is what you perceive. Being under siege will entice you to temporize. Taking cover will incite feelings of living in a glass house. Resist these temptations. Time's in the imperative. Throw stones against empty walls. You might even survive.

Expect to receive broadcast messages from the theatre of war when and if available. Expect these in nutshells. Don't expect them to harp upon the long and short of expiration. Forget about obituaries. Listen for new ways of understanding old expressions. Of grief, of eating your heart out, of passing away. Of being smashed to smithereens. Give voice from the bottoms of your hearts. Be wise after the event.

Anybody who wants to broadcast on our community station we will list in our weekly program: topics like ceramics, self-improvement, memoirs. Nothing discouraging please. Nothing negative. No goddamn whining to see the stars again. And for heaven's sake, no gardening tips.

Those of you with children will find games and corre-spondence courses provided. It will be up to parents to educate their children to the new constriction. Unlike some shelters this one encourages children, but it would be delinquent not to remind you that having any more at this time would require a sacrifice you might not like. Childless couples should realize their own space is limited and no new rooms are available should they suddenly give birth. We inform you of this with a heavy heart.

Singles among you should remember that no doubling-up is permitted. The single rooms are just not adequate. Those found cohabiting will be asked to give up one of their rooms to families in need of additional space. A single room needn't be lonely for anybody involved in community activities. We have a small bank of information available about other singles listing their interests and aspirations. Dial the number in the manual by your telephone. Be brief. This shelter is on a party line and many of you may not be familiar with party-line etiquette.

This is the case with children in the habit of using phones whenever they feel like it. Children should be discouraged from using the phone unless they ask permission. Please, no goddamn pranks. In the last war no one, let alone children, had access to a phone in the underground bogs they used to call shelters. The telephone has been installed to prevent you feeling down in the mouth. Use it wisely.

What else? Golfers are reminded to give up their clubs and putters. They are going to have to replay a lot of life's links in their heads. They're going to have to mow them and hoe them and irrigate them alone. By the way, ladies, there is one hibiscus in every apartment, which likes to be watered once a week with a pinch of fertilizer once a month. If you spot thrips, murder them or they'll eat your root.

WHOOP WHOOP WHOOP—

Always whoop from the abdomen, never the thorax. The worst whoopers will not survive in the event of another bomb. Fallout in the corridors may cause a slow and painful—

Give up what you knew about the good old ways of taking cover. Lay the groundwork for a new way of feeling at home. Lick your rooms into shape. Gird up your loins for a long lean time.

During which it would be better to toy with new ideas and mince no words. Your perception is idiomatic and begs other space. War is hell. War lasts. It is the original sin. Heaven blazing in the head.

When you feel like throwing in the towel when you feel like burning your bridges when you feel like kicking the bucket . . .

just remember: to get a new lease on your room, refurbish it. You are apt to believe that grass is greener on the other side of the fence. This is a fatal mistake. Nothing here is the same old story. Not looking for greener pastures, not keeping up with the Joneses, not making a beeline for security. Nothing flies the way of the crow. Out there is definitely no man's land.

You're all in for a long haul. Feeling down in the dumps will become a residential virus. By the look of you, it already has. Expect to find yourselves up the creek without a paddle, fishing in troubled waters, going down for the last time. . . But don't give up. The war in the world may disappear. Don't presume, so may the world. Acquire detachment.

In a moment you will be asked to take off your clothes. This act will be your final preparation. Your first precaution to ensure that as little fallout as possible reaches your rooms. There's no need to be embarrassed. In the end we'll turn out the lights and you may shed your clothes by the light of the Exit sign.

Remember—what you are used to is now old hat. Like pulling up your socks or flying by the seat of your pants. You are accustomed to buttoning up, belting up, pulling yourselves up by the bootstraps. You used to be clothes horses.

No more. Here your baggage will be stored in lockers until it's safe to return it to you. Everything you require, showers and robes, will be found inside your rooms. Inside your covenants. Inside yourselves. You're among the lucky. You're taking cover.

All your troubles are packed in old kit bags. You've decided that discretion is the better part of valour. Displaced and anxious you are willing to turn the other cheek because the alternative is a slow and painful death.

But cross that river when you come to it. Right now you're tired and anxious to retreat to your rooms where you can cherish old possibilities. Like wading out with the tide on a clear August day dreaming of your best friend's wife's buttocks. Like barbecuing fritters for the gang on your backyard Hibachi. Or playing tag with your spaniel in the park, where he did his business, scratched up the lawn and came bouncing back. Down here we encourage the exchange of snapshot albums. We delight to imagine you seated here. Spitting images.

Yet these are erstwhile pleasures because in the end you may suffer nausea, run out of oxygen, deplete your food, fall apart inside from radiation. Waste away, suffer, go up like smoke under a direct hit, perish.

For the succour of all you will discover in residence an interior decorator. He's another reason to keep your phone free. We encourage the arts and feel the cost of a decorator will meet with your approval. He comes with the shelter and although you will never meet him he'll help to brighten up the dark days and months ahead. His services are subsidized by the questions you admit.

Does anybody exist at the end of the line if he doesn't speak? How else do you know if the forest exists? Why do we need a voice at the end of the line anyway?

Anybody interested in receiving one of his calls can count themselves eligible. He wants you to know he is not a crackpot. He merely wants to change the way you listen. So when your phone rings and he refuses to speak—give him the time of day. Sit back and take a load off your feet. Let him breathe in your ear.

He speaks in no pictures you'll recognize. He may not even be a he. Listen to him breathe. He is used to reticence, indifference, hangups. He hates darkness and isolation. The darkness he finds obscene. He breathes and even pants.

Your world may light up. It may not. You may call him an impostor. He may be one. Greatness lies not in being strong, but in the right use of strength. Our decorator's strength is in his fingers. He dials, he calls you up with new sets of old numbers, old combinations with new prefixes. He'll try to turn you into voyeurs. The effect could be narcotic. You may feel like rearranging your rooms. You may begin to see the forest for the trees, that you're still in the swim, that unlike Heraclitus you are able to dip your foot in the same river twice.

Pay attention when our decorator in residence rings and fails to reveal himself fails to tip his hand fails to live up to his promise fails to meet you halfway fails to darken your door ...

For in here your received notions of human nature will undergo change. Nature will not survive man's assault on himself. The luxury of ideologies leads only to the grave.

Your blood cannot survive invading anemia. Your senses cannot survive radiation that blisters your skin cooks your eyes gnaws your eardrums ulcerates your tongue oxidizes your nose.

The sensible thing is to check for leakage every day. Check your gauges. Report changes in levels of radioactivity.

You are all contaminated. All victims of what is everywhere in the air. Take stock of changes in yourselves, any desiccation, any deterioration, any convulsions of your tongues. The way you speak measures your degree of resistance to residential virus. To severe dislocation. The penalty down here for talking shop is fallout. It hangs in the air like dust.

205

mmmmmmmmmmmmmmmmmmmmmmmmmmAAA
AAAAAAHHHHHHHHHHHH ...

Make up your minds to empty them. The dialect here is new. Old-fashioned war permitted a return to normal life every morning. This is no longer possible. Your nightmares last all day every day. There is no way of distinguishing day from night. What you forget no longer exists, what you don't remember no longer infects you:

no more clover in July no more asters in September no more plane trees or lotus or dragonflies in autumn no more milliners no more pianos no more concert halls no more stadiums no more theatres no more chicken coops no more Toyotas not to mention legislatures congresses courts no more brass bands no more lexicography no more Chinese food no more trust company officers no more archery no more bicycles no more comstockery no more Visa and MasterCard no more libraries no more junk mail no more Constantinople no more cappuccino ice cream no more gerrymandering no more Sunday newspapers no more hindsight no more friends in cafés no more parachuting no more Hovis bread no more popery no more waterbeds no more stockbrokers no more sciroccos no more adjudications no more blueberry-picking no more lapis lazuli no more ferry schedules no more hugger-muggers no more topping lifts no more donut diners no more cosmography no more eggs no more area codes no more Malvern Hills no more simony no more butter lettuce no more butter no more mystagogues no more jujubes no more store detectives no more Latinists no more cryptography no more kid gloves no more tabernacle choirs no more mergansers no more oysters no more pointillism no more natural light.

No more fresh air. Those who insist on poking your heads outside will return with radiation sickness. You will keep throwing up. You'll lose control of your bowels. You'll bleed from your noses and your ears. Your hair will fall out. You will probably die.

Here while it lasts is a less noxious world. Breathe in, breathe out. You will discover you have noses. You will smell what is denied your common sense. You will smell apple skin in the air, cologne on dogs, chocolate in daffodils. Grass bleeding, a lake stirring, the sea rotting. You will smell the engine rooms of freighters on the night wind. Train stations, golf balls. Hair in the sun, motel swimming pools, metronomes. Chicken feed, $10 bills, printer's glue in the spines of books. Shingles in heat, cat gut in racquets, missals in church. Baseballs, teabags, tarpaper. Bark on trees, violins at concerts, cement in mixers, turkey in the straw. Salt marshes and roller skates. Fingernail filings, African violets, decaying teeth, watch straps. You will smell turpentine in sagebrush, ammonia in brie, popcorn in lobsters. Sprinklers, pitch, tires on asphalt, suitcase handles, blowholes, Bombay, holy water in fonts, goose shit. You will smell furniture polish at parties, sewing-machine oil in rifle barrels, lights at a play. Spider monkeys, newsprint, lobelia.

Do not believe the source of life is extinguished. Do not believe it isn't. Do not be generous without being kind. Don't believe the quiet person has less to say. Don't be sanguine about the place you're going to. Don't, on the other hand, repine. This is no place for the senseless. Not even if the place makes no sense at all. Your sentence now is life. The idiom can be translated but never commuted. Love starts here in the vernacular.

You may not be Chinese. But you're becoming oriental. You have glittering eyes. Your eyes amid many wrinkles are wise.

The world is on fire. This place is covered. Take off your coats. The light is going out. Stand up and shed all your clothes. Do not be ashamed. Use the light of the Exit sign. Stand up.

Tell yourselves not to be afraid. Tell yourselves the fear is in your minds. Address yourselves to the cave inside. Take off all your clothes. The light is going out. Tell yourselves you are taking cover. Tell yourselves to shed the jejune remains of style, your flirtations with persistence, your resolutions to lead less solemn lives. Tell yourselves this place is ideal. Tell yourselves the world is on fire. Tell yourselves the light is going out. Tell yourselves to stand up and take off your clothes. Don't be ashamed. Use the light of the Exit sign. Leave your clothes where they are. Leave yourselves by the Exit light. Stand up. Do not be afraid.

THE EMERALD CITY

Lust requires for its consummation darkness and secrecy;
and this not only when unlawful intercourse is desired, but
even such fornication as the earthly city has legalized.

– St. Augustine

IN ONE EVENING, two remarks: Kendra says I remember
smells like some people do faces. Arlene says nobody can
change their own smell. It's an odd evening. To have known
these women ten years, husband and lover, and until now
never discussed your nose or smelling with either. You might
suppose that after a decade of double-dealing, the coincidence
of one evening is a slight price to pay for the variety of many.
But such cost over time is inflationary. It breaks down
relationships.

Two into one won't go.

The sum of a triangle's three angles is two right angles.

What you learn later about the propositions you memorized at school isn't necessarily what you proved there.

"School was easy," Kendra might say upon reflection. The mirror becomes her.

"School?" Arlene would claim nothing so long ago deserves reflection. "Why would you want to go back there?" (Her interest in my high school reunion is nil.)

Still it's true. I *do* remember smells. Tar, say: my grandfather claiming hot tar a good antidote for whooping cough, and taking me, where rigs spread smoke from low-down nozzles, to stand on curbs and fill my lungs. To this day I don't know what whooping cough is. I thought then it swelled lungs so they flapped reluctantly, like the wings of a crane, straining to rarer air. Even now I associate the smell of tar not unpleasantly with coughing symptomatic of bubonic plague, black plague. Maybe the memory compensates for a sizable regret. As a child, I was often teased for having a small nose—so no matter what the disease, I can still recall its attendant smell. Wabasso flannelette sheets with measles, Sunkist orange peel with chicken pox, Vick's VapoRub with a cold. . . Most other men misprize their noses. Maybe if you have a nose, a city is a poor place to cultivate it.

Arlene says my rambling associations make me a hound in search of their gist. Guilt always makes you feel like a dog. Or worse, a fugitive trying to cover his tracks. Poetic justice requires a fugitive to seek his refuge at home, with a wife and daughter, say, reading Uncle Remus and Brer Rabbit. I don't have a daughter myself. A son, yes, by someone else's wife, but I never see him and suspect he can't read.

In truth I do see him on visits to Kendra and Jay's, but never by himself. Around me he's either making flitting sounds like laser beams, snuffing out his enemies, or on his way to bed. He has hair my colour, off-red, hardly red at all. Jay, whose own hair is dark, has never to my knowledge questioned his boy's paternity. Jay is nothing if not robust and I feel no jealousy over Kendra. (Her own hair, thank God, is light.) I like Jay. Once you cut through the lawyer's soap he has an agreeable smell. I suspect Kendra's early interest in me owed mainly to her suspicion of her husband's sterility.

"Things I've told you," Kendra wonders. "You know my secrets...I couldn't dream without you knowing."

Kendra knows a thousand and one ways to keep me in thrall. The problem's our son, orphan of our pleasure, who is dull and hates school. If she were to start reading him *Arabian Nights* every night, he'd be 2.7 years older when she finished, an adolescent and just as brainless. She says he mainly enjoys Buzzball on Jay's video game, which uses the TV screen when Jay's hockey and golf are out of season, or not on. The solution (the *problem)* lies with Jay, legal and moral father, whose hopes for his son have never bothered to "factor in," as Jay would put it, the realms of fancy. Straightforward and spontaneous, Jay attracts clients easily and has an influence over the boy I only dream of.

Visiting my son on his ninth birthday, and alone in his bedroom, I find he's discovered points. All over the walls have appeared bilboes, falchions, cutlasses, scimitars, rapiers, stilettos, hunting knives—sheathed in ivory, wood, steel and leather. Naked blades are rare and apparently unprized. I sit on his bed and study his armoury till it grows blunt. Reminds me of nothing in my own experience, sets no wheels turning, gives me no pleasure beyond the vague symmetry in its hung pattern.

On the floor's a copy of *Popular Electronics,* a magazine with a sour gutter. If you can't tell a book by its cover, you can always tell something by its smell. This smell depresses me.

Outside in the tree a bird calls, below on the patio my wife is singing for her supper, here on the bed I'm thinking of lumber. Is the magazine's pulpy smell conjuring up the thought?

"Hear our cowbird?" Kendra in the doorway causes me to remove my nose. "Arlo climbs out on the roof once a day with sugar water for that bird. Have a look."

She leads me by the hand to the window. A bird flies to the dogwood at the end of the yard. In a wire cradle a blue plastic dish hangs from a cedar bough beyond the dormer. How does Arlo manage not to fall off the roof?

"Oh," replies Kendra, "he's got Jay's agility." Adding quickly, for my sake, "Something he's picked up."

"You shouldn't let him, should you? Nothing to grab onto if he falls." She looks back outside. "The tree?" In jeans and a plaid shirt how unfamiliar she seems, even after a decade. When I see her alone she shows up in dresses or skirts. I like her dresses, the reach within them endless, the unravelling pineful. She is looking into the yard now. "Have you noticed, by the way, how well your tree is doing?" She means the dogwood. "You're a wiz." I planted it for them when Arlo was born.

"All these swords too," I go on, "he could cut himself. You let him play with these?" She looks. "Jay does. They're his collection, from an uncle who died of legionnaires' disease or something. Jay thought we could get rid of the rocket glue on Arlo's clothes and bedspread if we gave him a grown-up hobby, to teach him responsibility. So I hung the things." She looks at the unkempt bed. "I can't see that it's helped," she says. "Can you?"

Sometimes you lie in the bed you make. We should drop our conversation and go downstairs to the patio. But as Kendra contends, butter spread over bread goes farther than butter spread across toast. *We* get along like bread and butter, seldom feel stale, never see one another mornings when awful things are said between husbands and wives. Both of us are sitting on Arlo's unmade bed. The danger of deciding to use it would be in sabotaging our nurtured secret, in a sudden ungovernable urge (bread and butter dissipating to a hot roll). With Kendra and me, things don't have their place, one thing dissolves to another. The dream gets better.

The perspective too. Conversations we've had years earlier recur, excite. Kendra, who studied Latin at university, was recently wondering about the heraldry of words. We were sitting in the window seat of the apartment we meet at, in the East End where we're unlikely to run into anyone either of us knows. No one blazons crests on words, she claimed, and it was her use of the world "blazons" that set me thinking of the September sun embossing the cluttered little gardens I could see behind houses across the alley. They resembled backyards I grew up in. Later, making love, I remember she had used this word four or five summers earlier . . . "blazons." In a similar conversation about heraldry, also in September, after Arlo's birthday. I whispered the coincidence in her ear. This new angle on an indifferent subject made our lovemaking very vital that afternoon. Dangerous, I don't know why.

Kendra is at the wall. She has resisted the enticement of her son's bed too easily, in my opinion. "Funny," she says. "Arlo never looks at this collection anymore. You'd think he'd be thrilled, showing it off. Taking down a sword now and then to impress a friend?"

The only blade missing is a letter opener. The kind my grandfather used on books he carried home from school and tried to read aloud. A migrant horse trader from Carolina, much later a school janitor, he brought home soiled uncut books marked DISCARD that my brother and I would look underneath like skirts, pressing each gathering at the edge till it made a hoop. (One of these DISCARDs was eventually responsible for my obsession with gardens.) The book that tickled my grandfather was about Uncle Remus talking "darkie." I mention this to Kendra. Discarded books that smell of the nineteenth century: "They still do, in my mind's nose."

She says, "You remember smells like some of us remember faces. Or places," she continues. "I remember the Rome I studied better than the Rome Jay and I visited on our honeymoon. I should go back to Italy."

Looking around Arlo's room I see no trace of my gift to him on his last birthday, an old *Boy's Own Annual* from the same grandfather, Arlo's great-grandfather, the janitor. I suppose a year is a long time to expect a child to look after a keepsake. Ten years is a long time to go on having an affair with his mother.

A shriek from the garden hurries us back to the window. On the lawn, Jay is chasing Arlo and two other boys around a rosebush in his apron and chef's hat, hollering at his son in pretended outrage for swiping an uncooked hamburger patty. "I'll whale the tar out of you, you thief!" The thing about Jay and me is that neither of us minds playing the fool. Kendra turns smiling from the window and touches me warmly in the groin. I touch her back. It's exciting to be doing this in full view of the garden. Downstairs, unhooking little fingers by her mock orange, we emerge into the patio's evening sun. The scent of cooking beef fills the air. Arlene is eating celery sticks in her amused, savouring way. I'm still in love with Arlene. A piano teacher, she has a sweet, natural fragrance and speaks *obbligato*. She's adroit, loves animals and always nails her colours to the wall. Wearing a pointed gold hat, an elastic stretched under her chin making little sutures down both cheeks, she for one is willing to enter into the spirit of any celebration. If I were married to Kendra instead of her, she might attract me as a lover more than Kendra. The points of duplicity are moot. Both are intelligent women. A weakness of mine, a strength.

> If two angles of a triangle are equal, the sides opposite these angles are equal.

Arlo has fallen into the roses and has bees mad at him. Jay drags him out, telling him to behave, to come and say hello on the patio. He's reluctant, his two friends hang back. His mother introduces us to his friends. We wish Arlo happy birthday. Shyly he answers questions about summer camp, the first week of school, the GIMME GRAVY stencilled on his T-shirt. Like mine at his age, his eyes are already weak, so he wears glasses that he hates and seldom cleans of their constant film. Fingerprints and sweat. He rubs his bare arm, complaining that his dad has made him get scratched on the thorns. I point to his bird dish and compliment him on his ingenuity. He looks pleased. Jay complains that the trouble today is boys have nothing left to build. Pre-packaging ruins initiative. Kites, for example.

Jay seems as fidgety as Arlo, who clings awkwardly to his scratched arm, making a one-footed H.

We eat our hamburgers, the sun goes down, Arlo blows out his candles. His gift from us is an inscribed copy of my little book on greenhouses. He's disappointed. Kendra shows him my picture on the back cover. He isn't impressed. He's seen me on TV—a better place all around to be seen. Politely grateful, he excuses himself and invites his friends inside to play Buzzball. Jay debates "the law" with Arlene—and I'm thinking of lumber again.

Kendra sits in silence too. What is she wishing? The evening's festive mood has gone down with the light. Hunger satisfied, the looking forward disappeared, another beer to stay the gesturing hand. Jay's hand, he's summing up: avowing his feelings of the moment at thirty-seven. The coals are wizened now. My dogwood in the dew smells as fresh as cedar.

"...so expecting things to come along becomes addictive." He gulps at his beer without much rhythm. "The bad part is when you start to push it. You know? Trying to make things come along? Wherein, you see, my problem. What used to come along was basically a surprise. To wit, a compliment here, a partnership there. You didn't expect these—I didn't. They were surprises. Now, though, everything's got *me me me* written on it ...

"Listen, I'm talking about surviving, huh? If nothing comes along, fine. I can live with that. I mean I'm definitely not on a ladder. That's an important factor, I guess. Ladders are

meant to be climbed when something needs *fixing*. Period."
Another gulp. "Anyway, here I am trying to stay off the ladder
altogether . . . even if having to *remind* myself is a sure way
of totally disappearing up my own asshole. Up the ladder?"
He laughs, sounding depressed. He looks at me, fraternally I
imagine. "Wish I had an oasis like yours. When I see you on
the screen, God, I think, *there's* heaven . . ."

Well, I tell him, that is what he is supposed to think. It's all
a very got-up oasis.

"And I'm not even *in*terested in gardening," he confesses.

Driving home, Arlene admits a new respect for Jay's
honesty. "He was talking about being subversive," she says.
"Warning himself. It bears thinking about." The hint is *I*
should think about it. She thinks I spend too much time
with seed manufacturers, booksellers, nursery workers and
producers. Jay's confession about stamping himself himself
himself on the future makes her say this is exactly what I do,
it's my addiction.

"You're afraid to be generous anymore. You're greedy. As
if the future even existed, for you to mortgage it in meetings,
phone-in radio shows, hybrids, the tomato hornworm, promises! You've lost your spontaneity. There's someplace, you
know, called Now. Home it's called." She gets out of the car to
open the garage. "No one can change the way he smells."

What this means, must mean, is you are who you are.
Period.

Anyhow, it sets off recollections of childhood, high school,
gathers up what Kendra said about my remembering smells,
and causes me to brood over Arlene's charges. I lie in bed
working out a rejoinder. But when I have it, turning to her
with it like a dog its bone, she's asleep. Dull if plausible she
would have called it. We wobble gently on our waterbed, like
jelly.

Subversive? Maybe the lies I've used to cover my tracks to
Kendra make me appear so. I appear busier than I am. I have

to. For there is Kendra to consider too. The demands of both women are different. Arlene demands less concentration than Kendra, more patience. Kendra wants a measured response to her recurrent melancholy, Arlene a bouncy disposition so she knows where she's at. With Arlene I feel that life is less tantalizing, with Kendra less certain. I owe much to them both for my wholeness. My integrity.

In the dark the scent of Arlene's skin in my nostrils is a fragrance that no amount of accomplishment on her part, I suppose, could improve. Unlike Kendra she is seldom bored, since the piano has brought her satisfaction, nimble joints and children clamouring for lessons. Schumann she plays well, the shadows in her technique seldom obscuring the music's light. Up until a year ago, that is. Since then I've noticed lapses. Sour notes, and not just at the keyboard. Her notion about marriage used to be not to make it a monument. I was free to go on gardening without the responsibility of a family. She decided against a family. "What the heck," she declared. "You have enough kids already." Her pupils, she meant. "Around here you're swamped." But this carefree tone has changed. Her playing sometimes suffers from the lack of her previous abandonment. She sounds distant. I've started to see how she wants to reshape me, handle me like a pupil, wish me more loving.

Next morning she wakes me with soft kisses in my hair. The dawn kisses of a bird fondly rearranging the wool of its nest. "I'm so incredibly sorry, dearest, for the way I spoke to you last night." We both snort. She wants toast and coffee brought to her in bed.

Leaving the house I call for toothpaste, "And while you're at it, some Intensive Care." I sound spry. "My hands feel raw."

"There's a whole bottle of Rose Milk left."

"That stuff stinks."

So I begin taping, with a sun that refuses to come out, and two cameras taking cues from my young, hungover director,

Jules Seabrook. Like our tennis matches, we make it all up as we go along. I just open my mouth and start talking.

"So as you sow . . . but so also as you divide—and I don't have to tell you regular viewers this—so shall you reap. Is this really true. . . ?"

A full garden in September is a bank of blue asters mobbed by bees. I like being up to my neck in them, bound to my stake as they are, cheerful, pullulating. Asters I say something about every fall before moving along to chrysanthemums, dahlias, cabbage, tomatoes, what have you. Jules gesturing out of range means cut the rambling or face his knife in the cutting room. This morning's headache makes his gesture sluggish and less inhibiting.

". . . Being gardeners yourselves, you regular viewers know how addictive gardening can get. Especially when you're expecting a handsome harvest—or just trying to solve a problem like slugs. You become a slave to your problems. Your letters tell me that how we judge other people's problems here in *The City Garden* is often a help in your own gardens, and your *expectations* therein." The legalese is definitely Jay's, so I follow that lead for a while, a matter of free association. The secret of TV gardening is to combine a little philosophy with plenty of practical suggestions. You end up talking off the top of your head.

"None of us are trying to force anything to grow—we're just in it for the fun, really, maybe a pat on the back for supplying the family with vegetables, and a few flowers for friends' vases. Half the fun, I guess, is expecting the *results.* The other half is not expecting anything . . .

"Like these asters I'm standing in . . . I wish we could've arranged for the sun to be out . . . it's the blue and bees in them that really set off this particular flower, in my opinion, from any other September perennial. Can we get a closer look at these? . . . We got these? All right? These particular clumps of asters, I confess, weren't split when I should've split them last spring, so you can see the blooms are smaller than they ought to be. Next spring we'll do a show on splitting off the young outside shoots from these older ones here in the centre..."

I turn palms upward and let the petals float between my fingers. ". . . Still. Aren't they something? Especially when you didn't expect—*I* didn't expect—*any* attractive blooms... That's when gardening's a surprise. When the harvest is definitely *not* always a sign of how well we sow. These lovely flowers are New England Asters, and you can see they'll grow four or five feet tall...*Aster novae angliae,* for you botanists."

Next week, watching this scene in the asters, Arlene talks to me on the screen as she would to some sportscaster. "Your grammar's bad... Why don't you take your hand off the flower? Get to the point, please..."

This has become a routine and begun to annoy me. "Hold your horses. There's a nice part coming."

Later, in another part of the garden, I'm trying to do justice to City of York roses. The camera has me from the waist up. The fragrance of these white blooms would stun a heretic.

"And by the way," I'm saying, "I should tell you of the holy man who got lost in a reverie..."

"Must you?" says Arlene. "Jokes?"

"Cut it out."

"Too bad Jules didn't."

". . . When this holy man returned from his dream," I go on, "a friend asked him what he'd brought back from the dream garden. The holy man thought for a while. Then answered that when he reached the rose bower he'd intended to fill the skirts of his robe with roses to give as presents to his friends. But, he said, something happened. He found the perfume of the flowers so intoxicating that, well, he just let go of his skirts..."

Here Jules has cut to a lingering close-up of a rose. Arlene, who has been stroking the cat on her lap, says very dryly, "I think you should fire your gag writers, honey." The cat stretches. "Unless that cloying close-up is Jules's idea of satirizing your Persian poet."

Sa'di, she means, who has become a regular guest of mine, his *pensées* have, and viewers write in to ask where they can buy a copy of his book. "Is he an organic gardener, or what?" inquired one woman. "I checked under Lifestyles—under Travel too."

I tell Arlene that I threw this story in for her.

"What, to excuse your forgetting my birthday for instance?"

"I was thinking what you said last week about people trying to change the way they smell."

"What *I* said?"

"The odour of self."

"What about it?"

"Subverting it."

"Sure it was me?"

"Listen to the rest of this—pretty soon I go on about the pleasures of the nose ..."

"Well, you look like a nose between two thorns, sniffing that way. Your eyes are glassy."

She laughs her thick, deep-throated laugh. She thinks I'm vain for wearing contact lenses. Why can't I wear glasses on TV like I do at home? The smell of the cat makes her cough. Her coughing irritates me, so I go and turn up the volume. This annoys *her*—she thinks I'm being unfair—and she leaves the room, dropping the cat in my lap. This is when the dog jumps up and barks twice: something it never does in the house. The cat spits. The dog makes for the cat. The cat's claws dig in like thorns up my shirt. Suddenly I find myself in the middle of two feuding animals that never feud, never lose their tempers. Neither do I, except when provoked. The animals cower. By the time I look again the closing credits are tracking up the screen.

"*Shit!*" I look for our black cat to fling into the fireplace.

"Language!" warns Arlene triumphantly from the kitchen.
"Shit! Shit! Shit!"
"Smarten up, please."
"*Me!* You ruined my program."
"Well," she calls with some finality, "you ruined my life."

We seem to be back in radio days—copying the Bickersons. Before slamming the door on my way out, I tell her to drop dead.

Backing out of the garage I spin my tires in displeasure. But without giving them enough gas. Instead of burned-rubber smell, I get worse, a burned-clutch smell. I roll down the windows talking to myself, myself, myself, and crawl down the alley.

Somewhere, up another alley maybe, somebody is breaking the law. Normally I adore this smell of burning leaves. Like the smell of marijuana, it's a smell the city denies us by law, except on one dirty weekend in November when you can burn all the leaves you want. Their smoke is the smell of mortality. I know—my grandfather died commenting on it, how much it calmed him down.

Reassured by the sight of a woman cutting zinnias in her front yard, I lift my foot from the gas to coast. (To save gas, my grandfather would turn off his car on hills, and then we sank quietly.) This neighbourhood is built on slopes and hills. Vistas still burst upon you, as they did in childhood, with a light to fill the bay and wash these mountainous shores, where we grow gardens in a rain forest.

Coasting, I reconsider my legal marriage and how it has deteriorated in a way Kendra's and mine has not. Have I, as Arlene claims, "ruined" her life? I had thought that her miscarriage was an accident. A year ago she came home from a mysterious walk, said dully what had happened and sat down dripping to watch a rerun of "I Love Lucy." Black and gummy with blood, her dress encased her legs in a shroud. I carried her to bed and dialled the hospital. It seemed fantastic to ride by ambulance through a city shimmering in Indian summer, rainbow-coloured sails in the bay, gardens growing as quietly as hair. I knew she was pregnant, she told me she was. Should I have encouraged her to *have* a family?

Stab of remorse, the cruellest cut. How can marriage parry such guilt without fading away?

At dawn, when the thought of return had overcome the desire to linger, I saw that my friend had gathered in his skirts roses and sweet basil, and hyacinths and spikenards to bring with him to the city; whereupon I spake: "Thou knowest that the flower of the garden will fade, and the seasons pass away, and the wise ones have said: 'Whatever is not lasting is not to be cherished.' He asked: 'What, then, is to be done?'" . . .

Rescued from the DISCARD pile by my grandfather, *The Rose Garden of Sa'di* was the little Wisdom of the East book that decided my life.

A garden whose waters were shackles of light:
A thicket whose minstrels enchanted the night.

I recited this distich for my teacher once and she said I was very sensible and would someday study botany. Botany? "Gardening," she said. It wasn't. But turned out to be, since it was a gardener I became—when, employed as a government botanist, analyzing insect spoor for the Department of Lands and Forests, I lost interest, quit the service and started up *The City Garden*. With my own TV and radio shows, I have become the author of three books on gardening: *The City Flower Gardener*, *The City Vegetable Gardener* and *Starting Your Own Greenhouse*. Mine's a career in blossom. When you think that gardening books can have the timelessness of a poet's books, and that good gardens might still be grown by people reading your books in a hundred years, or even looking at Jules's videotapes (if they haven't faded)—then you feel a responsibility. Even in outer space, assuming that living there you can create an atmosphere to smell something in, the laws of growing will always begin in the seed.

Arlene laughs at me. Kendra has more faith. Arlene's the down-to-earth type who keeps my feet where she feels they belong. Kendra's the one who stimulates me by the nature of her forbidden fruit. (By *virtue* of it, I nearly said.) Unlike Kendra, who keeps up to date on alternate lifestyles, Arlene would say she herself has little yearning for caprice. I require both women.

Yet something is happening to recast old propositions in a new light. The coeval pleasures of a decade are not equal to coincidences that start impaling you. The loss of one woman has begun to seem the cost of retaining the other.

Arlo figures in this. The next time we see Arlo is shopping. He and his mother are looking into the window of a card shop along Dunbar one Saturday morning. Arlene and I greet them. I ask about his sword collection, is he treating it well? "Yeah. All right I guess." And school? "Crummy." Then Kendra asks casually, "And what have you two been up to?" Subterfuge, for she and I have seen each other two nights earlier, over dinner in a restaurant, taking a chance we never do in public.

"Well," says Arlene, "I was hoping you could tell me."

She says this offhand, as if turning a threadbare greeting back on itself, saying nothing in preference to too much.

Almost involuntarily, Kendra follows up. "Pardon?"

Arlene pretends to be looking at a card that has caught her eye. "Hmm? Oh. *I'm* fine, but I never see *him*." She studies me, then Kendra. "Didn't you see him for dinner recently?" Her question has the effect of one of Arlo's blades, pirouetting in my stomach. Kendra scrambles for something to say.

These convergences of life transfix us. It turns out Arlene and Louise Caine happened yesterday at the same time to find themselves with appointments at the hairdresser's—an accidental double booking by "Norbert"—and Louise happened to mention she'd seen me, *as* it happened, eating in a restaurant on Commercial Drive the evening before. Surprised, Arlene pressed her for details, wondering who I might be with.

"'It must be Kendra!' I said to her," (says Arlene to me, mockingly, walking down Dunbar). "'I wonder why he didn't mention it?' I said." We've left Kendra and Arlo behind at the card shop. "I've been waiting for you to say something," she says. "So when *she* asked, I decided I had a right to ask."

"Well, it embarrassed her."

"Should it have?"

"We were discussing Arlo."

"So she said. In a restaurant?"

"Arlo's been having trouble at school this year. Hates reading, won't settle down, gets moody. Kendra was wondering if I could suggest anything."

"Are you suddenly an expert on Arlo? What about Jay?"

"Jay's got his own problems. His partners passed him over for a big case."

"Oh, you discussed Jay's problems too."

"She's an old friend."

"Yes, you introduced us."

"Coming from the Maritimes she didn't know anybody."

"And now what—are you thinking you chose the wrong lady?"

"Look, I suggested she might want to send Arlo to you for piano lessons. You heard what she said back there. She *wants* him to take lessons."

"You *did* choose, didn't you?" Her insistence muscles up against any casual reply. Nothing has yet reconciled us over the dog and cat fight, and that days ago.

She says carefully, "Arlo couldn't learn 'Ba Ba Black Sheep' unless Kendra held his head." She ponders me at the crosswalk. "I'm trying to understand. Are she and Jay unable to discuss their own son?"

"We didn't want to bother Jay."

"We?"

"*She*—didn't." This pronoun shuffle is too fast. The mistake is in trying to cover up—bothering to. She picks up something in the air that travels to the same locus in her brain as mine. The impulse is slow, like sunrise on a wet morning. Still, it arrives. The most terrible of all illuminations between husband and wife: the admission, the recognition of betrayal.

Nothing is said. I can only look away, trying to reroute my thoughts. By staring at me she tries to home in on the secret she has accidentally discovered, here on the curb, and doesn't fully understand. A man in a car honks, huffs in resignation, adjusts his sunglasses. We cross the street. We enter the store and shop its aisles listening to distant couplings and uncouplings of steel carts. Driving home we say nothing. The air smells heavy with seawater; it seems transfiguring.

When the first child arrives at the door for a lesson I slip upstairs to phone Kendra. Arlo answers so I don't hang up, as I do when Jay answers. Instead I disguise my voice. "Hello, is your mother there?"

"Yeah." Breathing audibly into the phone, he hangs on. Then he says, "I read your book."

"Oh? Well... Good for you, Arlo."

More breathing. "I liked it."

The receiver bumps the table, before Kendra picks it up. "Arlo," she announces, "has finished your book. More or less. So there." Her tone is self-mocking for she has finished it for him—reading him parts, Scheherazade.

She goes on to say, "I wish I could tell you how upset I feel. How be*trayed*." She's referring to our encounter this morning.

"I don't think I sounded very convincing. About the piano lessons? Did you tell her how difficult Arlo's become?"

"She knows."

"Good."

"Everything," I say.

The briefest pause. "Everything?"

"I don't know where Louise was sitting. She couldn't have seen us leaving . . . could she? Weren't we the last to leave?"

I feel like telling her it is only because Arlene never sees Arlo that she has never seen the resemblances between me and my son before now. Colour of hair, weakness of eyes, the small noses. . . But this would only take us back to our quarrel at dinner. It was *my* never seeing Arlo that Kendra and I were discussing. Quarrelling over Jay's influence on Arlo, his lack of fancy, you name it.

"Fancy?" asked Kendra, forking her salmon.

"Fantasy."

"Well, he's always fantasizing about space."

"Who, Jay?"

"Arlo. It's a world he gets quite excited about."

"I'm glad to hear he's excitable."

"That's supposed to mean what?"

"He's always so . . . indifferent."

"Shy. Around you he's shy. He never *sees* you, after all."

"Exactly."

"Besides, boys change. Their interests do."

"I just wonder if Jay's the right influence."

She looked down at her plate. "What are you suggesting?"

What was I? "How can anybody grow up, really, not knowing his lineage?" I asked.

"Does it matter?"

I said, "To you, of all people, I thought it would. He should read more. I'll bet he has trouble with cereal boxes."

No time that evening, even if we'd felt an urge, to go to our apartment so we said good night, dissatisfied with these growing differences over Arlo. Maybe his learning piano from Arlene should have come up after all. It might have enabled Kendra to assess the benefits of Buzzball in her son's life. Given her another perspective. I don't understand why I should feel so possessive of this child. With the passing years, he has fascinated me less and less.

The slow, dissonant fingering stops. Arlene's voice downstairs is saying, *I want you to learn this. I want you to place your fingers like mine. Do exactly what I tell you. Try this. Now play.*

Suddenly an explosion, deeper than notes, of the overwhelming bars of the "Fantasia in C Major" causes me to wonder if the child on the bench, with legs too short to pedal, has arrived on a wand of my wife's waving. Inspired instruction knows no bounds. No correlation between her instruction and the response, between her words and the illumination, prefigures the rhapsody. It is like love. I sit listening to it, stirred to imagine a pupil's fingers could contain within them codes for such blossomings.

"Hello...?"

I return Kendra's voice in my hand to the cradle. It is as if she no longer exists.

I slip down from the den and out.

The city is green and growing greener by the day. Lawns and boulevards defy the coming winter in shades deeper than dry summer's. I sniff the fall. These days that start with foghorns end in brilliance: rim of mountain and arc of sea. What a romantic vision of high pressure, circling in upon us from the Pacific on satellite maps, tales within tales. (TV informs us from every angle.) Poised thus on the edge of country and continent, we are always being told we are beautiful, we are smug, we are green. We are always being told we are Hong Kong, San Francisco, Rio. That we are Lotus Land, Shangri-La, God's Country. That we are a poster in a travel shop in Venice.

We are all these. Or so we come to believe, and erect dazzling towers to resemble all the other Babels of bigger and more important cities. How we shine at sunset!

But it is still a poor place if you have a nose. Walking the city you try to remember that a nose is the rooting organ of all mammals. The dog reminds us to go digging, and I do.

Against a tree I remove my contacts and go blind. The release is wonderful. The equivalent feeling would be an orgasm or a powerful movement of the bowels. I am absorbed now, like a pig eating, or grandmother smelling lavender.

My nose grows bigger.

Here by the curb is the smell of leather-scented motes drifting inside the tinted sunlight of a locked Mercedes.

I walk on, out of my neighbourhood.

Here on Broadway is the smell of garlic from pores of a Greek woman standing at the bus stop.

In Chinatown comes the abiding smell of pork trotters and cauliflower.

If I could answer Arlene's charge of greed, my rejoinder now would be that *blind* greed makes the dog in fact spontaneous. At least I haven't lost my spontaneity.

Tomorrow, Sunday, I'll catch whiffs of the lemon oil that Jules uses to varnish his ash racquet. He likes to flail the air on court to intimidate me at the net.

As I say, you compensate for having a small nose.

———————

Thus are Arlene and I politer than ever to each other. She won't confront me, and I'm too inured to life's biformity of the past ten years to imagine it's through. She's waiting for me to act: her eyes look away, but see. Her intuition's like the knowledge of flowers closing at dusk. Fading, her scent is sweeter now. Even apart from her I will always admire her arched foot.

Near the end of every program, nose to the grindstone, I like to turn to my mailbag and answer questions from viewers.

A. Slugs? Get rid of slugs with grapefruit skins. Or tin cans. When the little beggars crawl inside, throw them in the trash can.

A. Clubroot on your broccoli is caused by the coast's acid soil. Burn all your diseased plants and don't sow the cabbage family in the same plot for four years, better still, five.

A. Your impatiens is *droopy* because you water it either too much or not enough. It's *yellow* from overfeeding or underfeeding. Be your own judge.

A. You can stop worms crawling into your cabbages by making tarpaper collars for them. Not for the worms, the cabbages. This way you never have to use a pesticide. (As for the rabbit: snare it with cheesecloth and ingenuity.)

A. Bury your compost under seaweed . . . suffocate the stuff . . . before wrapping the whole heap in black plastic.

Counselling others is easy. But doing justice to your own life is trying to weed out received ideas about heart, home and courage. If Arlene is right—that nobody can change the way he smells—it's a proposition the bloodhound might verify. The fugitive too. No matter how much scent a woman reapplies in the bathroom before coffee and liqueurs, *he* can detect an otherness in lingering traces of urine two hours after she leaves the house. Doesn't matter next visit if she changes perfumes: *her* smell seems the same smell, neither pleasant nor unpleasant. Just an odour that makes her commit a subversive act to disguise it.

Perfume, aftershave lotion, deodorants, bubble bath . . . none of these, if Arlene is right, alters the smell of kidneys or changes character. If Arlene is right, we put on smells as we do ideas, and come to believe that we smell like we think we do, instead of the way our noses tell us.

My fading Arlene, do we take the perfume for ourselves? Knowing full well ten thousand others use the same soap, mouthwash, cologne, toothpaste? And do we think in flocks? *Home is where you find it. Absence makes the heart grow fonder. Discretion is the better part of valour.* Incontrovertible bits of wisdom to pull out of cedar chests, smelling of mothballs, leading to proverbs and even myths. *The grass is always greener on the other side of the fence. Mighty oaks from tiny acorns grow. The lion is king of the forest.* Sometimes! Sometimes! Sometimes! The real answers, like the ways we smell, seem to lie deeper.

Who but the dog knows enough to dissociate a person's smell from his deodorant?

Who can track his own marriage to its lair?

Coincidences such as these in my own life raise the hue and cry: jury duty, my high-school reunion, *The Wizard of Oz*. Doing, going along to, reading—each for the first time—all at once. They complicate an already busy fall. Suddenly life feels driven and unsettled. And by temperament I dislike travel.

I prefer the city. I consider it my moral obligation to get along here. Of course anyone who does this with success is an impostor. He pretends acquiescence. Pretends to forgo revenge in the interest of saving his neighbour's face. Jay has criticized our Just Society to me as dealing *too* evenly with somebody who doesn't value this facesaving. Somebody who refuses to listen to another point of view, who shovels over what threatens him, who has only the talent for pointing and cutting. A man who can't compromise. A man in other words who lacks a green thumb. Therefore, says Jay, the Law: to ask questions of those who are a law unto themselves.

Selected without warning to sit indefinitely on a jury, to listen to arguments about whether or not a crime has been committed in the case of a twenty-two-year-old woman— I'm in the doghouse with Arlene who thinks I'm avoiding her. Kendra thinks I'm avoiding *her*. Jules is frantic. With the last month of the season upon us, and my attendance at court looming, he and I must tape four shows in seven days.

We set a record. The trick's to pretend a week has passed between each show, to match the continuity of time between each viewing. There's a lot of juggling with camera angles to exclude the still un-grown parts of the garden discussed yesterday. In the greenhouse—where it's easy to rearrange flats, hanging flowers, sick plants, and where I answer my viewers' questions—I spend more time than usual explaining fall as the time for consolidating, winterizing, planning ahead. I extemporize. I doctor diseased plants. I talk about the fragrance of flowers. (I, I, I . . . *Listen* to yourself.) Outside I wander through my recently planted colchicums, such masses of lavender and white goblets, like crocuses. Likewise through my *Amaryllis belladonna,* explaining that soon large pink trumpets will show up on two-foot stems and carry right through November, when my favourite fall-blooming bulb, *Nerine bowdenii,* with pink trumpets will bring *The City Garden* to a pretty close. I advise people to protect the bulbs of their autumn queens from frost with peat and frame lights.

I really wonder what's going to happen between Arlene and me. Between Kendra and me. Among Arlo, Kendra and Jay. Among me, Jay and Arlo. Among—

Reading *Oz* in recesses at court, I wonder what my son would make of it. Kendra has said his imagination is fertilized by deep space. But what about by what Dorothy says to the Scarecrow: "No matter how dreary and grey our homes are, we people of flesh and blood would rather live there than in any other country, be it ever so beautiful. There is no place like home." Arlene, unlike Kendra, would agree. Given the chance Kendra, sunny dream, would circle the globe.

The Crown says no amount of rationalizing by the defence can change our certainty of the crime (rape). The accused is a blackhaired rascal with the features of an amoral gnome. Listening, we are half men and half women. The dock in the distance occupies our days. Days pass, the city hums through lunch hours, the mountains stand up to the skyscrapers. The ridge of high pressure, the sun and blue sky have kept on and on... Like the citizens of Oz I discover that sunglasses help to cut down the sheen.

Still on jury duty by day, where the smells of the court-house sequester beneath glass and steel, I'm unprepared one evening for the smells of the anniversary reunion of my high-school graduation. Dustbane, desk varnish, chalk dust, formaldehyde, Ditto sheets, steam heat from cast-iron radiators: these smells my grandfather would have remembered too. He swept this school, then died as I enrolled here, his heart hooked up to an electrocardiograph screen. I visit old classrooms and Mr. Dodgson who pretends to remember me and who never liked my geometry. In the cafeteria, where the wine-and-cheese party is held, the tables and stools have been swept back against the painted concrete walls to allow anxious men and women to renew acquaintances from twenty years ago.

Few of us, loyal to the city, have lived anywhere else. We wouldn't want to. We sniff each other, this girl and I who were lovers once, over Easter of our last year in school—she seventeen, me sixteen. Offhand now, we act as if we never shared love's magic (I think she was enchanted too). I practise what I couldn't do as a teenager, I polish my laugh like an apple. In those days, with her body backed up against the leather of my grandfather's old Hillman, I was as meek as a cabin boy. Afterwards in bed, conjuring up her image like a harem, I was as bold as a sheik. Fantasy became a way of life. I could remove my glasses.

Does she still smell of almonds? This wine has spoiled my nose. To match her eyes she wears a dress as blue as hydrangeas, but because she suffers from hay fever, or used to, I wonder if this association with flowers isn't improper. When pollen was heavy in the air that Easter, a late Easter, her hay fever meant long drives instead of walks. We drove along the ocean. We drove up the river to conifer forests.

Determined to test Arlene's theory once and for all, I turn the conversation to TV, inching my nose forward to catch her breath. "You used to wear glasses," she says, stepping back to keep me at bay. "What happened?" Vanity, I explain. I have a public now, has she seen my show? Laughing, she says she never watches television. She says, "How much have you drunk?" Touching my chest to make her point stick, knowing I'm married.

How can I say I only want to smell her? That my problems began (and keep on) in her time? That the way she smells is almondy? Too late I ask after her, if she's the same or a different person today, you know, compared to yesterday when we knew each other better.

"Oh, not that different, I guess."

She wants to get away from my nosiness, this sniffing up to her, the strangeness. Maybe it's a myth that high-school girls shape us. Yet when one reappears she is like an open, old-fashioned window, curtains parted on a Sunday morning, in a brick building that you will never enter. Gazing up from the sidewalk, moved, you don't understand why the vision should make much difference. But it does. Her blue eyes wondering, Louise Caine stares at me here, now and forever noncommittal.

Have I become greedy?

Case closed, we the jury deliberate in a small, low-ceilinged room over the forest of evidence presented us, and decide our verdict. We defer, agreeing there are shades of guilt, and decide to request leniency of the sentencing judge. These women are the stronger advocates of leniency, convincing us men of mitigating circumstances. Somebody, the Italian baker among us, says the guy is lucky the law isn't codified according to Islam, or an ayatollah would sentence him to a minimum of sliced-off hands, more likely his pecker.

The judge himself says the convicted man should have better explored the safety valve an imagination offers. He sentences him to two years less a day removed from society. When the gnome protests, the judge commands, "Off with his head!"

But I am imagining this, for I have replaced the judge by my great and terrible self. I ask the Tin Woodman to take care of the details with his axe.

Watching TV in October, Arlene and I sit eating cold-cut suppers. She makes no comments about my performance, my grammar, my sincerity, and this irritates me. I know what she's thinking. Even I feel my integrity impugned by answering fake letters written by myself, Jules, the sound man, anyone with a pencil in the rush of completing our season. Her sarcasm would help me save face.

Q. My fibrous rooted begonias have mealy bug and what look like bagworms, only they're not, maybe leaf miners. Is this due to some sort of deficiency? As one now bitten by the "begonia bug" I'm wondering if I should just throw them on the compost and start over.

Q. I read someplace that fall's the time to seed Siberian wallflowers so they'll bloom next April. Should I keep these pots outside AFTER September? (I don't have a greenhouse but a friend says my garage is the ticket if I punch out the roof and plasticize it. I'd been thinking about doing this anyway—ever since I read yr book.)

Q. We have a lot of *Armoracia rusticana* (horseradish) in our garden and can't figure out how to get rid of the stuff. The wife's tried digging it up, but says the only answer's a very stiff cleanser, like Ajax, or else gasoline. How would you get after this nuisance? Gas?

Q. What you said about asters makes me wonder if my phlox haven't suffered from the same laziness. (Mine,

not yours!) The blossoms this year look pinched. What
do you recommend for phlox? Likewise splitting?
Q. What are you always telling us to smell so much for?

In my Paradise, in the blooming, buzzing multitude of
questions—a charlatan. The oldest smell I know is the worn
one of my Sa'di book. Its sweet decay settles me ...

Diminished here at home, I sit thinking that with the
season almost through I still have a winter of radio to do,
sponsorships of fertilizers and garden tools to record—for
broadcast next spring—a nursery centre to look after and a
staff there to keep on its toes.

And Arlene thinks all my goings have just been excuses to
see Kendra.

When I look out at my own garden it's nothing the size of
Jay's. Unlike the garden where we film, it seems small like my
nose. On TV I definitely appear better off than I am.

"I suppose you're still seeing her?" asks Arlene.

"What? Not at the moment, no."

"I suggest you make up your mind." Her tone is sarcastic.
"She'll be wondering."

"Are you?"

"Wondering?"

"Leaving me."

"I've already made plans," she says. "I'm staying in the
house."

The foregone separation leading to wider separation
equals the received separation. This saddens me. When your
moral congruency (or so my duplicity seems to me) is threatened, you choose your survival.

You agonize. You pretend you actually have a choice of
wives. The act of the Sultan, two at once, in reality is *never*
having to choose. Between the flesh and the trance, for *him*,
falls Allah. (Gimme Gravy.)

So this farce of my having two women in one marriage compounds. When Kendra marries Jay, do I retaliate by marrying Arlene? How does it happen, once each of us is married, that we meet by a lifeguard stand one February and start over? What is Kendra's smell to have led me to her in the first place (or the second, at a winter beach)? If Jay expects a child, will he take Arlo's appearance for granted? Why should Arlene, who lives for the moment, care if we never have a child of our own? Would my leaving her constitute a betrayal of her commitment to me? Would her leaving *me* mean Kendra can finally make up her mind?

Stay tuned.

I need more questions like holes in my bed.

Still, Kendra and I meet to talk over options and angles. Such angles.

Plane geometry lacks perspective by definition, however, and it is Kendra's forte to see the distance. It is her equivocation that delays a solution. She still hasn't told Jay what Arlene knows. Arlo has no idea that Jay is not his father.

It makes me mad the way an apple cart is upset so easily: Kendra, me and Louise in the same restaurant, Louise and Arlene having the same hairdresser, these two having an appointment the same day, same hour. . . If coincidences aspire to unity, it isn't one of geometrical design, in a mosque, definitely.

Relationships end up suffering. Arlene would doubtless like to find out when she is to become a liberated wife. I try to imagine liking my son and can't.

At the apartment Kendra and I meet and end up discussing Arlo again. He now has mumps. What if he dies, she worries. (I feel like telling her about Arlene's child, our child.) She says she shouldn't have come today. We are sitting in the barely furnished living room on a cloudy October afternoon. I mention that the fear I smell must be my own. She's frightened too, she says.

Did she know, I ask, that women handle stress better than men because they have far smaller doses of the male hormone testosterone?

"Botanists," she answers, "know a lot."

We are drinking from an old wineskin that a friend of Kendra's brought her back from a trip, which Kendra keeps on the wall along with prints of Shiraz. I've filled it with dry Californian burgundy that tastes faintly of goat's bladder. We ourselves seem transients here, squirting messy mouthfuls in hopes of settling on a more permanent future. We try love.

Roughly, I carry her to bed.

As I do she is telling a story about Arlo when he was younger. Her perfume smells new. I lay her down on the bed. She gets up again. The curtains closing on their tracks sound like monkey screams.

When it's nearly dark outside, I wake up to an empty wineskin and my lover has disappeared. I seem to be hanging above the bed looking down on its emptiness, floating as if I had a cold and were young again. I remember taking Kendra in my arms, her long hair in my hands, and raking my fingers through it. It wasn't combing. It hurt her, I could see it was hurting her, her white eyes blistering to tears, her face turning as dark as a sunflower—shouting at me to stop. I apologized and said it would never happen again. "What are you *talking* about?" she said, pulling free. "What do you *mean* it'll never happen again? You deliberately hurt me! Are you trying to strangle me? And these scratches!"

I don't remember making love, though I'm sticky with the flotsam. As if in a dream we made a tar baby who squawked in a brier patch for betel nut and dates. An old voice was making Uncle Remus's old voice say, "*When Brer Fox fine Brer Rabbit mixt up wid de Tar-Baby, he feel mighty good, en he roll on de groun' en laff. Bimeby he up'n say, sezee: 'Who ax you fer ter come en strike up a 'quaintance wid dish yer Tar-Baby? You des tuck en jam yo'sef on dat Tar-Baby widout waitin' fer enny*

invite,' sez Brer Fox, sezee, 'en dar you'll stay twell I fixes up a
bresh-pile and fires her up, kaze I'm gwineter bobbycue you dis
day, sho,' sezee. Den Brer Rabbit talk mighty 'umble. 'Roas' me,
Brer Fox,' sezee, 'but don't fling me in dat brier-patch... Skin me,
Brer Fox,' sez brer Rabbit, 'snatch out my eyeballs, t'ar out my
years by de roots, en cut off my legs,' sezee, 'but do please, Brer
Fox, don't fling me in dat brier-patch ..."

The laughter coming from the sitcom next door is hysterical.

Over breakfast I tell Arlene, "I stopped off at London
Drugs. I bought some Intensive Care."

She asks, "Have you made up your mind yet? I'd like to
know." When am I leaving, she means.

"This evening."

"You're leaving tonight?"

"Tonight I'll give you an answer."

"You sound like a blushing maiden," she says. "All I want is
you to choose."

This has become a game for her, watching me squirm. She
is calm, unfluttered, prescient. Who am I to go anywhere, she
thinks, without having to agonize. She thinks she knows me
better than I do. She does. She dresses according to her own
knowledge, casually, at home in a Madras shirt with an Eaton's
label.

That evening when I come home from the nursery I make
her sit down to await my last show. "Please?" I pop my contacts, rub my eyes in rapture and put on my glasses. I make her
supper. The dog and cat get shooed outside.

Eating, I discover that Jules has cut my introductory ramble and made his own beginning, splicing in vegetables and
flowers in search of the continuity that our presentation on
location lacked.

The phone's ringing adds to this chopped-up feeling. When
I answer no one says hello, and I wonder uneasily what man
might be phoning Arlene.

With the show almost over I'm there suddenly in this dream garden, mouth moving, delivering the spiel that I thought was my beginning. I definitely look shrunken.

"And so we come to the end of the season, friends, though nothing in a garden really changes, seeds blazoned from the start, codes given … nothing really changes.

"'What d'you mean,' I hear you regular viewers saying, 'nothing changes? Look at the flowers, fool, look at the vegetables. You blind? Remember March?'

"March, yes. Come fall I look around me here in *The City Garden* and take stock. I breathe in, breathe out. I say to myself, 'Smell the flowers, the vegetables, the trees!' Couples in other cities, other gardens are saying the same thing, 'Smell the flowers! Smell the vegetables! Smell the trees!' These smells never change. These couples go on though their cities decay.

"Yes. The pleasures of the city garden keep returning, keep tempting us back come March, keep us saying to our wives,

If thou so desirest Jove's renewal,
Turn, return! be mine—mine more than ever …

When the credits are running up the screen, Arlene says quietly, "What a way to end a season." Her face is even wet with tears. "Spreading homesickness like manure from here to kingdom come …"

"It was supposed to be an opening," I answer.

Then I say, "I want to be allowed to stay. I think I want us to go on as before."

"Before what?"

Exactly. She and I have always made a triangle.

She acts restless, as if yearning for the cat to stroke, keys to press, a remark to be delivered of. Perhaps a place to be.

"What about Kendra?" she asks at last.

"I let her go."

"Did you? Truly?"

We continue our parts as we always have. She sighs.

She softens like a girl coming down on a bicycle saddle, the air filling her dress like a sail. I can smell the leather, the saddlebags, the chain oil.

The sea.

When she leaves it is to bring in the animals. I am left wagging, of course, wondering.

A wind has come up. You can hear it lifting the house. She returns in her silver slippers, like the Wicked Witch of the East, carrying our Persian cat.

I don't believe you can change, she says to me. *But I expect you to. You will never see Kendra again. I want you to learn this. You will do exactly as I tell you. Place your fingers like so... Now kiss me.*

I do. I remove her plaid shirt and lick her scratched back. Ours is a herbaceous life, dying down in perennial hope of flowering anew. It is as if Kendra never existed. Arlene is playing the part she knows, discarding her grief, renewing our love.

"That's right," she tells me. "Yes..."

And I recall the seed of a demonstrable old truth: that the sum of a triangle's interior angles is in fact a straight line. Just as the last picture in a hospital of your heart on a screen is too.

Is too.

THERE ARE MORE
DARK WOMEN
IN THE WORLD
THAN LIGHT

THAT SPRING he began calling on her often enough to leave his lock and chain wrapped around the Japanese cherry tree by her building. He saw no point in carrying the chain home every night. He would pedal home and park behind his Toyota Celica in the locked underground garage. Then in June she went away on holidays to visit relatives in Utrecht. She didn't *want* to go—she said leaving the West Coast in June was like eating curry for Christmas. "You know, Sad City." When she returned he pumped over and discovered his lock and chain had disappeared.

"Well, Dimwit, you'll have to park in the lobby from now on." She said the interesting thing about the Netherlands was how *many* people rode bicycles. "With wicker baskets, full of cheese wheels and glads." In Amsterdam she saw Anne Frank's house again, the redlight district, and far too many twenty-course Indonesian *reistafels*. He could see she had put on weight. She bemoaned her trip because of what had happened to her forehand since going away. And over coffee she made him open his present. "It's not anything great," she told him. A lavender candle, he discovered, shaped like a phallus. "They're for sale all over the Rembrandtsplein," she explained. He lit it, with a smile, and before it burned halfway down they'd made a homecoming of love. The candle cast a guttering, mellow light at dusk. Except its smoke got in their eyes, and she licked her thumb and forefinger to snuff the flame. The lustre slid from her eyes and her hair came down in ringlets. If only she didn't have to go back to work until at least her tennis improved, she murmured. She disliked the trust company and was thinking of going over to a real bank. "You know, an old-fashioned one with marble columns and chandeliers?" She wondered how many of those institutions were left.

He took his own holidays in August, though he would have preferred October, and went fishing in Ontario. The acid rain in the lake had killed all the fish. He was surprised and told his brother they should think of selling the family cottage. His brother, who had black spots in his nails from banging up wallboard, said no one wanted to buy into a dead lake. He should have warned him to stay in Toronto. Anyway, it was still an okay lake for waterskiing and reading books, but if he wanted trout fishing to try Algonquin Park. Instead he flew to San Francisco. Casting around in bars for a little action, he got off a few good lines with a young woman in pearls, who told him she was engaged to a financier in Connecticut. "Wants to retire by the time he's forty," she said. "People in finance burn out fast." She glanced around. "I don't really know why I come here, I know all this crowd." From her office, she meant, but standing there with a Heineken in hand she wasn't talking to anyone he'd noticed. They shared a few laughs, she liked Sissy Spacek and he didn't, and then she left, taking along her dry cleaning in cellophane from the coat rack. The bar was crowded and loud. A young Vietnamese with nobody to talk to said hi. He was in marine insurance, finishing a college degree at night in business administration, about which he wasn't sanguine. "People tell me to count on future," he said. "Now is first time in history population of San Francisco is not mainly Caucasian." He dropped his articles and drank

Pernod, looking uneasy among these lawyers and brokers. The bar was on Union Street.

In October he bought another lock and chain to bind his ten-speed Norco to the cherry tree. As before, he left the chain behind in the grass when he rode home at night. He really only used the bike to ride to her place, or occasionally around the park. But driving home from work one afternoon he noticed someone had stolen his bike from the garage. Luckily it was December then and raining every day, so what he didn't much ride he never really missed. In fact he rarely thought of cycling till the warm March sun returned, and he felt his legs could have done with a good pump. The police never phoned him back.

By this time he had known her a year and a half. She was still with the trust company and wondering now if they shouldn't take their holidays together. Trouble was, she had August, and he October. He told her if she had come up with her bright idea last January they might have coordinated their plans. "You sound just as happy I didn't," she said. Anyhow, it didn't matter that much because she was thinking of going to this tennis ranch in Scottsdale with John Newcombe. "Jealous?"

He walked back to his own apartment, sometimes as late as midnight in the middle of the week. One night he remembered to look for his chain in the uncut grass under the flowering cherry. But as he squatted to unfasten the lock he couldn't remember the combination. He had one of those blank moments when he knew if he waited for it, the name, or in this case a set of numbers, would come back. Presto. But his thighs ached and he abandoned it.

Every time he visited her after that he tried to remember his combination in the grass. Trying to remember was a game and he refused to look up the card he had with the numbers written down. It annoyed him he couldn't recall three numbers memorized six months earlier. His business was to remember numbers the way a squash player remembers angles. "Hey,

Ben, can we live with these numbers?" Figures in his world were numbers—just as chairmen were chairpersons. (The salespeople at meetings who were women insisted on the title.) At lunch he would sometimes grow absent, not hear his gesturing companion, and listen instead like a safecracker for the tiny sounds of tumbling digits. Once over Sanka he thought he smelled freshly cut grass, and dog urine. He sniffed his cup. By May the cherry blossoms had all gone.

On a Sunday morning that month he phoned to ask if she wanted to try for a court. "I've got on an apron and pancakes," she said. "Thought you were coming over." He'd forgotten. "If you'd rather play tennis," she told him, "go ahead." He thought it sounded like a test, so he apologized and walked over in his Adidas and whites and had pancakes. He enjoyed them more than he expected to, and spilled syrup on his shorts.

When she was running hot water over the stain he removed the rest of his clothes and waited for her in bed. Listening to her toothbrush he got up and drew the curtains closed on their cedar rings. As soon as she came into the room smelling of Dial and Ultrabrite he gathered her long, thick hair in his hand and bit the back of her neck. "That's how the Japanese do it," he growled. "Bullshit," she said. "They do it like this." He laughed. They both made big bellies and denounced pancakes as disgusting and probably immoral. "Think of the squatters starving in Calcutta," he told her. She sighed. "Mother Teresa isn't getting *me*," she said. "Besides, she only takes movie stars and pop singers." Standing there on a little rug from Jakarta they rubbed their stomachs together like inflated beach balls. He looked down her back and admired the long dark leg, bent at the knee, poised on its toes. "You exotic cunts are all alike," he said. "You'll go down on your back for a pancake."

Afterwards, lying there, they drifted off. The Dutch clock in the kitchen went cuckoo eleven times. Helpless with laughter she turned to him with love in her eyes. "I ought to tell you," she said.

She said the only time she'd ever gone out with a guy she didn't know was last night on a stupid date her friend Katie at work had set up. She gave this guy her number, and when he phoned he asked did she remember him from last August? "I didn't remember him at all. It was a really stupid date." He picked her up in his brother's Rambler, she said, with these spotty seatcovers that felt Mexican to sit on. All he could talk about was when he was going to get a Mazda and how great she looked, but he kept saying it in the stupidest way, like she was a Liberty scarf or a packet of spangled pantyhose. Besides, he didn't even know her. They went to Le Soleil Couchant, which was stupid because he said he couldn't afford the appetizers. She didn't care if she had an appetizer or not, but why go to a restaurant you can't afford in the first place? The view maybe. Or maybe he was razzing her. "I ended up ordering stuffed sole and I *hate* fish. He kept asking me the stupidest questions." Like what was her favourite food? Or were the colour of the sheets on her bed mauve like her blouse? And how come she wore her hair behind her ears, or did it just go that way? "This guy is supposedly a university graduate in forestry. He turned me right off." They ended up at a Whitecaps' game under the dome and sat in seats a mile up in Section 32, which was stupid because you couldn't see the game and he wouldn't move to better seats that were empty.

"God, he was a joke! His conversation consisted of what he was having, like, for lunch at the plywood plant where he's supposedly learning management." She snorted with laughter at the recollection, and the bed shook gently. "Fruitcake! It was insane. The only interesting thing he said all night was he knew Doug's sister, or Doug's cousin, or Doug's *something*— of Doug and the Slugs. And she wants to start a band called Movement. On the way home I could hardly listen to him. He asked me did I want to go someplace for coffee and dessert? No. Could he kiss me good night? No. Could he maybe see me again because, well, he was really intrigued by somebody different? No. It was stupid, really stupid."

She took his hand and placed it fondly on her stomach. "This morning I decided that's the last time I go out with anybody who isn't a friend of mine already."

Then she said, "A trust company's funny for friends like Katie. I mean I really like Katie, but our tastes are just different. She's younger I guess." She thought awhile. "I'm tired of withdrawals and standing up all day." She lay back and stared at the old schooner reproduced a hundred times in the wallpaper. "The men get careers. The girls just disappear. At a trust company you either quit or get shoved off to another branch. I'd like to get into mortgages."

He listened to what she told him. "I'm glad you're seeing other men," he said. "But this guy sounds like a liability."

She laughed. "Isn't that what you wanted?"

"What."

"I feel guilty, though. That's why I lied about breakfast. I wanted to make it up to you."

He said, "I thought my memory was going." And told her about forgetting his combination around her tree outside.

She found this touching, the lock with no Norco to mind, and they slept until the cuckoo roused them at noon. They woke up smiling. He looked into her dark eyes. "You exotic cunts," he said. He made her breast large by lifting it like a custard.

"Is this," she asked, "what losing your memory does for an appetite?" Later, on their way out to a court in the park, she bent down in her white tennis dress and played in the grass with his numbers. She was twenty-three.

He remembered her birthday in June when she turned twenty-four. He bought her roses, dinner and a modest remembrance. "I've never *kept* a diary," she said.

"Keep it in your vault," he warned her. In July when he turned thirty-two she hired a chauffeured limousine and stopped by his office tower to pick him up. Last year she hadn't done anything, she said, on account of her being in Europe. "Besides, I didn't know you as well."

He told her it was pricy on her salary to be treating him to this. She took him to the Four Seasons for broiled sockeye under Béarnaise sauce (she had Veal Oscar) and afterwards told the chauffeur to drive them up the mountain. They parked at an angle on Hollyburn and looked down at the lit-up freighters and city. She handed the driver, who even wore a chauffeur's cap, a bunch of dinner mints. They all gazed down and listened to old rock'n'roll songs on speakers hidden inside the grey-flannel roof. She had requested this particular tape because she thought he'd remember the songs. "Hey," he laughed. "I'm not your father." He sank back into the upholstery smoking her Schimmelpenninck cigars. "This evening must have cost you a month's salary," he said. "About," she shrugged. "Anyway, I'm not going anywhere this year. I told John Newcombe to buzz off." There was a chance she might get out of selling soon, into a desk job. She looked down over the sparkling world, up into the firmament. A group called the Platters was singing *My need is such, I pretend too much, I'm lonely but no one can tell. . .* "I really like these old songs," she said. On their way back down to the bridge she asked the chauffeur to park at Ambleside, where they walked barefoot in the black sand. The Beatles crooned through the rolled-down windows of yesterday, and the driver's cigar glowed like a paper lantern.

In August she took local tennis lessons to get rid of the loop in her serve and to improve her footwork. After dinner they often met in the park to play a set before dusk. She was a gifted athlete and beat him more often than he liked. Later on they walked to Ping Pong's on Altamira and had Italian ice cream in small aluminum dishes. She said that after tennis with him, and the hour-and-a-half lesson before that, she could eat a whole tureen of Malaga. But she kept a paring knife handy to remind her of the destiny of fat girls. Meryl Streep had a peach-and-cabbage diet she admired.

In October he dropped into Canada Trust to buy American Express travellers' cheques, waved at her behind a till and went away on his holidays to Hawaii. Not, however, before catching sight of a thin boy up the street with a ten-speed Norco. "This is mine," he said, grabbing the saddle. The thin boy and his friends turned to him with avid curiosity. He had jaywalked through four lanes of rush-hour traffic to nab the thief, who had his knee hooked over the crossbar.

The next day he flew to Honolulu in need of rest and recuperation. The Norco was not his at all. The pedals had toe straps and the saddle under his hand felt bony, it was so narrow. He apologized to the boy, who just smirked. His friends, sea cadets, laughed abusively.

That evening, packing his suitcase, he phoned her and let the phone whir nine, ten times before hanging up. He wondered if he had the right number, for the exchange he reached sounded custodial and distant.

It was a pleasure to think it was raining at home. He sunbathed on Waikiki, toured a few clubs, bought himself white loafers and then flew to Maui for the last week of his holidays. In Lahina, where he stayed at the Pioneer Inn, he struck it lucky with the piano player downstairs, a green-eyed doctor on leave from Los Angeles playing her way through the islands. She was living on a thirty-foot Yamaha with her poet husband. Meeting her was lucky because of the girl she introduced him to, her husband's flaxen-haired sister, who served beer in the same pub. Together they all went sailing one day to Molakai, the old leper island across the strait. They were into the sauce. The blond poet sucked unlit Lucky Strikes and pointed out where the whale pods arrived in January, asking Ben if he knew *Typee*. He hadn't heard of it. Just off a coral reef on Molakai they dropped their sails and the rest of their clothing. He and the poet cooked frankfurters over propane in the galley, rubbed Coppertone into the girls' backs and gave them the whole day off. The doctor asked herself why she was playing the piano in a bar every night when they still had savings. She laughed. Her sister-in-law, tanned dark from spending every afternoon in the sun, and before this two years in Africa, said, "I hope we can hang around these islands forever." She'd just finished teaching with the Peace Corps in Nigeria, where her eyes had been opened. He gazed a little drunkenly into her blue irises. She sliced pieces of watermelon and he admired her pale gardenia breasts. "Over there," she concluded, "we're definitely in a minority."

The three strangers mentioned books they were reading, and he felt left out. The doctor's breasts perked up like baby owls. The poet put his head in her lap and bit into the flesh of his watermelon rind. He gave Ben a volume of his verse to look through, neatly cut stanzas of long lines and no punctuation, each poem addressed to a different girl whose name always began with I. Iris, Ivy, Ianthe, Isadora, Irene. . . "All Greek," said the poet. "All tried and true." He put aside his rind and spoke earnestly to his new friend. "Every woman has a year in her life," he said, "month, week, even—dare I whisper it—a day, when she reaches a summit of perfection, a rare point in time like a peak in the Sierras, when she's neither child nor adult in any strict sense, and from which her body will begin to slide imperceptibly away. This is a sexist observation, Benjamin, certainly not a balanced one, because in toto a woman is a whole mountain range." He smiled appreciatively at his dozing wife. And later on, dopey with sun, he turned to his sister and murmured, "What you noticed in Africa, Hel, was there're lots more dark women in the world than light." To go swimming—in water as inviting as Helen's eyes—they hung an aluminum ladder off the stern and snorkelled down to coral.

Returning to Vancouver, he learned she was planning to move at the end of November. Because of the recession more

249

vacancies existed now than when she'd taken her present apartment. The new place, she told him, had a small view of the bay and she was surprised to be taking a step *up* in the world, since her real reason for moving was the cheaper rent. She was also checking out a sales job at a downtown radio station. They were looking, she'd heard, for better balance in their staff, and she guessed a woman who was ethnic might have a fair chance of success. She rented a U-Haul and he helped her park it. Her heaviest things were a sofa and the bricks she used to make a board planter. He took apart her bed and found the futon lighter to tote than the kitchen clock.

In one of the last boxes to be loaded into the elevator, lying among herb jars and a rolling pin, was the diary he'd given her. Riding down alone he opened it to see if she ever used it. Most pages that year were blank. There were a few entries like *Went swimming today at Aquatic Centre with Katie, promised myself exercise classes.* And *Met Ben downtown to see* Stardust Memories, *with supper afterwards at Las Tapas. Home for a juicy something, but it wasn't a screw, both bushed. He went home.* The longest entry read *Sometimes I feel like a mistake. Loneliness is a bad city inside you. I don't understand how so much can be going on with so many people doing it and I have nothing to do with anything except gloom. Bought a blouse at the Bay.*

That night, to ease the transition, she stayed over at his place. She'd forgotten how big his apartment was and what a view of the park he had, even in the rain. She loved his plants, his white rattan furniture, his full refrigerator. She remembered the Markgraf prints and the decanter of sherry. They drank some sherry. "Everything's so magic here," she said. "I envy your touch." He smiled like a pirate, his dark hair shorter than Richard Gere's by a businessman's inch.

Later she woke up beside him in bed and asked what he was reading. "Melville," he said. "The Greenpeace granddaddy who wrote *Moby-Dick.*" Outside on the balcony the cold rain was puddling, but inside by the bleached glow of his chrome lamp it was warm.

"I love the South Seas," she said, snuggling closer to the light.

At a meeting that year before Christmas he tried to remember the phone number of her old apartment. He wrote down different combinations of the last four digits, and none looked right. He remembered the prefix all right, since it was the same as his own. That evening he phoned her new number and she seemed surprised to hear from him. He told her he'd been away on trips to Toronto and Montreal trying to make his boss some money. Tomorrow he was going to Calgary to see if he could make some more. And her? "Okay, I guess. Still at the trust company." An aunt of hers from Rotterdam was coming for Christmas, and tonight she was picking her up at the airport, in a new old car she'd bought from a friend at work. "Do you know anything about Crickets?" she asked. "Don't tell me if you do." She wondered when they would see each other again. "Over New Year's," he promised. "When I get my act together." She told him she had recently had her legs waxed. "Let me tell you," she said.

He ran into her in March at the tennis courts. He was driving home and saw her playing, striding into the ball with litheness and grace. Her brown limbs shone under her white tennis dress, and her brief blue anklets flew over the green sunny asphalt. She saw him at the fence and waved. Azalea and magnolia blossoms filled the air. When it was her turn to serve she corralled the lime Dunlops at her feet and spoke through the wire. "Katie," she said, "is now better than I am. She took lessons in Colorado." He told her she looked pretty good herself. She smiled shyly. "This year I'm definitely going to Arizona in October." Hooking her finger in the mesh, she asked him how he was. He said he figured the recession had finally bottomed out and things were on their way back up.

"You forget my number or what?" she said.

He didn't pretend he had forgotten it, and rattled it off. She laughed. "That's my old number," she said.

"Is it?" He seemed pleased.

She looked relieved. He took down her new number again and said he would call.

A week later, driving by her old building, he stopped along the no-parking curb and switched on his emergency flasher. The Japanese cherry was in full flower. He had thought of it again at a performance of *Madama Butterfly* the other night with a lawyer he'd met in January at a party. He got out of his car and crossed over to the grass. He knelt down in the fallen blossoms and picked up his lock and chain. But the face was encrusted with rust so thick he couldn't dial the numbers in either direction, not even a hair.

FOREIGN AFFAIRS

E'S NEVER WRONG about suffering, this ex-diplomat.
He understands its spasms in his muscles and clonus in
his knees. How it can take place, as somebody said, while
you're eating or looking out a window or just dully rolling
along. Every year he has had at least one good attack, lately
two, when he's flat out in bed for months. Fatigue, tremors, dizziness . . . forgetfulness, jigsaw-puzzle vision, a tangled tongue.
He has long since lost his intimacy, or so Silas remembers
hearing was his wide-open way, with the far side of earth. Still,
he's plotting once more. Not to rebuild his ruined career, nor
have some say in the world, but to pack the saddlebag on this
chair he's in and get outside. Eat his lunch rolling along a sea
side promenade, smell the salt, feel voluptuous again. Any
spontaneous remission of his disease (he paws himself for
signs) takes longer and longer every year to recur. Already
June and he hasn't been outside in five months. Whimpering
for it now, his zest come back, he even dreams himself inside a
woman's body, where he hasn't been in years.

    whim   purrrrr   ing   g
    "You okay?" she asks.

As Nadine administers to his improving torso, he recalls the P & O ships that don't call this far north anymore, and haven't for years. San Francisco's their limit now.

He says to her, "The da   ay I sailed back from ab   road I could see men on the docks baiting their hoo   ks with shrimp. Pulling in shiners as fast as they threw in their li   ines." Speaking better and more coherently than he has in months, he can afford to reminisce. "W   ho ate these fish, I wondered, the Chin   ese? Were they carted over to Chinatown and peddled up alleys to Chinese re   estaurants, where you used to get a ga   ame of mah-jongg with the cook, if you happened to be Chinese, whi   ich these fellows weren't? Must have been a dozen men, fishing. The market behi   ind was where I once got an apple for a d   ime. Chinese women all over pic   king up broccoli and buying sprouts. For what part   icular holiday I had no ide   a."

"Like it when I do this?" asks the frizzy-haired girl.

He looks down at his chest to see what she means. "I don't fe   el a thing."

"You serious?"

"They whee   led me down the gangplank in a cha   air like this one. Only the tires were f   lat."

"How 'bout this, you feel that?"

"Look," he says. Wheeling around, shirt undone, heading for the sideboard in the hall: he brakes, draws open a drawer and removes a pair of Polaroid sunglasses. Breathes deeply on the lenses, wiping each in turn on his shirt-tail. Puts them on, shuts the drawer, rolls himself back over the cork tiles, his head hooked at a queer angle and jerking uncontrollably.

This predator, he makes fun of himself,   *"hee   hee well   Miss   Riding Ho   od   how do   I hee   hee   look?"*

"Like a spaced-out jerk, gimme a break."

He quits jerking and reaches for a Rolaid.

"*You are a veddy veddy young woman,*" he tells her imperiously, as Nehru might have spoken, the fluent mimicry unlike his own cracked speech. "*When a man has his nipples massaged like jujubes, he feels he must take on the world through green-coloured glasses. He* is *the world!*"

"You're sick, Silas. Bloody hell."

"I'm in remi   ission. Listen to me, *I   co   here.* My holidays are here! I'm understa   andable! If you care for me, you'll whee   l   me into the world. I want to take *i   in* the world. I can smell the salt!"

"Sun's too hot. Nell wouldn't let me. You'd melt to death."

So says his slender friend of twenty who appears to him to have the disease dieters get from not eating. He sometimes catches her, quiet as her reflection, studying herself in the mirror. Silas refrains from any more spastic gestures, to take her hands warmly in his hands.

"You du   umb twat," he says. He says warmly, "I've been nego   tiating with dear Nell for con   cessions..."

The sound of his nurse's key in the apartment latch causes Nadine to tuck in his shirt-tails.

When old Nell appears, the girl is saying sternly to her friend in the chair (putting on Nell for Silas's entertainment): "*This is the last time I come here, Si, if all you want is to keep telling me Nell's after you to diddle her in the sack. I think it's really unloyal of you to tell tales out of school and if I was your nurse,* hi Nell, *I'd give you a good talking to.*" She says to Nell, "He's now got it in his head, like, to take his holidays at the beach. I can't think of anything stupider, can you"?" To Silas, "I'm taking off, Si. Clay's expecting supper. I'll call you."

Nell stands in her street shoes with plastic Super Valu bags in her hands. She dislikes this floozy on sight, has ever since

Nadine turned seventeen, when Nell baked her a cake and the girl gave Silas a facial with the icing. Wouldn't eat a bite. Just plastered it on him like shaving cream. Since then, as far as Nell can tell, she's got worse. Dyed her hair punk red as if to excuse her state. What in Jesus's name is she ever talking about? Mouth on her like a rathole.

This year summer has come along like a hot towel after a close shave. The close shave came in January, when Silas was on his back in bed and felt he'd never again climb out of the depths. Didn't want to climb out of them. Last winter's exhaustion was the most penetrating, disheartening, enervating of all his "exacerbations" in twenty years. Even Nell was worried. She looked for him down the well like she might for a bucket come off its rope. Her words, echoing, drifted down to him submerged in darkness. He could not raise his fingers. She brought Krish into the bedroom to lick his face. But what dog has a taste for sick skin?

> *ding*
>   *dong*
>   *bell*
> *pussy*   *'s*   *in*   *the*

Krish went over his face like a washcloth, however. Cooler in the depths, Silas kept dreaming of New Delhi and would not be fished up from despair. He could hear foghorns.

Twenty-three years ago, aged twenty-seven, he'd been coming of age in the fluent way expected of men who aspired to success in the Department of External Affairs, when his body cut loose from compliance with his brain. The Canadian High Commission in Delhi was his second posting. As a second secretary for immigration, he spent half his time behind a desk interviewing Indians who wished to go to Canada and part of the rest at receptions given (it always seemed) by East European consulates in honour of touring string quartets and rival uranium salesmen; salesmen feeling out India's direction in the world. At these receptions everybody appeared to be lifting beaded glasses of vodka and iced tea and looking to Canada, through air full of imported cigarette smoke, for the confidence a Nobel Peace Prize had given to its leaders. Silas handled his duties, obligations and invitations with an energy his relaxed manner belied. He never felt relaxed, exactly. Even though one of the senior counsellors responsible for development told Silas that he possessed the "attribute of effortlessness" that any young man with ambassadorial aspirations required, but few acquired. "*Can't* acquire it," this diplomat seemed tired of reminding him. This man would have been happy to spend his own final years in Ottawa. Silas, nimble in his observations, correct in his reports and interviews, was spoken of by colleagues as a young man on his way up in the world, expected to move effortlessly from country to country until he became in young middle age ("It didn't surprise me at all, his promotion") ambassador to one of them. He was admired and even envied. Brilliant, sort of, and charming.

Dressed informally in white Indian pyjamas, at home with friends in his bungalow garden, he would try to relax by mimicking the mincing precisions, the pompous meanderings of corrupt Indians when they spoke. Here with exaggerated gesture was the kind of release he required from the usual watchfulness his position stipulated.

Well, he might say over drinks Sunday afternoon, his servant having returned to the kitchen, . . . *I was coming down this veddy veddy crooked road, when an elephant, he must have been standing thirty hands high anyway, twice the height of the biggest polo pony, you know, was suddenly blocking my way, just like that out of nowhere, in the middle of the road, where* my driver had stopped to toot his horn. "What is it doing?" I asked. "Where is its mahout?" My driver tooted, the elephant started slapping the windscreen of my car with its proboscis, looking, I suppose, for something to eat, some peanuts or sweetmeats. "Baksheesh," claimed my terrified driver, "he is wanting some baksheesh!" "An elephant?" I replied. "Well give him some, get rid of him!" "Master," said my driver, "this elephant is hungry. We have no baksheesh." I grew angry. "What about these jujubes? Give him a jujube!" My veddy frightened driver took my bag of candies, opened his window and threw a jujube into the dust of this veddy veddy crooked road. "What are you doing!" I screamed. "How do you expect a beast with bad eyesight to be finding your jujube in the dust? Give me the bag." I got out of my car and confronted the elephant by proffering it a jujube. "Here, you. Take it," I said, "and stand aside so my driver may proceed down this veddy veddy crooked road ..." Well, I am obliged to be telling you, my friends, that I was no success whatsoever with this enormous beast. His hairy proboscis sniffed the jujube, sniffed my hair oil, sucked the jujube up one nostril and ... here is the really disgusting part ... sneezed. I have no idea where that jujube is today. It went whistling by my ear like a bullet. I shouldn't have minded so much risking my life, yes, if it wasn't for these villagers standing idly beside the road, giggling and clapping. Yes! "Is this beast yours?" I shouted. "If it is, see that he is removed at once from this crooked road, so my car may be passing by. Do you hear?" But they wouldn't hear. Wouldn't. The elephant began poking my pockets, the villagers swarmed round to look-see, look-see, my driver cowered. "Why don't you feed your beast?" I shouted at the villagers. "It's fleecing me! I have no food for it! I have a luncheon appointment!" I threw the rest of the jujubes in the elephant's face, got back in my car and told the driver to go ahead. "Drive right through the beast," I told him. "... So he'll never forget us. Push him backwards, bump his knees, toot your horn. There is nothing here, nothing. How are you expecting to get to the end of this *veddy veddy crooked road unless you use a little bumping and pushing. . .?"*

At this stage of his story, Silas might pause for a long sip of lime juice and gaze at the crows squawking for attention in the surrounding flame trees. A crow might shit. His guests might urge him to go on: if only to enjoy his making a fool of himself when his powers of invention evaporated, as they surely would in this heat. A third secretary at the embassy, from Wolfville, Nova Scotia, who admired Silas, would nevertheless tease him, "Go *on*, Silas. Amuse us."

The strange thing to Silas was how little his own mimicry relaxed him after all. He wondered why his eyesight had suddenly gone fuzzy and he couldn't see the crows. He felt askew. His friends missed whatever point he thought he was making (at least they never applauded his allegory), chuckling instead over the sleek tones of the accent they all resented in corrupt and self-important officials, who were nobbling their own country.

But not seeing the crows was really the second clue of Silas's decline, before he ever recognized that his lapses from fluency were in fact symptoms of disease.

The day he first suspected something might be wrong he'd peed on his shoe. A) He thought he was peeing into the bowl. B) He felt nothing as the very yellow stream splashed off his shoe. His foot, he later realized, was numb. This happened in the embassy washroom. He had occasionally before splashed floors, even his shoes, but never for a whole pee. Zipping up, he found the floor a pond. He didn't think till afterwards he hadn't even *seen* he was missing the bowl.

This, then, was the first clue that in his diplomatic world of graceful posture he might not be able to count on himself illimitably for posture. For that matter, grace. He felt disoriented.

The extreme heat that year sapped his vigour, prickled his limbs and left him stranded on reefs of fatigue. So far inland from the sea, such stranding seemed ridiculous, yet he slept surrounded by an ocean and could barely drag himself off to the embassy each morning, trudging through seawater up to his chest. His legs wouldn't bear their responsibilities. He could have put this down to the terrible heat, if it wasn't for his senses. These couldn't be counted on, either: he had periods when he smelled and tasted nothing. Little gaps sprouted between his touching a table, or a mango, and his actually feeling what his fingers were up to. And he was often interrupted by a faint ringing of a telephone, as if from the cellar, when he was stuck in the attic. Some house. Controlling his emotions, like his bladder, became a problem. Sudden bouts of compassion, for whom he was never sure, caused tears behind his nose to itch and sometimes fall. Sentimentality, shame. His brain, responsible for the short-circuiting of his body, crackled with little puffs of smoke that left his vision clouded.

He was especially stupid to travel, he later learned, in the hot season. Two weeks after his errant piss he was aboard the morning express to Agra, for three days of sightseeing in the Golden Triangle. A year earlier he'd travelled to Agra in an embassy car by way of introduction to the countryside where most of the country's population came from, including his driver. This time on the train his eyesight really let him down. The white light of the floor at his feet he thought a transposition of the rising mist from beyond the train window. Mist was rising off the fields like night smoke being sucked up by the sun from lava fields. Swirling through this smoke were faint smudges of lollipop trees. Silas thought the train was blowing up dust, if it wasn't fog, grain dust or the residue of a dynamite explosion. It seemed very beautiful, until he looked at his feet and couldn't see them for the white light.

But his sight came back.

In all its resplendence he again took in the Taj. Then, after a taxi ride to the Mogul ghost city of Fatehpur Sikri, he fell down like a lump in the middle of the Jami Masjid. His leg just buckled. With a temperature on the surface of the bricks of 120°F, it was enough to buckle an elephant. He got up and said to himself he was fine. A small boy handed him his guidebook. He told the boy he was fine. Next morning, listening to a tubby little guide on the other side of the Red Fort's urine-smelling moat, Silas had a vision. Two visions. He saw everything in the world twice. Two guides, eight minarets, four hands, two watches on his own wrist like some black marketeer's. Silas saw the world as if he'd forgotten to wind the exposed film in his brain. "Here they be playing hide and seek," the guide was saying, referring to the king and his harem splashing through the now-empty tank and dry fountains. "Here they be playing hide and seek, in eyeshot of the Taj. There."

Back in Delhi the young diplomat described his symptoms to an Iranian doctor, a refugee from the shah. "Sun," declared the doctor. "Too much sun. Take a week off, rest well in bed. Try that."

No more symptoms for seven months. No more awkward or involuntary movements, visions, tears. Grace and posture returned, as did his strength, and he began to learn Hindi. It had all been a bad case of sunstroke. So Silas travelled to Ceylon. After that, in December when it wasn't hot at all—cold, in fact, it was quite cold—his body went haywire. Messages received by his body weren't messages dispatched by his brain. Bladder conked out, balance went wonky, both legs caved in; his eyeballs began to flutter, his eyesight blotted. When he tried to talk it sometimes sounded like he was mimicking static on the shortwave from London. For a while his friends at the embassy felt mimicry had seized control of his ambition, unless (as he once overheard them say among themselves) he had had a sudden desire to become a stand-up clown, the fourth stooge. For his symptoms didn't show up all at once, rather one or two at a time, usually at some official function in front of local politicians whom his colleagues might reasonably have supposed him to be caricaturing.

Naturally, they thought he was drinking too much, which he wasn't.

Silas knew he was in trouble. This world, on the other side of the one he'd grown up in, was impoverishing his body. And the floor of his compassion dropped out: no matter how much he wept it wasn't enough to flush out his system and make it healthy again. It wasn't poor people he was weeping for, it was himself. He wallowed in self-pity. The Iranian doctor told him to go to bed indefinitely. Instead, weeping Silas consulted other physicians. But physicians in India were untrained to look for a disease that didn't occur in people of southern, tropical countries. *His* disease, he later found out, was a northern disease. From a numb torso his arms hung full of tingling. He handled cufflinks, zippers, buttons and shoelaces by a kind of trial and error he wouldn't have thought credible a year earlier. Where was he and what was he doing here? His body temperature fluctuated widely: some days he felt like climbing into the embassy's soft-drink cooler had he the energy to climb into anything. Nobody would have believed the exhaustion he felt. At times, he just lay down on the floor and wept.

A young doctor, just home from internship in France, finally diagnosed his disease at a cocktail party in the French embassy. Although it contained only lime juice, Silas was having trouble holding his glass steady. This man studied the way Silas moved (with much jerkiness) and asked him, when he got an opportunity, a couple of discreet questions. Silas responded carefully. The doctor asked to see him privately, in a day or two, and hinted there could be some neurological disorder. He sounded very ambitious.

"You me   ean," said Silas at a loss, "   I have a bra   ain with veddy veddy crook   ed connections?"

He didn't care if the doctor thought he was mocking him. He made himself *speak.*

Dr. Parecattil rubbed his palm over a gold wristwatch, cradling the glass. That was one way of putting it, he replied. And confidentially told him about myelin. "Myelin's a sheath of fatty tissue which insulates the brain and nervous system. It is like getting the wrong number," he explained thoughtfully, "when the insulation frays and the wires of your nervous system are crossed." He rubbed his round stomach.

Silas asked him diplomatically how he could get fixed up.

"I'm not saying I've got the answer," replied the other young man, smiling hopefully, "or even the right diagnosis. May I come and see you soon?"

"Sup   posey   oudohave   the ans   ?"

"If I do," said the Indian doctor looking right into Silas's eyes, "there is no cure."

Next day, visiting Silas's office, he explained that in Switzerland, where he had also lived, the place had one of the highest rates of this disease in the world. There and Saskatchewan and the Orkney Islands.

"Saska   atchewan?" said Silas.

"Your beef-and-beer culture," replied the doctor. He went on to say the disease he thought Silas might have could be "exacerbated" (the first time Silas had heard this word used in connection with disease) by sunlight. How long had Silas been living in India? Two years?

And cautiously the young man mentioned he had been checking his medical books overnight.

Silas sniffed.

If he was right, Silas's disease had been diagnosed first by a Paris doctor in the nineteenth century. Did Silas really want to hear any of this? (Silas, who could not lift his arm that morning, did.) Well, when this Parisian in his research cut open the head of a cadaver that in life had suffered symptoms similar to Silas's—and here Dr. Parecattil mentioned tremors, paralysis, general jerkiness—he discovered scars on the brain tissue. "He named this disease," said the Indian in scrupulous French, "*sclérose en plagues*." Silas wanted to mimic the sound of the words, when he realized what MS really was—as the doctor now began to call his disease—that it was multiple sclerosis he might have, and young Silas noticed for the first time the jumping nerve on his own sunburned wrist.

He thanked the doctor, agreeing to another consultation.

What an undertow, he said tearfully to himself in bed, what a way to sink without a trace. What would happen to diplomacy now? Without such a diplomat on his way up, what would happen to it? One thing, said the sympathetic third secretary from Wolfville, Silas wouldn't have to watch his Ps and Qs any longer. Whatever that meant. Silas wondered if he ever had, really.

P   ees   Qua   P   ees

He then gave up trying to do anything requiring arms, legs or concentration. His life was finished. His colleagues came in regularly after that, to stand around his bed, until he was well enough to be shipped back to Canada.

———————

Putting away the groceries, Nell has nothing to say about Silas's notion to plan some outings. The box of Tide itches her nose and she stops to pinch her nostrils: Silas watches her from the living room. He fondles Krish's ears. Outside, Mr. Fogarty is weeding the geraniums and Silas waves at him spastically. (Spastically on purpose, for if he looks too healthy, or else not healthy enough, the caretaker might make him get rid of Krish. No pets, adults only.) The setter was Nell's idea, one of her "cures," and she had brought him home as a pup, explaining to the caretaker what a therapeutic effect on her patient this dependant would have. Just stroking the ears would make a big difference, she said, to how much Silas jerked his limbs; it'd calm him down. Stroking and caring for an animal reduced stress. ("What about a budgie?" asked Mr. Fogarty.) Thereafter, whenever Nell spotted an attack coming on, she would put Silas to bed with Krish alongside him on top of the covers. Silas always hoped his nurse might come to see Nadine as a similar therapy.

"What's he want?" Nell asks suspiciously.

"Fogarty? He's saying hello."

"I wish he'd vacuum the corridor."

She hates dust. Any sign of nonchalance. Outsiders, unaware of what she has learned over twenty-three years of caring for a victim of an incurable disease, seem indifferent to the fine balance of her patient. Silas outdoors, as far as Nell's concerned, is a man on his way back down the well. She cooks his meals, launders his clothes, gives him sponge baths and enemas when he's paralyzed, changes his bed, shops, pays the hydro and telephone, cuts his hair, helps him in and out of the tub, flosses his teeth when he can't (often), shaves his face when he asks her, feeds the dog. He pays her a salary and still owes her everything.

"He's good with flowers, Nell. You can say that for Fogarty. The man believes in gardens."

"The man doesn't know anything," she says. "How can he believe in anything?"

"That's true. That's very true." (Better butter her up.) "You're right."

In training for the holidays he envisions with Nadine, Silas has been building up his strength by clanking like a bucket in his leg braces around the apartment. He keeps a cane, two canes dangling from the hat rack. He never knows when his wheelchair may break down and he has to hobble home from the beach.

"The man doesn't know anything," repeats Nell.

Nothing about disease, she means—not in men, maybe in plants and the furnace. She'd claim hers is a worthy knowledge, knowing everything there is to know about a man's body, and enough about the world to know where to shop for a double-coupon sale. That's something. Shopping's more than Nadine knows of the world. That young girl takes her health for granted, the fool, and in her condition. Nell mistrusts health as she might a man in yellow shoes and a pinstriped suit chewing a toothpick. (Too devoted to the Victorian Order of Nurses, she has never married.) "No such thing as a healthy man," she once told Silas, when he thought he felt well enough to take an airplane trip to Los Angeles. She meant an honest man. Sick men will always lie about how they're feeling (better), because they've never been trained to know how bad disease really is. Silas went to Disneyland and detested it, said she was right after all and renounced cheap charter flights forever.

Silas asks, "Wh   at's for supper, Nell?"

"Casserole."

He won't risk antagonizing her by asking what kind.

As if daring him to object, she tells him anyway. "Tuna."

"Love   ly."

Tact and finesse.

She looks at him suspiciously.

He goes on, "Fish takes me ba   ack, Mother would never cook it. I could have d   one with more fish. She'd rather buy brain. Sometimes I think the ma   atter with me is I didn't eat enough fi   ish." He smiles. "Thank you for getting tuna."

"That's the first time I've heard you liked tuna."

"I was just telling Na   dine how much I've missed in life by ne   ever being a fish   erman..."

"Her."

She shuts the cupboard smartly on his sugar-free, diet jam. Silas continues to stroke Krish's silky ears and studies *Family Circle* on the coffee table.

"Nell," he says. "I'm scared."

"Scared?"

He can always count on her to rise to a crisis by her refusing to ever acknowledge the possibility of one. He keeps quiet, looking dolefully at the setter. She comes into the living room. "What're you scared of? There's nothing the matter with you."

A bumblebee hits the window, thump, thump, trying to get inside.

"You've been up and walking around even," she tells him. "Your appetite's good, you don't feel overtired, why are you scared?" She feels his brow. "You're not scared."

Silas is looking out the window, at the Allied moving van on Bartholomew, at the muscular legs of a Vietnamese high-school girl jogging by on her way into the park.

"I don't know why I'm sca   ared."

"You don't know, who does?"

"You think I'm healthy?"

"I think you're looking for sympathy. You're not on the edge of any relapse I can see. Yet."

"No?"

"Listen to yourself. I can understand you, not like last January. And your limbs are steady." She holds up her hand. "How many?"

"Fo   our."

"How about your bladder? Sore?"

"No." He doesn't mention that his teeth still hurt, or that the muscles in his thighs throb dully. And he nearly said five. Five fingers.

"Nothing to be scared of then," she tells him. "Is there?"

"But I am."

Over their years together she has learned the importance of letting him discover in his own words where it is he aches, how badly he needs to pee, what he wants to say in the letters she writes for him to old friends scattered around the world. Or what he has to say to the presidents, dictators and generals he writes to on behalf of Amnesty International: *Señor Presidente. . .* "Why can't you write the fellow in English?" she asks, copying out Silas's formula laboriously in ink: ... *He tornado conocimiento con consternación de que el señor X, joven poeta, sique en prisión* ...

"I'm sca   ared the world is passing me by."

Relieved, she snorts with laughter. "Welcome to the club, buster. Myself, years ago I passed fifty and the landscape went by in a blur." She heads back to the kitchen.

Quickly he says, "You think I'm in good sha   ape then? For fifty?"

"Why don't you try skateboarding or waterskiing?" She enjoys her own irony. "Swim across the gulf if you're so worried. Climb Grouse."

"Thank you."

"Thank me? What for?"

"Suggesting a holi   day."

She returns to the living room in a hurry. "I didn't suggest any holiday."

"Tell you wha   t I want to do," says Silas.

"Is this to do with that girl? You're not in any shape to go travelling, if that's what you're thinking."

"I don't want to fly to L.A. or any   thing. Just wa   ant to go wand   ering in my chair, every day along the seawall."

His plan, he tells her, is to work up the strength in his arms so by mid-July he'll feel strong enough to wheel himself around the whole ten kilometres. Living close to the sea he never gets a chance anymore to look at it. Nor at the people who stroll in their hundreds, thousands, along the promenade. This is a real chance to test his eyesight. (Silas wonders if he can still take *in* the world without its exhausting him.) What he tells her is that he's been living inside too long, that he needs a holiday from looking through glass. An aphrodisiac, so to speak.

"N   adine'll take me," he says.

"*I* could take you," replies Nell. "If you're so set on erasing yourself." She sounds offended.

But at sixty-five she would hate having to lug the overweight Silas about in his chair, and in fact has not offered to take him outside in three years. Ever since Krish joined the household, she hasn't had time to walk dog and Silas both. And the dog needs it more than Silas. When he's well, it's Nadine who takes him rolling around the block, a fact Nell seems to forget every time he's feeling better and desirous of escape.

"That girl knows you shouldn't be outside in the summer sun. At least she knows that much."

Silas mentions that he intends to make a canopy of his golf umbrella.

"She's a floozy," says Nell. "She never washes her hair and she lives with who knows who in a pair of jeans and that mink shorty coat she probably sleeps in. Only it isn't mink, it looks like rabbit." (This is a persistent winter memory.)

Silas, reassured her resistance is breaking down, draws back nobly in his chair like a bewigged British judge.

"*Is the prosecution claiming that the accused young Lady has engaged in an activity incommensurate with her duties as a trusted volunteer worker and a friend to cripples?*" he mimics fluently.

"What?"

"*Are ya claimin', laidy,*" he asks unhesitant in Cockney, "*that she's a rotten two-bit laiy wiv a pox on 'er box and a longin' to spread'er germs?*"

She looks at him.

"You've got a mouth like a rathole too."

She deserts him to put on the kettle, take down her Royal Dansk Butter Fingers and prepare tea before her soap opera comes on. Afternoons are her own, and she spends them watching TV in her room. Silas hates tea. He hated it in India, he'd hate it in China, he wouldn't like it at Buckingham Palace.

Say tea and he thinks of brown hands on a hillside in the tropical sun picking leaves. Say tea and he thinks of crooked spines. *He'll* never drink to bad health; he made up his mind about that in Delhi. But he wouldn't say no to a Wedgwood Drum Biscuit.

"In China," says Nell, "they have a law the man helps to keep house." She's tidying up.

Silas grins. "Tha   at's in China. This is
h   ere."

He knows what she's thinking, and because she's thinking it and not saying means she has decided not to argue him out of his foolish risk-taking till he's feeling more vulnerable. She's thinking she's running out of cures: that he doesn't know how *bad* his relapses have become: that remissions aren't automatic anymore. They've talked to doctors (*she's* talked to doctors). She thinks Silas should accept the fact that after X number of years you just keep on going downhill. And never to be too careful on the way down.

If she can, she'll try to *cure* him of the idea of a holiday. For her instincts, bred to cure men, have kept him as healthy as he could have expected to be for twenty-three years, since he first hired her on his small government pension and she agreed to work for a low salary in exchange for room and board—and for the security being attached to a disabled man allowed. She's tried cures of all kinds. When he feels unbearably hot (frequently), instead of shifting him in her strong arms into a cool bath, she has invented an ice-cube collar made of a popped inner tube from his wheelchair, to drape around his neck. Into a slit she'll drop four or five dozen ice cubes, before collaring him and offering guava-fruit juice to sip, or, if he needs one, some new enema of particularly gaseous concoction, especially if he's lying paralyzed in bed with atrophied muscles. She also coaches him to empty his bladder and drink cranberry juice for urinary acidity.

But these aren't cures. The cures she tries out on his incurable disease are diets of low fat, no salt, no gluten—specially treated dishes like barley pilaf, soybean casserole, chicken tandoori, Cantonese shrimp and beans. Nell follows Swank, and won't believe that a low-fat diet has never *scientifically* demonstrated that it will, over the years, retard the number of attacks, maybe even eliminate them. For summer desserts she prefers raspberry Bavarian or easy cheesecake, because neither has any fat or oil, nor, as far as Silas can detect, any taste. He prefers Seafoam Nut Kisses, cookies that at least have peanut oil in them.

Yet because these diets take the long view, too long in Nell's trained opinion, she tinkers with short-term cures. Once she procured from a "research lab" in Arizona a phial of diluted snake venom. Silas remembers it came special delivery, in a khaki envelope with a path of stamps across it that looked like medals on a major's chest. After twenty years he had nothing to lose (she said), so he tried it. "Ho   ope's a virtu on a pa   ar   itch   l   ove," he told her, barely coherent. "Th   in   cura   aren't no   oted for their   ske   ske   ticism, e   h?" The injection made him throw up. That and scratch his ankles, of all things, till they bled.

Since then she's tried megavitamin therapy, physiotherapy (she took an evening course in physiotherapy) and electrical stimulation. She stimulates him with wires emerging from a battery her handy cousin in Cloverdale made for her in his garage, a Christmas gift for her patient. Each wire has an electrode she attaches to Silas's flabby muscles. But all her fiddling with the electrical charge has given him is a few laughs: the same effect as laughing gas. When he's been abed for weeks, and things look like they may never improve, Nell seems to derive solace in seeing him giggle. She should have had a job on a poultry farm electrocuting turkeys.

The only cure of hers approved by his doctor is the regular injection of ACTH, a pituitary hormone, which makes Silas look fat and a little corrupt. The doctor himself does little except remind Silas to avoid extreme temperatures, too much physical activity (humping and jogging, maybe?), infection and emotional upset.

"If science still has no idea what causes your disease," says Dr. Cabot, a young MD with a general practice, "it does know what makes it recur."

Silas was used to Dr. Storey, who had been with him ever since he returned to Canada and who hummed opera arias. But three years ago Nell lost her faith in that physician when he expressed reservations about her snake venom. She cut him loose. For a while she even toyed with the idea of taking her patient to a chiropractor on Altamira she'd heard about before she discovered Dr. Cabot's office up the street.

Right now Silas figures a holiday is better than a rest, snake venom or electrical laughter. He has to re-examine the world. So when Nell disappears into her bedroom with tea, biscuits and a hidden (she thinks) piece of sponge cake, he does wheelies over the tiles, back and forth, to test his strength. Then telephones Nadine.

"Silas? You sound spaced out."

"   Cat   atching   my bre   ath."

"Clay's on his way in so I can't talk now except to say when do you wanna poop down to the beach? That why you're calling?"

Then she says, "I can't come before noon. Noon okay?"

"Ye   s." He wants to go on and ask her a personal question. "W   hy," he manages to get out.

"What?"

"are y   ou so thi   in?"

"Me, thin? I like your sense of humour, Si. Big joke."

Half a butter finger in hand, Nell emerges from her room when he hangs up.

"Was that her you were talking to?"

"My beloved," he answers sarcastically. "*Hee hee.*"

"What've you been doing with yourself? Where's the dog?"

Out from under the dining-room table comes Krish blinking foolishly. He always hides when Silas takes his turns, careening like a wild man over the cork.

She says, "You've been playing with yourself again. Even the dog knows better than to get in the road. You deserve to have another attack toot sweet."

"I"

"Listen to you!"

She's all for putting him to bed, pressing home his wax earplugs, giving him a sedative. She swallows the rest of her biscuit and says, "If she wasn't Vincent's daughter," sounding like the soap opera she's tuned to, "I would not let that tramp past my door." She returns to her room with a small, involuntary burp.

Silas wheels himself back to the window and looks out through the plate glass. It needs a stripe of gull's dung washed off. He was asking Nadine about Vincent only the other day. How was Silas's old mentor, anyway?

"Dying."

"H im too."

"I don't know," said Nadine. "I never see him."

Silas never pushes for news of her father, not since she mentioned once how much she'd disliked growing up with him on the gulf island where Vincent had retired with his young Brazilian wife, Nadine's mother, and built himself a home. More than mentioned it, actually, for she also told him how much she'd hated the private school in Oregon where he'd sent her, and she refused to be "finished." Silas remembers her coming home on holidays and looking bonier year by year. She shed refinement early, if she ever had any.

"It's odd, isn't it?" Silas was saying to her one recent morning. "Vincent's like I should have been, after the career I never had."

"Were you really the ambassador type?"

"*My dear—*" he could still mimic the corrupt and sleek "*—is the Brahmin fastidious? The road to the top may have been veddy veddy long, but I, you see, was being the answer my country was looking for.*" As a mimic he seldom spoke without the fluency he'd lost, which is why it used to occur to Silas he should have gone into theatre and thus avoided his demise as a diplomat. Until he realized he *had* gone into theatre and fallen all the same.

Nadine's father, a generation older than he, had been his first boss, in Mexico City more than twenty-five years ago, before Silas was sent to India and Vincent to South America. In those years, especially in Delhi, Silas owned a vision.

"*A vision,*" he continued, "*that all the beggars in the world would have been loving. I was the Way and Light, you see.*" Here he was mimicking his younger, idealistic self. "*I was seeing a chicken in the Muslim's pot, strawberry jam on the Hindu's chapatti, and chocolate ice cream for everybody. I was seeing a roof for every family, an electric light for every shelter, running water, furniture, toilets . . .*" Yes, Silas certainly had known what it was to know something. He had had a vision, bless it anyway, rather far removed from diplomacy, perhaps, but definitely full of missionary zip.

If she felt like it, Nadine would undo his shirt to massage his chest with her fingers. And he'd talk of what he'd been seeing lately of the world. A call-girl racket in the second-floor condo across Bartholomew, he'd tell her, "a minor operation, with a live-in old man in a baseball hat, who keeps his eye on the plump girl living with him who gets driven away in an old Pontiac

every afternoon b   y this d   ude with a
tooth   pick."

He enjoys telling her of nosy real estate agents who drive
BMWs and dress in Dior suits. He'll describe a police assault
on a nearby building, when the street was sealed off and a
jockey driven away in handcuffs. Summer, he likes to tell her,
is the season for men who walk alone with other people's
insults, and talk to themselves in rancour; for the violinist in
the building next door who works squawkingly on a passage
until it sings; for crows irritated by the heat.

But this is the extent of Silas's world, when he isn't looking
at the ceiling, flat out in bed ill. At night, ill or not, he's likely to
catch the scent of skunks gliding through the shrubbery, on
their way out of the park to forage for who knew what among
apartment buildings, towers, alleys. He is awakened by the
noise of toilets above him flushing, water falling down pipes
in a rush. The truth is that above him, not ten feet away, sleeps
a woman he has never met . . . above her a couple . . . above
them. . . Living here in layers, thinks Silas, he's living in the
most densely populated corner of the Commonwealth outside Hong Kong. It's a conceit he enjoys.

"My at   tacks are getting lo   onger
now, noticed?" he asked Nadine last month. "Compa   ared
to when you were a girl, when Vin   cent brought
y   ou visiting. This last one was a lu   lu."

"Yeah, I came to see you sometimes, but you were sleeping. Anyway, that's what *she* said."

Nell was annoyed with Nadine for having caused this last
relapse, or so she believed, by keeping him outside too long
one cool December day, when he caught the chill Nell insisted
led later to his fever. He couldn't sleep. So in January she discovered earplugs. She discovered she could stop up his ears at
night with waxy wads wrapped in cotton, to help him sleep.
(More likely to punish him for listening to Nadine.) The earplugs at least kept out the caterwauling sirens, squealing tires,

cars revving their engines at the curb outside for warmth. Trouble was, earplugs made him snore, like a grain-fed hog, said Nell. She felt obliged to punch him. He'd wake the widow above if *somebody* didn't punch him to make him roll over. Then when his condition turned paralytic she couldn't even do that when he snored. She cursed Nadine. Luckily for the widow above, the wax had a way of loosening, then falling out of his ears when he swallowed, sometimes his tears.

Sounds of Nell's key in the latch.

"Do up your shirt," Nadine would say.

"Mo   mmy fix."

"Useless cripple."

"O   h? Take down your fa   nny filthy, na   ughty knickers and sit on me. H   orrible little girl."

"I don't like the way she talks to you," Nell would complain.

She made him do tongue twisters. Not a punishment for listening to his young friend, but as a cure for his jumbled tongue (disconnected brain). He was more successful at these some days than others: every morning she made him read aloud for ten minutes from a little anthology.

Where wizened wranglers wield weighty widows,
winsome wrinkles weirdly wangle whitened shadows.

This loosened his lips, tongue, even (fortunately, she felt) his bowels.

———————

The most useful part of Krish's anatomy is what Silas employs every morning to soften his cheeks. Shaving cream, he has discovered, lathered over dog spit make for stubbleless cheeks, especially when Nell handles his razor with the determination of a threshing machine. She dislikes beards. Funny the way

Silas's gaze afterwards in the mirror always feeds him so little esteem. Starved for affection, for a woman's body to be inside, he envies Krish for having lost his balls when Nell took him to the vet after a year.

At his toilet, Silas prefers to help himself but is resigned like a wrestler to the encumbering hold of other arms. Nell tugs, she complains, she warns. "In *her* condition," she tells him next morning, "she's not fit to be taking care of anybody. Can't take care of herself!"

When Nadine arrives dressed in sandals, shorts and a dirty sweatshirt, Nell can hardly be civil to her. She suspects her motives, convinced of another catastrophe like last December's, its inevitability. Sensitive to the tension and maybe even hoping to defuse it, Nadine asks the muscular old nurse if she's heard of the latest treatment for MS.

Nell sniffs and refuses to be drawn. "I'm aware of lots of treatments."

"Got to have a pressure chamber for this one. These doctors in New York put really sick patients inside a tank or something to breathe pure oxygen five times a week for like a month. It's like having air blown through your veins."

"Oh?"

"I should've torn out the article. Sounded wicked."

Nell snorts. "What kind of scientific data is it based on?"

"Search me. If it calms you down, why not?"

Krish, excited by the appearance of his leash, jumps up to lick Silas's cheek, paws on the chair.

"I thought we were lea   ving," says Silas.

Nell says, "You thought you were *lea   ving*, did you? You sound like you got a big fall coming, buster."

He grins, sleekly.

"I didn't pack you a lunch. You can't go anywhere without lunch."

"We'll buy him something at the concession," says Nadine.

"That's not food, it's nausea."

"*My good woman,*" Silas instructs her, "*you may pack my saddlebag veddy veddy tightly. Tomorrow.*"

Which annoys her. Frankly, his holidays sound like a moronic idea. "*I'm* not responsible, no. I only have to suffer the wonderful consequences!"

So she will.

Outside at last, Silas and his expedition zip down a paved lane in the park, protected from the sun by a red, white and green umbrella. Kris pulls and Nadine steers. Silas has his umbrella in one hand, dog leash in the other, his feet planted firmly on the footplates. Everything surprises him: the air, being outside in it, his skin like cedar bark after a good soaking. He feels sexy. The air through a window is nothing. This air steams. Tropical blossoms spin by. The rain forest smells green and endless.

The dog nearly crashes them into a stump when it swerves from the lane after a squirrel.

"Sp   astic!" roars Silas. "Dog breath!" His troubles compound: leash in the axle, foot on a paw, umbrella knocked goofy. Silas is certainly back in the world.

Never mind, he'll take as much of it as he can get.

Nadine apologizes to Krish. Silas thanks Nadine. They all go on, man and girl unconcerned, the dog with his doggy life.

Emerging from the piss-smelling tunnel near the beach, they discover a traffic school in session beside the wading pool and the disembowelled fire engine. They stop to watch. Children pedal pastel-coloured cars over the asphalt, past stop signs, through traffic lights, across painted white lines. A policeman with a microphone is chastising the violators. "Number , Six, you didn't stop at the red light!" "Stay on your side of the road, Number Three!" Number Five's mother insists on accompanying her child on foot, as if fearing the effect on him of an early encounter with the law.

"Want to try it out, Si?"

"I am   trying."

They come to the promenade at Second Beach with bodies everywhere. Silas feels like he's back in Asia. So many bodies, lying in the sand, sitting on logs, standing in the sea with the enthusiasm of converts awaiting immersion. These human positions, he thinks. The sun at its zenith is dazzling.

Nadine rolls him on. The world expands. He can't get enough of girls with globes stuffed into bikinis, musclemen with cigarette boxes tucked into their trunks, waltzing roller skaters, barefoot families lined up at the concession stalls, lifeguards waiting to go on duty, children. Onward he rolls, past the saltwater swimming pool full of spindly boys and wading grandmothers. A lifeguard in a white safari hat patrols the horseshoe wall with a megaphone in his hand; a lifeguard at sea bobs among bodies in his rowboat, far out where the tide has ebbed low.

"I ca   an't take it   all   *in*!" shouts Silas. Krish, adrenalin pumping from the trot, barks and turns his leash into a snake. Umbrella teetering, Silas aches from holding the torrid sun at bay. He's flagging already.

"Wait'll you see the sea festival in July," Nadine tells him, knotting the leash to his chair, calming him down with hands on his shoulders.

"Do I wa   ant to?"

"You're on your holidays I thought."

"   right. How many fre   ighters?"

Looking out to sea, counting, she drifts away from him. "Five."

"Ei   ight!" Breathing deeply he exhales like a diver.

She straightens the umbrella in his hand. "You okay?"

"Count!"

She counts. "…eight…nine!" She points beyond the shipping lanes to the mountainous west shore where another ship is anchored. "See its bum, in behind that first one?"

"*Stern.*"

"You've got a great voice, Si. You should be in radio." She straightens his Polaroids.

A small plane is towing a row of letters across the sky, making an advertising sweep of the miles of beach between the city and Point Grey:

RON ZALKO MAKES BEAUTIFUL BODIES

First day, first hour of his holidays and Silas, trying to take in the world, already feels sick and depressed with a burning tiredness. Nell was right, he'll soon be on his back for eternity. Hot and prickly, he feels a child's shame for having wet the bed. Wants to cry. Wishes Nadine would point him down the slope into the swimming pool.

She observes his weepiness. "We'll try again tomorrow, okay?"

"Wha   at about lunch?" He sounds like some brat whaaing for a treat.

"Nell'll fix you a nice one, Si. Today we just broke the ice."

But what Silas wants to break is trail, if only his own, over this hot, veddy veddy crooked tar ribbon, curling in and out of coves, the only promenade in the world to attract all a city's citizens, drawing them together from the hemispheres—Chinese and Italians, Chileans and Swedes—snaking by forest and sea, a sea these freighters will cut through full of grain, potash and lumber in exchange for luxuries from Asia like cars, perfumed tea and rattan patio chairs.

On fire with the sun, Silas feels like giving in to his unjustified tears. The muscle to hold his bladder shut won't work and he pees, scalding, in his underpants. Couldn't stand up now if he had to, not because of pissy pants, but because his legs have cramped up in their braces. Can't feel the footplates. Can't *combine* to feel his senses. Having a heat attack is what taking a sauna must feel like, steam from scalding stones.

The stones uncovered by the tide seem to drag at water on his knees. He remembers what deterioration is from the inside out. He feels drained. Covered in barnacles and mussels.

Hanging on in his chair, dog whimpering to be off, he guesses this will be the end of his holidays. It's a feeling he recognizes as if remembering it, the sudden dragging, the temptation to crawl down over rocks in his braces and drag himself in mercy to the tide. He listens for the tide.

But the world bursts in.

Transistor radios, children's screams, the sound of bodies exploding on water back in the swimming pool. These gaps in his life.

And Nadine, bending thinly over him, looking in at him through his sunglasses.

"Silas, if you feel like killing yourself," she is saying, "you can't, 'cause I just washed my hair."

Alarm and intimidation from Nell convince Silas to take a holiday from his holiday. The tiredness and misery he must endure, just to have a holiday! He sags. Not owning an Amigo means he's dreaming if he thinks he can build up enough strength in his arm to propel himself around the whole seawall without electricity. It'd be like learning to walk again, visualizing every step before he makes it, every thrust of his arms that at sea level grow heavy, especially against a breeze, no matter how much exercise they've had over his smooth apartment tiles. He can't imagine asking Nadine to *push* him everywhere. So when she phones that evening to ask him about tomorrow, he begs her to "sk   i   ip" a day.

"No problem," say Nadine.

"Just as well," says Nell (appeased). "Because a man from Sri Lanka phoned to ask if he could come and see you."

"Ma   an?"

"Am I supposed to tell *him* not to come either? I should've guessed the squalid state she'd bring you back in."

Lacking the vigour even to chew, Silas refuses his food (leftover casserole in a mushroom sauce) and falls asleep as if his skin enclosed molten lead instead of blood, stones not muscles. He sleeps fitfully, dreaming of Nadine's good teeth, her keyboard smile making loud music (too loud) in her dark, underweight face. "Nice smile," she agrees in his dream. "But I roller skate like I've got polio."

He reassures her. "I couldn't walk down the block without holding on to parking meters." Such a smoothie in his dreams.

At dusk Nell awakens him to offer soup, brown bread and margarine. "You were talking in your sleep," she says in her quiet, professional voice. She supports his head to spoon in the soup.

Slurping, Silas wonders if the man coming wants him to take back his old job as an honorary consul. Silas took up honorary consulling because periods of remission in the early years of his disease had never been long enough, in the opinion of External Affairs, to earn him another posting abroad. He remained on their books to the age of thirty, when he finally accepted a permanent pension, a disability allowance and a flattering retirement citation. But he required something more to do than sit in his apartment plotting walks with his nurse, what magazines to subscribe to, or the shapes of foreign languages he tried studying on his own. When he was well, much of the time the first fifteen years, he needed to feel useful. His striped-pants training required it.

Thanks to Vincent's influence, he became an honorary consul for Ceylon without ever having to leave Vancouver, and used a little office in the Marine Building twice a week, or whenever he felt strong enough to grant visas, talk to travel agents on the phone about Ceylon's comeliness and sometimes answer questions from provincial ministers about the possibility of expanding trade (umbrellas, newsprint) with Colombo. It gave him a feeling of being in touch. He'd only visited Ceylon once, on a week's holiday from Delhi, during which he missed seeing even the main tourist attractions like Anuradhapura and Polannaruwa. He'd spent most of the time walking up and down the beach in Galle Face Park, trying to recover from the enervating effects of dysentery. Despite his unfamiliarity with Ceylon, Silas was nevertheless appointed to represent its interests on the West Coast.

The extent of Vincent's influence was evident by the inquiries Silas received over the years from officers of the Canadian embassy in Colombo, asking to be remembered to the retired ambassador. Vincent hadn't served in Asia at all. His fluency in the Romance languages would have been wasted on Hindus, Muslims, Buddhists. By then Vincent had retired to his ten-room house on an arbutus-fringed knoll overlooking the Gulf of Georgia. He had his very young Brazilian bride. He had silver hair and the same old disarming gestures and laugh. Such charm made Silas doubt whether he himself, even healthy, could ever have become an ambassador, for growing older Silas discovered he loved earthiness too well, and diplomacy never really got down to earth. Too much pie in the sky, men nibbling canapés and shaping small talk into vases, to really nourish accord between cultures.

"Don't gag on it, eat," Nell tells him, pressing in his bread and margarine.

The only payment Silas received in fifteen years, apart from visa fees used to pay a part-time typist, was the privilege, as established by the Vienna Convention in 1963, to park on city streets without paying. But Silas used the bus. So the only diplomatic immunity he could expect was if on duty he happened to have an attack stamping a young lady's visa, stamping and breaking her wrist instead, he was immune from prosecution. "That's something, anyway," said Nell. "You never know." His only real perk was a monthly luncheon to

honour the city's consular corps. Silas attended five luncheons
and no more. His fellow consuls were old with fat around their
hearts. Each luncheon was formal, gracious, and he would
come home on his cane aping gestures, mimicking speeches.
Dutifully, he visited his office as well as sometimes the crews
on freighters from Ceylon, sending them to Dr. Storey if they
had a problem like venereal disease. In the end he had to
give it all up, forced to resign once more when he landed in
bed for almost five months, following the worst attack in his
life. His last link with diplomacy passed to a businessman in
Gastown, who imported sandalwood soap from Ceylon and
had travelled there once to buy silk shifts (in bulk, he claimed,
for a chain of convents).

He falls asleep dreaming of parking meters, the intensity
of the world, sunlit beaches. Not to mention a very healthy
gap between himself apart, listening, yes, to himself talking to
a walleyed tiger on a chain. He drops a quarter in the meter.

The man at the door is Vincent.

"Vincent!" cries Nell.

"Vincent!" cries sleepy Silas in his pyjamas. "I
tho   ought you were done for!" He tumbles into
his chair.

"My dear Nell . . ." says the old ambassador at once, taking
her hand in the hall and kissing it.

"And, Silas, how are you?" he asks with an eloquent,
motionless handshake.

"Ha   anging around for some   body
from Sri   "

Vincent lays a palm across his own breast. "I'm he."

Nell seems surprised. "You should have told me it was
you," she says. She says she was all set to turn away a stranger
at the door, thanks to a young lady Vincent probably knows,
who brought Silas home exhausted, yesterday. "But you're
feeling better this morning. Aren't you Silas?" Saying this she's
looking at Vincent. She adores Vincent, their distinguished

acquaintance, Silas's old mentor. His pale-blue suit matches his eyes. He has hair the colour of snow.

"I had to tell a white lie," says Vincent, settling into a soft chair and surrendering his oak cane to her. "I didn't want to put you to any trouble." Confidentially, he adds, leaning forward in an exaggerated way, "I didn't want my daughter to know I was coming."

"Na   adine?" Silas immediately feels stupid for asking.

Vincent says to him, "I know you see her regularly." He waves his hand. "You young people ..."

Nell hoots with laughter and plumps his cushion. Conspiracy's in the air and she relishes conspiracy. Ignoring Silas, she small talks about him all the same, thus maintaining herself as the centre of attention. The older diplomat has a languid way of stroking his tie and a cheerful manner of not appearing to notice anything in the room, including Krish sniffing his shoes. This sort of posture, if he'd ever truly acquired it himself, Silas has forgotten. He's aware he's still in pyjamas, but unlike the dapper Vincent doesn't care. Nell offers to make Vincent coffee.

285

"Have you anything stronger?" he asks politely. "A little sherry before lunch would be lovely. I have a luncheon appointment at twelve-thirty sharp. And a taxi waiting, I feel very important." (Something about him is missing.) He consults his wristwatch with a self-mocking air, then pulls lightly at his French cuff with the silver stud.

His request for a drink has flustered Nell, who always pretends to Silas there's no alcohol even for medicinal purposes to be had in the apartment. She will have to see, she says, caught between probity and hospitality, disappearing down the hallway.

"*T   ry your bedroom, Ne   ell!*"

Silas turns to Vincent. "Nell's a c   loset drinker, she ke   eps it in her closet. Thinks I'm unsteady

enough on my fee   t as it   is. But I can
still move around on m   y legs when I have to.
Touch   metal."

Vincent confesses he's been unwell himself lately, which
he hopes will explain why he hasn't called in the last year or so.
"Wanted to telephone, but couldn't make myself understood.
An operation, one thing and another, you know what it's
like…"

"You sound well," says Silas.

"You should hear Silas," says Nell, returning with a bottle
of shooting sherry and two glasses. "When he's tired, or having a relapse…" She pours. "I need an interpreter."

"To our health," says Vincent, raising his glass to Silas.

"Likewise," says Nell.

Silas gets nothing. He's still in his pyjamas wondering
what this is all about. Vincent's distinguished presence makes
him want to rise above himself, so he tries to look disinterested. He tries to match Vincent's meticulous gestures, but he
can't think of anything to say.

"It's really very kind of you both to admit me under false
pretences," Vincent says. "Sri Lanka has nothing to do with my
visit. I wanted to talk to Silas about Nadine, and I didn't want
her to get wind of my coming, if you can appreciate my concern."

"Of course," replies Nell. If she has any idea of what he's
talking about she fails to take his hint about wanting to talk to
Silas (alone).

Vincent chats about old age awhile, very relaxed. Silas sits
thinking that India, thanks to Canada, has the atomic bomb.
Outside is another hot day, too hot for a country that loves
ice-skating more than its Ps and Qs. Nell opens a window to
relieve the mugginess.

"…I was reading about farmers in northern Japan," Vincent is saying. "They seem to lose their brain fibre at an ear-

lier age than other Japanese because they fall into routine and don't exercise their brains enough by thinking and talking to people. They lapse into senility earlier. I suppose we can be thankful that—"

"That's why I left the prairies," quips Nell. "With him to look after there's no danger of *me* falling into routine. And I'm not getting any younger."

"*Some*   body has to grow food," says Silas.

Vincent admits it. "Green revolution or not, yes, we need a breadbasket."

"I'll cut some Cheddar," says Nell, "some hors d'oeuvres. Do you like pickled onions, Vincent?"

"My favourite kind."

And he reassures her lightly, since she's worried about keeping his taxi waiting, that he has more money than brains.

"Then you must be a millionaire," she says, going to the kitchen.

Thus flattered, Vincent turns to his friend. "Tell me, Silas. How is Nadine?"

Silas remembers his training and manages to show polite surprise.

"I never see her anymore," admits Vincent. "She refuses to visit me in my nursing home."

"I did   n't know that."

"I know she visits you," he says cheerfully. "Which is why I've come, to ask your advice." He sounds debonair, one old dip talking to another. It reminds Silas of an afternoon in Mexico City when the pipe-smoking Vincent casually asked him once if he knew where the ladies of the evening might be tasted. Silas knew, but didn't care to admit it. Vincent told him if he wanted to know, to come ask. Vincent prided himself in knowing things, in finding them out. About the private lives of Mexican politicians, the corruption of officials in high places and the pleasures to be had in low ones. It suddenly seems strange to hear him admit a limit to his knowledge—about his own daughter. Does he know how thin she looks? Silas doesn't ask.

Vincent asks, "How much do you know about the man she's living with?" His wrinkled face seems much older than his wavy hair.

"Clay?"

"You know him then."

Silas shakes his head.

Nell is listening from the kitchen. "Is he a nice young man, Vincent?"

Vincent chooses his words carefully. "I have reason to believe his influence . . . on my daughter is poor."

Old Nell would be very willing to corroborate this hypothesis with her own observations of his daughter. Instead she declares, "A father tends to worry more about his daughter than he probably should, Vincent." She pretends to bluffness in the hope of securing a little more knowledge. The way a hungry seagull might perch on a windowsill looking for scraps.

"I have information," says Vincent, "about him."

"Oh?"

"If you can appreciate my meaning."

Evidently Nell can. She hurries in from the kitchen bearing pickled onions and a slab of Cheddar. These she places on the coffee table, along with a cheese slicer and a plate of Stoned Wheat Thins, settling herself with obvious pleasure into the second chair and crossing her thick legs. Silas wishes she'd buzz off and leave them in private. Her white nurse's shoe, for she insists on wearing colours that testify to the presence of disease (red and white), jigs in anticipation of some revelation and reminds Silas of a cat's tail.

Vincent accepts an onion, a slice of cheese on a cracker, and balances these on top of his napkin. She has forgotten the plates. Silas is offered only the pickled onions. (He slept right through his Special K, toast and fruit salad.) Vincent nibbles awhile. Then appears to notice the dog for the first time and, smiling, offers him a piece of cracker and cheese. Nell manages not to look displeased. Vincent is so kind to animals.

"I have discovered," he says, "that the man my daughter is living with is a terrorist."

Nell's shoe freezes in mid-jig. This is knowledge. But what kind? The tone of its possession by Vincent sounds official, impersonal. Has he spies who open mail, tap telephones, buy information? His purpose in coming seems to Silas in keeping with his profession: to gain assistance by offering friendship, even confidential intelligence.

Silas recalls the hydro bombing last summer in the Interior; the firebombings last winter of a bank, a trust company, a video cassette store ...

"This man is terrorizing my daughter," Vincent tells him. "I'm worried about her health. I don't understand all the ins and outs, except he's turned her against me. I want to give her whatever wealth I've saved over the years. But she won't talk to me. I wanted to talk to her, about him, and she won't see me. This isn't an easy thing to talk about."

"Of course not, Vincent," says Nell. "Nadine isn't taking care of herself, that's my opinion." This boyfriend (she knows now) is an undercover operator. "In these matters, a woman should know how to look after herself instinctively."

After high-school graduation, says Vincent, his daughter just wanted to drift and not go on to college, even though he offered her anything she wished to go there: travel, a car, money. "Then she met this man she's living with, older. And she and I drifted apart. She never comes to the home where I live. She never came to see me in the hospital either."

"I can't believe it," says Nell. "She's such a nice girl."

Vincent says, "What do you think, Silas?"

Him? (He's wondering what's become of Vincent's pipe.)

"Frankly, if I can get her to accept my money, she won't have to live with him anymore. She depends on him, you understand, and he uses her. Intimidates her. He's a bit of an impostor. Does things like threaten her if she wants to see me, *thinks* of seeing me. She's afraid of him. I don't think she'll tell you her side of it, Silas, but if you tried, as somebody she admires, she might be willing to listen . . . I owe my daughter something."

"But what do you owe her?" Nell asks.

"Appeasement." He sounds plaintive. "I'm so much older than she, she never really had a father. She never really had a mother." Then he says, "You're like her father, Silas. Will you approach her? About the money, I mean."

Silas doesn't know how to answer, for he is out of touch with diplomatic initiative.

"Of course he will," answers Nell. "Won't you, Silas? Silas is good at that sort of thing. Trouble."

Silas is wondering if she remembers how much Vincent used to love angel-food cake, unlike Nadine, who grew up with little of her father's sweet tooth, even as a child. Neither did she inherit his cultivated airs. She used to keep her own chicken coop, learned to straighten nails against rocks, played with fishermen's children and scuffed bubble gum into teredo holes of washed-up logs. By then her mother, Jacinta, had mysteriously returned to São Paulo. Vincent alone became his daughter's support. He brought her visiting; he dressed her in pinafores. And then, abruptly, he sent her away to school. "To be finished," Nell liked to repeat with approval. Except Nadine left school as if she had never begun it.

"Anyway," says Vincent, nodding. "I'd better be going, my driver will think I've deserted him." He laughs and reveals his becoming, crooked teeth. He hasn't touched his onion.

On the way out he mentions to Silas he doesn't expect life to last. His own, he means, very much longer. He sounds off-hand, debonair. "My hair's a wig," he admits. "I've had gallons of therapy for throat cancer."

Startled, Nell hands him his sturdy cane with great sympathy. "Vincent, we had no *idea* …"

He bows graciously and asks them both not to forget his daughter has been deprived.

"Deprived!" cries Nell, after his departure. "Depraved is more like it. That girl of his is a floozy par excellent." And she pours herself another glass of shooting, hoping to savour the entire conversation with Vincent by going over it again with Silas.

Silas, his brain fibre suddenly inactive, feels in need of gallons of seawater to refloat it.

"Still," she says, "you might have been polite and answered. He *is* her dad."

"Dry u   p. Nell. Go drin   ink in your room."

"This is my room room."

"G   oinandwatchTVanddrinkyour-blo   odybladderfull!"

She swallows noisily, a little surprised at his malignity. "Silas! Dear, dear!" Trying to sound mocking, she sounds merely mournful. She goes into the bathroom and slams the door.

Silas looks out the window and hears a Smithrite garbage truck grinding away in the alley, followed by a settling-down explosion of a hollow steel box and then the amplified bleating of the monster in retreat. He can hear her tinkling in the toilet bowl. Then a scrubbing of teeth.

You can have—
Fried fresh fish,
Fish fried fresh,
Fresh fried fish,
Fresh fish fried,
Or fish fresh fried.

Nell disappears into her bedroom and emerges in street shoes.

Stella stole stealthily to the strand.

"I'm going out," she announces. "If that floozy ever comes here again you can tell her from me not to wash her hands in my sink. She can diddle you all she likes in the zoo."

Monday, wearing his catheter, portly Silas is rolled by the zoo on his way to Lumbermen's Arch. Today he's decided to intersect the seawall beyond First Narrows, at the other seawater pool, on the inlet past Lions Gate Bridge. His task is to endure.

Parking him beside a bench, Nadine raises his umbrella and the disappointed Krish, propitiated by its shade, settles down. Panting, the three of them sit looking at the world.

Silas gazes across the water at yellow mountains of sulphur, blue loading ramps, scows, a shining white city on the mountain. Gleaming veins of snow are trapped in the peaks above golf courses, reservoirs and Indian reservations. No integration in his brain, just excerpts: a Sanko Line freighter dragging its anchor along top of the water; a white ferry going out under the bridge; a man in a red bikini kicking a soccer ball against the wall of the unflooded, sand-bottomed pool. The harbour hums. A seaplane ascends. Cathedral bells   *pussy*   *in*   *the*   *well* drift out from the canyons downtown, over the floating gas stations of Coal Harbour, across Hallelujah Point and the Nine O'Clock Gun, up over trees and down to them.

Silas should have raised his umbrella sooner against the sun, for he has begun to feel its knock. He's pooped already, even scared.

"   me   back   "

"What?"

"Take   "

"You just left home, Si," she tells him. "I'm the one who should be tired!"

Maybe he needs to laugh a little. He's like the tide, up and down, in and out. So she stands up and dusts off her hands, preparing a performance she knows will cheer him up. She speaks to him very loudly where cyclists pass, walkers stroll and fat men are eating pickled radish in their hot dogs.

"*It's fine for you,*" she says in a husky, inimical voice, "*telling me to take you home. But what about me? Think I want to go back to that squalid place full of tin cans and underwear? Crucifixes and Coke cans? I'm sick of your smelly home!*" A few people look in their direction, then away, pretending not to hear. "*I'm not taking you anywhere. If you don't like it by the ocean here, stick it!*"

Vincent's daughter lashing out at tact, reticence, propriety always makes Silas snort with laughter. This time she sounds like Vincent. Silas's jerking head makes it look like he might be crying, and a woman in a skirt and blouse, not dressed for the beach at all, comes over to them and stands looking down at him. Krish sniffs her ankles. She glares at Nadine, who pretends not to see her and keeps on at Silas.

"*. . . I'm fed up to here,*" she says. "*Nothing pleases you. Zero. And you know what? You smell.*" She wheels upon the indignant woman for help. "*Don't you think she smells? Smell her. She oozes rot like an abscessed tooth. Jesus, she hadn't been to the dentist in her life, when I fished her out of a slum. Now when she brushes, she's brushing stumps. Look at them . . .*"

Silas obliges with a large grin full of drool. The woman draws back to full height, considerable in heels, and clamps her mouth shut. Nadine hasn't stopped talking.

"*. . . Why should I care if she lets herself go? I'm dealing with some emotional cripple here, let me tell you. . . Could you hold her still, ma'am, while I pick the gillies out of her hair?*"

The woman flees. Silas, confused, shakes however with spastic laughter. Nadine knows how much he likes irreverence. And to rant himself. Lip-whipping he calls it, letting go at the mouth against exercise parlours, personalized licence plates, the increase in junk mail. A little crowd has gathered to watch them. Nadine continues her performance by grabbing hold of his handles in apparent disgust and claiming, to everyone's amazement, that Silas never changes the diapers on his dog. The embarrassed little crowd disperses. And then quietly, straining more than necessary (it seems to Silas), she pushes him back up past the commemorative arch of red cedar, through the sycamores and by the monument to fallen Japanese soldiers of World War One. What exactly was she saying to him?

He himself can get worked up at fat dentists who fly south on weekend junkets to Reno. At women who love makeup and let themselves worship fashion. At fools nattering and laughing about nothing on TV talk shows. At elegant self-indulgence. According to Silas, diplomats and honorary consuls should all have to appreciate that their international failures arise from lip-whiplessness. Diplomacy does not prevent wars, only delays them. It cannot feed people, just reinforces complacency. And since diplomacy isn't in genes (luckily), Nadine has inherited no diplomatic protocol whatsoever. Still, her own plain talk has confused him.

Muscles sore from laughing, Silas nevertheless feels better now, even if taking in the world is an unrequited business. No wonder diplomats lounge behind protocol.

"I   've got to talk," he tells her. "To yo   u."

But she's standing in the road scratching her stomach, wet from the labour of pushing him, trying to figure out how to get his chair up steps to the wishing well in the little Air Force Garden of Remembrance. Surrounded by cool firs, it's an oasis worth the trouble, if he's dying for shade. And evidently a chat.

DAMAGES

"Listen, Silas, I know you're bushed, but if you could just like climb these steps in your braces, I could manage the bloody chair and dog. You'll like it here."

He obliges, anything to be cool, and wishes his canes were along in a quiver. She slides the seat under his rump not a second before he falls backward, beat, at the wishing well. The setter leaps sideways. Silas stares into the well, awaiting energy the way a dead lawn does rain. The water is deep-blue ink, inviting, but he does not ask her for a coin to toss in. She rubs nickels cheek to cheek under the peaked shingle roof and drops them herself straight into the blue.

"Didn't mind, did you? I'm wishing these days." Then she says, "Why not shut your eyes and rest?"

"Pro   omised."

Wishing he had a sugar cube to suck, Silas closes his eyes, breathes deeply, goes to sleep for ten hours and wakes up refreshed. His words rush out:

"Yourdadwantstogiveyoumoneyhesays."

Message delivered, he goes to sleep for another ten hours, her wanton, unfettered voice rousing him.

"I'm an ungrateful daughter who doesn't need any."

"   thinks you do. He   e's worried."

Up and down like the tide.

"When did he tell you this?"

"   "

"What else did he say?"

"Clay."

She writes awhile on the surface of the water.

"Like to know how my Fascist father knows all about who I'm living with." She lifts her finger. "You?"

Shakes his head.

She looks so young sitting in her shorts and sandals, stick-limbed, vulnerable on the well's stone lip. A sudden breeze could blow her in. A sudden breeze might revive Silas. In his sick-chair dream this well's a hole in the ground covered with rotting shiplap and long grass full of cow puddings at the fringe. Someone has warned him to stay off the planks, and when he won't an uncle ties him up in the barn to be beaten or forgotten. His child's body fights free, returns to the well, as if to a hole in his tooth. He has been here for the rest of his life, in or around a well, falling in and climbing out.

He motions to her, his saddlebag.

"Want an egg sandwich?" she asks.

Not him. It's she who needs it, her fingers as thin as pencils, her arms bamboo.

"Not hungry," she says. "How 'bout the dog?"

"W   hy are y   ou so thi   in?"

"Are you kidding?"

"Vincent," he tells her, "thin   ks Clay's corrupt."

"Vincent thinks," she says. "Clay thinks *he's* corrupt."

"Who?"

She looks down at Krish, panting on his stomach in the shade.

"Vincent tried to get Clay to leave me. By offering him a bribe. Without Clay, I guess he thought I'd have to take his money just to stay alive." Balancing on the lip of the well, trying to part the water with her hands. "Clay thinks I should've let him take the money. Then I'd have got my inheritance, or whatever, and we'd go right back to shacking up, or take off somewhere. Vincent couldn't do anything, 'cept worry some more about the state he says I'm in." She dries her hands on her shorts. "Clay thinks giving your word's less important than who you give it to. Lying's okay if the other guy's an asshole and deserves what he gets. Especially if it's not his own way."

As far as Silas can see, her legs are just bone and skin, with two small fists for knees.

"I don't agree," she says. "Even if we lied so Vincent thought I was back under his thumb, it'd be like allowing him the satisfaction of *giving* me something, even if he found out we'd ripped him off. But," she goes on cheerfully, "I don't want to give him the feeling of being exploited, not when he's dying. He'd take real pleasure in that. He'd feel like he was being punished for his sins, can't you just see him? Saint Vincent? Yuck."

No, Silas is incapable of taking in the multiplicity of the world he's seeing these days, let alone the duplicity of one he isn't. Made a reluctant envoy, he's mainly equipped to parry Nell when he must and go to sleep when he feels like it. He doesn't remember, if he ever did, how to mediate.

I saw Esau sitting on a see-saw. Esau saw me.

"You say something?"

Stalemate.

Why couldn't Vincent leave him alone? Silas on his holidays. Who cares about Clay?

"Clay?" she asks.

"Huh?"

She leans against a cedar post to keep her balance. "He's got a part-time driving job. And he's acting on a shoestring in a David Hare play. Guess you could say he's an activist like. He used to be a priest. At least he was in training to be one—is that the word? A Benedictine. What he couldn't stand in the end was not being part of things, like not being able to make things happen. I met him when he got out."

"Th   ings happen we m   ake."

She pauses. "We ache is right."

Staring into the ink, her dark eyes look hollow. "Life's bloody, isn't it? I've been trying to get on as a typist or something. I can't type. I don't have the stamina for waitressing. People say I couldn't last on my feet."

She brightens. "They wouldn't believe what I lug around the park, would they? The restaurants, I mean."

"In my pock   et, if you dig …   "

She digs deep. Krish sits up.

"Just for you, Si." She gives his quarter a juicy kiss and drops it from above her head, *gloop*, into the blue. Ears perked, paws up, the dog wants to become blue by diving in with the wish.

She wanders over to where a bronze plaque is screwed to a rock in the goldfish pool. Above, a crow leans rasping at Krish from a bough. Nadine reads aloud:

> *Not here they fell who died a world to save;*
> *Not here they lie but in a thousand fields afar.*
> *Here is their living spirit that knows no grave;*
> *Not here they were—but are.*

"That's nice, isn't it?" she asks.

Every day she brings him home tired and full of wonder.

"W   heredoyougetyourenergy?" he asks.

"It's goofy."

"Are you on drugs?" Nell asks her.

"Did you guys hear what the minister of agriculture had to say about the world?" Nadine asks them both. Here her voice deepens into the triple-chin sententiousness of a politician. "*I see the world as a big roast beef. And Canada is the best slice.*" She shrugs. "When Clay hears that kind of spiel it makes him smoulder."

"Really?" says Nell.

Try as she does to feel some sympathy for Vincent's daughter, who is being abused by the man she lives with, her resentment of Nadine increases daily. Her worry is Silas. Silas letting himself be abused by Nadine, Silas abusing himself. She resents Silas too. Ex-diplomat, ex-second secretary for immigration, veteran MS victim: can't he understand he can never get *too much* sleep? A fool carrying on to his holiday's end past

DAMAGES

Second Beach, Fergusson Point, Third Beach . . . pretty soon (or so he must think) around the whole seawall in a day. "Ha," says Nell. "Whatever happened to your letter writing?"

For two hours a day Silas is determined to cram his head like a hope chest, telling his amanuensis to keep pushing him farther and farther along "this veddy veddy crooked wall." At noon the sun grows hot, he squints, his eyeballs flutter. His journey is a road of tropical intensity. Symptoms of his brain's scars are the malarial prickling in his arms, the gator's breath on his neck, the loosening of his bowels from burrowing weevils. His eyes blur. He lifts his sunglasses and the world changes colour. No relief. He lowers them back to the bridge of his nose and feels as heavy as a sawdust scow.

"Ba   lls," he says to the descending fatigue.

"Want me to slow down?" asks Nadine.

"No   faster! No bre   eze!" And grabbing at the rims outside both tires to push himself faster, his hands bounce off the steel like birds flying into windows. Flap and fall.

"You okay?"

"Kee   p out   the bike lane   or   "

But Silas knows he's already run down. A racing tire up the spine might stimulate him, like a jolt from Nell's electric cure. He should quit before he ends up immobile on his mattress. Try to walk these days and he'd be crawling at ten paces (five, if the heat gets any worse). He can taste his suffering on long, wilting stems of teeth, in a mouth full of undergrowth, with leathery salal for a tongue and fern-tickling tonsils that make him cough. Krish, as if leashed to his brain, also whimpers after too much sun.

Silas opens his mouth to smile at a young woman jogging by. She smiles back. He isn't chopped liver yet.

But the thought of food turns his stomach. Would rather swim any day, wobble down stone steps and dunk his ankles at high tide. And if he can't stand up, get Nadine to trundle him in his chair somehow through the sand, far enough across to let the ocean slap his ankles. These days he's wearing sandals that smell of excremental tanning. He'd remove his sandals.

He studies her frame, the disease wasting her, and tries to account for her energy. Where on earth does it come from? He would like to fatten her up. He keeps telling her to eat whatever she wants from his saddlebag, that he's sick of *Swank's Diet Book*. Diet food, if any food, should interest her.

It never does.

"A fudg   sicle then?"

"We're half a mile from fudgsicles."

She just likes to do good works it seems (and he's the good works she's doing). How to reciprocate, put meat on her bones, help her survive? A diplomatic initiative, this, unlikely to succeed if she can't be rescued from herself.

"Where's Kri   ish?"

"Right beside you, Si. Why don't you pat him?"

But his arms don't feel all here. Pulling them in one direction is gravity, and his brain, light for lack of food, insists on lifting them. Dizzy, he could float home on days like these. He feels decadent for desiring her to push his carcass whichever way it points, for wanting to make progress around a wall, pushing her to push him a little farther every day, wearing them both down as his dreadful martyrdom runs its course.

Nell is witness to his decline and stubbornness. This holiday business, as she calls it, doesn't make sense to her. "There are other ways of seeing the world, my friend, like the camp for MS patients in Vernon, I think. Or Salmon Arm. Or what about writing some more letters to dictators?" As if travel by proxy is what he wants. "I could help you," she says. The only camp near Vernon Silas can think of is an army boot camp.

The lemon light each morning gives rise to heat-waving days. In order for the cripple and his friend to make less cumbersome advances along the promenade, they leave Krish at home. By the end of a week they've come as far as Siwash

Rock. Silas feels some accomplishment and remembers to watch, as a sign instructs him, for rock falling off cliffs. This is wilderness indeed.

She reads him an Indian legend commemorated on a small plaque in the wall. The sea's fifty-foot rock is what Skalsh the Unselfish was turned into as his everlasting reward by Q'uas the Transformer.

Nuked, thinks Silas, this rock would fall fast. B   oom.

"Some reward," says Nadine. "I'd rather be ashes like Pauline Johnson, floating."

Already halfway, they could make it around the whole wall today if they hadn't stopped to feed him Nell's mashed bananas. Silas feels bold.

"Whe   ere," he asks between swallows, "are you and Clay   at?"

She looks at the Filipino fisherman casting his spark plug into the sea. "Ask me no questions, tell you no lies. That's what he says, so if you want me to tell you the truth, I don't know." Which puzzles Silas. He swallows his mash. "We're together, living together, but if you want to know where we're at emotionally speaking I'd have to trust what he tells me, and he tells me love, only I don't believe it 'cause he doesn't want me to. You figure it out."

Silas can't. He resists the urge to mimic her and asks what she wa   ants from Clay (sometimes it feels like he's mimicking himself).

"Like to feel safe? If you can feel safe with a guy, that's something." She spoons him more mash from Nell's Tupperware, but he pushes it away.

"You like feel sa   afe   with me?"

"Not the same thing, Si. It's you I'm making an effort to protect, sort of. It's you who's supposed to feel safe."

On the rock above them a crow is trying to land in a dead tree, but a cormorant won't let it.

"I never think about it, Si. Honest."

Her thigh horrifies him when he reaches to pat her leg.

"   I'm not tr   ying to in   terfere with you and him. Your bees   wax is your own."

"Wish Vincent believed that."

"I bel   ieve it."

Touching her, patting her, does nothing but disconnect him more from the ideals he once held about women and diplomacy. No aroma about her of baking bread or being at home with happiness. "Wha   at do you ea   t?" he asks.

"What?"

He wants to take care of her.

"Tell you what," she says. "Let's see if we can make it right around today. Before the sun gets really hot."

So he never finds out if she's snorting cocaine, smoking marijuana or doping herself up in some other way to overcome what looks to be gnawing her apart. Cocaine is Nell's theory, Nadine jumped up on drugs procured by her live-in boyfriend, the terrorist, to keep her loyal.

Rolling on as they never have, with the west wind at their backs, they make good time along this darker, cooler side of the peninsula, where gulls on the foreshore hang out in hundreds for the tide to uncover starfish and crabs. Moss grows like a sweater on the bosomy sandstone cliffs. The air smells sweet with fir.

They roll on, they wind, they overtake sauntering girls, encounter earnest couples, steer clear of short men speaking loudly, sometimes to themselves. Past, under, over and through the world on a walk built for pulling people together. Past the red foghorn atop its white dollhouse, through the stench of cormorant dung on the cliffs above, under the bridge (traffic clanking the span), over a stream flowing into the inlet out of Beaver Lake, right by Chinese fishermen, Lumbermen's Arch, picnicking Indians, English cricketers, American tourists.

Beyond Silas's expectations, hopes, wildest dreams last February, this journey's got him huffing like an old airplane taking off. Winging past his pumping, tired body are the replicated figurehead of the Empress of Japan, a bronze mermaid, the tide coming in at Brockton Point like a train. *Wheeeeeeeeeee* they fly, umbrellaless now to the floating gas stations and a view of the city's skyline. Out of breath and swollen with pride at his endurance, Silas parks himself in the shady oasis of a maple and Nadine collapses on the grass from exertion and strain. Her paddling sandals echo in his ears.

"Don't talk, okay?" she tells him. "Shit," she says, "she's going to kill me for keeping you out this long."

Hottest part of the day, month, year. A crowd of Japanese tourists strolls over from the totem poles to snap the city across the harbour. Snap me! Thinks Silas. On fire.

When Nell meets them emerging from the elevator she's enraged. *Where have they been?*

"Oh," says Nadine. "Here and there mostly." Silas just grins. And Nadine says, a little annoyed, "Piss off, Nell." Silas rocks in soundless laughter, exhausted. This lip-whipping of Nell is its own delight, just as effort and risk are their own rewards, even if you end up collapsed in bed for a week.

What's here was there.
There's what was here.

Nadine phones in the morning, but Nell hangs up. Silas works on his tongue twisters. That afternoon he dials her number from his own room on a red phone.

A man's voice answers, deeply.

"Who?" it asks.

Na   dine says Silas.

"Isn't in. Who's calling?"

Sigh   lesssss

"Les?" A bold voice, conscious of its own value, careless and proprietary. Is this Nadine mimicking Clay?

She calls back, after Silas has fallen asleep. Nell's voice squabbling in the hall is what wakes him, not his phone ringing, for the bell was removed years ago. He lifts his receiver to mediate, but he's too tired to make a sound.

He loses connection with Nadine for a week. She doesn't call for fear of disturbing him, and when he phones he gets no answer. He and Nell quarrel in the heat; it's definitely their worst week together in twenty years.

"It's no good," she tells him. "Nobody can live with you, you'll have to go into a home."

His belief is that he's entitled to holidays and a nurse who leaves him alone to enjoy them.

So she leaves him alone. She informs him of her intention to take her *own* holidays and doesn't know when she'll be back.

If she means to frighten her patient into remorse, she fails. She packs two suitcases, gauges his response, calls a cab, gauges his demeanour, says she's on her way to the bus station to visit her sister in Chilliwack, receives no comment and so is forced to depart.

Wily Silas, ex-diplomat, he's careful to exploit the guilt she feels for leaving him in the lurch. He acts nobly, tacitly, as she leaves him, will *not* cry out. He pretends his jerkiness is worse than it is by trying forcibly to compose himself.

The ruse works well. Out the window he observes how hesitantly, how palely she gives up her suitcase to the driver.

Nadine, when she comes over the next day, is shocked, not about Silas wanting to diddle her, but about Nell's desertion. Straight away (as if he'd planned it) she phones Clay to tell him she's going to be staying with Silas awhile, and she'll be back for a toothbrush.

Talk about mistaken priorities, thinks Silas.

What could she who never eats conceivably have stuck in her teeth to brush away?

July.

Even preparing his meals in the kitchen, she never so much as licks a knife. She must just brush her teeth for the taste of his toothpaste. Her breath is never bad; a faint smell sometimes as if from deep inside her heart, like a bird's burp after a worm.

Everything that can go wrong with Silas, outside of an outright attack, has. He isn't charming. His eyes grow so dim at times he thinks she has purposely hidden the sun. The opportunity of a lifetime, he thinks shacked up with a girl—and all he can do is tremble and sound like a spaced-out Mingus. Ten years have passed since they looped the seawall. Can't control his bowels and, hobbling through the bathroom door, he falls out of his shoes. His muscles in general feel like hot plastic. And the meat he calls lips needs constant exercising.

305

> A fishy old fisher named Fisher,
> Fished fish from the edge of a fissure,
> A fish with a grin
> Pulled the fisherman in,
> Now they're fishing the fissure for Fisher.

Nadine has settled into Nell's room, studies herself in the mirror, watches TV and talks on the phone for what seems like long stretches in a language alien and remote to Silas. He assumes she's talking to Clay. She denies it and claims she and Clay are better off apart for a time. When Nell calls from Chilliwack, Nadine insists it's a free world if she wants to come back, do what she likes. Her tone suggests she too will do what she likes, stick around awhile.

One afternoon she goes home with a pillowcase to bring over some more clothes.

The Fogartys figure out what's happening because she lets the dog out to roam the corridor every morning. Mrs. Fogarty comes knocking to say her husband has sent for the pound. And looks at Nadine as if it's her the pound should be called for. This building has a no-pets policy, she says. Clearly, she'd like to know where Nell is and tries to peer in. Nadine calmly tells her to return Krish or face a lawsuit. The harpy backs down and sends her husband by with the dog on a twine tether, and a stern warning.

Krish's inglorious return has a miraculous effect on his master. Face wet from licking, Silas feels like he's been bathed in the Ganges. Again his health picks up.

A week after Nell's departure he's back in the world. Full of wind, lip-whip, crankiness. Pushing his chair, Nadine wonders how he could ever have thought about becoming an ambassador with the likes of *his* crankiness.

"The likes of *your* crankiness," mimics Silas.

He flaunt his bowels like a rooster its voice. Disgusted, she blows a long strip of wind right back at him, more or less exactly in his face. Silas cackles with laughter, which stings his spine.

Well, she must have eaten *something*.

He feels cocky. Having (he believes) defeated a rival in Clay he again grows expansive about the world. My God, he babbles, why do these treaty Indians make such asses of themselves, pushing stolen shopping buggies full of beer bottles, plastic garbage bags, blankets? Maybe they're poor, says Nadine. "Why do I make such an ass of myself pushing *you*?" Yes, replies Silas, but *he* doesn't dangle big pairs of foam dice from his wheelchair. "Big risk taker," answers Nadine.

On the seawall, stalled by stupor, a pair of these inebriated Indians, a couple, won't let them past. Silas catches himself mimicking the poor man, so sure is he of his own right-of-way. He even bumps his knees up against the steel mesh, driving the buggy back into the man's knees. Trying to make him feel guilty.

"What's the matter with you, Silas?"

Nadine pulls his chair away, apologizing to the miserable and unwitting couple with their ravaged faces, and drives him on around the bend.

And for what thanks, she must wonder, for he turns to mimicking her as if it's possible to embarrass *her* in public. She laughs at him. So he says to her boldly, in what he remembers Clay's voice to sound like, "*I want you to suck my lolly, honey.*"

"Oh, Si," says Nadine, "are you ever feeling your oats. Are you ever witty."

Horsing around, living with a young woman who massages his chest, who forgets *Swank's* and sends out for pizza and Chinese food. Who watches him fill his face with McDonald's quarter pounders without nagging him about manners or warning him about cholesterol. Who is always studying herself surreptitiously in the mirror. Where does she get her energy?

A feeling like love flows into Silas's dehydrated carcass. She squeezes him orange juice. She buys him Pepsi. She pares his toenails. "What big teeth you have, Grandma!" She flosses his gums and kisses him good night. Who else lives with such attention to detail, the miraculous birth of hope, the infectiousness of an expectant age? If he puts his mind to it (scar tissue and all) he might even invent a bicycle for cripples, water skis that never waver, a wheelchair that floats. A voice that glides.

Maybe even a dish to tempt Nadine. Oh, how he would love to tempt Nadine into the fullness of the living.

A letter arrives from Nell.

> Dear Silas,
> Your floozy will not let me talk to you, so I'm writing to remind you that without me, as much as I

refuse to blow my own "horn," you would have got shut up in a home long ago instead of your own apartment. Who cut up your meat for you as well as pumped up your tires? Who put up with the smell of your unfortunate disease and mopped and washed and gave you succour in general down the years? This old farm girl, that's who, who wants to remind you that I've never considered my obligation to you a burdensome chore as you seem to think, or your own obligation to *me*, if I could so put it, Silas, something I ever thought about. I may have made a foolish mistake acting on impulse, Silas, even when you forced it on me. All I'm asking is that you answer me this,—how long is this going to go on, or do I have to prolong my holidays indefinitely? (You're the only one who can answer how you feel about your own "future," I can't, or how you would want to live in a *sty*, because I guess that's what she'll have you dragged down to soon enough, although I'm a FORGIVING person, Silas, the Lord knows why.)

"Sounds like she's tired of Chilliwack," says Nadine, putting down the letter. "You really ought to phone her, Si, tell her she can come back."

"She   e's not my mother," says Silas.

"She's not your father either."

He asks her if she wants Nell to come back because she wants to leave him.

"Well," she tells him, "I can't stay forever." Adding, for his sake, the hyperbole he gets off on, "You wear me out, Si, you've got nuts like basketballs."

"You   *hee*   *hee*   dum
b   twat!   Take of   f your panties!"

She smiles coyly. "I think it's wonderful the way we get on. I'm going to hire you to instruct Clay."

"Kiss off, Jud   ass."

"Tee-hee," she says.

She's rummaging in the closet for his leg braces.

"What's this?" she asks, unravelling a nest of red and blue wires emerging from a shoebox.

Silas looks. "Stimulation."

"Kinky," she says. "Thought they outlawed this kinda jazz with *One Flew Over the Cuckoo's Nest*."

That evening she takes him strolling along English Bay to the bathhouse, where they park to watch the sea festival. His aroused vision of the world dilates. Like Krish he drools. His gaze is determined to covet everything. The filmy blouses of thin-strapped, heavy-breasted girls in white jeans and black heels. Helium balloons shaped like silver salmon tied to the wrists of oriental infants. Bowling pins in the air around a juggler's head. Krish, too, is agog at the drama. The mincing steps of male couples in pressed jeans and white sneakers. Sloops and yawls of drinking revellers anchored offshore in the twilight. An apricot sky turning tomato, and the mountains of Vancouver Island standing up to a pink apocalypse.

Ranks and ranks of bodies are walking in both directions past Silas, as in a film by Satyajit Ray. The traffic has backed up Altamira, all the way over to the harbour. Clumps of cops are searching out rowdy behaviour to deal with swiftly.

Past the bathhouse a rock band sings on a pipe-and-plywood stage. Nadine jerks to the time. Krish howls. World War Two Hurricanes roll acrobatically overhead, trailing smoke, followed by skydivers plummeting through the fruity sky. Who will hear the splash, see the white jump-suited legs disappearing into the green water?

Not an imporant failure for the popcorn seller trying to talk Nadine into a rendezvous later. His voice sails calmly on. A Bunsen burner shines out through the glass doors of his cart.

Plump Silas stuffs popcorn into his face and sometimes misses his mouth. "God," he thinks, "I'm becoming a character."

Nadine knows he's doing it on purpose, predictable Silas, looking for sympathy. He even starts to meditate with butter on his fingers, O M M M M M M M M M M M M M M M M M M M M M M M M M, anything to keep himself in focus after twenty-three years of disconnections. His eyes play over lights flickering on across Point Grey.

Lights of the anchored freighters have also come on. The sail of a sloop going nowhere in the bay is black.

O M M M M M M M M M M M M M—

"You got a tummy ache, Si?"

Mimicking the world, he tells her, the buzzing in his ears, the babble. "l could mi   imic waves once, trains."

"What about cement drying?" (This on their roll home, up a street where the old sidewalk is being torn up because chestnut roots have lifted and made it crooked.) "What's *its* sound, huh, Si?" Nadin puffing with the strain.

"You can't mi   imic being w   alked over," Silas says.

"We could carve your initials."

"That's mo   ocking. A mo   ocker and a mi   mic are different."

"Big difference, Si. I'll use your key."

And she does, parking him at the curb, bending underneath the rope to carve the old dip into posterity.

"S I L A S   W A S   H E R E," she announces in the time it takes her to write each word in wet concrete.

Is here, *Is* is what you should have written, he thinks. *There* is where Silas *was,* on the other side of earth, when he was too young to know anything.

He smells the dew, the chestnut leaves. Feels no coolness upon his brow, only an incipient fever. Maybe Nell's caution was the right way all along.

She drives him down the middle of the road, tar bubbles popping softly and sticking to his warm tires. Golden lights come on in the windows of apartment buildings; he imagines a ticker-tape parade. But there's no place he's coming back from, could ever have come back from, victorious. Went away as a young man, came back as one, achieved nothing.

The only local hero is an Olympic sprinter, in the newspapers a few days ago, who brought home gold medals from Europe fifty years ago, and last week inside one of these buildings shot himself to death in the bathtub. These men who once flew for their country have a long way down. Silas has been lucky. He's been let down gradually from nowhere lofty. Counting down, he is *here* and hanging on.

Yet the letters of his name are already filling up with darkness.

Stuck into the outside doorjamb of his building is a diplomatic note of protest.

> Nadine, Where were you? The world turns.
> Clay

"He's a poe   et," says Silas.

"Good old Clay."

Silas hates him and closes his eyes on the short elevator ride up. He sees smelt fishermen casting their nets like cages against the sky, and this distance between him and them across the sand, vast space, is how far he is from Clay. Trying to get to where the tide is would bog Silas down. Infinite bloody sand, he'd need a camel. He hates the way Clay's knuckles peek out in rows above his jean pockets. Hates the bulge in his crotch, his scruffy cowboy boots, the way his voice falls like canine urine over Silas, as over a fire hydrant to mark off territory. With no morality, let him count sand, this terrorist who wants to kidnap Nadine. Silas is on Vincent's side.

He never wants to meet Clay.

Before tucking him in, she helps him clean out butter under his nails, floss his teeth and blow his nose. The dental string twanging sounds like a banjo. First she puts the dog to bed, then Silas. She comes into his bedroom and kisses him good night on the temples. (Never, alas, his lips.)

"W hy are y ou so thi in?"

"Don't I wish." She cannot see herself as she appears in the mirror.

When she shuts the door he turns his lamp back on. From under the blanket, too warm anyway, he fishes out her wallet, opens the drawer of his side table and removes the cash left over from this month's household expenses. He opens her wallet and pushes the bills inside.

Curiosity causes him to remove a folded-over piece of newspaper in her billfold. A yellowing, dateless letter to the editor, signed "C. Wade," from an address on East Twelfth Avenue.

Sir, It has become clear the most violent countries in total are now Latin American. They are also the most in debt, with the greatest disparity between rich and poor. Death squads and military tyrants prevail there. Freedom to form effective oppositions is denied and Freedom's advocates are imprisoned, tortured and executed. Canada can't claim to have a clear conscience with respect to what's happening in these countries. Our churches stay officially neutral. Our diplomats continue to negotiate business and banking transactions throughout Latin America, as if these Fascist regimes they keep propped up were legitimate! We give tacit support to American imperialism. We provide dictators with the technology to make atomic bombs and send our salesmen to negotiate the best terms for us. The violence we help sow means the long road to freedom and independence in South and Central America—if it hasn't already been blown up and made impassable—is now sprouting with corpses. Will nothing shake our complacency?

Underneath the writer's address, in Nadine's hand, is a phone number jotted down in ballpoint ink.

Silas tries to fall asleep. He fiddles with the Snooze Control on his clock radio, flips awhile through the turquoise numbers and can't decide if he wants to wake up to music and the alarm or just to music. He counts to a hundred in French listening to an exquisite (he rakishly insists) bel-cunto aria. A toilet above him flushes and falls. He rummages in his head for tongue twisters. *The bottom of the butter bucket is the buttered bucket bottom. Five French friars fanning a fainted flea.* He never forgets a tongue twister. He tries to remember everything he saw this evening but his mind wanders to something amazing. He turns on the lamp to find a poem, hoping to read himself into tranquillity. He finally diddles himself to sleep but never comes. Such a weekend wanker.

He wakes up wet and thirsty, crying (he discovers touching his face). He's aware of Nadine's voice somewhere in the apartment and sleeps another three years. Such are the gaps between his hearing and remembering, himself or anyone else.

He dreams of warm white fish, of a grandmother he never had, who canned tuna fish once in a great oven of her own invention, sealing it with a lid of heavy ornate design. Years later he has returned to a sideless barn beyond which there's nothing but white light, to open the stove with a can opener. Amazingly, the white flesh is still as warm as the day his grandmother preserved it fifty years ago. In the barn are dray horses the size of elephants. Before he's allowed to taste the fish, she tells him to climb up hay bales and drop onto the backs of the horses to unharness them. But fire breaks out. The horses panic. Silas gets frightened and wakes up.

———————

To the sound of voices arguing in the living room. They possess no diplomatic inflections. The sound of him and Nell squabbling is what it sounds like, their twenty-year relationship reduced to nattering in a far-off living room where no true living has ever gone on.

"*Don't you think I smell? Smell me. I ooze rot like an abscessed tooth.*"

"*Eat!*"

Compassion for shopping-cart stealers pinches his spine and makes him savour the pain he deserves. Yes, how well he recognizes suffering. Eventually. He imagines hearing Clay's piss thunder into the toilet bowl at four in the morning, a bladder with the compression of a firehose.

A dozen years later, morning arrives to the sound of violent retching in the bathroom, nausea rattling her tonsils, Nadine throwing up. He listens to the cat tastro ophic sounds of her misery. A bird of no paradise in need of comfort. He says nothing to her when she comes in as usual to lift, shift and bounce him like a car with a bad battery, to get him going for the day. She looks wan. He doesn't wish to fail her, but senses he does by remaining polite and noncommittal in the face of her drowning.

The kettle in the kitchen puckers, whistles, screams. She goes out to make tea and he's left alone with his shirt buttons. She returns to fit him into his leg braces, in which he walks a few steps to his wheelchair before steering himself (rekindled for the world) out to greet his dog. Where is his dog?

The apartment door is just closing.

"W   ho's that?" he says startled. "Di   id you hear the door?" he calls to Nadine.

She comes into the hall. "Probably Clay. I forgot to say he came over last night, after you went to bed. Hope you don't mind."

"He was he   ere all night?"

"Yeah."

Well. He wonders if her hair is really dirty, or just aping the fashion in women's hair these days. Dyed and scraggy. Starved bodies in peasant dresses. He's unsure of where Nadine in her colourless cheeks is *at*.

Or where he is at. When she gets tired of him, he's going to need all his diplomacy to woo back Nell. He can't live without somebody to look after him. Which is maybe what old Vincent was thinking of—his own decline, hoping to woo back his daughter.

She does up his shirt without noticing the funny look on his face. He's staring at the dining-room table covered in half-eaten buns, glasses and beer bottles. Empty coleslaw containers and plastic forks. Nell's good china smeared with ketchup, the greasy remains of chips and chocolate pudding. And bones, everywhere. In the kitchen, Krish has his head stuck inside a Kentucky Fried Chicken bucket.

"Sorry 'bout the fucking mess," she says, picking the morning paper off the floor. "Clay and I had a pig-out." A Skippy Peanut Butter jar and an empty brick of ice cream. Silas can't decide what to say. Then Krish comes in licking his chops to greet him. Silas rubs the dog's throat and actually thanks Nadine for being such a good Samaritan, for taking care of him in a pinch.

"You mean Krish?"

"M   e."

This surprises her. "Looking after you isn't a Girl Scout act, Silas. Like visiting you, when I finished high school, it was just something I wanted to do. Shit, visiting Vincent wasn't what I wanted to do. You might've seen me twice as often if something better hadn't turned up."

He chuckles at her honesty.

She says, "I don't know if I will, since Nell's not here now, and on account of your being on your holidays and that, but if I suddenly get the urge to take off with Clay, I might...You know what I'm saying?"

He's never wrong about loneliness, this ex-diplomat.

"If he feels li   ike it, Clay can come he   ere, maybe."

"Thanks."

"To live awhi   ile?"

"I'll tell him."

She steeps some Nabob, pours skim milk into her cup followed by the tea. Tea is all he has ever seen her consume, and even now surrounded by dirty dishes and gnawed bones he finds it strange to think of her as a consumer of any food at all. "I need a laxative," she says. She adds boiling water to a mug of Sanka and hands it to him with a little milk. Then she takes up her tea with both palms, as if warming them. Her arms are bamboo, bamboo.

"WhatisClayanyway?" he asks suddenly.

"Clay?"

"Re   evolutionar   y?"

"Search me. You think he is?"

"Doeshegiveyoucocaine?"

She laughs sharply. "What?"

"Do you do do   ope with him?"

"Oh, Si. You have a choice way with words . . ." So out of it, she means, his slang embarrassing.

He's thinking she doesn't eat because her hunger pangs are usually drugged.

"Coke?" She sips her tea and knees Krish away from her crotch. "Probably he keeps a lid of grass around his place. Sometimes we might smoke that."

Silas says, "I thin   ink your father's r   ight."

"Right of Idi Amin, maybe."

She looks at him, trying to decide if it's worth the effort, explaining baseballs to a monkey.

"Vincent cared for my mother like a lawn. He walked all over her. He wore white shoes, I remember, probably still does. They might as well have been hiking boots. You know?" Silas doesn't know anything. "That's why she went home. He didn't approve of her in general like. Thought she was dumb and couldn't be shaped in his own image like he hoped." Her sunken eyes squint like an old woman's. "Maybe Clay's right. Maybe I should keep my mouth shut, take his money and split."

"Fifty-fifty?"

"What? No, split. Run away."

"W   here?"

"São Paulo. To see my mother."

She tells him Vincent always had to know everything about his wife, like what she was thinking when she sat out on the verandah, what she said in her letters home. He made her tear up letters if they sounded illiterate. He wouldn't even let her come into the city alone shopping. "Why are men like him always trying to piss on things?"

"In thei   r genes?"

"But you're a man," she says.

"I'm dise   eased."

He concentrates as he pours milk all over his Special K, on a trip to Florida he could win by sending a box top away before next November. Nadine is scrounging in the freezer compartment of the refrigerator for a lump of frozen hamburger.

"Guess he won't eat this," she says, unwrapping the cellophane lump and dropping it into Krish's dish. "I forgot to feed him last night, and he shouldn't have chicken bones, should he?"

Krish feigns disinterest and yawns at Silas. Silas kisses the air, a token of his affection, and the dog blinks in satisfaction. As an afterthought he decides to sniff the beef. A lick and a promise is all he earns from the frozen lump. Nell, who purchased this lean meat for human consumption, would crucify Nadine if she could see Krish meditating over it.

"What do you feel like having for lunch, if I pack your saddlebag?"

Silas doesn't feel like going to the beach, but won't admit it. "The usual?" he says. Tonight she's even promised to take him to the fireworks to mark the end of the sea festival.

"I'm taking my bathing suit," she says. "I've been thinking how awful I look, not my arms, but the rest of me is totally milk. I've got my mother's complexion so I tan fast. That is, if you think you can stand the heat. Remind me to bring your umbrella."

Maybe his beard has slowed down, anyway she forgets to shave him, merely combs his hair. This stroking must be what Krish feels: the comb's wide, white teeth making moan the ego beneath. He feels depressed. The seeds of another attack feel sown in his calves. (Are his braces too tight?) He throbs between the shoulder blades, already feels exhausted, has a headache. He's certain Clay's presence hasn't lifted his spirits much. Last night the sound of a foghorn hailing winter might have easily pushed him back down the well.

He feels tearful for no good reason. He doesn't *want* to resist where his tiredness cares to take him. Watching her at the counter cutting Cheddar, Silas misses her already with a yearning she has no idea he's feeling. How indifferent he is when she's with him all the time, how irritable too, at her noisiness in the kitchen, her habit of leaving drawers open, lights burning, the radio blaring. He is already remembering her. He feels disconnected.

"Yuck, listen to this, Si," she says, lifting the newspaper and putting aside the Cheddar.

"'Poor people in eastern India have begun to eat elephant meat, threatening the animals' existence, the *Hindustan Times* reported Sunday . . .'" She reads to herself for a moment. "It's because of crop failures, or something, and nobody's got jobs," she says. "So what else is new? Orissa's chief game warden says it's an unheard of thing, eating elephants. Sign of an ominous trend, he says."

Her mouth turns downward in disbelief. "It says 'When

an elephant died in the area, people from far-off villages came carrying axes, meat cleavers, and large hoes to chop off chunks of meat...'. Gross," says Nadine.

"W   hat else?" says Silas.

She reads, "'"People prepared elephant meat the same way as lamb," said a range officer. One villager said it tasted like lamb, but was a bit coarse. "But we are poor people and any meat is good for us."'"

She has forgotten to do the voices. Her finger scouts the margin for more.

"That's all. Elephant!"

He studies her pale and bony face as she rereads the story.

"Totally gross," she concludes, throwing the paper aside on the counter.

Silas comments, "I   it's like eating thems   elves."   319

At the beach, flying the colours, they meet head-on the healthy of every age. White-haired men in leathery skins hunting the tide line, boys in swimsuits throwing wet sand at each other's knees, girls like gazelles with their wallets in hand, strolling barefoot to concession stalls.

Parked in his own shade, overlooking the sea from a knoll, Silas tries to remember the name of his dog. It lies on his tongue like bread he can't taste, hangs in the air like a field he can't smell. He strains to remember what

"Kri   ish!"

His tail moving, Krish sits up dutifully, uninterested in hoisting his haunches on such a humid day for no other reason than a master's whim.

"Krish!" cries Silas.

The dog stands up, places a paw on his arm and licks his face in a slow, obligatory way. Revived, Silas remembers he forgot to practise his tongue twisters this morning.

At his feet in the grass, Nadine is oiling herself. She has stripped down to a meagre black bikini. When she stands up it seems clear to him she's dying.

She wants him to oil her back. "My bum is really white," she says, twitching it, "make sure you grease that too."

I want a dozen double damask dinner napkins

Touching her shocks him. Sharp bones, along with her spine and shoulder blades, appear out of paper skin, while the shoulders themselves seem pinioned to the torso. A rib cage clamps two lungs in place, barely, and her stomach protrudes like a malnourished Ethiopian child's.

"Lower," she says. "Do my bum."

His hands outraged, his palms feel guilty for cupping half her body in a gesture. He can't go lower.

"What's the matter, Si? I thought I turned your crank."

His hands feel prickly and spurts of real weakness pulse at his temples. He feels like throwing up.

She says, "I can see where I'm going to have to get my father after you with a shotgun, Si."

Kneeling down slowly on a towel she oils her own bum, the backs of her legs, and then realizes she wants to lie on her back. Silas is staring at her. None of the people suntanning on blankets nearby take any notice of her condition. Their blindness is mystifying.

He overhears two young couples discussing Dr. Spock's discredited theories of war. They sound so businesslike and conservative he closes his eyes. Radios tuned to different stations, screams from the pool, a seaplane. He opens them to look at her again, expecting a tapeworm to stick out its head through her ear, in quest of nourishment. The two couples are sharing fried fish and ice cream.

The fish sauce shop's sure to sell sauce for my fish
yes

He hangs on to the red, white and green. The sun must climb to the zenith before it begins to fall westward over the gulf.

Count the freighters.

Squeeze this umbrella.

Fondle your pet.

His pet has dug itself a hole under the nearby salal. Silas tries to look at a copy of *Time,* but the coloured plates are blurred, so he lifts his head to pee. The heat feels like a wool blanket covered in marmalade.

"The bloody blue I'm looking at with my eyes shut is bluer than the sky," says Nadine. "Violet. The colour I bet astronauts dream." She opens her eyes and looks right into the sky. "It's something I could do as a little girl, look right into the sun. I wanted to be an astronaut."

He imagines the languid way girls wait under the firs here at sunset for lifeguards to get off duty, summer after summer, girls in their cars, while the policeman's horse scratches its innocent behind on the bark.

"Hey," she says, hauling herself up. "Are you crying?"

He's certainly sniffling.

His umbrella falling seems to have knocked the Polaroids off the bridge of his nose.

"You need some orange juice," she says and digs into his saddlebag for a Thermos. Swallowing, or trying to, the spastic spills juice on his shirt and slaps the cup from her hand.

ba   ack   home

But the cat's got his tongue, sleeping on top of it by the taste of the fur.

"By the look of you," says Nadine, "you need a snooze." She retrieves the Thermos lid and screws it back on. She sponges off his shirt with her towel.

"Soon as I have a quick swim, I'll take you home." To cheer him up she reminds him of the fireworks tonight. "They'll be wicked, Si. Make you feel better."

The setter follows her down to the swimming pool. Silas has forgotten his own dog's name again. He tries to remember his old nurse's name. The thing is to locate the right circuits and re

Retrace them.

Now the dog's barking at this girl he knows wading into

He feels feverish.

The dog is bar

wherebodiesaresocrowdeditlookslikethebaptismofmulti-tudes.

This tide, for Silas, goes in and out about a thousand times.

He loses   of her among th   spla   shing each oth   with th   enthus   of

---

Fished up from sleep, Silas responds to his name. He names the dog and the girl. Does he want some supper, asks Nadine, before she takes him to the fireworks? He adjusts his vision like a pair of pyjamas. His legs feel as limber as licorice sticks, and therefore unreliable. All right, he'll have a little soup.

The strenuous struggle seemed superfluous

At least Nell knew from experience when his symptoms looked critical. Is he beginning to yearn for the old lady again? Talk about patriots, this ex-diplomat knows a thing or two about loyalty when it counts.

The crowd at the bay reminds him of an Indian funeral for some holy man. Ten, twenty thousand people waiting for the fireworks to happen, sitting in the grass and sand. His dog is at home, his umbrella is at home, his saddlebag is at home. His mistress squats by his wheel. Everybody is patient, awaiting darkness.

Crammed with pleasure craft, the sea gets scalded by the embers of pink rescue flares shooting heavenward from bored skippers. People go aaah. A police helicopter cutting arcs overhead makes Silas wonder what would happen if a flare hit a rotor blade. A snicker ripples through the crowd when a defective flare fizzles and dies without ascent. Already the air's clogged with smoke that stretches back across the city.

With darkness the crowd grows noisy. Air horns from motor launches are saying it's time. Pensioners are moving their spotted hands in pleasurable anticipation. Teenagers ask what are they doing on that barge, waiting for Halloween? Everybody's sense of time is suddenly acute.

But the barge blowing up fireworks is anchored too far out and the spectacle is disappointing. A few people even boo, though most say nothing and politely applaud the dramatic if distant sequences. Nadine says you can tell how far away the barge is by how long each boom takes to reach them. It's like an eruption in another country. Ash, gunpowder, smoke: to Silas the wonder is any of these stars can be seen.

"Did the Chinese invent firecrackers?" Nadine asks him.

He feels like scorched pasture. A monsoon seems about to burst inside his brain. A brain meant to leap to conclusions, like a bridge over space, but when he tries to think of his dog's name, even this girl's, he can't.

Could he find his way home? If he could somehow push himself down across the sand, launch himself in the bay, could he find his way anywhere amidst all these boats? Trying to cool off, could he sail calmly on through the death of flares and stars?

```
                the          ese
        wh          eels          mired i          n
```
"What's the matter, Silas?"
```
cha            air to          coo      l      his
```
On the way home people float past them as she pushes him through streets he hardly remembers. Her fingers keep slipping inside the finger channels as she strains forward in an acrid, gunpowdery air that threatens rain. Mixed in with

the smell of gunpowder is the smell of burning garbage. She moves like she's doomed to push him uphill forever.

When they arrive, apparently back inside his own apartment, the lights are on and a young man is sitting in the living room.

"Who let you in?" asks Nadine, surprised.

"I did."

Says Nell, grudgingly, in the kitchen wearing wet rubber gloves and an apron. She's confronting dishes, a mountain of them by the look of it.

"The world turns," says the young man, rising from his chair. He must be in his thirties, of lithe posture with a resonant voice and sharp Adam's apple. He's wearing jeans and a PAX MAN sweatshirt.

"Si, this is Clay."

"Nice to know you," says the young man. He fingers blond hair off his high damp forehead.

to   you

"What've you done to him?" asks Nell. "He can't talk."

"He's gelled, I guess. Too many people at the beach."

"If you ask me, he's well on his way to losing his pins. He's put on weight." She removes a rubber glove to place her palm on his brow. "He's burning up."

"Is he?" says Nadine.

She might as well have said, "Then call the fire department." Her interest for the moment is Clay. Shy and a little tentative with each other, in need of quiet conversation in a corner, these two have matters to clear up.

But the toilet flushes, and out of the bathroom on his cane walks Vincent.

"Jesus," says Nadine. "It's a congress."

"People are concerned about you," says the old man. He makes no attempt to greet her, turning instead to Silas. "Hello, Silas. This is a poor time to disturb you, I know. Please accept my apologies. It's rather important."

Nadine says, "Is it?"

"You listen to your father, young lady!" says Nell, wheeling suddenly as if in anxious possession of state secrets and nowhere to discuss them but underground, here in Silas's apartment where she's convened ambassador and terrorist alike. The least Nadine can do is show a little respect. The old nurse in her gloves stands like a surgeon about to operate instead of a scullery maid poised to tackle a kitchen full of dirty dishes. "What a sty," she comments. "My good china's caked in fat."

Vincent settles himself carefully into a soft chair. He's wearing a cream suit and maroon tie, colours Silas would normally associate with off-the-record negotiating, if he wasn't trying to remember the name of his dog again, who's sniffing everybody's knees, hands and crotches. He hasn't seen Nell in weeks, possibly years, and tries to bite her dress.

"Down!" warns Nell. His tongue settles into a loll.

Vincent says politely to Clay, "Perhaps you'd be kind enough to show my daughter a chair, as she seems indifferent to her own comfort?"

"I'll bring in a kitchen chair," offers Nell.

"I'll stand," says Nadine.

She and Clay remain standing, a little apart, and the silence is full of an atmosphere that escapes Silas entirely.

The snow-haired ambassador slowly reaches inside his jacket, perhaps to test his heart. "Nell," he says, "when she came home was opening the mail and found this." He removes a paper from his pocket and unfolds it. "A telephone bill, my dear. Long distance to Brazil, on two occasions, a total of forty-three minutes. Does Silas know he's going to have to pay this?"

"I'm not ripping anybody off," says Nadine. "What is this?"

"He's worried," Clay says.

"No kidding."

"I want to help, my dear. You know that. I'll fix up Silas for these calls."

"No."

She looks at Clay. "I'm free to refuse his bloody aid, aren't I?" As much a challenge, it sounds, as an invitation to agree with her.

"In your condition," Vincent says, "are you free to refuse looking after yourself?"

"I'm free."

Clay says, "He's decided you have a responsibility."

"Well, I'm really fed up with him trying to tell me what it is."

"How are you feeling?" asks Clay.

"I'm still wishing."

"I'm worried about you," he says.

Silas (out of it) wanders around in his mind like the setter, off sniffing a silverfish he's squashed with his paw. Everyone ignores the man in the wheelchair. Everyone except Nell, whose gloved hand on his shoulder wants him to know he possesses the good favour of enough people present to persuade them all to become amicable, if only he would speak. She's solicitous, a little unsure of her position after being away, but moving to retake it from Nadine. Her diplomacy is interested.

She bends over him soothingly. "We all want what's best for Nadine, Silas."

Nadine stares at her. "You look like a fishmonger in those things."

Silas feels the rubber on his shoulder tighten, then relax when Vincent says, "Nell is speaking the truth, Nadine." This distinguished ambassador mentions receiving several phone calls from a very worried woman—Nell here.

He returns the phone bill to his pocket. "I want to be candid," he says to her. "Nell doesn't think you've been doing Silas any favours, although I'm sure Silas could tell us of many kindnesses you've shown him."

Then he skips down the agenda so abruptly it's as if he's speaking in another language. "My dear," he says, looking at Nadine in a welling-up way. "If you do decide not to have your child, Silas and Nell would be the first to applaud your decision, because they know your health is number one…"

In the old days, Silas might have reached for earphones to get a simultaneous translation. Now, gaps in his comprehension mean he can offer nothing to the meeting, not even his inklings. He has understood, it seems, nothing whatsoever.

"If you'd just agree to see a doctor," declares Vincent, "he'd tell you it doesn't make sense to go on saying you want a child that's sure to be born deficient. My dear, look at yourself! What's the good in it? You don't have the means to support a handicapped child. Your friend here tells me frankly it was an accident. I believe him. But you can't allow an accident to ruin your life—if you'll allow me to finish—any more than your refusal to take care of yourself has ruined it already."

His tone is conciliatory, gentle. Clay, in a gesture of loyalty, puts his arm around Nadine's bamboo shoulder.

Nell presses Silas's neck under the earlobe.

"He's on fire," she says quietly. "His so-called holidays have taken the mickey out of him."

"What I'm willing to do," continues Vincent, "is negotiate."

Nadine says to him, "You mean I see a doctor to get my guts sucked out and you give me your money?"

Silence.

She turns to Clay. "Let's go."

Silas, who has been dreaming he has no presence, no clout, no wishes to be taken into consideration anymore at such a congress, spits in his lap.

"He's drooling," says Clay.

Nell wipes his mouth with her apron. She presses him forward, wedging in a cushion to relieve the pressure on his spine.

saw   flares

"What's he saying?" says Clay.

flares

"The fireworks were too much for him," Nell says. "Is that where you were," she asks Nadine, "the fireworks?"

"The fireworks were a disappointment," says Nadine.

"The fireworks were a disappointment," repeats Nell.

Nadine says, "Did you see them?"

"Me? You wouldn't catch me dead in that madhouse."

"I don't intend on just walking out," says Nadine.

"I beg your pardon?" says Nell.

"Silas is going to have to tell me he never wants to see me again, or I'll be back."

Sigh   less   's   poo   ped

"What Silas," says Nell, "is going to get is a good long rest, the monkey. Look at him. This here's the start of an attack on his whole system. I recognize the symptoms," she says, "if you can't."

Vincent, of course, understands the necessity of recognizing his old friend's state, the priority of his current condition. He hastens to say to Nadine, "Perhaps we could work out a compromise, Nadine, and leave Silas in peace."

His watery blue eyes drop to the tip of his cane lifted off the floor for his own minute inspection.

Then Nell tells her, "I think you ought to forget about Florence Nightingaling and listen to what your father's telling you."

"My father isn't telling me anything, because I don't have a father."

"What I'd like to say to you," says Vincent, "is that as a compromise I'm willing to trust you to do what's best for yourself." He is sitting very erect and intent on avoiding a complete breach. "I have to give my estate to somebody. You can appreciate that, can't you? Can't you, my dear? If you would just be willing to put yourself in a hospital, voluntarily, I'm willing to accept whatever the doctor suggests would be best for your health. That's my offer. I mean, there'd be no other strings. Your relationship with this young man is your own business. As far as I'm concerned I'll resist him because of what I think he's done to your life in general. Threatened your health, violated your priorities, brought you grief. So the money would go to you only. How you handled it, of course, is up to you. All you must do is promise me to put yourself in a hospital—right away."

veddy   veddy   crooked

Clay, who has suddenly everything to gain, looks down into Nadine's eyes.

He says to her, throwing away his lines, "I should tell you, earlier on Vincent and I were talking about Latin America, since he's supposed to be an expert on that part of the world, and I was asking him, wasn't I, sir, just where we're at in this country vis-à-vis the Fascists in those countries, and what he said to me was, just before you came in, we're nowhere, Clay, we've got a long ways to go, and I warned him the fighting's going to get a lot worse before it gets much better."

Ever the actor, he removes a package of Matinées one-handed from his shirt and puts a cigarette between his lips. The other hand is still around Nadine's bony shoulder.

"Your father actually sounded sympathetic," he says, a little mockingly, the unlit cigarette waggling in his lips. "He reminded me of a guy in my cab the other day, just back from pissing around under a palm tree, trying to sell what he claimed was international hardware. On his way to lunch and mad at a traffic jam. Couldn't understand how people just sat there not blowing their horns or getting mad. This guy said somebody could threaten to drop a bomb and the fools'd still be waiting at their wheels for the road to clear when it fell. 'A backward race,' he says to me."

The way Clay removes his cigarette by fingering its unlit tip is effortless, even graceful.

"This guy," he says, "opens his briefcase and I thought he was going to take out either his wallet or a bomb. Instead, he reaches up and takes off his hair. Lifts it clean off his head and locks it up inside his briefcase. His own hair was the same colour, but shorter, it made him look younger. 'These days,' he says, 'you can't be too careful.' Then he opens his billfold and hands me a fifty-dollar bill. 'Keep the change,' he says in this offhand way. All of a sudden he's out the door and hurrying away down the middle of the street. In the direction of lunch, I guess. Weaving in and out of the traffic till he's gone without a trace. Poof."

He's still talking to Nadine. "Nada," he tells her.

For the first time she smiles at him. Maybe she thinks she has won something. "Nada," she says.

The terrorist gives her shoulder a squeeze and removes his hand to light up, blowing smoke smartly through his nostrils before dropping his match through the open window into Fogarty's garden.

"Whew," says Nell. She knows when she's been listening to a whopper, waving her hand in the smoke's direction.

Outside the rain has started to fall against the window.

 dull   gung

Chuckling, Clay says, "I was going to buy myself a free lunch, you see, but I never did. I'm incorruptible."

Nadine says, "Since you've still got it then, give it here."

Her tone is firm. He studies her awhile, dabbing at a shred of tobacco on his tongue. Then shrugs and, squinting against his own smoke, reaches with both hands for his back pocket and makes a show, perhaps for Vincent, of fanning his thumb over bills in his wallet.

Nadine plucks the fifty-dollar bill from him like Kleenex and walks across the room to Vincent.

"What's this for?" he asks, uncrossing his legs.

"I must owe you a fortune for my education, Vincent."

"I don't understand."

Nell is taking Silas's pulse at the wrist. "He feels like death warmed over." She wipes his mouth again with her apron. "Stop chewing," she tells him.

But his eyes are on Nadine, his hands, his breath.

sit   twirl   swe   eet   hee hee

He seems to be huffing like an overheated dog, though the truth is he's having a pee, his own warm secret.

Vincent has risen on his oak cane to address his daughter (nobly, it turns out), Clay's currency in his hand.

"Honestly, nothing would give me greater pleasure, Nadine, than to hear you had recovered your health and to know, in spite of my lapses as a father, that in some small way I'd helped you on your way in the world . . ."

veddy veddy

"There, there," Nell tells Silas, who is gesticulating limply. At the same time, loyalties divided, she's saying to Vincent, who has a crisis on his own hands, "Oh, you poor man . . ."

Nadine has left Vincent and come to Silas. She reaches for his fingers, to tend their warm buds. Bridges close across gaps. She says to him, "I thought I knew what I was doing, Silas, straining and pushing myself behind your chair. I thought I was doing the right thing, sort of. You couldn't even see what I was doing, could you, Si? You just wanted me to feel safe."

"Why don't you quit pestering him now?" Nell says. "Look at the state he's in. He can't hear you, he's got his own pain."

But perhaps Silas can hear, for he seems to be remembering every word as he hears it, years and years ago. If only somebody would remind him of his dog's name, he could call him.

"You asked me where I was at, Silas," Nadine goes on. She nods in Clay's direction. "Here with him, I guess. Now."

Silas, the pig, is drooling again. About drooling he's never wrong.

"He can't hear you," says Nell. "He's dozing."

The girl's voice grows louder in its affection, as if she's out-side on the promenade, wanting him to laugh at the recollec-tion.

"*You hear what I'm saying to you?*" she asks. "*I'm going home 'cause no woman's an island, okay? 'Cause you're decay-ing, amigo, decaying. Living for nothing but yourself, eating my flesh and gnawing my bonywonies. What we say in Portuguese is kiss off, amigo . . .*" Mouth on her like a rathole. "You under-stand what I'm saying to you . . . dear Silas?"

The ex-dip, rocking spastically, witless and at sea, drool-ing.

Maybe, on the other hand, he's enjoying himself.

From her years of experience Nell knows when the advan-tage has fallen her way, a treaty as good as signed, and so she can afford to move tolerantly, in defence of her patient's well-being, or what's left of it, and not a minute too soon.

"Leave us in peace," she tells Nadine, "no more of your squalor . . ."

ding

                             dong

           leav

                       in

  g

Slumped in his chair, corpulent, whimpering for a

"You tried, Silas," the girl says. "We both tried to get away." She draws Clay to her side. "When Clay and I scrape enough together we'll probably take off and have this kid with my mother. We'll take a holiday."

"Slut!" hisses Nell. "Why don't you listen to your poor father?"

Such an unbearable situation for her, old and perspiring with the excitement of her own homecoming, she gathers

Silas's head between her large breasts to arrest its swaying, to wipe his mouth, to apologize for having left him in the care of no one.

"Thanks, Si, for that money you put in my wallet. I might buy a dress. Five dresses."

"C'mon, sugar," says Clay.

Nell watches him take the girl out, his arm around her hip. Good riddance to bad rubbish.

Vincent is watching too. His training will not desert him (even in defeat), nor will the suitable possession of charm in crisis vanish. He can count on his charm to pull him through, though not out of suffering, about which it seems he is always wrong.

"I apologize most sincerely for this scene in your living room, Nell. I don't understand the young anymore."

Grey eminence to his end, an ambassador recalled.

"Amen to that, Vincent. You just let me know how you're making out in that old-folks' home, will you? Like I say, I want to come and visit you one day maybe for lunch." It tickles her to look down fondly at the top of Silas's head in her arms, to spot dandruff in his thinning scalp. This Pièta of old Nell and pooped-out Silas. "You never know," she says, "when you might need a friend like old Nell. When you get on, you need more than your own company. Don't you, Silas? Say good night to your old friend, Silas."

                              goo
        goo
              hee
                       he
                       nose
        a thin
                  g   *or two*

She has him   the shoulders now, big mus   cular
Nell   fro   th   prairies dragg   in   him off
to   b   lik   e   a   sac   o
f   whea

13 WAYS OF
LISTENING TO
A STRANGER

S O *WHO CARES if he's a recidivist* says Howard *so long as he respects the TV news hour and isn't responsible for the SMELL in this house.* Howard won't lock his door. He says Kerby's a shoplifter, not a thief.

What's the diff? Andrew asks him.

Lots says Howard. *Thievery is antisocial.*

Here comes the whale you guys so can it. Old Gerry asking for quiet so we can find out more about whales landing dead on beaches in White Rock. Yesterday we got only part of the story and a full twelve seconds of footage. *Lookit* says Gerry. *Goddamn WHALE.*

Around here we're conditioned to lifting words above TV.

Gerry's divorced and a laid-off sawmill worker in his fifties *too one-stroke* he says *to do anything else.* He's never had a holiday, outings hardly. The beach, he confided once, he remembers for a memory of his son as an infant. Gerry was tending him in the sand at a picnic like a small fire in the wind. He cupped his hands around the cheeks, banked up the blankets, he didn't know what all he didn't do to keep his son warm in the ocean breeze. He's the only man I've heard admit nursing mothers aren't the only ones who feel sexual twinges breast-feeding babies. *Nursing fathers feel it too, bottle-feeding. Boy, I don't want to sound like a PERVERT* said Gerry. *Just a fact. You feel twinges in your organ.* And he said *You can really love a baby.* He guessed his son would be somewhere in his twenties now. Could barely remember the little boy. Gerry could hardly veil the sorrow coming back to him from a distance, when he listened.

More shots of the dead whale on the beach. *Jesus* says Gerry. Greenpeace has asked an American biologist from the Marine Animal Resource Center to come across the border to perform an autopsy. He's attacked the whale's carcass with a Japanese flensing knife. Spectators on the pier, on the beach. Guts tumble down the mountain of carcass to hill up in the wet sand. *Lookit the tongue lolling* says Gerry. The whale's tongue is French kissing the sand and the mouth, like the end of pleasure, curls up in a little smile. Gerry whistles.

Seven or eight of us are boarders here, men without families, taking our supper after the news hour from Mr. and Mrs. Carlin. Mr. Carlin has muttered he thinks the smell might be a dead mouse, caught between studs in the wall, joists in the floor, rotting. *Keep it under your hat* he says. The missus is after him to call in the pest people and not ignore what's getting worse. We all agree with Mrs. Carlin. Call in the pest people, the marines, anybody to figure out what the matter is. It's a question of having to breathe shallower and shallower every day now.

On TV, Tony Parsons is saying officials fear it's likely too late to matter if they retrieve the liver or not. The whale's been beached five days. Enough time for vital organs to deteriorate.

What was it says Howard *an ALCOHOLIC whale?* He'd be surprised says old Gerry. If he wants to hear the dope just listen to what he's being told. Howard watches. We all watch. The American biologist cuts and saws the washed-up grey whale for blubber, blood and lymph-gland samples. *In its last two hours of ignominy* says Andrew. *B-lub-ber* says Howard, popping his lips. This isn't the first whale. Two or three dead whales have washed up at Mud Bay and Boundary Bay in the past month. A helicopter camera shows an aerial view of driftwood on a shoreline, then, cutting lower, of bones like a wrecked ship's ribs. Then back to the sawing biologist in White Rock.

When we're watching him who should wander in but Kerby, the shoplifter. He does a long take at the carcass. *That is a DEAD PARROT* he says. *What d'you mean it's a dead parrot?* He answers himself. *It's DEAD!* he screams. *Is NOT* he answers *that parrot is just sleeping.*

Choke it, Kerby growls Gerry. Kerby falls backward into the pink armchair in a frozen bow.

The autopsy is intended to find out if these whaling casualties might be related to toxins from a rumoured spill at a paint-and-chemical plant. *Shit* says Gerry. *Should see what sawmills pump into the river. Incredible there ain't salmon dead stiff from here to Yokohama. It's them chemicals, I know it. Chemicals in the water, chemicals in the air, chemicals in our goddamn food. Goddamn chemicals every place. These guys* says Gerry. *Whadda these guys in factories care? They don't care.* He says he feels cheesed off, browned off and hoofed out. Hoofed out because he got laid off when the lumber markets collapsed. *Thought you were talking about whales* says Howard. *I am* says Gerry. *The pissing factories are poisoning us.*

We might find something says the biologist. *But it would surprise me.* Andrew doesn't disagree with authority. *Another beautiful mammal down the tube to pesticides* he says. But Kerby is back for an encore. *PLUMAGE!* he screams, rising from his chair. *LOOK AT THE PLUMAGE! IT'S WILTED!* Kerby can boil up his face like John Cleese.

Gerry glances at him. *Boy, what a jerk.*

Say what you LIKE! shouts Kerby. *I know a dead parrot when I see one!*

When this joker leaves us to wash up for supper, Andrew turns to Howard. *I'd lock my door if I was you.*

Gerry would like to know where Andrew gets his info and fancy words. *ReciddaWHAT?* he says. *Sounds like somebody who does sumpin' to little girls in the holly.* Howard thinks we should all gang up on Kerby the next time he wants to watch a Monty Python rerun. But Andrew is cautious. *Let's wait till we're all here and take a vote.* Howard snorts. *Piss on the vote, Andy. Man wants to watch limey fags being funny when they're not deserves* Three's Company. *WhatEVER.* Old Gerry won't believe Kerby's got a criminal record *and even if he does he wouldn't steal from us.* Howard says Andrew is a worrywart. *I'm telling you* says Andrew. *Lock your doors.*

Nobody does and everyone squawks when a thief visits our boarding house one afternoon a week later. Most of us are out doing the little we do when it isn't raining. The sun keeps us in the streets and on benches longer than usual. Stuff is stolen and Mr. Carlin doesn't know anything about it. *TOLD you* Andrew reminds us all. But even his own door was forced, locked or not, and he has lost some spare change. Howard says it couldn't have been Kerby anyway, *Kerby was working* he says. At least he thinks he was working. Kerby is a sales clerk in menswear at Woodward's, where Andrew claims he does his shoplifting as an inside job. *THIS had to be an inside job* says Mrs. Carlin. *I don't let in strangers, we keep an eye out.*

So there it stands. Thief at large, mistrust, the loitering smell getting worse. Old Gerry says *Imagine if it was a WHALE rotting. PeeYOU.* We're not encouraged and don't breathe deeply anymore. In our rooms we've closed the rads and opened windows. It really is a disheartening smell and bespeaks putrefaction. Mr. Carlin has called in the pest people and they can't find the stink's source. They suggest he hire a carpenter to do a little prying behind walls.

Oh sure says Howard *tear down the walls, turn us into a dorm. DoRRm* echoes Kerby, rolling his Rs like Eric Idle mimicking a Dorset farmer. Howard, who lost a fountain pen from his unlocked room, says to Kerby *You'd like that wouldn't you, a dorm.* He's just as mad at Kerby as the rest of us in the absence of anyone else to blame. Howard is a lapsed Catholic who retains belief in the obligation of guilty consciences to *act* guilty.

If we was all *WIMMIN* says Gerry *we'd of stood up and demanded the smell be got rid of when she first cropped up.* He's serious. *When somebody or sumpin' raises a stink we're willin' to put up with it till it's too late. I'm thinkin' of moving but I can't afford it. I can't afford to even THINK about moving right now.*

He says he doesn't miss the sawmill so much as a paycheque. His hands have softened since he used to roll hemlock boards onto piles off a greenchain. He shows us his leather apron, worn bright as glass, he even straps it on for old times' sake. *And you wore these oven mitts that smelled sweet on your hands. Afterwards like.*

Not that this takes our minds off our noses. Colin, the womanizer so-called, comes closer with a tale about the peach he's dating. He skins her fuzz right in front of our eyes, before eating her up and leaving us a scarred red stone when he's through the door for a night on the town. *Boy* says Howard *I didn't smell this place AT all when he was doing it to her.* He's shaking his hand as if he just touched the stove. And forgotten he's late for his workout at the Y.

Colin, for all his good fortune with women, is a straightforward man of twenty-six who designs greeting cards, hoping to copyright his own line. He is usually asking Andrew to take his picture, outside on the porch, or in the park with a nice backdrop in the rose garden, for his dossier. His real prey are distributors. Andrew does his best to oblige. Colin poses, Andrew clicks. Andrew tells us the snaps of Colin all look good, *as good as he can expect,* but Colin's never happy. He won't believe he isn't better looking than what his Polaroid spits out.

It's his spitting image says Gerry when Andrew shows him a snap Colin has rejected. *He's never happy* shrugs Andrew.

Mrs. Carlin observes *It's always the prettiest girls who worry and primp.*

This is wisdom we appreciate, can use to justify our own lack of much lasting success with women, pretty or otherwise. *Women want to be considered EQUAL* says Howard *and still think they have to paint their lips and eyes and cheeks. They're bloody clowns sometimes.*

You sound like a misogynist Andrew tells him. Howard looks at him like he wants to swat Andrew in the chops. *Kiss off, Andy* he says. Doesn't know what a misogynist is but knows enough to know it isn't somebody who gives you a massage. *Sounds like a newfangled word for dame* says Gerry. *Starts with Ms.*

We're all sitting around the parlour the Carlins haven't refurnished in thirty years. Everything is worn down and nearly out. Not like the smell, it's smelling stronger and stronger. Howard keeps wondering if Andrew has insulted him. But Andrew as the most sympathetic of us all is unlikely to hurt anyone. Just the reverse. He helps Mr. Carlin with chores when he doesn't have to, brings Mrs. Carlin flowers, which he picks illegally from the park, an act of exceptional daring for Andrew, who respects rules and would never even walk against a red light. It's just that he can't afford a bouquet any other way.

Howard says to him *That dictionary of yours is a compensation for something deficient.*

Hey says Dale. *Knock it off.* Mrs. Carlin excuses herself to start dinner. Dale is our latest addition by eight months. Reliable and better educated than most men in reduced circumstances, he gives the impression he would be generous if he was better off. He has travelled the world, taught school in Australia and dodged a war in Vietnam by coming north to Canada. *Don't forget* he calls to Mrs. Carlin *I love raisins.*

He turns to us. *I love raisins in ice cream. God, I would probably love them in meat loaf.*

As if we don't know says Mr. Carlin. *Yeah* Howard says. *Last week it was raisins in our cookies. I personally prefer chocolate chips.*

So do I says Andrew. Howard looks at him. *If Colin and Kerby were here* says Andrew *we could get up a petition and take it to the cook.*

But Dale is shaking his head. *When you can taste raisins as big as nipples, guys, the chocolate chip is a zit on the backside of a monkey.*

Howard guffaws. He's laughing at Andrew, whose nostrils flare a little to suppress a smile. Dale can be one of the boys when he wants to be. Andrew would like to be, notwithstanding his books and love of order.

On Saturday afternoon I find myself outside Colin's door upstairs watching him rub himself against a men's magazine. *Hey* he says, turning towards me in the hallway. *C'mere.* When I walk into his room everything is tidy, the bed made, his mirror on the wall trimmed with snaps of girls and even one or two of himself. His drafting board sits under the window's light. *Look at this* he says. *Smell it.* He hands me the magazine, a perfume ad for something called L'Homme. I study the advertisement. *Try L'Homme Right Now* it says. *Open flap and rub on wrist. You'll love it!* I sniff the scented fold Colin has been rubbing on his wrists. For a moment the smell in the house vanishes. *Order now* it says *and begin your L'Homme adventure today!* I wonder if L'Homme adventures aren't what Colin enjoys anyway. *Smells nice* I say. Colin sniffs his wrists. *Not bad. I'll get Kerby to pick me up some. Beggar owes me.*

Seems he's on his way out to celebrate the acceptance of a set of Father's Day cards by a major chain of drugstores. *It's a start* he says and shrugs with false modesty. *Well, Colin* I say *that's fan-bloody-tastic. You told Mrs. Carlin?* He looks at me. *Her father still alive?*

She might cook you a special meal to celebrate.

Jesus he says. *I'd rather eat at Burger King. I'm on my way out with a chick to the Keg.*

Big deal says Gerry, when he hears where Colin's eating. *Listen, this calls for a SPECIAL celebration. I'm gonna tell Mrs. Carlin to lay out a nice supper for the occasion. On Father's Day* he says. *Wild* says Kerby, arriving home from work to learn of Colin's success. *Last time anybody besides me around here made money was when Howard opened a cheese shop. Let's hear it for free enterprise!*

What's he talking about? says Howard. *Bloody CHEESE shop now.*

Maybe says Dale *he's getting it mixed up with when you tried delivering flyers.*

Howard thinks the biggest rip-off in his life occurred when unemployment stopped coming and he got ink in his skin for peanuts. *Eff all is what flyers pay* he advises anybody tempted by a route. He'd rather hoist dumbbells at the Y.

Kerby says *You guys'll go on living off welfare long after this SMELL drives us all into the streets. I'm getting TB as a result of this stink.*

Old Gerry doesn't say so but you can tell he likes the idea of a Father's Day celebration, and not just to celebrate Colin's success. He excuses himself to go to the toilet. *My kidneys. Chemicals or sumpin' on the lumber over the years.* Gerry's become an environmentalist.

Poor old Gerry says Dale. *He's got bad pipes.* Then he says *Makes you think what the plumbing in the late Glenn Gould's brain must have been like. All of a sudden bursting. You know.*

What? says Howard.

What? mimics Kerby, unknotting his tie. *Typical American, Dale, you trying to throw dirt on our national genius?*

Who's Glenn Gold? asks Howard.

The smell in the house isn't any better, in fact it's getting worse, and the pest people have come back and still can't locate it. Mrs. Carlin has begun to worry what if we can't locate the smell, what if it's part of the wood in the floors and walls and ceilings? *Don't be ridiculous, woman* Mr. Carlin has told her. But the house *is* old, a boarding house at the turn of the century, still a boarding house today. A lot of men have passed through here. Turrets, gables, some gingerboard left where the weather hasn't eroded it away, the place from the outside looks like the ark. Kerby's theory is a dead pigeon. *You betcha* says Howard. *Seriously, Howard* he says. *Rotting in the attic. Infested with lice.* Mr. Carlin informs him smartly everything is wired tight against pigeons under the eaves. *Well* says Kerby, wheezing. *How come I HEAR pigeons every morning in my room? On TOP of my room. In the ceiling someplace.*

That's a can of worms says Mr. Carlin *I ain't interested in.* Kerby acts surprised. *Mr. Carlin* he says *you don't believe me?*

Nope. There's a stink all right. Not pigeon stink though.

Parrot maybe?

When Gerry comes back into the parlour buttoning his trousers he turns on the TV. *News hour* he reminds us. Kerby glares at him. *Just when we're having a philosophical discussion, Ger. Howard here was saying he'll go back to Mother Church if only Glenn Gould would play his organ. Right, How?* Howard yawns.

Dale must be wondering if Kerby's flair for smart-ass talk is any different from being a thief. He's alway robbing the house of sensible direction, his selfish ego. Dale decides he's had enough of Kerby's nattering and asks him point-blank if he stole an electric shaver from his room.

Dead quiet. Except for Tony Parsons talking to us, only we're not listening. Even Gerry wants to hear out Kerby. *Nope* says Kerby. His lack of surprise at being challenged disturbs Dale, as if Kerby expected it. *No?* asks Dale.

Nope he repeats.

Let's watch the news says Gerry.

Wars, famine. More shutdowns.

After the news hour comes supper. It's a long time to wait for supper, and only Kerby approves since it gives him time to get home from Woodward's and freshen up. He never bothers to watch the news anyway. *At twenty-one who's interested in news?* asks Gerry. *Makin' FUN of the news is news.* Mrs. Carlin doesn't say so but serving the meal after instead of before the news makes her feel superior to the ordinary landlady, although her food is definitely ordinary. Maybe she hopes her silver and china will help us forget the bland taste of the food. These heirlooms from her mother are nothing less than exalted, and she keeps them sparkling, watching us hunkered over her Chantilly forks with a sureness that sooner or later some transformation of our manners will occur. This is no more likely than a metamorphosis of her cooking. Sausages, hamburger, greasy lamb chops, stews, boiled chicken . . . *Blubber food* remarks Howard, worried about cholesterol. *What's food anyway* shrugs Andrew *except fuel?* Andrew eats little. *What OUGHT to begin in the stomach* mutters Colin *is romance.* Usually Mrs. Carlin, who sits at the head of the table, is too busy explaining to Dale why there're no raisins in the casserole, or complaining to her husband about the smell, to hear dissension about her cooking.

We wouldn't know HOW to celebrate.

Even together we are not interdependent like women in a group. We are irritable having to stand in bank and bakery lineups on Altamira. We don't trade easily in gossip with strangers, don't value it much among ourselves. Most of us are still young, without prospects in a world that expects us to work and, worse, to judge ourselves by what we have. We have the false freedom of the idle. Having to live together gives us a washed-up feeling. And this smell in the house just more or less reminds us of our futures. We don't breathe deeply for fear of forgetting what the past had promised. We've learned to get along on UI, and when that runs out, welfare. After we pay for room and board what's left over is bus fare to look for jobs. As if there was someplace left to look. Colin, it's clear, has initiative. He is always saying *I'm getting out of this place when I get a few bucks in the bank.* Andrew is the one who doesn't seem to mind the house. He likes us to depend on him for little things, like Colin for his photographs of himself, Mrs. Carlin for his setting the table and helping serve the meals, Howard for someone to bully. He's the one who supplies womanly sympathy, in place of Mrs. Carlin you could say, at least you can trust Andrew not to ignore your complaints. Kerby doesn't like him much, that's because Andrew doesn't trust Kerby. Andrew is stubborn when he believes he has the right. Andrew believes Kerby's out to sabotage our house from the inside.

Kerby's like the smell we can't put our finger on says Andrew. *Elusive and insidious sort of.* Andrew worries about losing his small but he claims a valuable collection of first editions. Sea stories he treasures. Old Gerry who has never had time for books and big words thinks it wouldn't be a bad thing if Andrew *was* to lose a couple books. But he's joking. Gerry who's lost a wife, a son and a job is tired of losing and wouldn't wish the same on anybody. He never talks about his wife and only says he used to have his own house. It was there in the backyard a crow once attacked his son in a baby carriage under the pear tree. *I trapped the bird inside the buggy and bust its wings with my bare hands* claims Gerry. *I think the baby thought he'd been Jolly Jumpered to death. The buggy had axle springs.*

Gerry says he remembers Saturday mornings because his son resembled a dolphin. Gerry climbed the stairs to his crib. He'd find his son rocking on his stomach, making little squeals, fat, whiteskinned cheeks shining and his mouth turned up in a gummy grin. *He had this bulgy forehead* says Gerry *and this bald head.*

Gerry's still in favour of a celebration to mark Colin's success. So is Andrew, who has talked to Mrs. Carlin about a party in June. Mrs. Carlin is too worried about the smell to think that far ahead and thinks we could be driven out by then.

Don't worry about the smell, Mrs. C. says Dale *it'll take care of itself. Smells do.*

No one is so confident as Dale, who goes out every morning before breakfast, to roam the city looking, we guess, for work. After supper he'll leave for the library downtown or go to a movie or walk to the beach. He only has to sleep with the smell. And he claims it doesn't affect his dreams. He just says happily *I escaped Nam and killing Asians.* But that was years ago. What's his story since? Dale is always holding something back, aloof at times, a man who commits himself to parlour life, such as it is, just so far, because he needs a buffer zone to think. A demilitarized zone Colin calls it.

Those of us who hang around the house are beginning to worry about the debilitating effect, in Andrew's parlance, of a smell we can now smell when we're away from the house, downtown or else in the forest in the park. We agree it isn't in our clothes so much as in our memory of it. This rotting smell, it seems to penetrate and lock itself into our brain cells, *if you can imagine* says Howard *those cells as microchips.* Gerry says *he* imagines them as jails. *Mexican jails.* It's putrid and depressing. A mouse has died, maybe a rat, and the smell from its small carcass has filled the entire house and infected our brain matter.

Sometimes, Mr. Carlin's feet can smell like rotting salmon if he's been cutting the grass or pruning the holly. But that's a smell we understand and can avoid by leaving the parlor. It's local. *When you lose control over the environment* says Gerry *that's when you get desperate.* Andrew wonders *What's the diff?*

A carpenter has begun prying behind places in our bedrooms, trying to trace the smell without tearing down the walls. But there is no centre to pinpoint. He'll lift a floorboard and sniff between floors. Howard's theory is the smell could just as easily be downstairs someplace, in the furnace even.

It smells bad everywhere. *Smells bad everywhere* he says. *We could die from lousy ventilation and lung bugs.*

Meanwhile things are happening for Colin. Women, publicity. A wealthy Chinese girl is after him, picks him up in a sports car that we all gaze at him slipping into. He tells us *Hey, I ask her to listen to her knees, she does it, eh?* And he's still skinning Peaches, as Howard calls her. Kerby's envy rises. By the time he's Colin's age he'll have a TR of his own he swears. Dale is the one who spots Colin's photo in the evening paper, in a column called We Asked You, about rezoning the West End. *Do you agree or disagree with the city's proposal to preserve the present character of remaining residential houses?* The caption beside Colin's photo reads, Colin Downs, age 24, 1497 Bartholomew, President and Chief Designer of Concord Cards. *I don't see the point of it. If developers are willing to put up new highrises, why not? Too many people are out of work. Those old buildings are rotten anyway.* Dale reads Colin's words out to us in the parlour.

Who took your picture? Andrew asks Colin. *Some guy took it when I was talking to the reporter* says Colin *I don't like it.* Gerry looks at the photo. *It ain't bad, Colin.* Kerby says *Makes him look punk.* Then Howard says to Colin *What're you going around saying they ought to tear down the roof over our heads for?* Colin's answer is that as soon as he gets his bearings in the field he's OUTTA here. Get Well, Good Luck, Happy Birthday, Congratulations, Happy Easter, Be My Valentine: funny cards on recycled paper are where it's at for Colin.

I like the name of your company says Gerry. *Concord Cards.*

The big CC says Kerby. *Day comes when we can say we knew him when's the day he's living in the British Properties looking down on us scrounging a living in the city.*

Dale looks at Kerby. *Or pilfering a living?* he asks him. Kerby isn't listening.

Colin asks Gerry why he wants to celebrate the selling of his first greeting card. *I already celebrated at the Keg* he tells him. Gerry says he thought it would be kind of nice to celebrate on Father's Day, kind of appropriate, given the nature of the card. But Colin just excuses himself. *I can't stand the stink* he says *Sundays least of all.* He disappears upstairs to sprinkle himself, I imagine, with L'Homme before venturing out, like some earl from a mouldering castle.

Howard has finally started locking his door. *The antisocial element in this place is beginning to get on my case.* Socks of his have disappeared. And cufflinks. *My old man's. Nobody ever saw them 'cause I never wear 'em. I kept the box in my dresser.*

The heat's on Kerby to own up and he won't. He won't even admit to Andrew having once had a problem with the law. *I'd like to know why you think that. I'm no con. Hey, I pinch the odd tie off Chunky Woodward but listen. It stops there, eh?* But Andrew has hold of Kerby like a cat shaking a mouse. *I KNOW* he says *what I know.* Says he's seen him writing with Howard's fountain pen. *That right?* Howard asks Kerby. *Hey, mate* Kerby says to Howard in cockney *your shirt's on fire.*

After this the pilfering drops off, Howard's pen reappears in the kitchen, though not his cufflinks. Dale is still missing his shaver. *Then nothing's changed* warns Andrew. *Keep your doors locked.* He sniffs a little, simpers. *Andy, you got to let the smell escape* says Gerry. Howard looks at Gerry. *ESCAPE* he says *shit.* Andrew tells Gerry to keep his window open. *I do* says Gerry *we all do. This smell just wears you down.*

It'll go away repeats Dale. We accept his voice as one of wisdom and general experience of the world. And have a good laugh just the same. *Go out* he advises us, smoking his pipe. *Sit on the beach and smell the wind. Clean out your mantras.* Howard snorts. Howard always snorts. *Jesus* he exclaims. Dale came of age in the sixties and laments the wreckage of their ideals. Howard says it's all right for him, he can probably afford to move out whenever he wants. He's got family in Philadelphia sending him money. *Irregardless* says Gerry *we like him.*

Everybody likes Dale, he has his hand on the key to some inner strength that eludes the rest of us. *He's tranquil* Andrew says. *Deep sometimes.* Howard says *For all we know HE could be the house thief. Confidence men run deep.*

Smell runs deep.

What's food anyway asks old Gerry *but thought. Hey?* He's trying to come up with a menu he thinks might interest Mrs. Carlin for Father's Day and he's biting the end of Howard's pen he's borrowed. Thoughtfulness, does he mean, or planning ahead? Maybe he means fuel. Fuel for thought. Gerry is putting a lot of thought into the celebration and Andrew says it's touching to watch. *Poor old Gerry* says Kerby *the guy who's lost a son, cooking up an excuse to celebrate Father's Day.*

When a silver fork, then a knife go missing on different evenings, Gerry is the one to rush to Mrs. Carlin's cries of alarm. He is outraged, to put it exactly, as if this kind of pilfering is more contemptible than bedroom stealing. *This is SERIOUS* he says. *Mrs. Carlin's silver's what keeps the likes of US alive.* He sounds silly, refusing to turn on the news hour till he lectures us on our responsibilities to our hosts. Howard snorts. *HOSTS!* Old Gerry lights into *that* remark. He lights into Kerby, he lights into all of us for complaining so much and doing nothing to contribute to our own order and well-being. Next afternoon Mrs. Carlin discovers her knife and fork in the garbage bag Andrew is about to carry out to the dumpster. *I must of swept them into the garbage cleaning up* she says. *And we nearly threw these treasures out!* Tearing eyes attest to the importance she attaches to these baroque heirlooms.

Don't ya see says Gerry, unashamed of his hectoring behaviour. *We're FAMILY. I believe that.*

His support during her two-day ordeal makes Mrs. Carlin a little keener to encourage his Father's Day party for Colin. *That's real nice, Gerry* says Colin, bored to death by Gerry's proposal. *But I don't need any party.* In fact he doesn't even know if he can come to a dinner in his honour. Dale looks at him. *You'll make it, Colin* he says. Colin looks at Dale in a puzzled way. He's got no intention of coming to dinner on a Sunday when he's never here anyway. Peaches cooks for him. Or else his wealthy friend from Hong Kong takes him dining in the sky somewhere.

Colin leaves the room to attend to his sketches. He shows me one he's working on at the moment, a birthday card on the cover that says I KNOW IT'S YOUR BIRTHDAY ... and when I open it, says . . .'CAUSE A LITTLE BIRDIE TOLD ME!! The sketch inside is of a muscular eagle smashing a tennis ball with his racket across a net. Under the net it says MANY HAPPY RETURNS!!! *It's a jock card* says Colin. *For a jock. Got the idea from our pigeons in the eaves.* He wants to know what I think of it.

Nifty. How'd you get an eagle to look happy?

May then June. Trees on the boulevard outside are umbrellas in full canopy. *Fulla crows* says Gerry sombrely.

Dale's RIGHT Mrs. Carlin exclaims, sniffing the parlour. *It IS going away.* And she hugs us right through the news hour one evening, before we've begun to notice for ourselves we aren't locked so much into the stink.

It seems unnoticeable at first, maybe because it's stuck inside the way we think of this place every time we come back, so we just close our minds and try not to smell what we think is still here. But it *is* fading. It's going away. Our terrible smell is going away. Mrs. Carlin can hardly contain her happiness, *for what's happiness but relief?* says Andrew.

R- O - L - says Kerby *A - I - D - S. Nudge nudge, wink wink.*

We settle down. We dare to breathe more deeply. Compared to the regular news hour, the Saturday news hour is more retrospective and the Saturday before Father's Day, Pamela Martin, who's substituting for Tony Parsons, summarizes a Greenpeace report blaming a spill of wood preservatives at a local paint factory for the deaths of at least nine grey whales in the inland waters north and south of the international boundary between March and June. *Holy crow* says Gerry. *NINE. Listen.* They're showing old footage of the same whale as before, lying sideways on the beach in White Rock. *It's sick what things can happen* says Mr. Carlin. *It's chemicals* says Gerry. *Hear?* He's right.

Authorities estimate forty-three tons of pentachlorophenols and tetrachlorophenols from the Cloverdale Paint and Chemical Company Ms. Martin articulates *were dumped into the Serpentine River and washed to sea, where they settled into pools and ravines on the ocean bottom.* Gerry doesn't like the beautiful Ms. Martin so much as he does Tony Parsons. Still, his attention is glued. *The whales come along like vacuum cleaners* she says *to feed and end up sucking toxins into their systems.* Cut to a genetics professor at a news conference, who guesses surviving whales will end up with liver damage and immune systems unable to resist disease. *Or to repair usual-type wounds and injuries* he says. *Plus it will probably impair their ability to reproduce.*

Gerry listens. And he listens when a forensic toxicologist from Oregon predicts nine deaths are just the tip of the iceberg, maybe several icebergs. *Didn't I tell ya?* cries Gerry. *Goddamn. It's the dyin' of the LIGHT. For sure.*

He means it. Deaths of these animals have moved him deeply. Howard thinks Gerry is moved too easily. Andrew says Gerry is probably worried about dioxins in his own system. *A fear is piercing him* he says. Dale wonders aloud where Gerry's son might be. *No one has ever asked him, right?* Howard would like to know the difference between dioxins and toxins.

When we finally sit down to dine on Father's Day Mrs. Carlin generously tells us Gerry has bought the shoulder of lamb out of his own pocket and prepared it with a mint sauce and roast potatoes. She looks on approvingly. Colin has shown up, as Dale predicted, and graciously consented to be our guest of honour. *It's my pleasure* he says like a good businessman. Kerby has contributed four bottles of dry red wine, Howard the avocados, Dale the dessert and Andrew orange blossoms in little urns. For some of us this is a first taste of avocado pears. We toast Colin, young Colin as old Gerry calls him with some pride. He wishes him continued success with his greeting-card business. We all drink to that, and eat up the avocados, the lamb, the potatoes, the sauce.

There's no occasion says Gerry *that food can't IMPROVE it*. And we drink to that too. *Food is delicious!* we all say. *Food is wonderful! Food is life!* And eating this heavenly food we believe fervently in what we say.

After Dale's big chocolate cake, *with RAISINS* he says, after my coffee, when we're all sitting around the lounge smoking Colin's cigars, there's a ring at the front door. Andrew comes back bearing a telegram. *It's for Gerry. Mr. Gerry Turner* he reads.

Old Gerry stands up and acts like he receives telegrams every day. There is dignity in the way he stands there. *Telegrams are always bad news* he says calmly. Nobody disagrees with him. His dignity in the face of inevitability seems quaint. The TV is on, flickering soundlessly in lieu of the boarded-up fireplace, something we can turn to if the conversation goes cold. We all turn politely to watch a car chase in California.

Then old Gerry is standing in the corner by the doorjamb weeping softly and studying his telegram. This makes the whole room uncomfortable. Probably nobody has seen a man as old as Gerry crying before. Our fathers never cried. Mrs. Carlin stands up and says she'll bring in some fresh coffee. Mr. Carlin gets up to turn up the volume. Engines whining. Only Andrew goes to Gerry, he's the only one who knows how.

It's from my son Gerry finally says. *Lookit this.* He hands Andrew the telegram to read. *It's from his son* says Andrew. Andrew looks it over. Then he reads *DEAR DAD STOP HAVE NOT SEEN EACH OTHER IN YEARS STOP BUT AM REMEMBERING YOU TODAY STOP LOVE MARLOW.*

Hey, Ger that's great! says Howard. The rest of us stand up and form a circle of gentle backslappers, congratulating Gerry and Gerry is crying unashamed tears as he looks at each of us with real joy in his heart. His wrinkled skin just glows.

It couldn't have ended better says Mr. Carlin, happily. *It's like Gerry arranged his own Father's Day, eh Ger?*

Gerry says Colin. *You didn't tell us your son's name was Marlow.*

All Gerry can say, in a glad tremulous voice, is *I musta mentioned it. I musta mentioned it.*

We go to bed happy that night, feeling good that someone among us has thought to send this telegram to Gerry. His room is next to mine and in the middle of the night I'm aroused by a muffled sobbing. It's muffled in the way pigeons coo roosting when night falls.

I get up and put on my dressing gown and go into the hall to tap lightly on Gerry's door. My knuckles rap the old varnish. *Gerry?* His light is on and he's sitting up in his bed with the telegram on the blanket. He wipes his eyes.

Neither of us says anything. After a while Gerry takes some deep breaths and calms himself. *I ain't sad* says Gerry. *I ain't crying 'cause I'm sad or nothin'. I'm just real happy.*

He blows his nose with a hanky he pulls out of his pyjama pocket. *I know you meant well. All of you* he says *sending me a telegram and all.* He sniffles. *Thing is my son died real young* he says *from meningitis and the reason I guess I'm mewing is on account of the sheer, I dunno, love I feel for the bunch of you and for some bugger in this place who was NICE enough to send old Gerry a telegram on Father's Day. I don't think it was a mean trick at all. I think it was real nice. You guys are family.*

What's the matter with Gerry? asks Andrew, waiting outside the varnish. *Sssshhh* I whisper. *He's just happy.*

These men, I think after, lying in my bed, their voices in my head. An ambulance is travelling up Bartholomew to the hospital, carrying a heart-attack victim through our tunnel of sycamores. And the other sounds, the shunting on distant wharfs of the North Shore, ships leaving one continent in darkness for another. Letting go, I breathe deeply and smell the old plaster and worn carpet thread. I listen. I value these sleeping men. I love them just as Gerry does. God, none of us knows the source of a thing like smell, or where kindness comes from, or where evil dwells. No more than we can fathom the vanishings of these.

DAMAGES

I AM GOING to confess something libellous. Can you sue yourself for libel? Am I liable to myself if I reveal this lamentable thing? The reason I hesitate is I wonder if it's worth my while confessing or would I be better off keeping quiet. I guess I like the contact. Like lots of women when I talk I risk losing a settlement against myself. It's not fair. By telling the truth I'm punished for indiscretion. I know the best defence against libel is to prove it's true. You see what a position this leaves me in. I could lie and say blackberry thorns really hurt me in the pleasure of filling my pail. But they don't.

The stars know this. They risk libel every night they turn on in the hills. The stars are foolish and who notices, who suffers? We do. Their watchers do, we suffer for them. We read libel in their glitter. We make a to-do about the showboaty stars and it gives them pleasure. Not till morning can we trace our scars, their scars, with our fingers. The skin declines to lie.

Take just one star. Look at the things Connie Francis has had to face. Bobby Darin. A gun, her father came after Bobby with a gun, so that was the end of a potentially huge romance. Bobby married Sandra Dee, not her. Bobby died. Then her brother was murdered. Her two, three marriages fizzled out. She miscarried. One husband beat her. She had typhoid fever and bled from the ears. A perfectionist about singing, she just made her pain worse. Lost her voice, attempted suicide, became psychotic. It got gross. She travelled in and out of clinics like a laundry van. A court found her incompetent to look after her own affairs. Twice. By the way, it was the mob in New York City who shot her brother—in the driveway of his New Jersey home. He was a racketeer.

These facts are part of our public record. I think it would be wrong to repeat them at all if magazines hadn't reported them, newspapers, if she hadn't told us herself. It's all true. Kicking a policeman, the lithium treatments, problems in her fourth marriage. Everything. I have watched her growing darker, I must admit, watched with more than wonder.

Take, for example, when a knife-armed stranger broke in and raped her in a Howard Johnson motor lodge, I too experienced a loss of self-esteem, failed to recover my usual good nature, and little by little lost my pitch till I *whrrrred* like a pheasant with strep throat. I couldn't have sung to save my supper.

"Something eating you?" asked Mr. Delmore, not looking up. "That . . . uh, tenant still troubling you?"

Nerves in need of the sun I told him, since it was December by then.

"Feed a fever," he suggested. "Starve a cold."

After the lawsuit she tried comebacks. She lip-synched on the Dick Clark show, I watched her on TV, and she flew home from L.A. feeling like a fraud. She who had sung for the Queen, sung in Carnegie Hall, been chosen Female Entertainer of the Century at Expo 67. She made herself go back to finish an engagement at the Westbury nightclub where she was singing the night of her rape. But nothing soared. She couldn't repeat the past. She was already passing into myth.

You felt it was all going to come out: barricading herself inside her house, inside her bedroom, where her wretched change of voice seemed to echo the men who'd violated her. A father who pushed her, husbands who left her, the stranger who raped her and was never caught. She herself blamed it on air conditioning. On the effect of air-conditioned rooms on her throat, after surgery to narrow her nose and the operations afterwards to fix up the first surgery's leftover scar tissue. It's hard to say. You admire vanity.

But who can write off the gagging fruit of evil?

Listen. *All* her hits came before the rape, before the marriages, before she found out her brother, rubbed out for squealing, was a crook.

> *Right to the end,*
> *just like a friend,*
> *I tried to warn you somehow ...*

I don't know who wrote that one—my father once said it was an old song, a real poco andante. He'd sniff his Dutch-Reform sniff at the Hit Parade, at how it sparked, then doused its stars. He was right. The stars flared, went shooting, died out. Frankie Avalon, Neil Sedaka—her father tolerated those two though he hated Bobby Darin, who went on to become a bigger star than either of them. Frankie befriended her, Neil wrote her songs. Such songs, even one song could have made her a star. Isn't it your memory of a song that stays constant when the flame that inspired the words is gone?

I could show you the river where Bernice Hailey and I were sitting in her father's Mercury when Tony Bellus sang a song on the radio that should have become a bigger hit and never did, not really, "Robbin' the Cradle." Or where I was when Ricky Nelson gave me the answer, "Uh huh," in a falling third to every question asked of me for a week, from his big hit "Poor Little Fool." I was at Mrs. Kabush's kicking the slats out of used lettuce boxes for her stove—not a thing in neighbourly conscience I could dodge, stocking her kindling.

"I'm in your hands, dearie!" she would scream. "I'd freeze and starve both without you!"

I just bet, I thought.

"Hold on, dearie, I'll turn up the radio!"

The old have ways of wheedling life from the young. What is dignity?

When I reported the record settlement for negligence against Howard Johnson, in the millions, to Mr. Delmore, he only stared out the window at passing traffic and said lawyers were so many farts in a closet. I think he said ten. He should know, he wrote the book on fustiness. Darkness. Not that litigation has ever threatened Mr. Delmore, he's too wary. I help Mr. Delmore to manage Stay-AWhile outside Lacey. We're the last resort for travellers who, because of indifference or just bad timing, are unable to reach the coast before nightfall. They come out of the Interior, over passes, down the Canyon, before making their mistake. Our highway isn't the Trans-Canada but a secondary route down the north bank of the Fraser, veering off at Hope. "Typical," mutters Mr. Delmore. He's been trying to sell out for years. Power lines buzz overhead and remind him of electric chairs.

He's an aging man with gas-station sideburns and a need of blunt pencils. He'd rather go to jail than mark anything, a cheque or crossword puzzles, with a pen. The nearness of an eraser encourages in him the conceit of retraction and the second chance. Around me he prefers to listen rather than comment, so I prattle, and dust lightly. He has no love for people who wear him down and all of us do. His face at the counter resembles the slumped side of an old boot, propped up at the chin with the heel of his hand.

When I say help him "manage" I mean changing sheets, vacuuming carpets, Cometing sinks. The things a wife'd get stuck doing for free to help her husband in any one-man operation of ten units. Mr. Delmore has that many peeling cabins around a weedy driveway and seldom more than four occupied per night. Nobody stays longer than a night. The Datsun trucks and Suzuki motorcycles all pull out by eight, eight-thirty, in the morning. Good riddance to the grumps. By noon yours faithfully is on her way home.

Except once. Just once in twelve years have I had to enforce noon checkout and I was not a success. This was when I first started. I was new and hating the job, my morale was rock-bottom. A young man with dirty yellow hair who hadn't bothered to close his blinds was still in bed, on top of it, in underpants. He groaned when I knocked on his door to explain who I was and what time the clock said. I heard nothing till he fumbled open the door, just enough to reveal a mole-sprinkled face and skinny chest. I looked away. He wasn't telling me anything, he muttered, if he was to tell me he thought he might drop dead from wild oats. He didn't look sarcastic so much as hungover.

I had to knock again, this time sharply with my broom handle. I walked to the window and rapped there too. He slowly guillotined my view with a downward pull of the blinds. So I walked over to the office and reported him to Mr. Delmore. Mr. Delmore looked at me, said it was nothing to get upset about, and pencilled in No. 9 for another day.

"What if he ups and leaves without paying?" I said. "Look, Mr. Delmore. I haven't been here long but I know a smartass when I hear one. He'll just out and away on those parked wheels."

Mr. Delmore raised his chin to window level. "Got his Gibson." Casually, he pulled out some baggage from under the counter and unzipped a canvas bag to show me the smart-ass's guitar. A shiny, expensive instrument.

"He give it in for safekeeping."

"Who's he afraid's going to burgle it? Other guests?"

Next morning I discovered the blinds still down and the same motorcycle on its kickstand. The licence said Saskatchewan or Manitoba. I knew how to wake the lazy ones by rattling my key in their locks to remind them it was time. This time I pushed forward and ran into the nightchain. Into the unresponsive gloom, wondering if I ought to shout through the crack, saying I was the cleaning lady. I tried.

The only rough part of the little episode was Mr. Delmore, finally, who had to come and lean in with a hacksaw across the chain. The minstrel in underpants offered no more resistance. We prodded him, God knows we tried to get a rise out of him...

As it happened he *had* dropped dead, and of course I felt shock as well as grief. I really did. What he died of Mr. Delmore didn't bother to phone the RCMP back to find out, after the ambulance took away the body. The heart, he guessed, gummed up with drugs. To the police he neglected to mention the guitar when they took away the motorcycle. Mr. Delmore is like that. Guests can do what they like to mess up, even exit their rooms in body bags, so long as they pay in advance and I'm around to clean up.

That afternoon I think he came near to firing me when I refused to enter No. 9 and he had to scour it himself. But he kept his tongue. If he found a syringe he kept that too. He was liable for nothing so long as no evidence of neglect surfaced to threaten him. Negligence of the heart didn't count. Such hopes as once beat in the dead boy's breast didn't concern Mr. Delmore. And he was safe from reporters. Our guest had become no star. Had not in all likelihood, coming west, even managed to see salt water for the first time in his life.

In the Carthage shopping mall that Christmas I listened to a choir carolling "O Holy Night" around the ears of Kmart customers. It reminded me how run down and depressed I felt. My spirit was taking a beating, my lungs felt padlocked, my priorities had been misplaced somewhere along the way.

Where? How very pissy the future looked. At twenty-eight that year I was still living on a dairy farm with my parents. You didn't need a little bird to tell you when you had a crisis on your hands. In the presence of a cat, barn swallows can drive you bughouse.

Tonight, looking back, I'm thinking of stars who peter out too. Who can't see themselves till too late to stop the damage, the libel of dying larger than life. I bruise easily in August, but I see farther. I see how we have three ages: young, not young, old. I see that the abiding age is the middle one. We are not young most of our lives. An evil age because we learn what decay is and face it sometimes with bad grace. I did. I understood history then without understanding the stars. The stars who flail longest against any intrusion of this knowledge and fade badly.

Aren't I a peach at hindsight? I could run a clinic for guests at Stay-A-While. As a matter of principle, I've stayed far too long myself since those days when Mr. Delmore's sideburns were still brown and boys carried guitars.

I was sure about the sun then. I believed in it, yes. But spring failed to renew me and made Christmas seem by no means the lowest I was going to sink. Whiny, I moped a lot. Mr. Delmore was dying to tell me to take a powder.

At home I behaved like a schoolgirl with no responsibilities to the parents who'd wheedled her into staying. I was to come into their farm—but who wanted a farm? I went silent. Noises gave me a headache. I couldn't pee without clenching over water. For someone who liked to talk, I was so far off the beam I was in danger of flying smack into silence. I made up my mind to fly south.

Club Med in Guaymas, Mexico, on the Sea of Cortez, is an Indian pueblo village above a lagoon with the dry Bacochibampo mountains behind. When I saw the violet hills and cactus desert I thought of our own B.C. Interior with the same Mediterranean climate that attracts stars to southern

California, along with reptiles and greasewood. I might as well have been in California, if you counted the swimming pools, tennis courts and restaurants.

I'm not athletic but was willing to make an effort. I played volleyball, bocce ball, ping-pong. I horsebacked into the desert, rafted on the Yaqui River, tried deep-sea fishing and caught a sunburn. I visited the quaint town of Santa Rosalia, ate too much, above all *talked* to anybody who would listen. I was determined to reacquire cheerfulness. Finally, in the evenings, I snuggled up to the mesquite fire listening to singsongs. I love songs. I love the way a singer trusts a song, the way she trusts a stamp not to poison her when she licks it. I listened closely those nights. Stretched thin, my throat wasn't up to flight.

Those were my two weeks on the surface. Black and white, cut and dried. No great fissures. My two weeks underneath are another story if this trip south isn't to sound distorted, even a lie. They say the greater the truth the greater the libel— the worse the libel they mean. I want to be brief.

I was talking so much, to anybody who'd listen, because of what happened after landing and busing in to the club. This I was trying to put out of mind. All Club Med bungalows are based on double occupancy, so if you go alone you end up, unless a single man tumbles for you in the plane or airport bus, sharing your room with another woman. The odd thing is I ended up in a double room of my own.

The other girl assigned to this room opened the door, looked at me, coughed, and backed out again with her luggage. I thought she had the wrong room—what she wanted me to think, in her straw Stetson. I was hanging up my dresses. Then it happened again, a second girl looked in, hesitated, vanished. Maybe her lip gloss needed freshening. Who were they looking for, Linda Ronstadt? Who was I, Linda Leper? Downstairs the G.O., a camp counsellor for adults, a French boy with lean tanned cheeks, introduced me to a third girl, from Wyoming.

"No," said the girl. You see she was expecting a ponce friend to show up any minute now. You like a lie when it's well turned.

I went back up pretending nothing was the matter. Pretended I was going to have a very nice time. Made up my mind to it. Pretended I was not an unattractive young woman. I kept busy, as I mentioned. Kept talking.

I talked to people in a breezy way and refused just because it was popular to shy off a kissy face. I took lessons in scuba diving to be included in a group: that group, any group. People were polite and this hurt. At meals no one shunned me, but no one lingered.

My room on the second floor was right below an identical room on the third, with a moonlit view of the Bacochibampo, where I'd hear two men at night, and sometimes a man and a girl, depending on who was changing rooms and shacked up with whom. Atmospheric conditions in a Club Med are randy, there's no other word for the weather. Swapping has lots of singles on the hop all night.

On the last night I woke up with a body pressing down on mine and smelled cocktails on its breath. It recognized its mistake right away and apologized. This calmed me down. It was nothing to get upset about, *he* wasn't going to get upset, he acted lazy and reluctant to leave. He knew he was an intruder, I knew he was an intruder, we both knew where we were. In that climate you learn to guard your privacy with a little less dignity.

"I think you have the wrong room" I said, turning at the same moment he chose to slip his hand down the side of my bare leg, under the blanket. In the moonlight I recognized the body as belonging to a Seafirst Bank employee from Seattle, not an unpleasant young man I'd made a point of chatting to on a trail ride to the waterfall. Arthur Perry. Peterson, maybe.

"Holy smoke," he said, suddenly embarrassed.

His fingers twitched and he looked away, down towards his fingers. In all the moments of my life none has seemed more glacial, more eternal than that moment. He didn't know what to say in a place that didn't cater much to talking, having to talk your way out of anything. Like the girls backing out of my room he couldn't think of anything to say. Small talk, anything, might have cheered me up.

Just listen to what he concocted, in this ticklish situation, listen to what this strong silent type said very carefully to me, who was more or less a stranger.

"*So help me . . .*" he began, whispering with real passion.

I thought for a moment he was just trying to make the best of a bad scene.

"*. . . So help me Christ, I could give it to you ten different ways to breakfast . . . do you understand? . . . and have you screaming from every orifice like Tonto in a teepee.*"

Whispering, he was coming on to me like life depended on his performance. He definitely sounded menacing.

"*Savvy, sweetheart? I'm saying I could eat your ratatouille like you've never had it eaten before. How would you like right now . . . to give me a dish of ratatouille and for me to wolf it?*"

He was moving the tips of his fingers over my burnt leg, rubbing it under the covers. He was staring down to where his fingers were misusing my leg.

"*Tell me,*" he whispered, "*how you'd like to feel the mouth of hunger so bad it gives you spasms for a week. Tell me how you couldn't stand supper from any other teeth. Who wants fast food, hmm, when her gravy train is pulling into the station for pork loin buffet? Tapioca pudding? Jesus, I got teeth so sweet for you they're singing in my gums. Listen . . .*"

He couldn't stop talking like this, turning himself on I figured, getting cruder and cruder like he was making up a libretto for buddies at a stag. Some of his other lyrics I remember are "*You can wait for it like a mare in heat, sugar, but try kicking me and I'll have you broken into saddle so quick it'll fry your curlers.*" And "*I don't take prisoners. When the sun comes up you'll find yourself either eaten alive or looping the stars. Both.*" And "*So help me Christ, I'm going to stuff you backwards*

like a Thanksgiving turkey... Brown juice is going to run out of
you so fast I'll need the gift of tongues to lap it up ... and spit it
over you till you get down on your knees and thank me to do it
some more."

I may not have this last lyric right, it doesn't have much
of a beat. It was pretty disgusting. Circling, he kept on like
this for four or five minutes, whispering, watching his own
grazing, invisible fingers. I wondered about his obsession. I
mean talking like that, hard and voguish, he'd begun to give
himself away. His whispering sounded passionate but the
words sounded hollow. He sounded like he was lying. If anything, too big for boots, he didn't believe his own threats. I was
concerned, but not terrified, the way I would've been with a
total stranger. I was tense but not rigid. The point is I was not
screaming.

He stopped then. Talking, he hadn't so much as removed
the blanket with his hand, but had kept rubbing his fingers
in menacing little moons on the skin of my thigh. I could tell
he was up against me in an uncomfortable position. But that
wasn't his problem.

His problem was anger had gradually got the better of
him. Silent, quiet anger. He'd stopped whispering. In the end
he was angry to the point of violence. You could have set fire
to the silence.

"God," he said at last. In a normal voice, glancing up at
my face, he said, "You haven't heard one word I've said. Not a
word, have you?"

His anger had given way to pity. He removed his hand and
sat up.

"Yes," I whispered. *"I have, Art."*

"No, you haven't," he repeated, irritated at this licence.
"You haven't heard one single syllable. I pity you," he said. "I
feel sorry for you, you know that?"

Maybe he was trying to cover up his own tactics, his own
violent language, his own embarrassment. His own failure,

for all I knew, to think up any more sexy threats. He stood up soberly in T-shirt and bathing suit, then flapped in thongs to my door—his thongs hadn't even fallen off—opened it and went out.

I thought about reporting him to our Gentils Organisateurs. I thought over his dirty talking, what he'd meant by it, just talking like that. And then the disgust, the pity in his venom. I felt sorry for him, for how foolish he was going to feel at breakfast for talking to me that way.

I don't exactly recall the hour that morning I thought I might have it wrong. *Him* wrong. No knife at the throat, no gag in the mouth, had stopped me from calling out. Worse, if I was being honest, I hadn't even felt insulted. This man was testing me, he was putting me on trial, and I just lay there ... *listening!*

I confess I cried after that, for a long time. The moon moved on. I cried for ages and ran my fingers over myself for a long time afterwards.

People at breakfast were nicer than normal because I didn't try to talk to them, and at our last breakfast it made them feel guilty. I must have looked like death warmed over. It was like they knew at last, what I knew they knew. That they were young and full of the future, or so they thought, and I was not. I went out of my way not to glance at Arthur's table, not to notice it, not to acknowledge its existence. I felt raw.

On my return to Canada Mr. Delmore didn't look up, but he had about him a generally sympathetic air. Maybe he missed me, laundering for the transient, unplugging their toilets.

"Sounds like your cold's got worse. Wintertime in Mexico too?" Only he pronounced it the Spanish way, Mayheeko, as if his adenoids were paperclipped.

I didn't want him to think I liked working at Stay-A-While any better than when I'd started, but couldn't think of anything smart to say, when he said, "Here. Take it."

He was holding out to me the canvas bag with the Gibson. "Take it," he said.

With his pencil he returned to a real estate flyer, the heel of his hand covering back up his wealed chin.

I still sometimes take out this guitar and think of the dead boy and wonder if he'd known suffering, and how well he'd played the blues. *"Who's sad and blue . . ."* strum, pause, *"Who's crying, too . . ."* The boohoo strains of a blue guitar. You can never learn the bridges too well.

Like tonight, I sit here in the window on the second floor, strumming, looking out at the fields. Mountains surround the meadows and from up here I can see the river where the brambles grow. A mist this morning was lifting off the mown hay and my father, old and stubborn, was calling in the herd. Bawling like a little sheik. It's a large Holstein herd. He came out from Holland to help drain the polder when this river overflowed its banks in the forties. He thought with his lore of flood plains he wouldn't need to stay in Perumbur past spring to contain the damage. But tempted by offers of cheap land he stayed on to do the Dutch thing and build a dairy farm. He built this house. We followed him, my mother and I, an infant.

The lamentable thing is I'm thirty-nine and still living with my parents. There was a time I would have lied about this. A time when I believed in the right to be free of oppression, that I had a right to be happy.

No more.

Listen, dearie! I can hear myself calling to the young a generation from now . . . But no one uses kindling these days. It's the young who blame their parents for the narrowness of age, including their own. The not young withdraw their accusations and settle down to compromise. We insist on paying rent in spite of objections they don't need it, no, they don't need it, please.

Notice how the tempo of my strings picks up to mock revolutionary fervour? The other day in a glossy magazine from

New York I saw pictures of Beirut guerrillas modelling the latest fashions in uniform. These boys, these men, in murderous pose—checked scarves over heads, bullet belts over shoulders. Asses over teakettles. I could have screamed! The myth of the young is their belief in the right to be free of oppression. What right is this? Who gives it?

Fashion's who. That tyrant of our age. The guerrilla as top dog, character of history, supreme individual. Listen, Mr. Fatigues, in your oversized boots.

What about me?

I often want to love and can't succeed in loving. I seek my own defeat without finding it, and am forced to remain free.

Like Elvis. Fattened on junk food and drugs, he fell off his toilet in the ensuite bathroom of a mansion where his heart, with no more room, lay enlarged and surrounded with fat. Bloated, beatless, his body needed fourteen mourners to carry its casket. Today it lives on in T-shirts and mugs. Is this dignity?

It's the stars who go to parties wearing the glass facsimiles of diamonds in safes at home. The false stones make those real stones look bigger than life. It's the same with the stars. To be bigger than life they leave their real selves at home. It makes them illusions like stars in the sky, glittering, long after dying into holes. Their light takes so long to reach us, so long to matter, sometimes we forget we're looking at history! Glitter has become its opposite: a dwarf, blackness, vapour: Time run out of gas. It's only distance that makes them appear to throb with life, poor things, unable to face death, condemned to be young.

This morning when I phoned Mr. Delmore to excuse myself from work he just grunted. Leery of being horsed around, he'd have to mop up, scour, sweep on his own. But he won't. He'll leave the dirty rooms for me as though I'd never missed a day. In real estate, as Mr. Delmore knows from long experience of trying to sell out, the three important things are location, location, location. In the case of libel I some-times think they must be detail, detail, detail. Tomorrow all the rooms will be dirty and I'll be hard-pressed to launder so many sheets. If you knew that sometimes I leave the unsoiled ones, stretch them tight over mattresses to look unused, would it shock you? The next guests never notice.

In spring the dike along the river protects us in these low-lands, an earthen wall of grass with a small road running on top, a trail, really, for the cattle. It stretches miles and looks natural. The river comes out of the lake. The delta comes before the sea. Where the river runs into the sea we learn, slowly, to read the sand dollar as a microchip of evolution—fossils implanted in its shell like scars in our own. Skin. Soul, it's the same. When your soul meets history you become liable for the damages. And they say you cannot libel the dead.

Some nights like tonight I accompany myself back to life, fret marks in my fingers, the memory of this song my deepest, no, wildest pleasure.

FLIGHT

HE FIGURES, why go home to a rented house with gutter weed when the most he gets there is a nice jack-off view of next-door bikinis from the sunroom? But what else can he afford? Numbers, including his own SIN, tease him, although those measuring engine capacity on the trunks of Japanese and German cars do more. They provoke him. He doesn't think. He pinches his house key and trolls it thigh-high along the paint jobs. Korean Ponies get a break, because of their drivers: single women on part-time salaries, he can prove it. But the Saabs he takes a walking tour around.

Give us a B, M, W, S, L, C, R, X . . . Yea Team! Most of them tend to replace numbers on their plates with letters, provided they get to the registrar first, or else fudge the spellings. EH-I, JAMEEE!, MACH-2, EPIC I, PR, etc. Their Italian rubber tires he takes care of with a pistol of sufficient calibre to rattle the chrome numbers as well.

Sure, dude. Go believe yourself

"D'you know what a robbed house feels like?" he asks his Shaughnessy hosts. "Like love lost. Someone's cleared out of

your life with something yours. It can really spoil a party."
He tells them you need to make the best of a bad surprise
when you come home, and hang on for the fingerprint squad.
"Those boys dust the jambs and drawers, as fresh as daisies at
two a.m. Their shift starts at midnight." His solution is not to
go home, except he maintains he's going anyway. ". . . Like the
pacifist Catholic, who refuses to wrestle with his conscience."
Arf, arf. He's been drinking, what of it? "A party takes the load
off your back and puts bearing in your balls."

At four a.m. he claims his artful housemate is saving him
a piece of blackberry pie—not a bad time to leave except bus
service has withdrawn till dawn. And no other guest is left to
drive him. He looks for rolls on the mantel and scrapes the
chili pot. He hangs on till seven, eight, breakfast of papaya
and herb tea with hibiscus flowers and cranberries. He makes
the most of this unsatisfying meal and looks in the fridge for
lunch meat: "All right, you jars, who's hiding the ham?" He
offers to send out for pizza, but can't get a response from his
hosts, abed since four. (Those parlours for Bohemians and the
proletariat have all closed anyway for the night.) He could
always ring up for Chinese, what his father's generation used
to ring for, his hosts' come to that, as tasteless budding bourgeois. . . Give us a DING, huh, give us a HO.

Here's the drill, so listen. But his father is renewing himself
with a second family and won't listen. Can't he see what's happening to the world?

In the pool outside he goes for a swim on a hungry stomach. He makes himself open his green eyes and look at his
fingernails, between his toes, the blue walls. Inside he expects
to find a hair dryer upstairs, but makes do with a towel job
and very little body until his hair starts to revive somewhere
around ten, when the sun comes out from behind clouds and
it (his hair) sort of puffs out like feathers. The snored-in look
is what he wants and would admit to. The party-crashing look.
By now this opaque girl who babysits for the family is hungry

too. She bounces down on the counter a thousand grams of bacon from the freezer. His swimmer's gut coils audibly when ice hits the pan. Fat in the air!

Shit in the fan. Some people's pleasure is another's cross. He hangs around, swimming and napping on the pool deck in his gaunchwear, sending out for pizza when lunchtime rolls around. But when the party looks like it could pick up again, music-wise, the hosts stay in bed, and their kids, taking dutiful turns on the trampoline, look appalled at how one leftover guest can command such tolerance from their folks. He feeds them anyway, including the babysitter and her boyfriend— a friendly freshman his own age with no hatred of cars—a number 15 combination. He has one more snooze, with his hostess's pink-dressed breasts in mind, before he goes home on a number 14, transferring to a number 9.

His housemate is out of town looking for a life preserver. Money, what else, to finance a noodle-packaging scheme for pork and chicken Chinese soups. There is no blackberry pie. There is a seventy-year-old wooden bungalow in decay, rented from a landlord now looking to level it, at which point his friend (who'd offered him a room here when an offshore swine decided to knock over his building downtown) would be expected to cart away his antiques. Even their burglars declined that job. Antique's the upscale word his friend uses for any basement junk of potential value from here to old age. This basement is as rank and neglected by them as the yard is by their landlord, a Portuguese contractor who builds houses, condos, and is wanted by the city for dumping toxic waste, extract of homemade deck stain—only the city doesn't know it's him they're looking for. Phone calls to city hall are not returned. Graft is rampant and capitalism flourishes. You could publish stuff like this: fire off a pamphlet for Hammer Co-op.

The afternoon sun is hot. Ash trees are growing out of the garage, the lawn is knee high. A rhododendron has gone berserk, maybe ten years ago, and morning glory snakes through blackberry vines that've suffered the back fence to disappear in their clinging. A cherry tree drapes the whole small yard in shade.

To pretend he doesn't spy on bikinis from the sunroom, he goes outside this Sunday and sits figuring at the swaying picnic table. He's trying to balance numbers and survive. He can still see bare backs through the pickets. They lie in long grass basking, baking, in the fallen seed. Renters proliferate through these houses that landlords decline to keep up, in exchange for moderate rents. But the word is out. *Buzzword.* For in a diminishing world of rented houses, rainforested lots, impoverished tenants, it's this word "renewal" that's become the euphemism for demolition, clear-cutting and eviction. Grass grows in gutters, suites carve up rooms, and pigeons land on roofs as often as pizza flyers on porches. Renewal is no longer an option, but policy. In time their own house will also become the pink townhouse with brass numbers across the alley.

"Hi, there." Arf. He'd invite the bikinis across for coffee but the Bing cherry's shade doesn't encourage it. So he's left to figuring with a pencil. He doesn't glance up to notice if there are any cherries. They're finished anyway.

What the bottom line comes down to is whether, if he takes up his grandfather's offer to house-sit in the country, he can live on welfare cheaper than here. Cheaper, but what happens to pleasure? The city offers pleasures he can't afford, unless he counts rich-bashing—Bingo!—cars and sometimes hospitality. (Still, he paid for the pizza.) The woman he really desired, with swell nachos in a black sweater, he didn't even get her name before she left the party at a decent hour with her husband. If he had would it've mattered, with such a difference in their ages? He can still feel the stiffening effects of the way her dark eyes spoke to him, as she sipped her husband's rye. Christ, rye. And boiling water made a toddy, he told her, while settling for ice and no seltzer himself, thanks. She poured. With her he could *go* for the bourgeois life of

pointy red boots and agree it needn't always be jangly bracelets and love in a cottage. Arf. They could dispute and bicker
too.

Still, the bourgeois world is too much with him, and the
age of noise bears no mercy. Car alarms bleat in the night, by
mistake, maybe not. There are radios now on motorcycles, gas
grass blowers on sidewalks, and no muffler on the lawnmow-
ers. Jets land, they take off—no one even minds the damn
seaplanes. The Coast Guard beats up the bay in a hydrofoil
to rescue foolish yachters from themselves. What about tape
decks on beaches, power shovels in yards, and junk calls on
the telephone? Main traffic arteries. "Let's move up the hill,"
the upwardly mobile mother will suggest. "Just as much traffic
up there," comes the answer. "Yes, but it's quality traffic." Diesel
buses, garbage trucks, articulated vehicles—bellowing, belch-
ing, bleating their lungs out in the burden of too-long lives.

Should he go back to school maybe? Nowhere to go appeals
to him more. He's just nineteen. It is the ultimate escape. There
isn't anything he can afford he wants, and nothing he desires
has a price. He isn't blind. Having a social conscience unlike
anybody else makes him weird in their eyes—they never say
why, they never get past his social gracelessness that really is,
he knows, satirical.

Here in the city, pleasure is about leaving behind an
impression of yourself. Burglars, builders, bores are in it up to
their hips. The only trouble with self-abuse in the sunroom is
it leaves nobody else with an inkling. It deflates on its own. So
all the good bad pleasures are about power, revenge, egoism.
He doesn't know what the good good pleasures might be.
Love, of course, he guesses. Having a good job and no elephant
to weigh you down. It's a joke how badly he yearns to be part
of the fucking tradition, with a party to go to, an address book
full of names, a bank book full of numbers, an old General
Motors muscle car. The all-American guy with his girl on the
gearshift. He studies his figures. Listen, he doesn't care where

he lives. If there is one guy he wants to escape it is the voyeur with the means and nothing else in his grasp.

Son

I decided to become a great man. It was in me to be so, the expansiveness, the generosity of spirit, the exhilarating release from obsession and pettiness. It would take courage. I would have to be brave. I was going to change the way people looked at me—insofar as they looked at me at all, this job I have—the way I looked at myself. I would accomplish more in the day's hours than I ever had before. I would be discussed, not always without envy, and I would make my mark on Time.

But this by itself was not enough. It would be enough to delight in my own talents, discover the consistency in my inconsistencies, and live musically. Breathing to the long phrase I would sound melodious, give of myself in a manner not given by me before, and behave with simplicity, compassion, wonder. I would be my wife's lover. I would cultivate my children with the fervour of a man aware of going *pfft* tomorrow. I would adopt an orphan, start up a foundation for dispossessed Haitians, enroll in a Spanish language lab. I would speak at banquets on issues of the day. So help me, I would.

I would address schoolchildren, art students, Rotary clubs, whoever in God's green city invited me—executive officers of trust companies (I know some) willing to listen to fairer ways of renewing mortgages without acrimony. I would wake up from my lethargic, sometimes cynical, manner of greeting the future and plan parties in my home. Dinner parties, surprise parties, neighbourhood bashes and garden brunches. Friends, not contacts, were to come first.

My door was to be open at all times, phone number listed, my way with the world frank. I would find the time after office hours to amuse and educate my children, compose a Russian novel, read poetry on my own far into the night. Think up songs and engage a librettist. Sing my heart out in the shower, learn to prosper on five hours' sleep, take piano lessons and certified instruction, possibly, in French cooking.

As much as anything I would discover the value—no, the pricelessness—of time, and think of wasting it as the unforgivable sin. Except for very special programs, I would give up watching TV. I would no longer insist on having supper watching the news. As a family, we were going to converse over meals and share our experiences, anxieties, jokes. I would listen to my children's jokes, try to answer their riddles, learn to interest them in the larger world. "Why did the little moron eat his shorts, Dad?" I would curtail my opinions. I would encourage them to bring me their homework, help my wife shop for their clothes, take them travelling as my greatness spread.

I would pay the babysitter extra to dress up as Elizabeth Barrett Browning and recite to them *Sonnets from the Melanese*. I would enroll them in tennis, the cello, Japanese. When time came, I would encourage them to borrow the Camry, treat their friends generously to our food and rec room, hold after-grads in their own home. *(Sonnets from the Portuguese, isn't it?)* Before shuffling off this mortal coil I would see them dandled, delighted, and dowried. I would drop the stern way I treated my first son—sour and sarcastic though he was—miss him more and send out a diplomatic mission. I would throw a party of reconciliation and maybe even kill a fatted calf.

In the spring, I would succumb to the lure of gardening and dig new rosebeds for my wife. I would learn the difference between a bud and a scion. I would plant wisteria and prune suckers from the lilacs. I would stop the laurel hedge from taking over my present, uncomfortable house. In fact, why not, we would move up the hill to a split-level view of the ocean from here to Binh Dinh.

What a change!

I would learn to carpenter and build my wife a gazebo for tea parties with her friends. I would encourage her to buy filmy clothes to enhance her softness, take vacations on her own, see herself as a woman of the world. And if she were to take a lover, I would understand and forgive. And also weep.

In my professional life I would be practical and reliable, considerate and unassuming. I would be great without being opprobrious, fractious, or flagitious. I mean abusive, touchy, or wicked—for I would learn simplicity and burn my *Thesaurus*. Those who wished to overcome me by the strength of their personalities I would treat courteously and without indifference. I would listen in meetings for silent cries from deep inside their hearts. The promise of greatness would keep me cheerful, sympathetic, and *wise*. I would command respect when I spoke in natural, winning ways—though my search for oratorical models would always take a back seat to quiet conversation with myself. I would neither natter, flatter, nor brag. I would speak with the deep conviction of having been, sometimes all night, at my desk over minds deeper, more encompassing, than mine. No longer would I complain. I would turn philosophy into action, compassion into deed, and flour into an elevated golden state when I baked bread in the kitchen for my family.

I would feel great in any clothes. At sales conferences and at the beach I would look terrific because of what shone from within! I would accept the religious beliefs of others, not as evidence of their shallowness, or confirmation of their received spirits, but as the benefits of doubt one always must have about impersonal matters of the universe. I would accept their need for religion as I would in others a need for astrology, lotteries, and unions. I would go up on my toes in secret pleasure at my iconoclasm, for I would enjoy sniffing out the radical hydrant of my heart. I would nourish my mettle by facing nothing alone. I would be great because of this willingness and ability to have it both ways.

I would make sacred the secular ways of us all. I would listen to great music, Berlioz's *Requiem,* and have the courage to sprinkle my Desert Island choices with rock 'n' roll songs—evergreen greats, golden oldies—which come from the passionate years when greatness was still a dream. I would practise tithing by giving money to charities (a tenth of my income to strangers is surely a requirement of greatness?). I would tithe, temper, and transform. (I would try to corral my alliteration, when provoked by tenderness.)

I would remember my childhood and go back to visit my parents, laugh at my father's jokes, fall in love again with Perumbur. I would purchase land by the river, build a summer house there, and share paradise with my children.

I would travel within the restrictions and responsibilities placed upon my time, by spending time at home. I would bear my greatness with unaffected lightness, kindness, and popularity. Like La Bruyère I would detect false greatness in the unsociable and remote, the careful and humourless. All the same, I would spurn greatness for the sake of being great (unlike the famous who cultivate fame for its own pleasure), and know that real greatness rests on more than solipsism. I would decline requests for interviews more often than I accepted them. Reticence would prove my distrust of the horn-blown name, my admiration for accomplishment that dared speak its own. I would become less jealous, intolerant, and erratic. Would I ever, would I always. I would stop whining for the world. I would finally grow up.

Father

"I'm looking forward to this," says his wife. "When do we start?" They're standing inside a picnic basket, creaking wicker when they move. A flame above is keeping things warm for them inside the colourful, billowing dome. Who wouldn't believe in Heaven? A champagne breakfast afloat over Pattaya's a long way from breakfast with mallards off the back patio in Perumbur. Country doctor, retired, he checks his watch and fingers a gondola cable, its pulse twitching to be off. "Once we tip out a little sand," he jokes, "we're gone." But it's hot air that will determine their departure, not sand. Loyally, she acknowledges the joke. His jokey style goes way, way back, to courtship in the Stone Age when her hourglass figure first led him into comic sublimation. Over the years he found house calls went off better with a joke. "D'you hear the one our Ted told me the day we took off, about the pacifist Catholic who refused to...?" So he gets carried away, so what's pleasure anyway but transportation? By bending over backwards out of their basket, he can read small letters stamped on the balloon's collar, and wonders how this ad could possibly be read from the ground. Convexity prevents him seeing the elephants, but much higher, encircling the whole top third of their present world, are Indian elephants attached trunk-to-tail, plodding lightly, it would appear, around the ethereal elements of silk and hot air. If someone happens to be settling early into a beach chair, that person could probably see the beasts hovering over palms, an illusion of weight, bulk, and seams.

Their mahout, or whatever you call this driver of the Elephant Walk balloon, emerges from the Palace Hotel with a bucket on a stand, two glasses and a wired-up magnum stuck in ice, followed by a white-jacketed waiter bearing a covered tray the size of a small airport, glinting in the sun. "Yummy, breakfast," says his wife. To the small sandy-haired man climbing the step-stool with his bucket, she declaims, "Our life, our soul, our gondolier!" Quoting? "I wouldn't know," she says. "Thought I just made it up." Doctor looks heavenward in a big parody of tolerance: Fly Cathay Pacific, command the little letters—in case he's forgotten. "You folks feeling hungry?" An American mahout, by the sound of him, his balloon having flown all the way from Paris, folded neatly in a cargo hold.

"We'll get flying as soon as I . . . Hang on, now." *Whoooooosh* . . . Increasing his bottled jet from Bunsen burner to acetylene torch to flame thrower, till the entire heated-up vessel is straining at its anchor, he prepares to cast off by making sure the toy table in their basket is okay to receive the waiter's hot tray. They his first guests or what? Housekeeping seems foreign to him. "All set for liftoff? Stand by in your places for liftoff." The wicker protests. But then, look, the three of them rising gently over the Gulf of Thailand, trying to salvage perspective, not drop it, as when passing from one element into another.

He knows immediately now what's been missing since leaving home for their look at Asia, and why, touring Manila, Bangkok, this Thai resort, he chose long ago to turn his back on cities to practise in the country. Very simple, just listen, between these intermittent whooshes when the mahout goads his balloon a little higher . . . the silence! It's the silence he values! No zoom of pink-turbaned Sikhs on rented motorcycles, no whining water scooter bouncing off waves, no go-go music from the rash of open-sided bars along Beach Road. Not on your life. Up here the champagne cork pops with the thrilling echo it'd make inside a vast cathedral's dome. "To us Asian impostors!" she toasts, including their American gondolier, who won't drink on the job—only pour, goad, and pilot them—all set to take the lid off breakfast. "Look," she points, "there's our hotel with the sunburnt prawn!" The emblem arches high over the Regent Marina's sign. She's balancing her effervescent glass by its stem, in the mood for a good chatter, despite a cold. "Why do we say swimming pools are kidney-shaped? Are they, really?" He's distracted by a—doesn't answer till she—"Yoohoo! Will the real doctor please stand up?" My dear one. "You think," he tells her, "the makers are going to sell any pools to the cocktail set by calling them liver-shaped? Suck 'em up!" Is what Don Ho used to tell them in the fifties, sixties?, on their first-ever extraterrestrial hols. After the floor shows they'd watch "To Tell the Truth" on a black-and-white TV in their room, looking down on Waikiki ... Voyeurs! "Lookit, I'm going to put my pistol in your holster and cock it," he would tell her with a mai tai under his belt. "Get ready to die, bad girl." Undoctorly of him, that.

"Go ahead and use the floor of the gondola," says the gondolier. Their life, their soul, their mahout. Gary Moore in a brush cut. "Good idea not to drop anything out of a balloon, you never know." Not even Kleenex, for she's blown once, twice, to rid herself of phlegm picked up from gusts of Hyatt air conditioning in Tokyo. And she's blowing to make her ears pop, since the balloon has risen faster than a—maybe her middle ear's infected. With a cold she's been lucky, not having to hear Asian din the way it's meant to be heard, not in Guam anyway, where for goodness' sake, they found themselves on an unscheduled refuelling stop, except they ended up on the ground for ten hours, and *she* didn't need the earmuffs offered at the shooting gallery they were taken to, where the rangemaster at the Wild West Gun Club—who ran the show for Japanese tourists—handed her a .44 magnum, compliments of Cathay Pacific, and told her to live out her fantasies with the paper men straight down range. The one in the middle was sitting on the fence when she got to him with a live, if less than full charge, *blam*, Son-of-Sam sound, blowing the barrel cool at her lips, and with her cold she couldn't smell the cordite. Better up here, where she thinks she can smell the salty northeast monsoon. He sniffs. His nose packing up or what? Either aging membranes or the champagne bubbles have succeeded in corking it. So he gazes instead. A country club has spread out below them as they drift inland, and the view makes up for his loss of smell. He feels like swinging. "You have a course at home," she says, "you never use. You're a member." *Whoooooosh* ... Man in charge gives them a goose to arrest the inland drift, and then uncovers her steaming eggs for breakfast. He *can* smell after all! Microwaving, like the neutron bomb, seems to put the heat where it belongs without cracking the china.

"Stand over here," she says, "and have your breakfast by me, Doctor. I have a woman's ailment I want to complain about."

It's like being in a beer commercial over the Canadian prairies, when a helicopter camera circles the balloon, and we see a waving couple, wind bearing them in the direction of foothills. Except a chinook would be blowing from, not to, the foothills, so where they'd really be heading with a Molson was Hudson Bay. She wants a cuddle. Can he cut his sausage and pat her bottom at the same time? Chew gum and have a gander? Time was they used to paint each other with the little tautologies of tongues, and have the world to themselves. Well, don't they still? Good breeding ignores a mahout. But what of the invisible cook who prepared their breakfast—could *he* possibly prove intrusive? Who knows anymore? Hairnets, plastic gloves, face masks *de rigueur* in the Rajneeshi commune for couples relaxing into missionary positions—and Safeway, where food comes from, today sounding like a condom factory! President Suharto, whose country's health clinics are next on their list, has the biggest growth industry in the Third World. *Should* they look for his condom factory on Java? All the president needs to get into now, for sustained growth, is razor blades.

"D'you hear the one about two ruby-dub dope addicts sharing the same needle?" he asks their mahout. "Social worker asks them if they aren't afraid of contracting AIDS. The older one says nah, they're both wearing condoms." Arf, arf. The gondolier laughs like their Ted in Perumbur. A sardonic sound, but it's a jungle everywhere these days; you need *some* kind of camouflage for self-protection. Take the last time they went for a walk in the city, they saw a seal rolling in waves along the seawall, dead. Plugged by a fisherman and brought in on the tide—or victim of a toxic breakfast afloat in the wrong element?

She can't finish her omelette for coughing. In fact the cold has sunk to her chest as they've risen. To release the phlegm and bring it up requires a patient hacking. No picnic for an *old* couple in a balloon, even when you can afford champagne instead of lager. What if one of them has to pee from it? From the champagne? The gentleman farmer in him spies the champagne ice bucket melting; but would she use that? A bucket? Possibly Kleenex. How did the Raj once pee in baskets atop its imperial elephants? With a very strict—nah, barely a one-arfer that one. He draws her attention overboard again to the parachute beneath them, rising from the beach, a man in harness towed by a speedboat: the apple of God's eye. "Yes," she replies, choking, "had *we* not drifted by hitched to a silkier apple." Their balloon's swung back for the ocean now, rolling down Beach Road over taxis as the wind picks up. "A knot or two," agrees their man, "judging by ground speed." The playground of Asia, catering to Iranians, Germans, Indians, Frenchmen, Americans—pedophiles, packaged tourists, homosexuals, transvestites, honeymooners, sailors. "All of us here for pleasure . . ." It's a little like Alexandria in the war, where he'd even managed to enjoy himself. "Listen, Molly, if you feel like spitting, don't care what the street signs say. Gob. We're nearly over the sea now."

He swallows the last of his French toast and peers down in search of the caftaned Egyptian in a fez who prefers his ratty-haired Thai women to walk several feet to the rear; or the three-hundred-pound Arab, creased by fat and bathing trunks, eating dates from a Cellophane pouch and joking with a prostitute who—*Whoooooooooosh* . . . Guests wave from the compound of the Royal Cliff Hotel as they sail up and over its hill. Consider the toadstool grass canopies along the golden sand. Consider the double-decker cruise launches at anchor. Consider—consider how wonderful he feels with no more edges to his life, how boundaries lap over, flow into, are wide open to possibility and unrestricted by any need to persuade a colleague, say. No axe to grind, no view to put, no personal changes to undertake on pain of failure. Lately, so *many* flights beginning and ending with the smell of jet fuel, their entries and exits at airports, turning him into a voyeur with nothing but time on his hands, sand. So? Honorary visits to rural clinics? Will the real doctor please stand up! Is he the man on the left, the man in the middle, the man— Still, he no longer misses the news. Watching the news from Afghanistan—is it months ago now?—he was saying Kalashnikov at home. Had he heard the name right, Kalashnikov? Rebels were manufacturing Kalashnikov rifles. In border towns the Afghans were copying Kalashnikov rifles they had captured from the Russians. Saying aloud the tongue rollers on the news he'd felt informed. It was a feeling he'd mistaken for knowledge and having a place in the world. Kalashnikov. Tamil Tigers. SDI. . . But lately he hasn't sensed any loss of place, though he's missed the news and something to get his mouth around. Ethical Mutual Funds. Tunagate. . . He used to be away to the races when a new world popped up on the news. Interferon. Smack. Now, having travelled *this* far, he's begun to lose the focus he once thought mattered. Attila the Hen? Consider yesterday's glass-bottomed boat—

"I think Ted's too sarcastic for his own good," she's saying, her coughing arrested for now. "He can't go on with that chip on his shoulder. I think house-sitting in the country will be good for him. A winter of frost in the fields is full of surprises." Providing we reap what we sow. Too earnest a son breeds another one rolling in waves of distemper and no life jacket. Poor Ted, even Devin, both adrift, business schemes coming out of Devin's ear. . . But so am I adrift, at my age still, in more knots of wind than I really care for, see, under the red, white, and blue? Colours of Thailand. And half a dozen other countries, including Heaven, you can bet. ". . . So anyway, when they get to the pearly gates, St. Peter salutes them, and one of them notices he's wearing only a single stripe . . ." The three-arfers have that little something extra, an indefinable atmosphere you could say, the appetite brought to them—or maybe it's the way the cook times his plates. Who can say? A jokey atmosphere for sure runs through little tragedies. Like these poor country clinics; even this Italian restaurant they've been going to, run by Thais . . . very funny, actually, very nourishing. "You folks enjoy your breakfasts?" inquires the mahout. What is it about the friendliness of Americans at breakfast, the highway waitresses, the—"That there you're looking at is the USS *Something* helicopter carrier—but if you don't mind, I'm gonna give us another burn, 'cause we shouldn't be drifting offshore. This wind has started to pick—" *Whooooosh . . .*

But it makes little difference, the wind's got them revolving like a slow corkscrew now, aided and abetted by champagne, and gliding towards American naval power, the same pair of anchored ships they cruised past yesterday, among their fellow passengers a hedonist French couple, grooming each other's tanned skins like monkeys, waving mischievously at ship-marooned sailors, young woman's breasts bouncing like volleyballs, the sailors hooting, the warship underneath them flexing muscle at Cambodia, where recent dry season offensives underway by Khmer guerrillas (according to *The Bangkok Post)* were drawing sharper than normal response from the Vietnamese. Was he starved after all for news? Molly thought so. Yet these ships made him feel like they were a lot closer *to* the news. Valour. They'd appeared overnight. Last night their sailors were already trickling ashore in civvies, headed for the Disco Duck, squashed inside little Toyota trucks that served as taxis. He and she had had to assure one suspicious boy Ted's age five baht was the going rate, so that would be ten for him and his girl. "Yeah?" This sailor said he especially didn't trust the glass booths where you changed money in the open on the street. So the doctor asked his wife if the navy shouldn't invest in Michelin guides, and not just condoms, for its sailors. "For heaven's sake," she is saying to their own guide, "we're heading for Coral Island. We were just there yesterday." *Whooooooooosh . . .*

Fire, air. It turned out the gondola they'd all climbed into yesterday, as soon as their launch anchored in the cove, had floorboards that lifted to reveal a glass bottom when they raised their legs. The guide had cut the outboard engine and they'd drifted a while over brown coral, looking for tropical fish. They didn't see one. Didn't matter. Peering from one element into another they saw only water, finally, so they passed over that, once the guide got his putt-putt going, to the shed ashore. (This earth, or rather sand, underfoot—as they ate a fish lunch and flapped away at flies—was nothing as nice as Phuket Island, said the French couple.) Coral Island had been a jungly destination, forty-five minutes offshore... Wait though. It's closer by balloon, even if the mahout refuses to look when they point it out to him. "Don't worry, folks, these knots'll die down, we'll catch the next bus back." *Whoooooooooooooosh* . . . Their gondolier, the fire fumbler. He rebuffs the big wind—or is trying to. Her coughing resumes. How her hourglass figure has filled in around the bottom, how this standing around's no good for the legs. She gets hold of her own throat and gives it a good throttle, because she wants to speak without choking. "Aren't we overdue?" she wonders. "I mean for the amount we paid—because by an hourly rate we've already been up in the air close to . . . I mean we're floating to beat the band in the direction of Malaya, aren't we?" His life, his soul for fifty years, a billion times lovelier—What's one more flight in an unscheduled tailwind? "For Godsake, Molly, let the man alone. Let's enjoy the experience." But it's hard sightseeing on your pins all day, the veins in a tourist leg start to look like rivers draining into—

"Say," he asks politely, "I wonder if we *are* heading a bit off course?" *Whoooooooooooooosh*. . . Maybe drinking champagne in the tropical sun is their real problem, lightheadedness, two airheads in need of gravity? Time to pull a valve maybe. Maybe if they both sobered up they could encourage their man to make landfall on Coral Island, bring them down with a bump in the jungle, where they'd be in touch with earth again. If he keeps on mahouting around with this Bunsen burner he's going to miss the whole bloody island ... "I mean we've already sailed downwind of the warships, Laurie ..." (Hard to tell exactly how fast you're drifting when the waves all look the same. Isn't that his name, Laurie?) "Keep your hat on, Doc. Doing our best. See if there's any more champagne." Cables pulsing, wicker in a tizzy, and her cough revving. Well, might as well lean back and enjoy this freedom from being in touch with any knowledge of how the world operates. The mastery of the thing! Listen, pretty soon they'll be throwing more than Kleenex overboard, just to keep up in the world! Magnum next, the ice bucket once they all have a pee to lighten bladders, their cutlery, the plates, glasses, tray next, then the whole damn table... Far harder for the rich ballast to pass into heaven, than the camel... "D'you hear the one," asks the sandy-haired gondolier, "about the sailor in the desert who thinks he sees an albatross drinking lion piss?" Coarse professionalism annoys the doctor—who decides this joker's going to get the best of him if he doesn't scratch memory for something just as cavalier to keep the orchestra playing ...

Scratching now, all he comes up with are cathedral tours in Europe when he and Molly never once commented to one another, nor, as far as he knew, to themselves, about religious experience occasioned by apses, holy stones, and little monk dolls for sale with moveable dongs. There wasn't any. Does this mean they aren't traditional? Father, Son, and Holy Ghost? Experience is what they were after, mild pleasure, a good enough time without being greedy. *Whoooooooooooooooooosh* ... They *have* given of themselves to their community and family, without regret, and never been, so far as they felt, excessive in their longings to get away; nor, during time away, wished to prolong their absence or indulge themselves without wishing they could be sharing all this with children and grandchildren. They were salt-of-the-earth folk when you got right down to the sniffy—Hey, Molly's started reading a magazine and looking quite calm in the middle of all this spinning. A frequent flyer by virtue of her stiff upper—Mind over matter. "It says here," she reads, "'Champagne breakfast in the sky with an exciting balloon ride around the resort.'" Glances up. "By the look of it, we're getting our baht's worth. How much fuel's left in the tank?" Her pages whipping in the breeze. He asks to peruse them. She gives them over with a warning that reading makes you dizzy. *Whooooooo*—Ignoring yet another quick ascent (this hot air's brutish the way it rushes the vacuum) he asks what she'd like to do upon their return this afternoon. "Mmm," she decides, "a snooze?" And what about a restaurant this evening, the Italian place again, or try somewhere new? "Oh, let's just have a quiet supper in the hotel and go up to bed early."

He pokes calmly through *Explore Pattaya,* Vol. 1 No. 2. Since this is to be their last night in the resort, he tots up pleasures they've had insufficient time to taste. Not counting water scootering, they've done no laser sailing or windsurfing, chartered no boat to go deep-sea fishing, ridden no hydrofoil, not played golf, or even gone for a demonstration by real working elephants at the Elephant Kraal near Pattaya's Orphanage (see map p. 16). They continue to sink like an elevator, but never mind, maybe they're saving fuel for a favourable updraft. "... We've also missed scuba diving, roller skating, shooting at the indoor range at Tiffany's (.38 bullets are nine baht each, targets six baht), horseback riding, hill climbing, tennis, waterskiing, archery, parasailing, badminton—is that enough for you?—camping at the YMCA camp on Jomtien Beach, boxing (evidently there's a training camp seven kilometres from Pattaya, where we could've rented gloves, speed and body bags), bowling, and darts. We could've also worked out on weights at Frank's Gym, just below our hotel, for an hourly rate of one hundred baht, including sauna." She's about to start hacking again. By the length of this, or any other holiday list, it's as if they've never partaken of the least of what life's party has to offer, so why bother travelling anyway? The clinics? He turns to the last page. "Come to think of it, my chevalier, we haven't really eaten any Thai food. . . Which does remind me of the Indian from Madras, who liked his curry hotter than an engine, so one day his daughter . . ." *Whoooooooooosh* . . . Cough's back, with a little nausea it appears, dizziness. Mucus penetrating her middle ear via the Eustachian tube. Up and down they go like a ride at Playland.

Their hearts in hiding, stirred for these years together, and they complain about catarrh and a little drift to the west? He can remember how sheer trudging kept them going in the thirties, that and the old rattletrap wedding gift to themselves, before their valley began earning enough to pay him, following his return from the medical corps overseas. When things seemed bleakest, they had put their faith in the future. Their son who amounted to the future, learned from them that renewal was ever possible. Trust to the future when things looked blue—like now, the sky above, the sea below. Up and down, pleasure and distress, they seem interchangeable when you get nicely humming on a morning air. "I don't think we really need this table, do we folks, now that breakfast is over? It'd give us a nice lift if we chucked her, hey?" So over she goes with the last of breakfast. *Whoooooooooooooosh.* . . Hard to say how close they're coming to water before these lofty reprieves. Waves slope longer to their troughs out here, they deceive the landing eye. But hang on, listen . . . Two men and a young woman in a boat, nothing to eat for a month, the first fellow taps the second on the shoulder and whispers in his ear—Three men in a boat, no water for seven days, the third one turns to the first one and says—Is the real captain the man on the left, the man in the middle, or the man on the right? Will the real—So anyway, they'd been standing around in this basket it seemed since the sun came up. To the east the sky had burned like their legs were starting to now. And when he couldn't stand it any longer, the older gentleman turned to the young mahout of his soul and said . . . "I don't think my wife is up to this much longer. You can see, she's suffering from nausea. I'd advise you to put us down the first chance you get." *Whooosh. . .* The flame is getting shorter, the burns briefer. So anyway, this older gentleman decided he'd just have to take matters into his own hands. Wh—he began to say. Blow! Wh—which of us is more valuable than the other if and wh—when it comes to sacrificing one of us for the sake of the rest?

What rest, he thinks, when we, ah my dear, fall. . . You see this older gentleman figured the younger man was going to jettison the past, so he wanted to make sure he—*Whooo*—Not much gas left in the old bottle now. Better blow for all we're worth. . . Wh—blow! So the old gentleman turns to his wife, you have to understand this, and he gives her one of those mouth-to-mouthers, deeper than the very ocean, with their tongues swimming around in there like bottom fish, tickling the grainy floor of the hemisphere itself, when—*Whoo—Who*—Flame's dead, hot air cooling fast . . . love alone on its way back up, and nothing to bottle it with for the next journey, a no-arfer, no coming up for air, no . . . Blow! Wh—Who is she, this mother? Wh—What elements conceive us? D'you hear what the doctor says to this svelte young thing comes into his office, Molly? . . . Arf, he says, sitting up like a puppy. *Wh—W*—So he blew out the party candles and turned to travel. But he got tired of travelling and decided to set about fishing with wh—what health of his remained in the narrowing craft of the world.

MEMOIR

OTEL KISSING is more passionate, I decided, because a hotel takes the individual kisser out of his or her own home. Or in case of a couple, especially an older pair of guests, out of their own home. Inhibitions fall away. Grudges and irritations vanish. This is the pleasure of travel. Or rather of a hotel—since you don't have to travel far to stay overnight at the Palace Hot Springs Hotel—the way it is sure to improve canoodling between a man and a woman. You have to remember, and this is the point. The best way for a partner to seem exotic is for you to feel foreign too.

So get out of town, come to the mountains.

Some such come-on is what I wrote down in the summer of 1951, on a sheet of hotel stationery, to show to the manager who had hired me at the Palace. Did I feel this was how the hospitality industry should attract business? That I would make my mark as a deskbound pimp? Of course, it was not then called the hospitality industry, not until degrees in hotel management came into vogue and made more sense than the kind of apprenticeship that once yoked me. My apprenticeship didn't make sense even then, not to the manager, who read over my proposal for an advertising blitzkrieg of the

Lower Mainland. "'Hot springs,'" he remarked drily, "will no doubt be taken in the lewd way you have in mind. But 'hotel kissing'? You make it sound like we're offering copulation with the building itself."

From the front office I rotated to the laundry room, where he said I would receive notice of further rotations in keeping with the terms of my apprenticeship. I waited.

When the hotel called the other day after thirty-five years, I felt no desire to accept an invitation to come back for a centenary celebration. I told the caller she must think I was a whipping post with a short memory. What I actually said was I would have to get back to her on that one. "But the dance," she urged, "the whole weekend's going to be wild." Some such come-on. I recognized the hyperbole, which held out to me, and I suspect a million other past staffers and guests, festivities befitting the grand old girl who still availed herself of a garter belt. Or maybe she said a Walter Scott. Something dildoish, probably, in keeping with my young caller's idea of an old girl's wild time.

She went on. As for returning stolen property, she felt the memorabilia contest might interest someone of my "vintage" who sounded like he "got off" on history of a local nature. She was flirting with me. I had to admit it sounded wild, but I would have to get back to her on that one too. Hanging up, I supposed I could win first prize by bringing back under the guarantee of amnesty—not a bar of witch-hazel soap, or a tarnished sterling fork piked from the dining room, the usual tourist peccadillos—but a chambermaid. I had used and abused their purloined property for many years now, and it would go over very well, I thought, very humorously, Della got up in the black uniform she wore during the summer we met as lackeys in residence.

When I put it to Della over dessert that I had had a call inviting us to the centenary of our dirty laundry she lowered her knife. "What," she said, "are you talking about?" The scene of her jitterbugging, I commented, the place where she'd tramped the corridors in underwear and less. "You remember, the palace of your first and, so far as I know, last passion for a future real estate tycoon?" She had heard this before. "Oh, is there a reunion?" Not, I replied, as far as I was concerned. She surprised me with her riposte. "Fiddley-doo. Naturally, we're going. It'll be nice for us."

And so we came.

It had been on the streetcars, under a raincoat, that I had learned to canoodle. This is what a wild time meant after the war, when privacy for high-schoolers was a raincoat to hide under from naked bulbs and the drafts of folding doors. A wild time on a streetcar consisted of jerky stops, lurching corners, and spotty acceleration. It is a wonder we learned anything, except how to control lip drift. Yet few places in life were so stimulating, except Happyland, beneath the timber girders of the Shoot-the-Chute, where overhead the boats went down even faster than we, in hiding, could launch tongues down one another's throats. It is unnerving how history slips away. Happyland gives way to Playland, and rides like the Giant Dipper are torn down. Who even remembers the Giant Dipper—or its reputation as an abortionist for girls in trouble? The timber joints of most rides get dry rot and rickets, the same way links that move these rides up their tracks and over the top, grind away to rust. I can still hear the wash of boats hitting the water.

After my botched apprenticeship, Della and I came back to the city as a number, later returning to the Valley where I set up office as a notary public in Carthage—but only after several years as a motorman on the interurban coaches, scrubbed from the Valley in 1958, the year I returned to school, the same year our little Alice entered first grade. Aside from a hundred million depositions and affidavits taken since then, contracts authenticated, bills of exchange protested, this has been my life. I wish I could call these millions hyperbole. The fact is I have not had my oil changed in thirty years.

I like to pull in to the Shell station on the highway and listen to the girl who works there clean my windshield and check my tires. This is the way she talks, broadly hinting of other things without meaning any of them. Years ago, as part of a famous advertising gimmick, she would have been asking to put a tiger in my tank. Her dirty hands on my oil pan would be enough to convince me that our daughter is right about her father, and men in general.

Alice is a lounge singer in the city, friend of a thousand men and property of none. She has taken the vow of single-hood, and is not unvocal about it. It is her conviction that husbands kill their wives—dump on their scruples, treat their friends coolly, expect submission, dole out the silent treatment if we don't get it, and, offered the least encouragement, screw around. She says that as husbands we kill them. They do not know until we are gone they have been waiting all along for their lives.

Our daughter has been unhappy. She seldom visits, and when she does will bring along tapes to pass the afternoon. She thinks it enough that she comes. I am sorry to say we bore her, the countryside bores her, she feels Perumbur needs a coke merchant. She misses the city, yet dreads Sundays alone in it. She's really an extrovert who looks to strangers for stimulus and approval. Caveat emptor. Through her I first heard the crooner Joe Cocker sing. The name alone was enough to make me think she was putting us on. I was recumbent on the davenport.

I say crooner, which is what you would expect from some-one of my generation, whose favourite song dates from our summer at the Palace Hot Springs Hotel. Each night that I went to bed under the eaves there, listening to a crystal set grounded on my bedsprings, Sinatra was singing "You're the

One." The song seeped into my brain. I was falling in love with Della Morra and learning, not so much the words, although I did learn those, but the control and phrasing in that rendition, to croon it to this girl. I did not want to sing it any other way than the way it lay in those grooves in my head.

Since last Easter, I have been listening over and over to the other song, on the tape Alice forgot to take home. The crooner in my time has undergone a change. He has lost his nerve. He repeats the same line with gaps and spasms. He twitches like a paint shaker in the hardware store. He sings falsetto. He screams at times and can't reach notes. He has a voice like our local gravel quarry, and I imagine, when he sings, the shape and firmness of his veins, resembling pumped-up peashooters. Yet it is his persistence in face of fear that makes his song sound true. When I hear the piano and listen to Joe Cocker sing "You Are So Beautiful"—if I were a woman, I would believe him. I am moved myself. If I sang this song to the gas station girl she would, I venture, fall in love with me.

But I too have lost my nerve.

Lost it, that is, until I did what I did tonight at the centennial dance.

I did not know until we got here who was behind the centenary celebrations. Like me, Frank Stockton had been hired to learn the hotel business that same summer, and he too had given in his notice by fall. He was very smooth. It was with Frank's hand more or less up her dress, upon my arrival in the laundry room, that I first met Della. For the next two months the three of us were inseparable, not because Frank and I were friends, but because Della could not make up her mind between us. Frank, after removing it from up her dress—and in what I wanted to believe was vengeance against ground lost—had turned his hand to real estate. He now owns commercial properties the length and breadth of this valley. In the media his reputation for having a fiscal finger in every pie is legendary.

Which is why I suspected his motives right away in this enthusiastic commitment to history of a local nature. What was he doing here?

I asked Della.

"Pimping, probably. Look at the forests."

Before dinner in the ballroom, she and I were strolling the lakeshore recalling a summer regatta, the nights we three soaked in the hot mineral water after curfew, the laundry chutes, the ticklish masseuse, our kitchen raids, the covert lovemaking of guests in bedrooms and stables. This hotel is not the original, which burned up in 1920, but a reincarnation, renovated further the year before our employment. We have our own bedroom tonight, our own bathroom, but it isn't the same sort of splashy room Della remembers servicing as a chambermaid. Today the building feels worn; history has worn away its grandeur.

For the sake of curious tourists, the manager would force Frank and me to recite how a few dirty miners had discovered the steaming springs on their way home from the gold fields in the last century, when sternwheelers plied the lake with prospectors heading into the Interior by ox cart and camel. The facts titillated those guests who pretended to care. By resurrecting a regatta in 1951, the village of Palace managed to entice speedboats from as far away as Washington and California.

That summer we had wild times like skiing barefoot and stealing horses. The blue stars threw down spears; we got qualmish stomachs from August pears. A pear rots from the inside out. I don't remember if it was the same with apples but the punch line in response to *them* apples was always, sure, but do you know how the worm gets in? It was a summer of remarkable wit.

———————

The dance was earlier tonight. There were six or seven hundred of us, swinging the night away to the Freddy Simms Orchestra, reminiscing among ourselves in swirling figures and seated at tables set up around the ballroom's sprung floor. There were balloons and streamers. There were corsages and boutonnieres. There was boogiewoogie. Della wore a blue chiffon semi-formal. We noticed Frank across the room, the centre of attention at a table for the manager of the Palace, two Japanese couples, assorted dignitaries who looked like boiled beets, and Freddy Simms himself, whenever the orchestra took a break and he came off stage for a drink of something in a yellow Thermos. Della suggested it would only be polite of us to go over and say hello to Frank, and ask him how he was.

"Tight, probably. Like us."

We underestimated his geniality. Not long before the home waltz Frank started gladhanding his way around the room, flush with the success he had helped to engineer. "Look at his wife," whispered Della.

399

I saw what she meant. Frank had killed his wife. I could tell by looking at her she was dead. I was surprised he had brought along the corpse. What I actually saw at his side was a dark, ravishing girl in a black gown, certainly—by the way she was holding his arm against her breasts like a pole vaulter getting ready for a run—not his daughter. Her black hair flared aggressively.

"Let's dance," I suggested to Della.

"My feet are gone."

"I don't think I really want a chinwag with Frank," I croaked. Her naked chair suggested an escape, had there been time to dress it in a skirt and waltz off.

To avoid him I walked away in the direction of the bandstand. I had been drinking a lot of Okanagan wine fermented from Napa Valley grapes. Not a blend I discovered sympathetic to prudence. The orchestra had just finished a popular number, near the end of the last set, so I climbed up and shook Freddy Simms's tanned, California-spotted hand. I chinwagged a little with the musicians, remarking properly on their instruments. I walked over to the old-fashioned microphone and looked down across the floor.

Then, into this silver watermelon of a mike, I began to croon.

No one quite knew what to make of me. I did not know what to make of myself, crooning, but the song felt liberating. The feedback was barely audible. I was picked up by a few unbuttoned musicians with sentiment in their fingers. A hush fell when I finished. I came back down to Della, right across the dance floor, and kissed her.

———————

The rest of course you know. As our host you went up on stage to thank Freddy Simms and his orchestra, whose big-band sound you said made it seem that they must have played here in another life because of the era they had so smoothly brought back to us at the Palace. You still have a silver tongue, Frank. You thanked everybody for supporting the centenary of the hotel, and reminded us, if we had not already entered something in the memorabilia contest, to get it in by breakfast, when you would be judging the entries and sharing them with us over pancakes.

"I notice we have a menu signed by Bob Hope, from 1948, the year of the big flood. So dig around in your luggage, ladies and gents, and find something old—you all brought a memento, didn't you, for old times' sake? Maybe the long-lost chandelier?" Your audience laughed and glanced up at the gold ceiling, trying to remember what it had once been like. To think if it had even existed. Perhaps an earthquake had loosened and dislodged it.

The last thing you announced, too casually I thought, was the impending sale of the hotel to Japanese interests, who

were planning major renovations reckoned to appeal to hon-
eymooning couples from Kyoto and Osaka. "I think we owe
our Japanese friends here this evening a big round of applause
for saving an institution. How 'bout it, folks?"

You did not disclose whether you owned a piece of the
action, Frank, or whether you were merely the promoter, the
salesman, the broker. I remember you once boasting to me you
were a backdoor man. I thought you meant *re* your aspirations
at the hotel, which you did mean, but not in the backroom
way of getting ahead. You were always louche. This evening,
did you want us to think you were returning something to
the old girl, before dumping her to offshore interests? Your
philanthropy made me think how those crooning machines
I once heard young Japanese clubbies singing into—probably
it was a filler on the news hour—made them sound very
smooth.

Long after the dance, Della and I were sitting alone in the
churning sulphur pool, when who should come in but a couple
with a flashlight. "I knew where to find these two burglars," you
said, shining the light in our eyes. "Didn't I tell you we used to
sneak down here after-hours, back in the dark ages?"

"Hello, Frank," we both said.

"This is Clark," you said, relocating the beam. "Clark, say
hello to Bill Williams. Bill Bills, we called him. He's a prince.
How are you, Della?"

And so there we were after thirty-five years, noticing how
only one of us looked the way we used to, free of gravity and
the rust of time. Your companion smiled, and slipped into
the rotating water beside me in her black, one-piece suit. She
is what, Frank, twentytwo? It is unlikely her wardrobe will
acquire colour for at least another ten years.

"You old dog," you said, coming down the steps wearing a
diver's belt, which was really your girth. "Who'd have thought
you had the woof still in you?" But you were looking at Della,

not me. "What've you both been up to after half a lifetime? Where's home anyway?"

"I liked your song," Clark said to me, floating closer with breasts like softballs. "Wild." I recognized her voice from the phone call. She put her hand on my knee, under the water where no one could see it, including me. Nothing heavy or unappealing. The movement of her nails had a trace of symmetry.

You and Della sat chatting—in the horizontal shadows cast by your flashlight lying on the pool's lip. You were looking at her the way you used to, Frank, peering at her underwater breasts for a better glimpse of the future, perhaps, moving your arm up against her thigh, she told me later, with your fingers sometimes threatening more foreign parts. Do you remember how you once charmed Charlene Downing, the Regatta Queen, but felt Della was the one, because she was distant, more alluring? Catholic? You are still a tom, Frank, sitting your kittenish companion down beside me and watching us at a distance. Were you, for old time's sake, anticipating the wild time to come?

I know I was.

The rules have changed since our time, in that rules exist where there used to be none, and the first of these is not to soak while under the influence of alcohol, which made us all violators. The rules pretty well cover the waterfront now: No bathing with nerve or cardiovascular disorders, high or low blood pressure, diabetes. You still have a handsome face, Frank, but the hot water made it perspire as if you were due any minute for a seizure down there, owing to your driven life.

Do you remember as a young man how you left Della when resigning your service to the hotel? You told me she was now mine. You were leaving and did not expect to be back. Addio, signorina. You who had already told her to expect a surprise that evening, and to leave her door unlocked. I thought you were leaving because you were fed up, as I was, with apprenticeship. I knocked. Her room was dark. She did not know it was me and said, of course, to come in. I am still ashamed to say that when I entered at last, it was under false pretences.

"Was that my surprise?" she asked, turning over at the end to face me for the first time.

So we both betrayed her. But I was betrayed, too. Nothing to be bitter about, Frank, except you both knew what I did not, for some time, recognize. That Alice was your daughter, not mine, and how later when I tried to forget all this I sounded anxious. A foghorn in heat is how Della put it. I seemed doomed to repeat the same line over and over. How could I tell Della Morra that she didn't really love me? Because her Catholic past made her refuse a ride on the Giant Dipper?

Remembering, I still sound anxious. Much to our daughter's disappointment, I've long had trouble expressing love for my wife. This is my flaw, Frank, but I suppose a very common one when most of us are killers by consent?

I am sitting up here in our room, in the small hours this morning, writing out this affidavit. As a voyeur, Frank, you would find nothing exotic in this, and be wrong. For I have discovered what I believe you were hoping to find tonight, by trading me your young girl for my old one. That the flesh of an older woman is imperfection worthy of desire. Some such come-on. Not a revelation that pounces like danger you spy burning bright in the bamboo, Frank. But the prospect appealed to you. You must have dreamed how singularity can inflame lust. How the blemish of the little local vein can give rise to an unaccustomed passion. This is what makes Della and not your pole vaulter—who you will admit can wear a little thin—exotic. Your idea of a wild time, Frank, is shagging softballs. You really cannot imagine what you missed out on there, when Della turned you down.

I will waken her before morning and see if she doesn't agree as she reads this through, that any memoir is an amnesty in its own right. "You see," I will whisper to her, caressing the knobs of her spine, unbuttoning them, "I am writing this for Frank's memorabilia contest. He is reading it right now, even as we talk. Frank is watching us here in bed, Della, with our conniving. I feel like turning to him, don't you, right now and asking him over my shoulder. 'You are, aren't you, Frank? Reading this for auld lang syne? What are its chances, do you feel? I mean, will you be reading these sheets of hotel stationery to your guests at breakfast, along with that menu signed by Bob Hope, and sharing the chandelier miraculously restored?' Della, my witness. My treasure. Here, let me lick this. My dear Della. You are so beautiful to me."

You are   so beautiful   to me

STURGEON

S HE WANTED CLOSURE but the vendor decided hold on, he couldn't accept, wouldn't sell. Having lied to her about his willingness to come down, he now seemed moored to a self-important dock he called his conscience. So a wasted evening, driving all this way with an offer for his "bosky get-away": five hemlocked acres with a teardown and spring-fed stream, off a dirt road cul-de-sacing in an oil-drum cache two miles from Steelhead. A marginal listing at best.

Something had given her a vile dream last night, not about his refusal to sell out, but a smelly little mirage about waifs in the Philippines. Maybe the vendor was mistreating his sons. They looked forsaken when she left, motherless. Three mustard-lipped children she was unlikely to see again, given the man's impromptu paranoia. She should've refused his shack two months ago when he told her more or less weirdly she had bad hair.

Driving home she calls her brother. They talk cellular, he in his fourteen-foot Lund in the middle of the Fraser, somewhere east of Mission. ". . . I hear they've parked a vehicle on the tracks and dinged the tires"—meaning the aboriginal people have, a purloined school bus, with rifle shots. With history on their side they could be *weeks,* Bryce says, charming the media. He knows several of them, nice enough toughs, buys their bootleg coho for his restaurant.

Their nation is blockading the Canadian Pacific tracks near Ruskin. In the dark he wants to know if she can spot any campfires near the Stave River Bridge. Where is she, again? Her brother blames the blockade on Oka and counsels her not to waste "Narciss's" money on advertising any more upriver property till the Mounties reopen the line. He doesn't mind counselling his sister on selling property. "Stick to the high-growth areas and, for fuck sake, don't keep not buying pepper spray. Okay?"

A year ago, attacked in an empty Open House on a quiet street in Lacey, she suffered a concussion trying to talk off a parolee with a crowbar. Colleagues agreed she was lucky to escape with her brain unscrambled. She wondered at the time, had she been killed in the line of duty, would they have come from far and wide like policemen or firemen to march behind her coffin in a long pastel line? Unlikely, all were on commission. One of them sponged off the tiles in the ensuite bath and sold her MLS listing two days later to a volleyball manufacturer and his Taiwanese family, without mentioning the crowbar caller. Agents she'd never met sent flowers, better suited to a mortuary than her hospital.

A real fire, this one a glowing beehive burner making sparks and fouling the night air with invisible smoke, has seeped into her air conditioning, its smell of cremated butt-ends and saw-dust from old-growth watersheds responsible for the same shakes, she thinks, exported into the high-end roofing market in L.A.

Bryce mentions he can see, horny on the hill above him, the abbey's Spanish bell tower luminous in moonlight. An erotic sight. His rudeness gladdens her. She can hear his throbbing outboard turning slowly over, keeping him stationary in the current as he mooches. Or whatever they call threading a lump of salmon roe over a hook the size of a baby's coat hanger and letting it sink to the dirty bottom of the river while he waits brainlessly for a bite.

He took her sturgeon fishing last summer and they spent the afternoon trying to persuade an anchor with retractable wing-things to catch hold like a vulture in the riverbed. It kept hopping off the bottom as she measured their velocity downstream without a bite or sunscreen. Her brother, like some sunstruck monk, had started abbey-chanting then, as if fishmongering in Steveston. *"Rotten roe, rotten roe . . ."* Bites, his gauge of spiritual transcendence, had left him burned and depressed. There weren't any bites. Skunked, they'd motored back.

Some miles downstream, and driving the winding high-way in light traffic away from him tonight, she can see his glittering river through trees, their connection immaculate. Giggling—two distinct *hee hee's*—he sounds high from an illegal substance. Probably the sturgeon flesh he's poaching, high on the crime itself, though possibly weed, sweetly perfuming the humid air over dimpled eddies around him like saucers in the moonlight. She tries picturing his restaurant's now dark-ened decor, till she can see cobalt-blue walls past flickering candle bowls and mitred napkins, warning her eerily away.

Won't ask him if he's lit up to port and starboard, remembering his deckless boat has no place for running lights. Ill-equipped to follow rules, anyway not while its skipper poaches, Bryce's dented hull resembles his recent life, bruised from idling among a backlog of patients awaiting radiation therapy, bumping around in a pool of shadowy X-rays. His life lets his restaurant take the hits. A sudden rise in the number of men with prostate cancer has given him the perfect excuse to fish while he waits—to goof off, she feels, from liability. He's told her he can't afford the quicker treatment in the States that would get him back into the kitchen sooner.

Would it?

She hasn't ever mentioned that an older acquaintance of hers, diagnosed like Bryce via a digital rectal exam, had gone regularly to Bellingham from Sardis and discovered visits to America hadn't solved his own slipping business. Just as prognosticated, after six months of cross-border shopping, the Valley's top developer (nauseous) died.

"...*Rotten roe*..."

He seems determined these nights to make peace with himself. She has never heard him blaspheme the Benedictines' bell tower with the same affection before. Never heard him blaspheme it at all. The wound-up cheeriness of his tone reminds her of how he talked at her house last Easter to Wayne and Kellie over his preparation of Peking duck. The same floating whine of dissatisfaction. *Spooky* how a guy, who no longer loves his wife, seems to expect continuing adoration from her children.

He is bedding down these nights where he can. Will admit no more. She imagines him living unhappily with a native weaver who smokes little cigars in her handyman's special off Highway 7 somewhere near Hatzic. One is vague, he is vague, on everything but his cell number. He says he takes calls on his boat, brick patio, and the toilet. "I have trouble *going* to the toilet..."

And complains that sometimes when he tries to pee standing up in his Lund it takes him so long—and its stream is too thin to detect—that riverbank fishermen feel he's flashing them like some groin-grabbing Michael Jackson after The Fall. This was two weeks ago, after dusk. Tonight she hopes the full moon will turn his pee into a sparkling tributary discernible from, attentive to, respectable distance.

He enjoys the June river because uprooted alders and jetsam from shingle mills float quickly past him in the broad current, leaving a surface smooth of all but wrinkled eddies.

The snowfields of the coast range, he'll report, are on their last squeeze.

———————

"Hold the phone, have to untangle my Walkman ..."

She guesses his cord in the downrigger could tug him, neck first, overboard. "Are you safe?"

"As in communicable disease?"

"Fish, idiot."

Recalling now what he's told her about angling for the white sturgeon: men rumoured to be drowned by these monsters were disappointingly *few* this century, since most of them (fish, not fishers) had vanished through overfishing and toxic dioxins. His chemicals had sounded like a redundant rock group, that day together on the river.

"There," he blurts. "Be able to tune in the riverbed now." Adding, "Still need a fish finder, though."

She'd encouraged him to share his new sturgeon lore as a way to buoy up self-esteem when his marriage was foundering and Crabcakes wasn't attracting the early numbers they'd projected. She learned sturgeon can live for hours out of water, so poachers will wrap them in wet newspapers to deliver live, unbelievably fresh, to restaurants. His restaurant.

That had been Bryce's introduction to sturgeon, buying them from blackmarketeers for his kitchen and serving the elusive dinosaur as a Jurassic Park dinner special. He was reborn a sturgeon fan in the course of an evening's shady transaction with local aboriginals. Longevity hadn't toughened the scaleless flesh, which could be cut into lean steaks and broiled till it flaked delicately if you cooked it longer than normal fish using lemon butter and thyme, after chopping through the barbed scutes.

"... Canneries round here were awash in roe, ninety years ago. You had caviar piled up on scows way down to—"

She had listened to him, wondering at such hoary hearts, slowpumping organs that let these creatures live outside water, and in it, suspended, along slough bottoms and in river caves for a century plus.

He now sounds like a native poacher, with his slant on how many fish a local boy should be allowed to take and when. He respects the sturgeon, hates government, and believes in family—even after dumping on his own (family) by quitting a superintendent's job with B.C. Packers to open a restaurant, just because he thought he was the best gourmet cook in the Valley. Possibly, he was.

Almost a joke between them, that she couldn't coddle an egg, but had agreed to underwrite a fish restaurant in a town that liked pork goulash.

Then, about six months ago, she began noticing serious gaps in the food chain at Crabcakes, concluding that his overhead, managerial incompetence, or cancer had begun to plunge him into crisis, cutting off simple supplies like broccoli and bread rolls. Politely, whenever she happened to be listing property near Mission, she stopped dropping by.

Bryce never mentions her absences. And seems to tolerate his own absences from Crabcakes without feeling the need to mention these, either. Except he will, by telling her his "second chef" Sarah is "covering" for him while he fishes. He'll tell her this without a quaver, though the phone in his restaurant goes unanswered, though she knows he's lying. His (like the natives') is a "food fishery." And he insists, "Got a kitchen to supply," when there's no question his place is *dark*—darker than his rectum.

Since childhood, and maybe before that, in shared amniotic fluid, her built-in mooching antenna has allowed her intuitions of a brother's unseen twitchiness. And his of hers, though he never says, knowing they don't have to talk about the twin thing to justify the business bit. Which makes dishonesty between them puzzling, knowing as she does his position at Crabcakes is hopeless whether he dies or doesn't. Death will not absolve his debts.

His second chef told *her* last week Crabcakes had closed down two months ago "for good." Sarah is worried now, unable to afford college in the fall for her graduating daughter who wants to study "Crim."

Bryce owes his underwriter an explanation.

But finds it difficult to admit failure, unless it slips out the way his cancer did, bad news masquerading as good when it helps to rationalize his over-the-top poaching expeditions after dark when he should still be at his stove. "I can always pull myself together with a bite." It sounds so masochistic, she longs to ask if this biting doesn't *hurt* him.

"You still got that widow's tire-farm listing?" Having de-downrigged himself, presumably by removing fishy-fingered earphones from around his neck, he is wondering again if—

She keeps quiet. Maybe he'll forget about "tying up" this widow's property with a deposit—in order to flip it to somebody he says he knows with recycling interests in Clearbrook, before having to surface with final payment himself. Bryce couldn't afford the first mortgage on a gum machine, the *deposit* on a gum machine, even if it were being sold by a thief willing to take a rye mickey for the entire rig and throw in the gumballs.

"Sarah was asking me yesterday at lunch if there wasn't some way we could jump our cash flow and live another winter." He's telling her this? With *her* house on the line as collateral, he's telling her Crabcakes is still serving meals and its mortgage payments aren't in shit default? How can she even believe he has cancer?

She now suspects her trying to cover both their assets accounts for her recent poor judgement, like agreeing to potentially commissionless listings such as a widow's tire-farm nightmare or a handyman's shack.

"Just forget it, Bryce. I won't deal in bad faith with Mrs. Sauvage. Full stop."

She accelerates, speeds on in silence. Has he got the message? As unethical to sell to a member of her own family as for her in her old Nancy Sinatra boots to walk right over a ... Sto:lo native in supine protest on the rails.

Sto:lo. If you were going to tease your name, the colon seemed a boffo piece to do it with, très post-mod: like studs in your nostril or gas rings in the kitchen.

She smiles and slows down. Loosens her cellular grip. Resolves to reprint her "Narciss" card at the earliest opportunity:

> Bi:anca T:se / NRS
> Med!allion Clu'b
> Go:Go Boots for Hu*s*le Plus
> (Play:mate, Au^gust 1973)

then braid her hair in a pigtail and hand out this card with green tea sachets and a copy of their great-grandfather's head tax paid in full. Stylish as cold pressed, extra virgin olive oil.

"You're amused," says Bryce. "If you're worried I'm soft-shoeing you on the commitment in Clearbrook, Bi, I'll give you his number to check out."

Whining again.

She flashes her high beams at an oncoming car. It flashes back to show she's blind and bullets past. Now finds herself in the dark having accidentally killed her lights. The green glow of the control panel has vanished, silkily, forcing her eyes to adjust like ears to a *hush*.

Moonlight beckons, reflecting off her hood, off a leather dash, pouring through open sun roof onto ebony seats and rugs, creamy on her arms. Light enough to drive by the moon and stars without electrical assistance to either port or starboard. And so she allows herself to speed on a hundred, two hundred metres in this manner without navigational accompaniment.

Wh:ee!

Temporarily empty in both directions the road like the river is carrying her west ... won't stop as it meanders ...

Liberated by darkness she floats right up through her roof for a picnic on the moon. Caviar in all this moonshine has the effect of making her think Bryce probably *longed* for his restaurant to fail, if it meant having highs like this every night when he should be serving up halibut off a hot range. Hence his desire to make a quick killing off worn-out tires. Off the used-up momentum of millions like his sister who drive carefully, responsibly, and never catch a white sturgeon in hay-scented moonlight, hell no, under a silver campanile looking like an abbot's bell-rung co:ck.

Lowers her arm with the thin instrument in lotioned palm, listening for imaginary bells. For a vintage 78-rpm crooner in love with Ramona or in the new CD version with herself. What she really hears is her last lover humming idiotically, refusing conversation for "security" reasons, although she'd bought herself a scrambler. A cabinet minister who used to enjoy surprises, peering down on her fast car and calling her up from his ultralight.

"We're all in the gutter, Ms. Tse, but some of us are looking at the stars."

She wondered, when the tire-farm widow said this to her, if the unfortunate woman knew more about real estate and its connivance with the truth than she was letting on. The listing had been between her and a RE/MAX guy and she got it by overvaluing this dump and promising its vendor the moon.

All right, stars.

Gutter too culpable? She—

"How many kids have Hef and Kim got now, Bi?"

_____

His voice brings her back down to the disappearing road. "What?" Reaching for lights to save herself from a head-on collision at the bend.

When the road is white like this, shining, death by darkness seems impossible to believe in. Surely his own illusion is induced by grasssmoking on the river.

At times, when he wants to skirt the truth, he'll ask for domestic news of the Mansion, his expectation in no way diminished by his twin sister's now twenty-one-year-old lost place in paradise as a Bunny. Something has since happened to the hutch—earthquakes and fires, drought and mudslides—to give it wrinkles, faults, broken veins. California, that is, the dream. The Mansion seems immune. As far as ex-Bunnies know from the tabloid grapevine, Hef is going strong again after a minor stroke, his young wife and family the fuzz on his peach.

She says nothing.

Her fling with fame had lasted five months, from eight weeks before she was to appear as the Miss August centrefold, to the time she hopped away from the last of Hef's pals in pre-Kim pursuit through games room, zoo, and waterfall grottoes where virgins appeared and disappeared in his underlit pool. She was nineteen, looked seventeen, and had come to L.A. on an unexpected invitation from the Mansion, soon after emerging from the magazine's Canadian files as a potential Playmate. Spinoff from her title faded fast, after Hef lost interest in her chances of making it in Hollywood with small oriental boobs.

To fill dead air he returns to the Sto:lo, repeating himself. "Seeing any fires?" Rushing in then to speculate on motives, whether his fellow fishers aren't hot to trot with power gone to their feathers—the road closure now *de rigueur* for any self-respecting nation—or whether they might not be genuinely aggrieved at historical mistreatment and shoving it to the CPR as a four-square corporate target. No shutting him up. "...We're all in the same boat, I reckon, with the multi—"

She drops his voice into the adjoining bucket seat to take better control of the wheel, when a Greyhound bus, heading east, sends a block of air cycloning across the line. Navigating clear of disaster, along a friendly shoulder, she pushes in a James Keelaghan tape and rescues her brother's voice.

"...used to fish sturgeon, in the dark ages."

"The reason I'm calling, Bryce ... is to ask if you know anything behind these reports of Virgin sightings on Doreen Kynock's family's farm. Remember Doreen Kynock?"

No response, no muffled motor burping in the background. His background. "Bryce?" She turns down the tape. Her scrambler accidentally disconnect them?

Then his dirge, growing louder, *"Rotten roe ... ROTTEN roe..."* Mocking her tape perhaps.

Anyway, amused. "Doreen?" he asks.

"Was she in our class, or the one behind?"

"She *flunked*, Bi." *Dor?* she hears him thinking.

Croatian Catholics from Bosnia-Herzegovina, staying with Doreen's aging parents, have recently spotted the Blessed Virgin Mary in a pear tree. Irradiating the fruit like spray, making these pears questionable eating come August, since something toxic has killed off the rusty juniper virus speckling their leaves.

She reports to Bryce what she's read of this local happening, without mentioning her listing up Polder Road from the Kynocks.' The Virgin is now appearing every Tuesday afternoon at 1:30 and they (the Croats) have promised her (Doreen) if she (the Virgin) will only cooperate, they could go for the longest serial sighting in the history of BVM appearances.

"What Vatican Guinness book keeps those kind of records?" crackles Bryce's voice, through interference.

She mentions it is really only one of the Croats, a Ms. Meike Dragicivic, who sees the Virgin. "Can you hear me...?" Secrets or at least heavy messages in Croatian, rumours of which have spread faster than herpes in a hot rub. The Kynock farm is suddenly attracting hundreds of weekly pilgrims, clogging the road with Caravans and Cherokees.

"So?" His voice clear again. Uninterested.

"... I was just wondering, big brother, have *you* had any recent contact with Doreen yourself?"

He could be forgiven for wondering if this is her version of his Hef-and-Kim question, to keep the conversation rolling by diversion.

It is, in a way. She's hoping to divert a few of the devout on spec, those with stars still in their eyes, to Tuesday Open Houses at Mrs. Sauvage's nearby tire farm. Who knows where the Virgin might decide to appear next, perhaps stage-managed by a complicit Doreen Kynock, spreading spiritual values in her role as Ma:ry, while upping property values in the surrounding polder?

"She's a sexpot," remarks Bryce.

Still? But she knows what he means.

Doreen would never have been invited to pose for *Playboy*. You'd never have had to see Doreen Kynock nude to know what she looked like without clothes. Always wore them too suggestively. Never realized you needed to dress tastefully, especially as a sex object, to be sexy. The hint of mystery was a required fiction if fiction was required, as in Doreen's case it wasn't. Dor was clueless. She dressed like a harlequin in heat.

What would she be wearing to welcome the Virgin?

"Not much," suggests Bryce. "I've run into her at the Wild Goose Inn." Giving it the rude name, where guys his age meet for stags, annulments, uncontested divorces. "She's a table dancer, decades past prime."

So, he's socializing. Or else drinking by himself to avoid people, hoarding his scorecard like a skating judge.

"She's one grinder you don't really *care* to watch."

Even though Doreen had once adored him, unrequitedly, in a cotton T-shirt with "Hip" over the left tit, "Hop" the other.

"...I doubt it's Doreen seeing the Virgin," his voice staticky again. "For one thing, she wouldn't be living with her parents. Unless she's between marriages. Heard her husband—"

"Bryce?"

"...tried to knife her."

"Bryce, listen." They could dance around all night like this.

"She ought to see a counsellor, not Mother Mary."

"Tell me the truth, Bryce."

"What I heard."

"I ran into Sarah the other day, when I was chaperoning."

"She's no friend of Doreen's, that I know of . . . *Chaperoning?*" His wireless voice, ironic in its weed-easy inflections, despite the air's electrical resistance.

"For fuck sake," she tells him straight, unwilling not to say what's distressing her. "I *know.*"

417

She listens closely, waiting for Bryce to come clean over what has befouled things between them. The collapse of Crabcakes. She wonders if her run-in this evening with the backwoods vendor hasn't unsettled her. Her eyelid twitches. She can't wear a *watch* anymore without sooner or later spoiling its time. Hair and accessories marred by vibes she picks up like some assailable tart.

The vendor, dressed in a lumberjack shirt, was showing skin where his stomach tugged buttons in directions they didn't want to go, a pitch-black navel chug-a-lugging the light. Something immense about him, smothering, had disturbed her. She could never trust a balding man with lank yellow hair not to pass gas in her face. Not one living in the rustic equivalent of a welfare tenement, probably hiding sons from their mother.

The little hot dog eaters had listened, unsurprised. Three unwashed boys, shaded by poverty and second-growth rain-forest infested with alder, burping quietly. It was getting dark.

Was it her Mercedes SL in his yard, where jet ski engines lay around in clumpish parts, that made him glad to announce he couldn't, "now I had the chance to sleep on it," come down from his asking price? Matters must have soured overnight, after his acceptance of her telephoned offer from a Hong Kong propeller merchant.

When she responded that it seemed unrealistic to expect to get *everything* he was asking, he just flipped.

Mall sprawl was now killing this greedy effing valley. The once-natural world had become golf courses for rich dicks. In fact, natural was now unnatural. Or hadn't she noticed the Indians being goaded into unnatural blockade tactics as a result of excesses threatening their survival? *Their* tactics had made him rethink his priorities. Selling out, sweetheart, was off.

She said she would try calling him again in the morning.

"Hang up on you, then."

Where had she seen him before?

Biking to the lake this afternoon, across flat farm land, she'd glanced aloft for ultralights. No, that was yesterday after-noon. Today she'd driven home to change into clothes more suitable for her resort listing. Her secretary had discouraged slacks, judging Mr. Douglas's mood likely to be "jeanish."

"Thanks, Holly."

Still-bright American pennies, the lucky ones in her loaf-ers, had then conjured up these same kids and last night's nightmare, just as she was setting out: underchinned men on a charter flight to the Philippines, where impoverished boys from eight to eleven were available in a Club Meddish setting of swimming pools and treats, sybaritic meals and Riesling wines. . . Pink-fleshed men, buckling up doeskin belts and rearranging their desert boots, as a chartered house prepared to lift off its foundation after the lumbering fashion of a Boeing 747.

Chartered house?

As if in *punishment*, this nightmare. Who knew why? Perhaps for selling some heritage turkey she can't remember to developers she knew would doze it.

She still describes as "peeling" the motel room she lived in after returning from L.A., age twenty. She describes it graphically to realtor seminars from Semiamhoo to Chilliwack, spinning Coffeemate like detergent into her Styrofoam cup with a plastic paddle. Getting *into* real estate had allowed her to sell this stinky motel for its disgruntled owner, invest in personalized notepads instead of breast implants, and eventually to move into her own manor, where she could recharge a cell phone and pasture a horse. To *lose* her property, now, would betray the legacy of a pioneering great-grandfather, her (his) driven nature responsible for sweeping her to the top within six months.

Old Tse, unlike the Sto:lo, resembled Doreen Kynock. He too had hoped to go all the way, but with style. A Chinese who panned for gold and thought We:st.

Gre:ed, Mr. Douglas would call it, in his snorting screed against development.

Her ancestor had tried to buy into the national dream, shouldering baskets of it and dumping rocks into Hell's Gate, helping lay the CPR railbed, refusing against odds to give up on the dream. Taking in dirty laundry and not dying till after she was born.

Bryce might die this fall, before he turns forty. Twelve minutes after she does.

———

"By the way," he says, ignoring her obscene remark about *knowing*. "What're you doing up this way tonight. Agenting?"

The dishonesty between them is naked now. He can't not know she knows he's lying.

The mystery is why he bothers, except to make his dream more dangerous. Crabcakes is his dream. He's lying it still exists . . . that he's part of it, for Godsake, the gourmet chef still dreaming up his own risky revue.

She isn't indifferent. Can't *afford* to be and survive herself. He should come out and tell her the truth. That his dream is gone, along with ripe old age, his kids' kids touting him as a way better cook than their grandma. So what's putting him on air tonight, hearing nothing he doesn't *want* to hear—the grass prescribed to cancer patients?

Or, she wonders, is the weed bootlegged too. The poacher's rush making danger the drug of choice for him, like lying. She thinks he could now walk from boat to shore.

"You still there?" he asks.

She says, "To answer your question . . ." And mentions frankly her aborted sale. Of white-trash property taken on for the sake of Crabcakes and how its cabin smelled of a backed-up drain. "'Worse than sour," she says, "other side of sewer."

Pause. Him thinking.

Her ready to say goodbye.

She wonders whether to speed up or to let herself be passed by fast-closing headlights. Her desire is to avoid moving over.

"If your restaurant's gone under, Bryce, like Sarah told me, I'm going to need commissions from even scumbags to bail out your mortgage."

"*Sarah* told you that?"

Fuck. "I *know,* Bryce."

But her echo, like his moonlit reflection in the river, carries no bad news for a poacher. He just ignores it.

Could he be telling her the truth?

Odds are against truth. As if among the illicit acts giving him a rush his biggest thrill is self-deception. As if trying to deceive his twin is an unaccountable act.

"Said you were chaperoning?" He asks. "Where?"

Guiding conversation the way it doesn't want to go.

"High-school grad. Keeping my profile high by doing community service. Dishing out my card if asked. Being friendly and available."

Silence. No more *hee hee's*. Reception again crackly.

"I can't believe Sarah told you that," he says after a spell of motor-revving to reposition himself in the current—probably letting out more line to judge by the *whiz* of his reel.

The headlights crowding her rear-view pull out to swoop by, music detonating inside a painted van with bubble windows. She checks her hair for frizz.

"She quit, Bi. I swear. I'm still wide open. Hosting the public and being a creative Chinese cook..."

Adding, their clear contact suddenly restored, "Except for one evening a week ... tonight, when I fish for supplies. My customers crave a fresh menu."

His voice brazen in her ear. "You think I'm *fibbing?* I think you should drill Sarah about her agenda."

"Meaning what, Bryce?"

"Wants to marry me, little sis. Fact one. Can't get me out of her mind, *she* says, fact two. In short, a misguided woman ..."

This twist confounds her. Indifference to Sarah supposedly prompting his spurned admirer to avenge herself. Sarah as liar, not him. *No way, him.*

"You asked about chaperoning? I was chaperoning the high-school grad. Keeping my profile high by doing community service. Dishing out my card, if asked. Being friendly and available."

"You said that."

She said that.

"What's the matter?"

"I believed what Sarah told me."

"Come and have supper, Bi. Any evening you like. Tomorrow if you like."

Maybe he's planning to drown tonight, so she won't catch him out at his darkened door.

"The restaurant's usually full for supper, not like lunch. So your host *may* have to neglect you ... Anyhow, you'll eat good. I'm about to catch a nice sturgeon for your dining pleasure."

She isn't sure how a two-hundred-year-old fish might taste, having led its life on the muddy bottom of Nicomen Slough, already a mature fish when old Tse arrived here as a young man from Shanghai to wash other men's tailings for gold.

More reel-whizzing in her ear. Then his voice, unexcitedly: "Got a bite." Is he just telling her this? About the big one soon to get away, his fading life reduced to the predictableness of an effing fish story?

Last Christmas, snorkelling through Hawaiian trigger fish, she had tried to imagine him poaching sturgeon on cold nights, as if his obsession were as natural as riding reindeer across a roof.

She imagines Douglas, the backwoods vendor, telling her excessive fishing is what brings these long-lived sturgeon to the surface now as monsters. "Common as salmon once, now as unnatural as goddam monsters." His rubbery lips gobbling wieners, telling her how poaching among Sto:lo used to be known as fishing. How dairy farming had become an unnatural act of dumping tires.

Trying to brain her with the treehugger's equivalent of a crowbar.

As Bryce would like to (he's huffing now), all of a sudden scrambling her head with stuff about comas, fish or no fish on his hook.

Sturgeon dive. Rise at. Motionless. As death.

She thinks he must *enjoy* fishing in little grunts. Limits? Upstream. One. Yearly. Downstream. *Daily.*

He's definitely fighting *something*. "Rod bends. I come alive." He sounds alive.

Tonight, east of the bridge, he is over his limit by about six months. "Of course," adding lightly, "if Fisheries shows up. I'll just drift. Till I'm west of the bridge."

But the forbidden *is* more fun. Even believable, he hopes. And since he's pretty sure of an imminent and indefinite sturgeon closure all along the river, poaching will finally be assured, *everywhere*. This same river their ancestor worked, panning it, her brother now regards as his personal pond. Mourning himself in it like a heart throb.

Telling her how dead sturgeon washed up by the dozen last year. Sturgeon living on the bottom for aeons, eating garbage like spent oolichans. Then curtains. Creatures so long-lived, he whispers, the females don't bother spawning till age twenty.

All this by way of deflecting the truth.

Maybe she ought to take his lying as an offering, given what a stick-in-the-mud she used to seem to him as a little girl.

Has she missed the joke of his vain audacity?

His reel's not whizzing anymore. He seems to have lost his bite. Maybe she should just show up at Crabcakes and be surprised, not by the absence of diners, but by a beatific dinner prepared specially for her, sturgeon done in a traditional Bosnia-Herzegovina sauce, its high-grade protein an antidote to disease and extinction. At this dinner her brother might finally come clean, over a fresh flower in the exact centre of his tablecloth, surrounded by his empty parquet floor.

"You'll be open? Tomorrow evening?"

No answer. Silence now. "Bryce?"

"Yep. At your service, madam."

She challenges him to back *down*. . . "You know, Bryce, I just might come." Warning him against mendacity.

"Make sure you do." He is unwilling to give her any power over him, over his life, by dissemblance. "Seven-thirty?"

"Make sure I do," she echoes.

"Over and out, then."

Gone, like that.

"Yes," she replies. And not even this last word is hers. "Goodbye, Bryce."

She puts down her phone on the bucket seat opposite, and glances left, long and fervently to the white river.

She can see his ghost crossing it, leaning over his boat for a last look in the moonlight below.

She will not go. She will go.

The moon is a flower on the river. Her German engine purrs. She makes a mental note to buy pepper spray.

She knows his face like her own face, down to the deviated septum they share, one nostril slightly smaller than the other, this single blemish on their beauty like the blockage in an artery.

Having listened now to the deeper edition of her own voice, she wonders. Could she look over the transom and see his bewhiskered face reflected back at her in the star-salted river, would she see it was her face too? Who are you? Who, if not yo:u, is your brother's keeper?

TELLING MY LOVE LIES

An Elegy

"OUR FRAMES OF REFERENCE have changed," she told me the week I was home. "What your father and I have in common these days is what I say we have."

I felt for this man. My mother had to remind me again at breakfast, after he came in from the barn, that if his memory cells were vanishing like petals in a windstorm his brainstorming cells still had a good tread. My father agreed through a mouthful of waffle, right, he was managing okay in the opinion department.

For example, watching me drive him down along the river later that May morning in 1980, to visit the federal penitentiary, he delivered this:

No matter where you live in Canada the pop music is imported, family cars are foreign, the highways long. According to him, driving in your own country had become an international event. Throw in the French kiss, even one banana, a backseat copy of *Time*, and you bad rewritten our national I.D. at the level of asphalt.

This level was fine by him, of course, a specialist in bald tires. Tires kept us together. Wasn't Canadian Tire a brilliant name for a company and the tire a more patriotic emblem than the beaver? "In my opinion, that name says it all." Even if most of our rubber like the national debt came from other countries it was rubber that kept us together.

"Count on rubber products," was his behest to me.

He hadn't forgotten his behest to me, stippled into his memory like a tattoo. *Rubber Products. Valour and Country.* You could forget the bloody beaver.

He interrupted himself to stare appreciatively out the pickup's windshield at a glinting current of steady traffic rolling the other way. Our front wheel was whupping from the accident caused by his seizure. So I kept us under the speed limit. "Be a big believer," he entreated me, counting vehicles. Chances were good that scalps of some of those wheels would end up in TIRE MEADOWS.

He was the equivalent of a colonial plantation owner, tapping rubber trees for the white goo that became black profit, advising his offspring how my future should carry on his past. So far it hadn't, he knew, and wasn't going to. I did not know if opera singing was the exact opposite of tire-farming, but it must have come as close as the well-known duet of chalk and cheese, in Puccini's beloved opera *Olio e Acqua.*

"I take it you're being humorous."

"Witty, yeah."

My teenage friends used to narrow their eyes at his rubber fields, unzipping to leak on his B.F. Goodrich inventory in our poplar-lined drive. I was mortified to be the son of a man who'd turned his dairy farm into a tire dump. I was ashamed of having had such a blackish youth amid once-emerald fields.

"I take it you're being witty."

"Humorous, yeah."

Stretching the point now, I can see how his obsession with rubber might be viewed as prophetic back then—if not in the way he expected. He didn't live long enough to see condoms take off in the marketplace, not long enough to see the latex condom become a kind of international flag of operation,

blowing like a windsock from every airport's control tower
where sex is a commodity for disembarking young singers
like me, and every other kind of tourist scrambling for a place
in the sun.

2

At the time of our penitentiary visit my father had two years
left to live. He would die in a mystifying traffic accident. His
affliction, about as rare as AIDS then was in 1980, seemed
partly responsible for his death. Unhelpful to call it marble-
loss, although this is what it amounted to with epileptic over-
tones. The neurologist had no idea what had caused his brain
seizure, leading to his recent physical collapse.

And I thought they could trace the serial number on these
failures.

Earlier that morning, my first in a week home from California, I'd learned from my mother the extent of his affliction before the neurologist put him on an anticonvulsant to
stop his auras. The auras had been washing over him agree-
ably, or so she reported my father telling her, for two or three
years before this, each one amounting to a mini-seizure, a
little stroke in the brain he didn't know he was having except
to remark to her on its gratifying premonition of a pleasant
BM—beginning in his intestines, but then, changing direction, and pushing up through his trunk and flooding down
his arms. She said he claimed to think a lot about death at such
times. Quite pleasantly, in fact.

"Erotic."

Erotic? I tried, but could only picture a mini-seizure as
resembling a match scratching on brain putty and never quite
catching fire inside the humid temporal lobe where his trouble was located. She mapped the geography of his affliction
enthusiastically on the oilcloth, before breakfast, with a red
lacquered nail.

"It isn't the occipital lobe, if that's what you're thinking."

"No."

She tapped her map. "It's the lateral lobe."

"The lateral lobe."

Her swirlish nails had always surprised peeing callers at TIRE MEADOWS, used to farm mums who deplored such honed razor blades. This was several years before punk came in—otherwise they might've viewed her grandness with less suspicion. She liked to think she was not an unfashionable woman, given the work-glove milieu she was forced to endure. Only dresses by Omar the Tentmaker spoiled her grand design.

"He was enjoying himself, mon cher, in a manner of speaking." Still on auras. Evidently my father hadn't made the connection between his premonitions of death in the last three years and his growing forgetfulness of events over this same period.

The failing memory had become her chief concern. He'd completely forgotten a weekend plane trip taken together last year to visit her sister in Calgary sick with kidney stones; and, worse, couldn't recall it when she tried filling him in on the "dreary" tower restaurant where they ate pepper steaks, not to mention that her sister's haggish cat had been "ill" in the lap of his new houndstooth slacks. "I might as well have been talking to the cows," she told me before breakfast. By October he'd even forgotten their visit to the PNE in Vancouver for the Holstein heifer competition, followed by a Giant Truck scrunching in the Agrodome of half a dozen worn-out Renaults.

"... Goes without saying he was riveted to tires big enough to drive up and over a whole car. Now he can't remember the tires *or* the heifers. I've never heard louder engines, anywhere."

My father had evidently mentioned his fickle memory to Perumbur's G.P., joking about his Alzheimer's at a prostate checkup, the agreeable sensations he was having in an out-of-body kind of way complete with pleasantly unpleasant premonitions of death. But the doctor hadn't recognized what turned out to be his petit mal symptoms.

"You remember how casual Hopkins can be. When he retires the great man wants to tootle around Asia."

Not until my father had a grand mal seizure, and my mother rushed him back for another appointment, did the light in the physician's brain finally switch on.

Driving them in for groceries, my father had suffered a shuddering paralysis and collapsed in his pickup. Rigid, gagging, right out of it. Luckily, he ran into the gatepost, wrecking his suspension but stopping them dead before reaching the paved road where sloughs on either side were skindiver-deep with winter runoff.

The violent jolt bloodied his teeth against the steering wheel. By now he'd lost consciousness. Gone purple, choking on his tongue: before my mother, listening to the sound he was making, "like keening at an Ibo wake," felt she should stick in her fingers before he suffocated. Prying open his mouth she broke her nails.

"Have you read *The Idiot*?" Dr. Hopkins asked him.

"It sounded insulting," said my mother. "But then you have to remember Hopkins is as sideways as a skate." Trying to get a straight answer from Hopkins, I could recall, was like consulting a high-school counsellor for a hunting licence. No comprenez, no dice.

He suspected my father's earliest full-blown seizures might have started some time before this first daylight seizure. During the night he meant, sleeping. He knew this was difficult to document.

"If you had a seizure in your sleep, Bill, Jane wouldn't have noticed it unless she happened to be awake. Even then, how likely a witness in the dark? She might've heard something, of course. Did you, Jane?"

She volunteered that some mornings her husband had complained of aches clear through his body, like he'd been run over by an eighteen-wheeler. She put this down to arthritis, the dairyman's disease, from decades of stooping and lifting, squeezing and pouring. Her information only bolstered Hopkins's theory of nighttime comas.

He sent them straight to a neurologist at the Royal Columbian, for tests like standing on one foot and trying to remember unmateable words—fudge, horn lessons, Buick; numbers: 58,17,143—and this specialist hospitalized my father for a week to monitor his cells and blood pressure, and to gauge his reaction to anticonvulsants.

Then they waited for a turn at the twenty-first century. To have his brain imaged by a CAT scan my father had to inform hospital staff he had no cerebral aneurysm clip, middle ear implant, or any stimulatory device like a pacemaker. He had to put aside his loose change and credit cards. His good health was supposed to be worth it.

Since March, two scans—both tests placing his head like an egg inside a wind tunnel, and my mother's nerves on eggshells, from driving him back and forth on the Trans-Canada—had turned up no tumour, or even scar tissue from a possibly traumatic birth. The neurologist, studying the inner brain routes, must have wondered at the all-clear results. "He was very polite," decided my mother. "Très cosmopolitan. European Semite."

The results, while compounding the mystery of my father, were a relief to them both. If the seizures' source remained unresolved, at least the pills had stopped them, provided he stayed on anticonvulsants the rest of his life. He was also on Elavil for depression, and Tums Extra Strength to counteract the bone-sapping side effects of a drug binge.

My mother had rattled an amber-coloured plastic tube next to his placemat at the breakfast table and set it down again like a salt shaker. I picked it up and tapped out one of the pretty yellow capsules, engraved MSD 45. In my palm it resembled a premature jelly bean.

He was no longer allowed to drive. And he had to expect a "diminishment of libido," as this nurse, charged with the responsibility of keeping their bed on an even keel, confided.

According to her he'd never felt better in his life. Alert, nice to be around, sans hangups d'any sort. My mother isn't one to deploy a simple compliment when a fancy phrase might better complicate her effect.

My father came in from milking, pleased to hear us popping off in French.

3

Because the lot was full I parked the pickup on the street. That week the B.C. Pen was shutting down after 102 years, with an Open House for the public to cruise inside its castle-like walls before letting them fall to crooks who built condos. Inmates had relocated to a new facility in Agassiz.

431

My father wanted a glimpse of his family's criminal past, which constituted one of his earliest and lasting memories. He had decided to test himself today, to see if he could remember what he'd never actually seen, a revolver, said to be on display.

He recalled his mother's stories about the famous inmate who once owned it. She knew him as a young girl when, to her awful delight, he had unpocketed it. His secret weapon was always the highlight of her recollections, that and his piggybacks.

So my father's memory was really, in this case my grandmother's. His recollection was *her* recollection of what had happened in her brief acquaintance with a train robber. This piece of family history, received as gospel, was no more forgettable to him than the parable of the prodigal son.

He seemed unsurprised that his childhood memory should remain entirely untouched by recent seizures, though perhaps his deterioration had begun by spreading backward in time with earliest recollections still his most vivid.

His mother and her older sister had met the be-weaponed "Mr. Edwards" while herding their stubborn cow across CPR tracks in Silverdale, some miles upvalley from Perumber, and even more miles upriver from the prison where this holdup artist would eventually land when it was still a new institution.

"Need some help, girls? Uppity cow gotcha mad?"

An old southern gentleman, slender, soft-spoken. My grandmother remembered a tattoo of a dancing girl on his right forearm when he flashed them his pistol. Aunt Betty corroborated the pistol, but disagreed over the existence of any tattoo. Neither girl had suspected an iota of "Mr. Edward's" criminal past—nor of his future in which their farm indirectly figured. My grandmother was five or six, not too old to be piggybacked but still too young to be suspicious of a stranger. He loved children. A feeling reciprocated. He'd shown up day after day, evidently reconnoitring their land for an escape route, reminding them playfully not to betray his secret.

His was the first train robbery in Canada.

Not until the wanted poster appeared did the old man's true identity become known to my forebears.

"It was like a revelation to them," my father reported. "Instead of hating him, they stood up for the guy. He'd told them stories and flaunted his gun. Helped them gate the cow every afternoon. They loved this masher more than ever. Probably owing to their father's religiosity and such ..."

I knew he was remembering accurately what more or less happened. I'd heard my grandmother tell her version of this same romance at Easter and Christmas dinners.

Our prison tour began in hot sunshine and a long line, snaking through a little oak door in the large Fantasyland gate. We climbed stairs to Admitting and Discharge, my father hobbling some from his arthritis, into a large room where each newcomer had had a military haircut in the chrome barber chair, followed by a disinfectant bath. My father approved both measures.

"Sent up the river," he joked, his once-baritone voice now fraying into a higher register. "You can bet a guy was pumping his paddle to get outta this load of grief."

This may have reminded him of his own predicament, because after a while he said:

"I never said it to your mother, but those turns I was taking? Before I got put on medication? Bliss. I think you know what kind of bliss I mean if I say bunk bliss. Shacked-up bliss. I miss my auras."

He was peering into one of the monkish cells in Block B7, left as it had been for the tourists before its last resident vacated. Grey white-striped blanket, a wall-mounted TV, gravity-defying centrefolds on the ceiling with sprouting nipples.

"... Happiness of being and body you can't imagine. All I remember of my big fit is this joy, before I blacked out. And then when I woke up—for some reason, guilt. For cheating my body out of the death experience? Some weird crime like that."

Concluding, a little sadly, "Taking the pills has stopped the bliss business."

Of all the cells we saw later, in the Hole and in the north and east wings, he would remember liking best these few with the river view, staring down at log booms and lazy sawmill smoke threading the cage of the Patullo Bridge. I never got an opportunity before he died to see how long he'd remember our visit. Longer, maybe, than I knew. For during my week home I would soon discover the reliability of his unreliability open to question.

We found an exhibition of prisoners' paintings for sale in The Hub. *Treed Hills. Screw in a Tuxedo. Doodles Like Graffiti. River Scow with Woodchips.* "Con jobs," joked my father.

He was quite taken with them, really—I think because he could see through them, how they'd come about in response to some flimsy Art Rehab agenda. He pinpointed this as the explanation for an otherwise useless waste of time. The prisoners' paintings were all about "lying their way outta here. Kinda glamorous."

His opinion caused me to conjure one of my own. To me none of these "Stop-Points of Interest" seemed as exotic as the flimsiest jail set of a *Tosca* production in some school lunchroom. I said opera, with its emotional sort of truth, you saw through right away. I was trying to reinforce his own opinion. This made it glamorous, I suggested, the total commitment to two-dimensional cardboard and passion.

"Interesting," he remarked.

And looked over to see if I was mocking him.

At last, the gym. Menacing objects confiscated from inmates lined a few portable shelves, including carved wooden pistols alongside Bibles opened up to pages gouged out in the shape of these fake weapons once concealed in the hands of putative penitents.

"Is that not clever?" said my father, admiring their industriousness. "Artistic."

The family pistol, a real pistol, was mounted by the trigger guard on two nails inside a glass case. The card said it was the weapon Bill Miner had used to hold up the CPR express on September 10, 1904.

I glanced at my father to see if it was the weapon he remembered, as it were, the same pistol his mother had seen in the flesh. A pearl-handled, black Colt .38, with an obscene prick of a trigger, a dorsal-fin hammer, and a plumpish cylinder with six little tunnels.

"That's the one," he said.

And insisted his mother could still remember the night the Express was held up, a few yards from her farm, associating the sound of her gate opening after dark with "this oddity" of a train stopping where it had never stopped before.

The squealing brakes woke her up.

He was clearly moved by our adventure into his family's past. "And *this weapon*," he said grimly, "was centre stage." It was his certainty of the fact, his arthritic grip on reality, that seemed to reassure him.

The more he studied the pistol the more he recognized its details. Clearly, guilt by association improved his memory.

If short-term memory was a problem, he was still flawless on the prenatal stuff.

He examined the wanted poster pinned up beside the stark family heirloom, a picture from which his mother and aunt would have recognized their gentleman friend: jug-eared, white-mustachioed; above a printed description of his colouring, and his inspired escape from these same walls.

My father was calculating something on his fingers. "Hey," he said. "I'm exactly the same age as *this* guy, sixty-five, when he Houdinied outta here in nineteen-seven for the States."

"Dad," I said. "Aren't you fifty-eight this year?"

"Me?" He suddenly looked sheepish. He thought over the possibility of seven lost years. Then sighed, a little pissed off for having misplaced his future if what I told him could be confirmed in an independent audit by my mother.

"Lately, I seem to be throwing away the odd half-decade."

Another Miner poster—issued by the Pinkerton Detective Agency in 1903—for a train robbery in Corbett, Oregon, exactly one year before the CPR holdup, showed a much younger man than the one posted in 1907. I glanced through the fine print.

The family felon had been "liberated" from San Quentin in June 1901, where he'd served twenty-five years for "stage robbery, less good time allowance." Under "Peculiarities and Marks" the description concluded: ". . . Mole on breast near point of right shoulder. Walks erect. Is said to be a sodomist and may have a boy with him."

So what was his dancing-girl tattoo, a decoy?

4

I had been born on this same day, in 1957. At precisely three-thirty that afternoon, as my father and I drove whupping home, I turned twenty-three. Back at the farm we found my mother making a birthday supper, and she wasn't surprised to learn her husband had come home seven years older. "He's like a fox terrier, if you let him loose. He counts in dog years."

Was it that? I felt older than my age too. Baritones do, I believe. Growing up I sometimes wondered if our worn-out tires gave me the world-weary sense my friends found comic. It took the horizons out of adolescence. It made me passive-aggressive. I hated TIRE MEADOWS for its contradiction in terms.

I was staring out the kitchen window as my father departed to milk his six last cows. The driveway was rutted from transport trucks still arriving twice a week to dump tires. Our once-green fields were heaped up into black ridges. In between lay pockets of pasture, kept clear by the bulldozer he hired monthly in a losing range war to maintain his cows and preserve the tax status of a farmer. A mile away they were removing part of a mountain for gravel. The light we'd lost here to tires was beginning to show up there.

"You're right," I said. "It really has some gaps."

"What does?" asked my mother.

"His memory. It's not like he forgets something called fish and chips then remembers. The idea of fish and chips is totally foreign to him."

I had treated him to a late lunch downriver at King Nep-tune, baffled to find this swiftest of fast foods a surprise to his taste buds. "I could get to like fish and chips," he said. I didn't think he was joking. He poked at our exotic order. Cod rolled in a tawny crust, potatoes cut into oblong fingers. The whole cliché meal swamped in tartar sauce.

"Fish and chips is a new one," said my mother, dumping pasta with a swishy flourish into boiling water. "Usually it's some event with him, like he can't remember it ever *happening.*"

She smiled through the steam. "Have to envy him his virgin tongue." For such a confirmed farm widow her nails still looked seditious. "Maybe dying is all about discovering your taste buds." Comically, she smacked her lips.

"*Is* he dying?"

"You mean, at a faster rate than us?"

She said this with the aplomb of a soprano trailing her exit line. "Voilà. Where's my colander?"

She was preparing my favourite childhood meal, chicken thighs and rigatoni. A meal I could take or leave now, accustomed lately to hauter cuisine. My mother thought at worse I'd find her home cooking droll.

"They prevent constipation," she said.

"Pardonnez-moi?"

"The bay leaves." Little petals were mottling her tinned-soup-and-sour-cream sauce. "And you know what your father always used to say about going to the bathroom."

By now the three of us were sitting at the dining-room table, after my mother had changed into a new azure dress and adjusted the dimmer switch.

"What was it I always used to say?" he asked, grateful to be noticed.

"Well," she warned, "it wasn't the prettiest thing you ever said."

"No," he agreed. "Bet it wasn't." He winked at me.

The mood elevators had had a noticeable effect on his humour since my last visit home, between graduation in Vancouver and postgrad coaching in San Francisco. My mother had been giving in at the time to his growing depression and absent-mindedness. His life had been controlling hers, in an increasingly resentful way to them both.

She turned to me and in her grand manner repeated what he always used to say, but which I certainly did not remember him saying:

"'A crap in the bowl is worth two in the bowel.'"

The laugh I was then polishing at opera school, the room-hugging *Ha-ha* that I'd eventually need as a bon vivant baritone beloved of after-performance green-roomers and, I was sure, media interviewers, went off. It was as phony as a three-dollar bill (a two-dollar bill in the country where I was newly resident). Its boom could blow the awning off a lawn party.

I call it my Shotgun. It serves the same purpose as the soprano's Hoot or the mezzo's Chortle. Pulling the trigger clears heavy air. Flirts outrageously, whether or not there's anybody to flirt with, anybody to impress. Its only danger is wounding by accidental ridicule. The tenor, incidentally, Whinnies. Very sincere. Always gets the girl by Whinnying in his oats.

(Not always. *I* ended up with her once, as Strephon the Arcadian Shepherd, in a college production of *Iolanthe*. Phyllis is the girl, Ward of Court. Sung beautifully, I remember, by fellow student Roberta Pardy. What's happened to Roberta in these fourteen years since? Or Marshall van Neer, for that matter. He was wonderful as Charles Tolloller, MP. Where are you, Marshall?)

"*I* don't remember him saying that!" I boomed cheerily, about my father's depressing toilet-bowl proverb.

"Thank your lucky stars," whispered my mother, jouncing her silver bracelets as she hid coyly behind a billowing diaphanous sleeve. "C'est incroyable!"

My father looked wounded.

At least he did until wrinkling his brow upward, saucering his eyes in a look of mock astonishment at her amazing disclosure of a confidence. I remember he used to do this if

I happened to overhear words pass between them as a child I wasn't meant to overhear. This would tip me off not to take them seriously. Wanting me to know they knew *I* knew.

"Not pretty, she's right. Surprises me that. I was quite a philosopher."

I laughed again. (Is it a French sage who says the man who exhibits a tits-and-hemorrhoid sense of humour deserves the laughter he gets?)

A laugh to belie my years. In auditions a baritone, unlike a tenor, must give an impression of ripeness and maturity. Corruption is all. I still didn't know then if I would amount to a professional singer of any distinction. Twenty-three is very young to know how corrupt you can be. If, at eighteen, I knew how to lie in public, I was still trying to understand why it seemed necessary to keep it up in private.

"*I* don't remember him saying that," I repeated.

My mother now said, a little pompously, "I suppose you don't remember us coming down to visit you in San Francisco either, last October. You're as bad as he is."

She turned to my father. "One memory going is bad enough, William. Two looks like a family trait. I hope his isn't going the way of all flesh, like yours seems."

My father turned sheepish again, as he had that afternoon at the Bastille. He looked down at his plate and poked the orange lump of chicken with his fork tines. Fingernails rimmed with muck.

"Did we take a trip to San Francisco last October?"

You could tell exactly from his tone how shame arising from loss of memory should sound. At the time I made a mental note of it, and have since called it up in the role of Sharpless.

"Don't you remember Chinatown?" My mother sounded like she was scolding him for forgetting some bargain they'd got on half a kilo of ginseng.

He looked up, puzzled. "I don't, no."

She sighed. "Or the restaurant, where Fin was one of the singing waiters?"

"Him?" The idea of a singing waiter seemed to tickle him. He chuckled. "Did I have fun?" It sounded like a private joke they'd shared more than once. His teeth, where he'd smashed them three months ago against the steering wheel, had gone dark. "Did I have fun?"

"We had a grand old time. Fin, what was the name of that restaurant again?"

"Max's Opera Café."

"That's it, yes." She smiled, remembering my performance serving them and then, as a special request she said, serenading their anniversary in front of the whole restaurant. "I remember you sang us a funny aria."

It was true I sang a funny Figaro in English, "Now your days of philandering are over ...", even a tragicomic impersonation of Elvis Costello doing Rigoletto's "La donna è mobile." I usually finished up an evening with a heartfelt Marcello, "Our love is still alive ..."

But they hadn't heard me sing any of these arias, and I wondered if I shouldn't stand up now and knock one off, to compensate for depriving them of the wonderful talent they'd helped nourish since adolescence.

"Excuse me, will you?" said my father.

Our merriment on top of his medication was pushing on his bladder. He got up slowly and hobbled out to the toilet.

When I heard the door close I turned to my mother.

"What're you saying? He never used to talk about his bowels, did he?"

"No, but it pleased him."

I paused to digest this. "Well, okay. But—"

She started being coy again with her sleeve.

I said, "Aren't you worried he might remember?"

"What would he remember?"

"For one thing, the truth. That you and he have never been to San Francisco. At least, not to see me. What's with the BS?"

She dropped her arm, abandoning veil and flaps, squaring her padded shoulders to give me an imperious look in the candlelight, a look that over a finer meal I might have mistaken for majestic. She then picked up her knife. "I'm telling my love lies."

I couldn't help it, I laughed.

"Lies? Why?"

"Why?" She sounded like I ought to know why, given her account this morning of his affliction. "Wouldn't you want a little filler in your life, if you'd had your memory neutered?"

I had no idea, if I would or not. Filler? Not quite mercy killing, more like mercy feeding. Fish and chips for the experientially famished.   441

"Our frames of reference have changed. What your father and I have in common these days is what I say we have."

She put down her knife and picked it up again. "He has a right to the same little pleasures you and I take for granted. His memories just need stimulating, is all."

She speared a mushroom with her fork and put its sleek skin to her lips. She smiled. "I crack a big whip. Pour le bon motif."

It was as if she, too, were snacking on Elavil. Heartiness was in the air.

The ideal husband returned chuckling to the table. After tucking in his shirt he resumed pecking at his pasta and poulet, wanting to know if there was garlic in the sauce. My mother assured him there wasn't. "Cherry head," she called him.

Or garlic in the birthday cake? "I hate birthday cake with garlic," he joked. "Anyways, I remember Fin prefers onions in his cake."

I'd never heard them together so playful before. If this is what it was. She reached across and pinched a bay leaf from his plate. I poured us some more wine from a bottle of Sonoma Valley Chardonnay.

My father wasn't supposed to drink more than a glassful, but he didn't object to a refill. "Mud in your eye," he said.

"Mud in yours," I said.

"You got plans for the rest of your stay?" he asked. "Make free with the pickup. Needs a wheel realignment, as you know. But it'll get you wherever."

Before I blew out my candles he sang me "Happy Birthday" with good diction and a flawless memory for the lyrics.

Forgetting to make a wish, but pinching the wicks, I said I might borrow his truck to visit the lake tomorrow.

"Uh huh."

I also mentioned needing to rehearse one or two roles during my stay. I'd try not to get in their hair.

"Not in our hair," said my mother, patting hers.

"No sir," said my father, keeping his hand on his glass.

After my third piece of cake I opened their gift wrapped in pillowy tissue paper and a yellow ribbon the width of a shoelace. A pretty cashmere scarf.

"I know how you opera stars are always being careful not to catch colds," said my mother. "Isn't your fog down there hard on the vocals? We thought you could wear blue in the sunshine without looking like an Eskimo."

My father was grinning into his Chardonnay.

Nearer bedtime she confided she hoped dinner had tasted exactly as I remembered it growing up, or better, because she'd slipped in three garlic cloves. She sounded whimsical and a bit tipsy. The garlic was supposed to be for my father's own good. But I think she wanted me to know she wasn't unfamiliar with the kind of nouvelle ingredients I was helping serve at Max's Opera Café.

I wondered if it was true. I hadn't tasted any garlic.

Later that night I was returning from the bathroom when her low voice stopped me outside their bedroom door. She was talking to my father. The voice was muffled in the darkness, but distinct enough to follow from the hallway.

"... me either. You wouldn't let me sleep two winks last night."

"What was I after?"

"You know what you were after. Tonight, you just better give me a little peace."

"What if I don't?" My father sounded quite interested in the consequences.

So was I.

Something garbled from my mother here. By the sound of the gurgling and sloshing, she was adjusting her six-foot frame to get comfortable on their waterbed.

Then she spoke again. "The first time I ever saw you, Bill, you were standing with sweat trickling down the gully in your bare back. Remember, haying? I almost had a bird. I wanted to come over and prick one of those drops, in the bushy hair over your neck before it started ..."

"Do it. Put your hands up."

Silence. Followed by a fainter voice, hers. "If I don't...?"

I swear, on one of those hollowed-out Bibles in the pen, I heard him drawl sotto voce:

"*Then I might have to pistol-whip you.*"

I did wonder, returning to my room, whether I was overhearing a therapy session or a honeymoon. Things had got operatic since my last visit home. My old bedroom had new bordello wallpaper, sheers, and a Carnegie Hall poster of Sherrill Milnes.

The window was open, its curtains the same diaphanous material as my mother's dress, billowing like a tent in a sandstorm.

A dog or a fox barked at the hen run. A cowbell clanked once among the tire piles, some cow desperate for a bit of pasture in the wending valleys between tasteless, lickless rubber. On occasion, searching for a salt block, a cow could go missing overnight, necklaced and locked by its own horns inside a Dunlop.

I tried to fall asleep, counting tires.

It was like trying to doze in a clearcut, with the rings of every stump sprung loose, twisted and jumbled up like Hula Hoops until they obliterated the landscape a million times for every year of my father's greed.

(Given a choice, I think any son coming of age in similar circumstances would've preferred Sartre's idea of hell to Walt Disney's.)

To try on the cashmere scarf, I flossed it under my balls for an agreeable two minutes before criss-crossing the tasselled ends around my consequent erection, arching my back like a catamite and knotting these tightly above my ass.

Then I jerked off into the night air.

5

Being home had stimulated my own memory in the manner of a bad joke. The *smells* of the place ganged up on my brain cells to smother them with trivial associations. I went back to counting tires. Soon found it was tires I was trying to forget.

I tried jumping sheep through them. The Arcadian past closed down on my face like a coffin lid. I could smell the tired air and decided this was getting silly. I might have to get out of bed to close the window.

By my late adolescence we'd become secure without ever being comfortable. And so it remained. My mother called this farm our cash cow, sardonically, as milk sales had declined in the twenty years since my father had begun replacing cattle with tires, from a total of seventy-five Holsteins and the daily equivalent of a sea of milk, to the present hobby total of six cows and a few gallons to sell as calfmash mix.

Our dependence on milk had shrunk with the swelling revenue from tires. The rubber fields, as they hilled up over the pasture, had begun to overwhelm the landscape like coal tailings in the British Midlands. In winter, if the puddles froze, ice-skating between the crevasses felt claustrophobic, dark.

The dump grew, though so gradually the tires never seemed, at least in my memory of them, to be anything but *here*. They never really grew. Yet they must have been growing. When I awoke on the morning after my birthday, May 5, 1980, they'd spread up to the house overnight. They were rubbing against the windowsill.

I woke up dreaming. Closed the window and went back to bed.

I couldn't remember a time when tires didn't make me wish the fetid rainwater trapped year by year inside all of them, breeding mosquitoes, irrigating rodents, couldn't be siphoned out to fill my father's bath and waterbed for the rest of his living days.

Yet weren't we doing our share to keep the highways safe from accidents and the rest of the country pollution-free?

My father's opinion of the tire business had undergone a change since he first got into it. In more recent years he'd actually begun to dream of returning his farm to the green space it once was. This in response to the environmental movement, just then beginning to gather steam, but really in answer to his new idea for profit.

To wit:

These rubber fields would continue to rise in his belief that someday he'd be able to augment the tire-bounty fees he charged to tire stores and auto wreckers, by turning over for a recycling profit the very tires he'd accepted for profit, thereby defeating all laws of capitalism by having people give him money for taking in their junk, and then having somebody else give him money for carting it away.

Ergo the equivalent of hanging *on* to our cash cow—yet not only *not* having to clean up after her, but being paid to let someone else do the mucking out.

No wonder neighbouring dairymen looked down on him: as well as a polluter he was an arrogant SOB.

My father really believed the future would see his farm become a win-win, profit-profit kind of operation—a kind of halfway house for tires without ruining the neighbourhood. And profitable for the whole chain of entrepreneurs up the ladder, who were soon going to possess the technology and ingenuity to recycle bald tires back into new ones, reselling them to wholesalers and retailers, until their products once again rolled through our farm on their balding ways to four-ply reincarnation.

"Believe in rubber products."

With growing confidence he'd repeat his belief that recycling was going to make him a millionaire in the eighties. Even then—in the seventies, his memory still good—he was ahead of himself, having launched his business in the sixties when dreamboat whitewalls were still the fashion but growing skinnier by the year. (I remember as a child when they vanished entirely along with inner tubes from loads arriving at the farm, so he could no longer scribble figures on these funguses with his saliva and a grease pencil.)

Over the past year my mother had been writing dutifully to me of his green dream, on heavy bond paper of creamy hue, with an embossed crest of TIRE MEADOWS printed like BRIDGESTONE around the upper rim of a laurel-leafed tire. *(Residence of William and J. Francesca Speranza Sauvage . . .)* The crest might as well have said OCEAN VIEW or FOREST LAWN, the euphemism made us sound like a graveyard.

Except nothing got buried here (or else everything did) and any hoped-for decomposition was imperceptible. Tires these days lasted forever because of tougher manufacturing standards: steel belt radials, indelibly efficient treads, fibre-glass compounds in the rubber itself. They were now impossible to get rid of.

"A rubber tire is a tough nut to break down," complained my father, still hopeful.

My mother had been ending her letters to me, mockingly, "Believe in rubber products." Though remembering to add, out of loyalty to her husband, "Even if they *enterrent* the farm, they still help keep you IN VOICE. Speaking of *in*voices . . ." You took her playfulness at face value and chucked the letter.

My father, knowing how much I spurned his idea of a family company, continued to hope I was the future he envisioned. My mother on the other hand expected me to succeed in the opera world and was willing to keep sending money till I did.

She felt I'd paid my dues as a teenager with a très drôle nature (her nature) in aiding and abetting le père's double-profit fantasy for recycling the common tire.

Example, tire slashers, a farm for juvenile toughs to come out from the city on day trips to carve away to their hearts' content. I urged us to dish out knives and collect them at the gate when they left. Make a killing from the Corrections Services, then sell the shredded rubber like excelsior to packagers of French-Canadian crockery.

"I take it you're being humorous."

Tire chairs? For the hemorrhoidal?

"Witty," he said.

My mother enrolled me in singing lessons, to help spike the sarcasm. She was still whisking me off to choir practice and piano lessons. Stuff to get me away from the depressing influence of the local crop. Stuff to stop me calling it *stuff*, for heaven's sake, at a time when I was still more interested in athletes than artists.

My only chance to help my father's recycling dream, and to put a dent in his inventory, happened the summer I got a job at Perumbur Lake. The floats needed new tires and I loaded two dozen into the pickup and donated them.

It was like trying to lower the level of the lake with a tea-cup. "How much you soak 'em for the tires?" asked my father.

"I take it you're being witty."

"Humorous, yeah."

Even he was struck with the growing evidence of his ambition, for all who passed to see. While farms around us were growing in value, ours had declined because the land itself had disappeared. Given the dramatic rise in property values, I think he now wished the price we got for accepting tires was enough to prevent him from wishing he'd never started.

How to relive the past. Rubber baby bumpers, said a million times, equals the present and so constitutes an absurd family of headaches. Sartre? Then some other French swot, babies on the brain.

When he saw his fields begin to fill up my father knew he'd need a dozer to push his inventory into higher and higher piles to give him more dumpage space per square acre for our product.

"You snicker when I mention 'product,'" he told me, "but that's what it is. Instead of haying I bulldoze. I build up our return. Every pile represents dollars in accounts received. This is a very visual-type crop, Fin. Even pays for your cup and garter. Your mother won't tell me how much the Bauers cost. Without tires, though, you wouldn't be playing the national game. Not in summer hockey camps. Too frigging expensive for a dairyman."

In the kitchen at breakfast my mother was standing by her stove. "Did we keep you awake last night?"

"No. Why?"

"Him. He gets insomnia from his medication. I thought I heard you."

"Visiting the john, probably."

"Waffles or crêpes?"

"Crêpes sound good."

"He hates crêpes."

"Waffles then."

"I've made crab and mushroom crêpes. Avec garlic."

My father was still in the barn. I thanked her for the poster in my bedroom. Where had she got it?

"Milnes' people sent it when I wrote him a fan letter in New York. One day your people will be doing the same, for fans like me."

I was warming up at the piano. I always recall Beverly Sills saying in an interview she never knew in what voice she was going to awake each morning. That morning was like coming up for air. I had the bends. It took me a while to catch the rhythm of breathing from the diaphragm.

Hay fever on a grassless farm seemed a contradiction in terms. When had my asthma begun?

My mother looked on from the kitchen, bemused by my vocal foragings. I was relearning the role of Rocco in *Fidelio,* since a university degree in Vocal Performance had foisted upon me bad habits—in Act One's F major trio, for instance, starting "Gut, Söhnchen, gut . . ." To attack this phrase without forcing it was a small yet critical detail when coached at a persnickety level of hypersensitive ears. My mother's ears were more attuned to gossip.

"Why don't you phone up Holly Harker for an assignation?" she suggested. "I hear she's home again. Things didn't work out with what's-his-name."

"Kupe?"

"Rupert. Yes. The dairyman." She pronounced his occupation as though her own husband had always been above cows.

Holly Harker was Seth Harker's younger sister. Five years ago she'd agreed to go along with me to my high-school grad when I needed a date who wouldn't get embarrassed by my belting out "O Canada" to the assembly like one of these Gallic Quebecois on "Hockey Night in Canada," before segueing into an elegy for our friend Michael who'd drowned, a song he'd liked, "Yesterday."

"You might ask her up to the lake. I could pack you a pic-nic."

"She used to claim to like quince," I said. "We got any quince?"

Eat well is one of John Goldsmith's guidelines for singers, as it should be for teenagers. Laugh a lot, avoid places with foul air, treat your body like a valued instrument, and pee pale.

As a teenager your whole life can go bad from the start.

6

After breakfast I drove up to the lake. Five years ago that week Michael had drowned. I passed a slim woman in stretch gear pumping a racing machine across the flood plain. At the boat launch I noticed tires I'd hammered to floats seven years ago still in good flexible shape. Which was why my father espe-cially disliked Firestones. They'd probably outlast the floats. Might even outlast the lake. Flank Narrows was where the lake ended and the tidal river began. The last smells of sea gave way to a light wind tasting of snowfields.

Mr. Douglas lived part-time in the houseboat tied up to a pile of four rotting logs. He was away, though you couldn't be sure, looking at his weed-hulled, dirty-curtained scow, if he wasn't just hiding. I knocked. The muscly man, insepara-ble from his T-shirt, didn't appear. A 200 Johnson outboard, bolted to his stern, would need mechanical labour in excess of its value before it would ever restart. I don't know where he'd got money to pay me in high school, unless misappropriated from the Forest Service. The Forest Service had erected two fibreglass outhouses for users of the lake. Recreation came cheap here.

So had I.

In season Douglas would supervise the boat ramp with its muddy trailer slip. To birders he rented out kayaks and canoes. When the season began, my job had been to bail out the canoes and keep things afloat for the duration of summer. Teenagers would drive up and launch ski-boats, throw each other off the floats, hang out at the aluminum trailer that advertised Joe's Disappearing Tattoos at one end and an Eats and Pop counter at the other.

The scene hadn't changed. Discarded safes and candy wrappers, rusted outboard gas tanks lying without hoses in a ditch of purple loosestrife. Only the car park seemed unlittered: no vans or boat trailers, dirt bikes or hot carbs. The heat of summer just beginning to burn.

I could see smoke rising from a solitary cabin across the narrows. Downstream, at the end of a thirteen-mile meander, the Fraser swept away this slow current to the gulf. The lake itself disappeared in the other direction, twenty miles north into wilderness.

On the marsh's boundary a flock of starlings suddenly wheeled and dove to sanctuary. Two recent watchtowers had cropped up on the dike's gated gravel road. Birders must've climbed these to spy on nesting sandhill cranes. No end to their petty peeping from day to day, as I once told Mr. D. He liked the youth he hired to amuse and keep him happy.

The woman on the ten-speed had arrived and was resting sveltely, watching from shore. Without her helmet, with her dark hair loose and luxurious, she looked Chinese.

I found a bucket hooked above the cat mattress and carried it ashore, where I waded in to the submerged canoes. Douglas felt that sinking his fleet discouraged borrowers and deterred the thievish. I hauled up an aluminum bow and bailed.

From the pickup I fetched my mother's picnic basket, nestling under a velvet blanket like Red Riding Hood's cape got up to resemble the curtain at Covent Garden.

"Nice day," called the cyclist.

Waving warmly I slipped out past the L-shaped floats, paddling for Mallard Slough. Snow-tipped peaks pinched in under a weatherless sky. Geese, nesting in cattails, jiggled their heads like street trade, hissing when I laughed.

I could still reverse myself and head into the lake, a place of happier memories, away from woolgrass and bog. Michael and I, Seth Harker and his sister used to powerboat six or seven miles uplake with Rupert Kupe, to visit shorelines where the mountains dropped three thousand feet into clear water. Glacial falls, deserted lumber camps. We'd climb ashore to clang stones off a rusting steam donkey. Or water ski near Goose Island, watching Seth slalom, as Rupert drove and I listened to Michael over the engine's whine.

"That Pen Island!"

"That Goose Island!" I corrected him. "Not according my father!"

"How come I've never heard of Pen Island?"

"You choirboy! Your voice change late! You get a pimple!"

Michael was Chinese. He sounded coltish when he laughed and I wondered about his pot calling my kettle black.

Holly Harker would listen from the bow, eyes closed, face sunburned. In a bikini. When the boat stopped for her brother, she might tell Michael he was right, by disclosing some fact to which only she was privy. Convicts had once quarried rock on Goose Island, to help build the federal penitentiary. She would open her eyes and smile mischievously, at me.

"Hear?" said Michael, laughing harder.

We picnicked on a sandy beach and drank cheap B.C. blush. From that same summer, at the end of grade eleven, I recall Seth christening Rupert's new Sea Ray with an empty wine bottle he'd refilled with his own rich pee.

Broken glass wasn't all we left behind.

Michael, with his sinuous draftsmanship and a box of oils, contributed the now famous pictographs: eyes and mouths by an apparent faux-naif on a rockface. Photos of them would appear that October in a local newspaper as proof of non-

European presence long before explorers arrived. "Right on," said Michael, his small teeth flashing. The accompanying article would locate his pictographs and propose the Forest Service declare them a sacred aboriginal burial site. An Elder of the Sto:lo nation would concur, wondering about compensation for their historical neglect.

Michael was hoping to persuade his parents to finance his attendance at Emily Carr College. He envied me a mother who actively encouraged artistic talent. Forced to be devious Michael wanted to pursue a career in wildlife oils, but his parents, strict Baptists, had no idea he was harbouring any secret desire let alone practising his art already. Empathizing with his sneakiness, I invited him along the following spring, up Mallard Slough, to sketch the birdlife. I thought he might teach me hatching.

I was celebrating my birthday. Steering clear of goslings we canoed through widgeons and goldeneyes. Michael stopped paddling to draw a long-legged bird, a great blue heron with the wingspan of a bridge, his pencil gliding across the page. After this we hiked up to tiny Mallard Lake, where I tried a pair of green-winged teals. An osprey, sailing on a thermal, wore out my eraser.

Hindsight is easy. Had we known what would follow lower down, we could've camped here and saved ourselves the return hike and ruin.

"No hunter allowed," said Michael, back at the slough. He was feeding crumbs to the mallards. The sky had clouded over and the air inside our tent had grown muggy.

Sketching me at the fry pan, he decided he wanted to be fed a sausage half cooked, a risk we would both come to regret after evening settled in.

In the morning, canoeless, I didn't know a search party was out till a Sea King helicopter circled at noon. Half an hour later the RCMP arrived in a pair of Mr. Douglas's canoes, the creek too shallow for the rescue boat they sometimes deployed in the lake. "Oh, good," they called. "You're okay. No injury to report?"

I now paddled up on the beach to the site where we'd camped five years ago. I removed my mother's lunch, then clothes, and sat down on the stones.

I ate readily through her picnic basket, bananas for quince, before lying back to digest in the sun. I felt my skin for any burning or rash. When I opened my eyes an ultralight was circling at a thousand feet, but it flew away when I guyed it with my mother's ridiculous velvet blanket.

7

Back from the lake I found my father in his barn, silent beside the milking machine. He seemed in mourning for seventy empty stalls. Maybe he'd forgotten to take his mood elevator at breakfast. The light was muted, the air close with ammonia and hay dust. It made my throat itch. I prodded the blue-veined, whiskery udder he was preparing to slip into cups. The pulsator glugged dully, waiting to suck. I took the washcloth from him and wiped down the swollen hooters. I recalled their spongy, sometimes freckled flesh from my years as a dairyman's son. I checked for signs of mastitis, as he'd taught me. I stripped away a bead of leaking milk.

When he attached the cups, each making a straw's slurp at the bottom of a milkshake glass, I raised my eyes to his green Brunswick hanging under the hayloft.

It looked full of hay and probably unused since the night Michael capsized it.

"Dad," I said, listening to the piston-like squeezings now underway, my palm lying in cow hollow, as smooth as tent canvas between hip and ribs. ". . . Remember the time you

helped Michael and me carry that canoe outside, to go camping at the lake?"

He didn't seem to hear me.

"You trusted us not to screw up, Dad."

After a moment he straightened stiffly from the other side
of Lucille and turned, following my gaze. "Yeah?"

Then bent over again to check on his machine's rhythm.

"You packed us a lunch, too."

"I did?" He lifted his face to mine, as if expecting to hear
what kind of sandwiches he'd made.

"Don't you remember, Nôtre Dame was away visiting her
sister in Calgary. You were sweet about it, asking Michael if
he liked chicken thighs. Michael enjoyed you."

My father now smiled. "What's Michael up to these days?
Haven't seen him in ages."

I managed to look surprised. "He's dead, Dad."

"Dead." He frowned, distracted by a loose cup.

"Drowned."

"Jesus. In the canoe?"

"No, fooling around. Cracked his head open in a swimming pool."

"Christ." He looked relieved.

He now checked to make sure the milk was running
unimpeded through the plastic tubing to his bucket.

"Was trying to remember," he said, upright again, "why I'd
hung that yacht up like some museum piece." He was trying to
remember, like any normal person, why the past had temporarily escaped him. I envied him.

I also felt pity, because like my mother I'd now figured out
how easy it would be to have my way with him, to rewrite his
experience on the tabula rasa of his affliction. She was right
about new frames of reference.

"I should probably thank you," I said, "for straightening
me out."

"When was that?"

"When I turned eighteen? You jumped down my throat for getting lost in the wilderness. On that camping trip, do you remember? The ruckus over Michael and me?"

I thought he looked slightly pleased. He clearly didn't remember, any trip or ruckus, but was happy to be reminded of rehabs among sons still possible in the world.

I could now tell him anything about the past and he'd be unable to refute or correct it. It gave me an odd feeling of authority. A control teenage sons dream of having over time and fathers, especially when asked when they got in the night before.

His last cows were waiting to have their teats sucked and diddled on the machine. He used to have three machines and we would work them the length of the barn. I was seven or eight. Sixty flatulent cows eating hay, grinding teeth, collared by scritchy stanchions: the sort of pastoral fugue I associated with incarceration.

I mentioned Holly Harker. "Her dad was home when I called by. Remember, Wallace Harker? Seth's dad?"

My father stared at me.

Had he forgotten his old friend, Wallace?

Dad had swindled him ten years earlier, on a tire-dumping contract Harker was keen to get for his own land and which my father promised he wouldn't bid on himself, telling Harker there was enough rubber to go around the world fifty times to breakfast. "We'll all be in clover."

With his knack for misfiguring the future, he'd probably begun to compare his utopia with Wallace's and decided his neighbour didn't deserve what my father had built up for himself. His neighbour was a deadbeat and a socialist.

Wallace was furious when he heard and swore revenge. A cold war between the two men, neither of them ever speaking to the other again, made it difficult for Seth and me. Our friendship suffered in the mutual hostility of two feuding farts. I don't think my father ever stopped worrying that Harker's acreage, a natural dumping ground because of poor land, would prove more convenient for trucks having to wind past the gravel quarry to reach our place on Polder Road.

"... Yes, I was reminiscing with Holly about that little episode with her old man."

"Right," said my father, bending over to check the action on Lucille. When he reappeared a thread of spittle was hanging from his mouth, and I thought the blood pushing to his head might have caused him another aura.

"What little episode, exactly?" Turning away and stepping heavily over the manure trough.

"Well, she happened to mention her dad's often said he was sorry the two of you never made it up."

My father thought this over. "Yeah?" I was watching his butt. A baritone is either wide in the chest or broad in the beam. Weight somewhere is required. I have my father's beam and overalls only make us beamier.

"I guess he could've had you in jail, Dad."

I think I wanted to shock him, by revealing as if for the first time the greed of his tire-farming past. Of his collusion with tire jockeys and exclusive, no-cut contracts.

"He had it coming to him," he replied.

"Pardon?"

"Getting outmaneuvred."

"... Then you remember?" My voice lifting an octave.

He turned to face me with a defiant expression. A kind of fierce calm. "Why d'you think I still keep the Remington loaded in the house?"

The sharpness of this response startled me. The bitterness of his memory seemed undiminished.

"Don't let your mother fool you."

I began stroking Lucille's rump. "Fool me, how?"

"I recall more than I let on to her."

Staring stubbornly at me now, like a lobster at its tormentor. "For a lot of things, Fingal, my memory is still pretty good."

Shame made me feel like a teenager again. I lifted my hand and it smelled of rubber.

"She just wants to juice things up, give herself a new interest in life."

I was waiting for him to wrinkle his brow and make saucers of his eyes. "I find it kinda glamorous," he went on in the same unglamorous tone. "Seeing how her brain works when she thinks mine's skipped. Disappointing, too, when I know she's fibbing."

Holding himself stiffly now, as if aching from every joint, he sounded rueful. "Instead of going snake, I listen to her. Gives me some control. She thinks she's the one in the driver's seat. So we're both operators. It's all a big pretend."

I was embarrassed. His tabula rasa now resembled a secret sketchbook on betrayal by wife and son both. It could've been all the forlorn empty stalls, causing him to sound disappointed at the way farming life had turned out for a man who believed he cared deeply about tradition. But I sensed it was the way he felt his son was still bullshitting him.

Over supper my mother asked how Holly had liked her lunch. She was fishing for more than compliments. She wanted to know if I was on the right track with ma vie sensuelle.

"Loved it. We had a grand old time. Paddled the canoe up Mallard Slough."

"Oh?" She looked pleased, despite her best effort to show concern. "Where the Wing boy drowned?"

"No," my father said, looking at me. "He drowned in a swimming pool." Sounding a little sarcastic, as if the lobster and his tormentor had switched roles.

My mother looked at me. My father looked at my mother. I changed the subject, to the blue scarf.

This reminded my father. He suddenly said, "What month is this?"

Seems he'd recently found a bill for about a hundred yards of dress silk, and a few pairs of pumps, and been unable to figure out if payment for the circus was overdue.

That night I did wonder about the nature of families and if any philosopher, French or otherwise, had ever composed an elegy to shame without first experiencing imprisonment.

In the years since this week home I've come to hear how the overture to *Don Pasquale* resembles a blissful seduction, full of passion and joy, with moments of tenderness and sometimes sadness. Its conclusion seems comically rambunctious in the way copulation is.

Singing the role of Dr. Malatesta, I now wait for the curtain, thinking how this overture sounds like a tragedy.

8

I recently turned thirty-three. Not yet a household name in the opera firmament, if that isn't a contradiction in terms. I sing in regional theatres across North America, do summer stock, contract for roles like a utility infielder and maintain my base in San Francisco. For Dallas Opera I've sung a replacement Sharpless in *Madama Butterfly,* performed *Masked Ball's* Renato for Calgary Opera, Ping in *Turandot* for Indianapolis, a Malatesta in Baltimore, and Escamillo in *Carmen* for Sarasota. Lately, I made my debut at Santa Fe as Silvio in *I Pagliacci.* These days I am preparing Rodrigue in *Don Carlo* for Opera Theatre of St. Louis.

This last was what put me in mind again of the penitentiary and my visit to it with my father.

That spring had been the spring Terry Fox started hopping across Canada, from St. John's to Victoria, to raise money for medical research after losing his right leg to bone cancer. He was planning to run the length of the Trans-Canada Highway, but, four months after my visit home, had got only as far as Thunder Bay when they discovered cancer in his lungs and he was forced to abandon his "Marathon of Hope." He'd run over two thousand miles, without crossing half the country. He vowed to complete the run.

Canada, according to my father who should have known, now took the faith of a cripple.

My mother sent newspaper clippings to San Francisco. L'héros was one year younger than I, but already famous. He came from a small town a few miles down the highway, and was travelling with his girlfriend who followed him in their camper truck at a turtle's pace. "She cooks for him," P.S.ed my mother, making sure I knew what the gossip of a Canadian hero consisted of, "and changes his leg."

My father quipped in a P.P.S. that their camper's tires would never wear out at a measly twenty-four-miles a day.

My athletic compatriot turned out to be the hare and turtle rolled into one. He won the big race by losing it.

He died at the Royal Columbian the next year, where my father died a year later. His death came as a shock, because it came in the wrong way. I went home for the funeral, but left before the inquest. I think my mother would've liked me to sing "O My Papa" at the service, lilting like Eddie Fisher on Elavil. Instead I sang Verdi.

My grandmother attended in a lavender coat and Aunt Betty, now eighty-seven, in a walking frame. My father's family was long-lived and no more susceptible to memory loss than normally governed by old age. The past tried but could not consume them. Both remembered Bill Miner's pistol in detail but argued at the reception following interment over the tattoo on his forearm. My grandmother remembered a tattoo, but her sister remembered none at all. How each could be so certain seemed a wonderful example of how death is cheated by detail. Neither seemed so alive that wet October afternoon, sunk heavily into my father's sofa, as when they bickered over the tattoo of a dancing girl on the forearm of a robber.

I refused to chip in with any documentary evidence from the poster I remembered, because nothing could have erased the conviction of opinion on either side. After almost eighty years their youthful memories had taken on the indelibility of dream. The consensus of my family's oral history confirmed the hand-held pistol in detail and this seemed as far up the arm as they could get without dissolving into disagreement. It was something.

By now I'd finished at the San Francisco Vocal Arts Studio, with the renowned coach Ricardo Tibaldi, and was wondering if I had a future in opera or not. There were a hundred baritones of my generation. Roles were plentiful, opportunities few. Tibaldi with his Grey Flannel perfume advised me to carry an adrenaline pump for my asthma and a small grip for the overhead luggage racks. "Forget the carousels when you're in a hurry. Fly first class and require a limo." He was a good-natured womanizer, whom I still visit for help with demanding roles.

I quit my job at Max's Opera Café and concentrated on serving a career instead of food. A debut with the SFO seemed years, if ever, away. I needed work with the Pocket Opera or else Opera in the Schools to keep up my confidence and bank balance. I thought of going back to live in Canada. What did it matter as an Italian baritone where I was based, Alberta or Alaska, singing Puccini's Sheriff Rance in *The Girl of the Golden West* for Edmonton or San Diego? Have Pipes, Will Travel. Ditto Laugh.

My mother had no idea now what she was going to do with TIRE MEADOWS. Sell out, if she could, but who wanted a dairy farm full of tires? Who wanted a tire dump with no space left to dump in? Who wanted a tire farm with nowhere to recycle the product? The profit in the place had run out. The land had long ago disappeared.

She sold the remaining cows to Rupert Kupe and stopped any more dump trucks from arriving after my father's death.

Perhaps his death had been an accident, as the inquest concluded. Maybe his mind *had* drifted to the centre line, causing him to walk into the path of Wallace Harker's car. What was he doing on the road anyway, walking alone with his back unguarded? My mother testified he'd gone out that afternoon to milk. Had the way to the barn finally slipped his mind, like the last line from a zeppelin?

She phoned to tell me Harker was suspected of manslaughter but wouldn't be charged. Tire marks had allowed the RCMP to trace the hit-and-run car to Mrs. Harker. Wallace said he left the scene of the accident because people still remembered bad blood between him and his neighbour and he was scared of them jumping to conclusions. Homicide was not his idea of order.

"Poor man had no idea William wouldn't have remembered him, even if he'd stopped the car and offered him the tires."

I avoided the inquest, remembering how an earlier one, into Michael Wing's death, had caused my hay fever to worsen. Also I had no desire to deal with my father's estate. If some legacies never changed, mine had. I made up my mind to stay abroad and make a home there.

Here.

Where, headed into my mid-thirties, I now find every fermata counts increasingly against the past.

A decade since his death my mother still lives in growing despair of her dwindling capital. Lately, she has decided her only hope of resuscitating it is through her husband's dream of recycling their tires. God help her. I suppose we are all waiting for our Godots, but how does she endure the place? She has long lost her farm status and taxes have soared.

She calls to say things in the recycling world have moved on since my father first thought of contributing his billion tires to reincarnation. Melodramatically, she tells me that early in the next century I, heir to a woman of no importance, can expect to cash in, provided I hire someone after she is

DAMAGES

gone to manage the transmigration—sell the tires, then sell the land.

"I know you don't want anything to do with the place, mon cher, and I don't blame you."

"No, you're wrong."

The provincial government she claims has begun collecting a tire tax of three dollars per tire sold there. This money will be used to finance new schemes to recycle the three million tires junked a year.

"The door is open to you, to make your fortune."

Doormats, rubber crumb, rubberized asphalt. The world is my oyster.

She says cement plants now burn tires for part of their fuel. This portion could increase with the new technology. She mentions a technique called pyrolysis, and says one day I could find myself in the loop for exports to the States, where they're using tires in power plants.

"Burning, Fin, has come miles since your father tried it. After the big Hagersville fire they had to crack down."

A heavy rainstorm had helped snuff my father's fire the June I graduated from high school. His burning tires would've lit up the surrounding mountains till Christmas. The smell, in one of those memories accumulated from odourless news clips on TV, reminded me of South African necklaces.

I sang poorly at my high-school graduation. I had been testifying at the inquest into Michael's drowning. How an unexpected storm had come up and I thought the wind and rain would make his navigation of the narrows dangerous in the dark.

"Holly Harker," my mother adds, "still phones to ask about you. More than once she's said how much she enjoyed that picnic tu et elle took up Mallard Slough. I *am* sorry to bother you about the farm."

She is very polite. And despite her despair sounds as healthy as a Holstein.

"Don't be sorry," I tell her just as politely back. And laugh like a tenor. "Remember how much I enjoyed bantering with Dad about recycling Goodyears and Michelins? You're dead right about the new technology. I look forward to taking over TIRE MEADOWS when they put you out to pasture."

Why do we go on talking like this, year after year? To cover the shame of knowing the other knows we're lying? Or are we each in our own way vying for control of the family album?

Just before she dies I'll probably come home and formally announce my engagement to a nice Marin County girl. Death-bed deceptions have their place, I sense, if the diee's doubt can be erased by the deception. At present San Francisco is full of such deceptions, small white ones, partners swearing loyalty to partners who are dying.

Like opera, life seems full of deceptions if you're determined to make an art of it. Ergo the performing artist, in flagrant delicto, the perpetual outsider. Not so bad. Being outside gives him his sound. Each to his place, beholden to a predecessor, Leonard Cohen sounding like Johnny Cash on tranquillizers.

I remember hearing Cash's Folsom Prison album as an adolescent, listening over and over to his rich rhythmic voice. But I couldn't deny my father's voice, breaking through in me as my glands then were like chanterelles. I couldn't deny my genes. How to escape a residency we both regretted, to get outside and be free?

On occasion I will be invited abroad, to poorer countries, for operetta roles in Gilbert and Sullivan, or Strauss, which count for little on my resume. I've even woken up in Argentina to find myself singing Andrew Lloyd Webber at a breakfast for civil rights workers in hot pants. But these junkets pay for themselves and keep my ego stroked. Stoked? In a provincial town in Brazil, say, I'll receive a kind of baroque hospitality alien to my non-reception in North America. This will match the unexpected nineteenth-century opera house, which is stunning, like the dark skin available back in Rio. It gleams against a jungle. I would love to return someday to sing *Tosca* with Pilar Lorengar, kissing the hems of that old hoofer as I, Scarpia, lie there dying on the floor of my apartment in the Farnese Palace.

I would kiss Joan Sutherland's hems, too, but she has retired and hung up her size twenty. That doesn't stop me from hoisting my dream sails above the Sydney Opera House, like some reincarnated Peter Dawson, local baritone long dead. Death shapes most stories and mine would have me on board as Germont singing "Pura siccome un angelo" to Mrs. Bonynge—and, from that same ecstatic scene in *La Traviata,* "Di Provenza il mar, il suol" to Marshall van Neer. (Where are you, Marshall? You were a wonderful tenor. Have faith!)

I find it perverse Germont is the role I dream myself into heaven with, singing a lament to my son of his fate far from the shining sun of Provence, and how I've suffered since Alfredo departed the joy of our family home. I sang this aria to my father at his burial.

Whoever lives longer can choose to recycle the other's story in theirs. This is the law of the jungle, ignored, I am sure by French pundits in favour of the absurd. I feel ruthless sometimes, thinking how *I* sing is the highest law of all, how *my* story is the last word in the family album. Like love, a corrupt business of dog eat dog. You sing to be encored.

(Take heart, Mother, this story is for you in case you're left alone without me one day. Pick it up and put it down, where you wish. You will have the last word then. You may even rework the ending.)

9

No.

The reason I am writing is to explain how the facts that came out at Michael Wing's inquest were opinions and how my father could forgive everything except the truth.

The truth is Michael couldn't make up his mind about me, although *his* version of our wildlife expedition wouldn't have mentioned this at all. Regrettably, his was the version that governed the inquest. The inquest ruled drowning by misadventure.

The version *I* testified to, as the reason for his leaving our tent, was my friend's nagging fear he'd betrayed his parents by not telling them where he'd come—that they'd be worried he hadn't gone home that night. His parents' lawyer countered they *had* known where Michael was and had vigorously disapproved his going. The inquest's story of Michael was of a sensitive, responsible son, whose feelings of responsibility to his parents were acute. Did not drink. Did not chase girls. A good son.

This story should've supported my own.

My mistake was having sworn earlier that neither of us had been drinking. Unfortunately, the autopsy showed traces of plonk in the deceased's bloodstream, from a bottle shared over our sausage cookout. Coroner's opinion was I wasn't telling the truth about what led Michael to abandon our tent. In ruling death by misadventure he upbraided me for seeming callous at my friend's "odd" decision to return to my father's truck. I supposed Michael felt he could sleep more comfortably there, his stomach apparently upset. He was an excitable friend.

But I had lied poorly. Somehow, had failed Michael. My reputation never recovered (whispered suspicions spread like a weedy ground cover) and I was glad to escape into undergraduate life the following September.

I was glad to come abroad five years later. Home had become increasingly exotic to me, as had its shame. My parents were ashamed of me. To return to live in Canada would've destroyed my illusions of the place. To be disillusioned at four in the morning was far worse than to know you had illusions and were still willing to stand by them. Even my father discovered this. Until wandering away from his own illusions, he knew they were everything, when everything else was fading. Corruption was all. Just as central to the map of his brain as rubber to the Trans-Canada. Anyhow, my Canadian driver's licence had expired and I had (have) never renewed it.

Patriotism wouldn't help my career, not at this stage. It would also kill the current relationship I'm in, as my partner has no wish to leave San Francisco and family to live in Toronto or Vancouver. We're content enough. I get to travel, he gets to sleep around. We both sleep around. His father owns three restaurants in Chinatown. We live together in the Castro, in a two-bedroom walkup off Clipper. We maintain a discreet dignity, never compromising ourselves by betraying the other's soul to another partner. Body, yes. In leather clubs on Folsom Street. In apartments as far away as North Beach. Anywhere, really, to keep up the wonderful illusion of romance, especially while young. The curse of desiring to live heroically in a non-operatic age is, of course, the current plague. My father would've approved.

Lately, we hear playing, as a kind of anthem song from the apartment next door, "Tell Him No" by the Everly Brothers. It seems to be replacing the old gay anthem, "Chances Are" by Johnny Mathis.

Would I could be so popular as those artists. Am afraid my discography is limited to pirated tapes from recitals and performances. These underground masterpieces circulate in the community and I'm cherished among a few for chestnuts like "Au fond du temple saint . . ." singing the role of Zurga with Richard Margison as Madir, in *The Pearl Fishers*. It's like being on the moon when I overhear myself coming out tinnily from some open window in the sunshine. A man inside is dreaming of me.

But where is my role in the great AIDS opera? Who will compose it? Probably a straight shooter from Broadway, some outsider with a mid-Atlantic accent and a mistress, a wife and a soccer team he coaches for his daughter's sake every Connecticut weekend after a papaya breakfast for good skin and a smooth pee. Puccini, after all, didn't need to contract consumption to compose *La Bohème* . . . only to create illusion to parry disillusion.

The condition of being in love is what I decided on my eighteenth birthday I'd like for myself. It led inevitably to corruption. I still throw myself into roles that would charm birds from a marsh. Can't help it. And this leads to wounded feelings all around. I desire ecstasy through other men, and while I'm unwilling to pay the price of dying I am willing to live with death constantly in mind.

What else is new? Death death death is the singer's dictum, and everything he performs is an elegy to the temporal voice. Or should be. I tell people what I think they want to hear, that I have/have not tested positive for HIV, in order to enhance their belief in my art. I want them to feel some of the happiness I feel as a baritone even of modest talent, as a lover even of unreliable declaration. Ironic, being in the business of perfection, to have to strive for it with corruption so much on the brain.

Sometimes I wonder in light of my father's auras what lies in store for my own brain. Have begun to wonder on stage if bliss wasn't always the beginning of my end.

To make art of life I find nothing more trustworthy than my conductor's baton, this baton. My instinctive loyalty is to it, confining me to ecstasy and grief upon a fixed stage. My nightmare is I'll fail my vision and discover poltroonery at my centre. So illusion is everything. The collective artifice of librettists, designers, singers, composers and dancing masters—all of us in the bliss business, our gaiety transfiguring all that dread.

Should I expect to experience my father's seizures?

Blackout, heaven blazing into the head.

Some of our friends believe the pulleys, racks and costumes of their S and M machinery are all part of the stage they live upon. I think this illusion the right one. Except their apartments resemble ancient inquisitorial prisons: blindfolds, tit clamps, cockrings ...

Ours favours less impersonal props and more traditional roles. "You like my weapon? I'm going to shoot you with it." This excites Richard. It excites me. I talk to him in my husky baritone—Puccini's own voce bruna—as melodiously as I can. I tie up my partner's wrists the way I once tied Michael Wing's, with a scout's half-hitch.

Richard isn't squeamish, doesn't spook if I laugh at his sensibilities. He struggles eagerly to escape. A stage designer, he is used to people walking, so to speak, over him. He's really the one in control. He contains me. He allows us freedom within his three walls (where Michael's sketch of the cook and fry pan hangs framed) and laughs at my thinking a mere stage pistol can be the centre of the action. A big pretend by us both. "Put your faith in rubber," I tell him. "Or die." Richard has a wolfish laugh. My blue cashmere softens pressure on his wrists.

In our own way, we're happy.

Even my father's directive is ludicrously, prophetically borne out. We've become believers.

Yesterday I found myself on Nob Hill visiting a black-and-white photo exhibition of AIDS victims in Grace Cathedral. The church was empty. Cool blue light sifted down from the nave's stained glass windows. Birthdates were given, death dates left open or closed, as required. Roommates pictured in kitchens and dens, posing with parakeets or dogs, a vintage Buick, dressed in T-shirts and chinos. Caught before the appearance of Kaposi's sarcoma, with its disfiguring and agonizing lesions.

A note said it's often possible to forget you're infected, because the virus can live undetected in the lymph nodes for up to ten years before launching a final attack.

I felt close to tears. I thought of the mothers who had arrived here from Wichita and Red Deer. And of the ones who hadn't arrived. Of the lovers, themselves infected or not infected, who nursed roommates. Or hadn't and disappeared. I wondered why it took us so long in the early days to shut down the bathhouses and plug the glory holes. We've all immigrated here from outside boundaries we never knew could've saved us from pneumonia and meningitis.

Yet at what cost, compared to imprisonment and falsehood? To risk all in a gamble over a drop of blood, as Sheriff Jack Rance does, hoping to capture the gentle tenor, highway robber Dick Johnson, is to know the value of everything and the cost of nothing. That, I think, is the price of wanting to live operatically: seeing through to the exotic, as Puccini did, and deeming this its own reward. Not a bargain, by any means, killing the thing you love!

Richard claims I am turning into an artistic director.

Afterwards, I walked down Russian Hill to Fisherman's Wharf, and along with all the fish and chippy tourists stood gazing out to Alcatraz across the green salt-smelling bay. It seemed a propitious time to invite an aura: the sky cerulean, the buildings behind me white and Mediterranean, the light crippling. I considered taking the boat tour of the now deserted prison rooted atop the hot rock, something every citizen has eventually to do for a picnic of bread and water. I could see water tanks and windows winking in the sun. What glory holes over there?

When he was released in 1901, after spending thirty-three of fiftyfour years in prison, Bill Miner left California and landed in my native province. I thought now I understood the source of his elaborate facade, his ability to take people in, including my ancestors. He too had been an outsider. A confidence man. A bandit who couldn't resist the abiding temptation of his nature, of his deceit in love with courtliness, and who ended up in handcuffs and jail, a gentleman recidivist.

Even in prison they couldn't see through him any more than they could through Wilde in Reading Gaol. His true identity resided in the sincerity of his facade. Shame seems quaint now. A performer's curse, Mother. It just gets to the point where it is no longer possible, or desirable, to separate life from its stage.

THE
AMERICAN
CALLER

OSA, the Cuban nanny, had walked Michael home from preschool with his vital statistics recorded in one of the new kits given to his class by the police. Michael's file, along with his mugshot, included printed instructions on how to use the enclosed swab to take a DNA sample. Heather was to rub it up and down inside his cheeks to harvest the genetic spoor. When extracted the cotton should be damp with her son's saliva and sealed in the enclosed envelope; she was to store this somewhere dry and preferably dark at room temperature. Rosa held Michael's blond head when the procedure began. The boy refused to retract his blossom-coloured tongue until he saw his mother lick the envelope and prepare to post it in the bathroom cabinet.

His sample would last indefinitely. It would still be there for him at 102, should he require it, assuming it had not been removed to investigate his abduction in the remaining years of defenceless childhood by a weedy stranger, threads of whose van's shag carpet would need to be chemically mingled with traces of the missing boy stored here above the sink. She wondered if the likelihood of old-coot kidnappings really made it necessary to arrange for the storage of Michael's genetic data in perpetuity. She hoped the sample would reside undisturbed for decades beside the seldom-opened bottle of Tums and then be tossed by herself, or Michael's loyal wife, in a hot whirl of menopausal housecleaning.

The police had requested the undersigned parent to keep her child's I.D. form up to date with height, weight, and hair colour. They asked her to make sure Michael knew his phone number and area code, snubbed strangers, never visited a public lavatory alone, and knew which houses on his street were safe ones. Moreover, Heather should know where Michael was at all hours, not leave him alone in her car nor print his name on ball cap or winter coat. If ever he happened to be stolen from her he should remember she would *never stop looking for him* no matter how long it took to find, comfort, and bring him safely home.

Twenty years, though, would she look that long, say, after the trail had gone cold? Despite every good intention of scrupulously monitoring Michael's childhood, Heather was unable *not* to hear a cologne-splasher with unattractive sideburns telephoning her two decades hence, who failed to recognize either his mother's voice or what city he'd just rung up. He would sound fervourless at first, a bit bony. She sensed his difficulty in talking to a stranger, or at any rate to her. She must be joking, he said. His mother?

"So," she'd say, "the name Michael Greeley means nothing to you?"

"Nada."

But he left the door open for her, a crack, because now that she mentioned childhood he claimed to remember a heavy man dressed in black clothes and a mask. This uninspired bit of opera made Heather wonder if he was testing her gullibility. He then asked her about a brown teddy. She coolly assured him her son's toys and clothes were all upstairs in his closet; he might recall these in more detail if he thought about them.

Was she being fair? She wondered about the ability of a former three-year-old to remember much of anything.

So he came at it from a different angle. He wanted proof that she was who she claimed to be. He didn't mean to sound grasping, but would a trip north, you know a quick jaunt, maybe help to jog his memory? Not that a working stiff like himself could afford the flight.

There was silence. "Listen," he added, "I understand your pause. You're wondering if you detect the whiny street voice of a heroin addict on methadone."

"No, please. Don't hang up."

His call had weakened her knees. How very deeply she still missed the love and loving of a child. Sitting down, surrounded by work files, she was trying to negotiate outside her understanding of certainty and surrender. She was in no hurry to cut him off.

He proceeded. If she was sincere, and he now felt she was, he would require a return flight. Proof of good faith in case her hunch about him was wrong and thus inconvenient, especially for the traveller. Plus, he told her, a return ticket would ease an American citizen's entrance into Canada, n'est-ce pas? "I've never been to Canada, so I'm in your hands. If you're interested ... my name is David Toms."

When Heather arrived at the airport to greet either lost son or scam-man—possibly both—so did two men with wallet badges. "Ms. Greeley?" She recognized neither detective as having worked with her on Michael's case twenty years ago. These new Columbos wore blue jeans and ear studs the size of cin cins. One wore a toque. Heather had driven straight from work in her Armani suit with power shoulders. Last night, thinking ahead, she'd rinsed the grey from her hair hoping to look the way she used to, in case David Toms needed help remembering her.

When he did not turn up, after arriving passengers from the American southwest vanished into the rain, the detectives relaxed and complimented her discretion in contacting them about her American caller. They had tried to trace the call with some kind of crim-crack—Crim-Trac?—software. They figured it might have been a local call.

"But I sent the money to Albuquerque."

"These extortionists poach from all over."

"How would a New Mexican hear about a bygone abduction in Vancouver?"

"Cyberspace. He cruises the information highway in a ripped-off laptop."

"He finds your number . . ."

"He calls."

"You decide to take what's on offer."

"Unfortunately," suggested the taller Columbo in a fingerless bowling glove, "your money is now history."

"It's not the money," she told him, "It's not knowing."

"Exactly," said his sidekick, a father by the look of his Yogi Bear notebook. ". . . Just one thing, Ms. Greeley. Would you recognize your son after twenty years? You appreciate what I'm saying?"

She wondered about hair colour. His voice too would have changed, years ago.

"I guess what I'm asking—would you happen to remember what his father looked like as a young man?"

They were still standing in the foyer, beside a low Plexiglas corral, inside which two tall Clayoquot figures wearing conical hats stood on concrete pedestals with upturned palms to welcome new arrivals. Heather fingered the key ring to her Japanese hybrid.

"I did mention to your predecessors that Michael's father was basically a one-shot sponsorship."

The men stared at one another, obviously not intimate with a file predating their software.

"I suppose a DNA swab would settle it," she suggested, impressively offering to release the sample still in her possession. It seemed to her an elegant solution to the delicate issue of identity.

They were unimpressed. Why would a "person of interest" such as her caller agree to be tested? And what would his refusal prove? Frankly, they were still at square one. They did wonder though if young Michael had been implanted under the skin with a microchip. That would make identifying him—and by default her caller—a whole lot *easier*.

Heather had never heard of the procedure.

Left alone then, she circled and re-circled the cedar statues, waiting patiently for her caller to emerge from Immigration. Outbound vacationers ascended the nearby escalator, departing from another level where she could glimpse the Reid sculpture of aboriginal paddlers. No one appeared on the monitor who showed the least interest in a middle-aged woman disguised in younger-looking hair. Seeing this past self reflected in the sliding glass door made her son's return seem unnecessary, as though he'd never disappeared. She allowed herself to drift back to the present on a deep, dispelling breath. No one had been taken from her. The future remained open, amendable. She was still looking at Michael's rosy tongue in the bathroom mirror.

———————

Closing the cupboard door on his freshly sealed DNA, Heather bent to kiss her son before going upstairs to change. She planned to file in her desk the form from the police, after rechecking his height against the latest horizontal line of vertical dates on the kitchen doorjamb. Was there a future watershed year when such lines would begin to descend, his weight drop, and hair recede? A ringing phone caused her to stiffen briefly, then pick up her toothbrush. She heard Rosa answer downstairs and waited to be summoned. This would be Michel Rozelle, the sponsorship she otherwise remembered as Michael's father, calling back with last-minute details about tonight.

His enthusiasm encouraged her to ask him, a little ungratefully, "Will you remember what I look like?" He responded "You still have your own teeth, yes?" Heather laughed, tapping chin with toothbrush. They had not met since their one time together in Toronto four years ago, but she had followed his career with intermittent interest. He was in town this month starring in his own one-man play, a recent triumph in London and Paris. A ticket would be waiting for her downtown at the Playhouse box office.

As the sold-out audience settled she read Michel's description of himself as "a jongleur" and his show as "based loosely on the 'there and then' during those years I remember growing up in Quebec City after ma mère died." He had dreamt of rocket flight among the stars, at the same time as his twin sister's trajectory was aiming her at a TV anchor job in Detroit.

Heather smiled often at his uncanny staging, a sweat lodge and a gym horse, a jetliner and a tavern, as if he had started out by fooling around with scenes from his own life and then discovered how they might serve his story. She was moved by the way his story flowed through light and shadow, video screens and feminine impersonations, especially of a maternal love embracing Michel's bereft young world in a kind of cosmic glue of space-walking pandas. For a barrel-chested man, Michel moved lightly on his feet. His miked voice allowed him to sound more natural on stage than actors who projected themselves unaided. His intimate tones let her see how the prosaic life of Levon Hardy had been translated by Michel Rozelle into a fantastic, hopeful dream of *ashes* (Levon's ashes) shot into space and tumbling freely forever in a capsule.

He had an ear for such mystery. Spacey electronic music resembled the sound of broken lyres.

They shared drinks by candlelight in a brick building on Homer she drove them to after his performance. Shorter than she remembered, a little overweight, Michel listened carefully to the story of her life since they'd last met. Maybe he was listening for a character to deploy in his next play, and Heather heard in her own voice something of Levon's commanding sister in *The Shadow Side of Time*. Unlike men in her firm, who could be told nothing they didn't already know, Michel was different. His guilelessness prompted her to speak winsomely. And she enjoyed having the effect of an actor who knew how to inhabit a pause.

She remembered feeling like this at the conference on indigenous rights where he first turned up. From the floor he was asking of panelists, among them Heather, apparently disinterested questions about the aboriginal notion of time, and pressing Ms. Greeley on whether her own province had so far failed to settle treaties because native people entertained one blessed hope of time of which lawyers were unaware. The audience of delegates, including lawyers, laughed. Heather waited. Then she spoke calmly and succinctly of treaty rights which were either extinguishable or non-extinguishable. You could not have finality and an ongoing relationship both; coexistence favoured open-ended tide.

This must have impressed the ingénue in him. Later, in the hotel bar, he more or less flung his soul into the bad light to banter with her. After a second martini Heather decided she wouldn't mind waking up to his full-hearted, slightly accented voice in her ear. She knew nothing of his having burst on the theatrical landscape like a comet earlier that decade. She thought he was one of the underdressed lawyers from Montreal and had already forgiven him his cords.

He laughed charmingly now, at her complete misrepresentation of their barroom tryst. "My recollection is scandalously less dramatic."

She paused, then told him. "You have a son."

He let her words sink in, rolling his olive slightly by its pick to catch the colours of striped fish orbiting in a nearby aquarium. "Is he witty, I hope? *Mon fils*?"

"He was kidnapped last month."

"My God."

Heather spoke her lines quietly, surprising herself. "He's been home just a week now. I can't be late, in case he wakes up." She examined her tiny watch face in the fishy light. "The police won't talk about what he went through before they found him in a makeshift shelter near Osoyoos."

"The homesickness. I cannot imagine it."

Over tapas she invited Michel home to view the sleeping child.

She was renting the same rambling house on Napier where Michael was born, and where Rosa was now asleep before a balding, heart-fixed Letterman. Heather noticed her nanny's Guatemalan friends had jettisoned pizza boxes in the kitchen. Their predicament as illegal refugees left them partial to the petty addictions of cardboard food. She was planning to speak to Rosa about greasy paraphernalia like belts and bandanas in the trash.

She tiptoed Michel upstairs, where he stood quietly gazing at the sleeping child's face. Was he seeking a resemblance? The light in Michael's room shone against the boy's yellow hair.

"My son?" he finally whispered. A little politely, she thought. The poster of an astronaut swimming umbilically in space had also caught his eye.

"I named him after you," said Heather, canting forward into the crib. Then overcome, righting herself, she took a long unsteady breath. "I can't tell you, Michel, at four a.m. the grieving ... the godforsaken *longing*."

Tenderly, he touched her wrist.

She collected her son's clothes from the wicker basket and carried them downstairs, where she set the washer for fifteen minutes. This domestic scene left her famous guest absorbed in watching Michael's cycling laundry through the porthole.

He asked if she still enjoyed treaty work. At her admitting she did he complimented all lawyers negotiating ancestral land claims and seeking accommodation with temporal myth. He sounded heartfelt. He confessed her original discourse had lingered much with him. "Extinguished, not extinguished . . . this is like the missing wall to keep the playwright looking through it."

She poured him a glass of Glenfiddich at the kitchen island. For a moment she felt like the imaginary bartender in his play, to whom his alter ego listens. "You might be interested to know," she said, "since you are a 'jongleur' of time, the kidnapped child's biggest enemy is time. Michael was very lucky. In three-quarters of abduction homicides, the child is murdered within three hours."

Michel listened, unshockable. He heard the spin cycle come on, the tick of zippers and little cleats. He asked about the raven carving on her windowsill. Accepting a second glass of scotch, he checked the clock and prepared to call a cab. He graciously shared with her what she had not read in local interviews. Two years ago he had taken up with a man from Haiti, a performance artist. They were happily cohabiting in Paris now. Or did he say collaborating? Anyway, Heather felt free to acknowledge the man in her own life, a resident ENT who was hoping to become a Médecins Sans Frontières. Unfortunately, she admitted, it was too easy to imagine him lighting out down the line soon for some place exactly like Haiti.

"Let's be in touch," said Michel, touching her arm warmly. "I would like to keep informed of your son's course. I am always nostalgic for the present. I am already nostalgic for this one."

Outside, the happy good-night air seemed to fall from a December sky of his own, theatrical making. He was a man who noticed small things, like taxi headlamps, and how they bleached the moonlight from her tangled yard before he vanished.

When the phone rang, years later, the timbre of his voice sounded familiar. "We missed at the airport. Let's just say I didn't care for the suits you brought along."

Michel's voice. *Maybe* Michel's voice. She wanted to believe in her son's return.

"David," she said, her knees weakening. "They were in blue jeans, David. And ear candy."

"Whatever . . . I'm downtown without your address. You gave me zilch to go on."

"And you me."

She imagined him in a concho belt, and one of those Navajo vests favoured in New Mexico, loose enough for David's barrel chest, and she felt tender now about his misjudged sideburns and overdosed cologne.

"Well, since you ask, your father was a famous playwright. A genius, in fact."

"My father?"

"I named you after him. Michael. Not that he ever knew. Do you remember Rosa?"

"I don't remember you. You're supposed to be my mother."

"Your nanny was the last one to see you. It was a relay kind of thing, the afternoon you disappeared. I was running late from work, meeting her at the field where she was playing second base and minding you till I arrived. You were in no man's land apparently, by the dugout. Neither of us ever blamed the other, and I was quietly proud of that."

"Jesus," muttered David Toms. Appalled perhaps at how effortlessly he had been snatched by strangers, at his mother's stupid pride.

"David. Please listen to me. I have to ask, do you remember a picture on the wall above your bed?"

He pretended to think about this. "Is there a clue?"

"An astronaut?"

"I remember a heavy man in black clothes and a mask," he claimed.

She went quiet. Her caller was repeating himself. She was offended by this image of a bogeyman, by the simplistic whim of a bargain con artist who figured he could... Maybe she'd be further ahead calling off their get-together and hanging up.

Nothing prepared her for what then occurred, inside the long pause where she was loitering. Something like an ecstatic sound challenged her disappointment. Pierced it in the manner of a carolling voice. *This man has to be my son!* Her unexpected grasp of his shopworn language had illuminated the dark figure this caller was remembering from the moment just before someone embraced and carried him off as a little boy. *He is still spellbound by the loud, blackcoated man in the mask at home plate!*

"Listen to me, David. Are you listening? Write down this address and give it to the taxi driver."

"How do I know it won't bounce?"

"Don't trifle with me, David. You are not actually who you think you are anymore."

"Yes, ma'am."

"I know this sounds abrupt. Don't get upset."

Infallible now, she felt compelled to explain how they urgently needed to revise their relationship vis-à-vis one another. She went on to acknowledge things were going to be more difficult for him than for her. Twenty years was a very, very long time. And so if he felt uncomfortable with anything about to be settled, anything that didn't feel right, he could withdraw and leave Vancouver on the return flight tomorrow.

"Mañana?" he asked.

Mañana. She held the phone a moment more. Heather Greeley expected she would know David the minute he stepped from the taxi and moved lightly, predictably, through the coppice gate.

She bent down and removed her son's clothes from the dryer. They were warm and waiting for him now as if Rosa had hung them in the Caribbean sun an hour before. She climbed the stairs to his room and pushed open the door. Peering in, she glanced around for the astronaut to hang, who had come down when she repainted these walls the colour of deep space. Heather knew full well that over time gravity returned dust from even far-out orbits to the land of its birth. She entered the gloom, hoping he would remember what he could never have relinquished, the colour of her hair.

THE
ANNIVERSARY

For Floyd St. Clair, R.I.P.

S HE "loves" star-dripping Rajasthan, the night air our hired car's rolling through, these sagey desert scents. Smells evoking her Okanagan girlhood of bunchgrass and rabbit bush. "Be that as it may—or was—I'm tickled to be here this evening without my girdle ..." Popping off like a stand-up in the breezy back seat, cuddled by her mate, when our driver stops in the dust to pee. "Oh! Is that my surprise?" Indicating on the horizon a faint glow where a saucer-shaped galaxy is shedding its halo into darkness. Expectantly, covering my hand: "A lovely sight."

Accelerating now towards the night's crystal roof—"past dozing camels, I bet, stuck in sand out there"—startling a fox into sight, brushed from our headlights in a flick. One's impulse is to have our driver brake and snare the sharp-eared wonder. He'd just say, "Too cunning, sir." And she, "Too dry a stick at your age for vixens."

When the throbbing motor drops us, the unattended revolving door seems paltry for so vast a galaxy. "Stardust?" Asked dubiously of the road's settling dust, cuffing my tuxedoed shoulder at our stutter-stepping entrance through weeping glass. "I *can't* take your arm, Harold, we'd stumble ..."

Pushing single-file through the air-sealed passage, into basting humidity and butterflies, as if our coming has shot confetti from a man-of-war.

"What a perfect touch," says she, luffing her silk shawl and relaxing into heavy air. Butterflies everywhere, as far into jungle foliage as we can see, quivering through jasmine and frangipani clear up to the glass firmament.

Or are those higher creatures parrots?

She can't tell. The whole place "dumbfounds" her. "Drought outside. In here, swallowed up by green flapping wonder!" Tapping into this wonder with her nose. "Smells like honey. Like all good rain. The bee's bloody knees."

Banter's easy when air is tropical. Young again, green and flapping, we're on our first equatorial posting to forests unspoken for. Breathing deeper than we have in years, from the kneecaps, cocktail hum pulsing in our ears like cicada legs.

"Who are all these people?"

Not that we see any people, not yet. Just murmuring voices. Inside propagating foliage, ears come before eyes. Noses before either. Composting humus giving way to top-of-the-chain pheromones, mugging us both like satin. "I know they all can't be here for our whichever anniversary, Harold, so what's the grand occasion?" And reassuring her mate, in case she looks disappointed: "Quite a surprise, Hal dear!" Squinting around, resolved not to dive into her purse too soon for glasses, speaking up instinctively on behalf of her (our) steamy past. "I hear a *party*..."

Convivial babbling to befit this operatic affair, chorused by running water, birdsong, hedonistic frogs—soon, no doubt, unaccompanied piano arias proclaiming undying love and rabid cherry blossoms. A disembodied buzz. Everything in Babylon worth knowing, including hubbub of flirtations still masked and fugitive, before the desert back then rose up and wrecked romance. She smiles radiantly, expecting contact with homo erectus at any moment.

When nothing gives, she fishes up eye ware.

A glimpse of blue. A stray couple like ourselves in evening togs, furtively strolling the gallery high up against a span of black glass. We'd need birding lenses to identify even the race. Is that the moon beyond? Cheese? Curvilinear struts echo contour of royal palms, bloodlines of a hothouse universe, steamy smells of gravity down here where mutating organisms the size of fibres fall from leaves the size of davenports. We're at home in a cloud forest.

She thinks we should climb the spiral, wrought-iron staircase to join our species above the epiphytes and lianas. Then she could "figure out and remember if I have to" who all these people *are*—"down here in the soup"—because her husband won't tell her ... "Pretty please, sweetheart?" The jungle's muddle reminds her of Togo. Java. "Sure don't resemble a Canadian rainforest ..."

"Yes, leafy, isn't it?"

Homo erectus at last, fellow our age with silver hair, dressed in rumpled tan windbreaker and soiled knit tie, pitched up from the hopping undergrowth. "Good evening, sir. You used our humble side door for solo tradesmen. . . ? Welcome just the same." His shoulder-length hair has escaped garden shears ever since, probably, the desert outside was sea-bottom. Manner, though, is kempt and modest.

"Normally we see so few visitors, given our remoteness. . . I'm the live-in curator but I might as well still be the house hermit."

A wry voice we like right away. Bit pommy. Precise and formal, a little reedy, in concert with the relaxed breathing the foliage seems to encourage in his slender figure. In ours, too, not so slender anymore, lovingly entwined ever since the Ark was lewd. He pops a breath mint. "This evening our plants stand agape, rejuvenated by your presence." Bowing graciously, willing to play along, as if to accommodate our odd entrance with his own show.

Listening to him, she's lifted her bangled wrist pretending to brush an itch or tickle, turning it slightly to reassure herself with fabricated scent. Not certain he *does* smell, but difficult to tell in here among fetid and transcendent odours.

"I like to think I'm here for the photosynthesis, madam, if that doesn't sound too fervent. Mother used to comment on my liking to sniff plants manufacturing their food like fussy little factories. 'They'll put hair in your ears.' I would now say the genes in my blood seem quite addicted to tropical leaves. You'd think they were tobacco." Voice smiling as he speaks, lips fixed in an upward curve. A breath mint in melt somewhere under his tongue. "Perhaps you would allow me to guide you through them? Not my genes, of course, the leaves."

"*What's he talking about?*" she whispers, still wrist-visiting.

His way of clinging suggests we won't be climbing soon to the gallery for a bird's-eye view. "You *could* choose the recorded tour, madam, but headphones have a way of disturbing the hair in your ears."

"*What's he* talking *about?*"

Worried she's forgotten how to banter, returns glasses to handbag in an effort to compose her tongue.

"I was starting to think deaf wouldn't be too bad," he continues, face brightening, as if we aren't to take him too seriously. "Luckily, I had this organ to remind me what I was missing." Pats his leaf-addicted nose. "Still my eyes and ears. Dog listens with its nose. Why not an old factotum?" Smiling, checking his wristwatch against deafness. "What say we get started?"

She peers in my direction, sternly now. Who got her into this? Who's this possibly smelly old man tempting us with the verbal equivalent of an apple? *And where are all the people, anyway?* Fixed in muscle memory, from lusty pre-retirement days, this instinct of hers to work a room no matter how humid the air or stuffy the do, pretending to admire somebody's sand-iron shot to the last green midst clubhouse gossip and tinkly flute glasses. *Where are the flipping waiters?*

DAMAGES

Hang on though, who minds being on the wagon when a butterfly lands on her arm and another her handbag, a third my lapel as if pinned like a boutonniere? Has suddenly rethought her disapproval of his offer to safari us deeper down the forest path: "Okey doke. To where the party's greener?" Whimsical this, peering around, willing to be led to the other side of kingdom-come so long as his "nose" for the place *doesn't get lost in the wallpaper.*

"I'm hanging on, Harold, in thrall to the prospect of libation. Not necessarily anguish, you understand, but anguish if necessary. Prosit!"

"Prosit!" Stock echo from straight-man partner, sanctioning dissipation she hopes will follow. Let the shindig begin. Still hasn't guessed, nor could she really, what the evening's shindig's about. Maybe thinks she's forgotten what she was supposed to remember. Will smiley curator spill all as we pedal after, longing for nightlife and a drink? We *love* a good flapping party.

R-r-r-r-i-i-p-p-t-t-t. Frog, clearing out.

In a tropical fish pond, the splash from a cherub's dicky-doo. Sculptor's imp, now mottled and grey, still peeing with a baby's prostate.

"You don't drink?" she asks him, gazing pondward.

His parry's one we've heard before from clubhouse foresters hoping to boost the bottom line abroad in say paper products: "With our shortfall in revenue, madam, we welcome anyone for special occasions." Hard to tell if we're dealing with an abstainer who's happy the party sounds like it's still a good night's tramp through wet bamboo—the other side of dry-zone eucalypts, maybe. He chuckles.

"Short-staffed, it falls largely to the few to care for and nurture our many specimens. This one, for example, has its own reward . . ." Meaning the asoka, its flowers yellow and orange where we halt beyond the drippy boo. He breathes into himself the thickening mist, sighing pleasurably.

*May you live to be a hundred, and may the last voice
you hear be mine.*

Startled, we glance around. "I know that voice," she says.
"Where's it coming from?"

"A long-standing acquisition, madam, unique of its kind."
Examining his watch, palming a thin white throat as if to relax
rogue tendons. "Commonly known by its redundant nick-
name."

Reaching again into her handbag. "Where did it come
from?" Glasses back on nose, as if to recapture memory out
of dense foliage. "I don't see anything except *leaves*. Blossoms."

Curator shushes, asking us to take a big "singer's" breath.
Demonstrating how by removing hand from neck and placing it on his own diaphragm, inhaling a deceptive sackful of
air, followed by a classic exhalation of measureless duration,
eyes somewhere on cloud nine. ". . . Breath, elixir of voice.
Please. The air is *yours*. Own it—inside and out—breathe!"

When we do, feeling like Cathedral Grove nature-walkers
blissing out on magic mushrooms, we overhear the unmis-
takable a cappella voice of—well, The Voice, emerging in song
from among the asoka flowers:

Night and day, you are the one
Only you beneath the moon or under the sun
Whether near to me, or far
It's no matter darling where you are
I think of you
Night and day . . .

She turns to me, beaming. "I recognize it now! You planned
this, didn't you?" Fondling her mate's forearm like a believer
in his ageless power to awe in the unlikeliest of forests.

"One of his steamiest," admits curator. "January. Third
year of the war. Less inbred and noisome than his hit the year

before about never smiling again. This voice gives you duck-bumps. His legato comes from bel canto, did you know?"

"Yes," she happily replies. "I mean, no."

"That man, for a crooner, knew how to power his breath."

His own, with unfurling minerals, seems to animate The Voice to fever pitch:

Under the hide of me
There's an oh such a hungry yearning burning inside of
me . . .

Silence, in wake of the decaying note, urges our ears ahead to chatterboxing cicadas.

"His jazz diction"—he adds—"one could certainly go on about that."

I'm sure one could . . . her usual riposte to the bore with party tricks, but sensing his feats aren't mere elbow-grabbers, holds her tongue. Figuring, if we stood here long enough, breathing like aerobic Zens among sodden plants, we might get to hear his whole jazzy discography.

"Listen," he cautions us. Stopping near a narra tree, or what looks like a narra, swarmed by jade vine with penis-looking blossoms tumbling whitely to the ground.

It's quarter to three,
There's no one in the place 'cept you and me . . .

"Same great sound, eh?"
"No, madam, breathe deeper."

So make it one for my baby
And one more for the road.

He smiles at us, indulgently now. "Admittedly sounds like the same voice, madam, but in fact nature's mimicry. Trying ambitiously to adapt, camouflaged to partake of this region's ideal light and moisture. Survivor of high-life aspirations." Here, a permissive sigh. "Where we find it rooting spontaneously, we let it ramble. This one's a member of the genus rat pack, a subspecies known to flourish in the west central desert of North America. You've been there?"

"You don't mean that smiley little man with doo-wop hair, converted to Judaism because of what's-her-name, blonde and freckled just like the sixties?"

Nothing wrong with *her* Trivial Pursuit.

Curator coughs politely, pinching his sinuses as if to tune them. "We do have better simulations in the dry zone, in among the sagebrush where they belong. Hardy copycat specimens of remarkably original inflections. They lie half an evening's walk, to our farthest range, catalogued under Nevada ersatz."

She laughs, a musical sound as if to signal her finally getting the evening's joke. Resultant rush of exhalation—her relief at tumbling to his facility—stirs up a vocal medley of old hits from among the sword ferns on our increasingly wet way:

> *Swanee, how I love ya how I love ya, Swanee, my dear old . . . If I didn't care for YOUUUU . . . I'm just a prisoner of Love . . .*

"Well!" Still laughing. "I can see where it might be a fun job, yours, living with this collection of exotics. Not easy, though, remembering names! How many thousands do you have, speaking strictly by species? You'd have to have a very green ear."

He nods, appreciatively.

"A green ear helps, yes. Especially, madam, in trying to preserve exotics either infamous or unheard of. A green ear's the lingua franca my intrepid predecessors once carried with them on expedition to the world's four corners. Those men discovered the Garden of Eden before it needed gardeners. The jungle's silence reinforced their respect for vociferous growth. They listened carefully . . . and brought back cuttings. We owe everything here in our keeping to their foresight."

Heaven, I'm in heaven . . .

She looks doubtful.

"Well, blessed be the attentive, I guess, they'll disinherit the desert. It's not a virtue I recall paying much mind in our own days and nights in the jungle. My hired hubby was too busy scouting hardwood to hear any doomsayers. A loyal company man. You, sir, on the other hand, are obviously a man in sync with his past."

493

Now this is not the end. It is not even the beginning of the end. But it is, perhaps, the end of the beginning.

Another blast from the past to beguile her. "It's uncanny, the growly resemblance!" From a candle nut tree—Malay apple, maybe—set back from the path twenty feet and obscured by mango leaves smelling faintly of turpentine. For the life of us, she can't figure out how he cultivates his specimens *(I don't see evidence of lip drift)*: whetting her botanical interest when she's dying to wet her whistle at the bar *(can't locate* it *either).* Getting her to huff and listen, when she can't see anything but trees and more trees with rain clouds closing in.

We shall not flag or fail. We shall go on to the end.

"It's like wine from water," she declares, "verbiage out of foliage." Wondering if this isn't the point of glasshouses, after an arid journey like ours. Supposes it must be. "All this fruity breathing, reminds me of a spa without the hand-chopping up and down your bulges."

Bulges? Curator, leading on damply through clumpish thorn palms, insists we stop alongside their black spines and inhale heartily. This time, breathe as we might, the latest voice never comes distinct. Cylindrical *whupping* overwhelms it. A kind of yelping stuck in pollen, inside a calyx we can't even see. Fifteen-foot leaves drip moisture down our necks.

"One of our oldest and rarest specimens," he expounds, beaming, a man of patient wonder regardless of mist and damp, hardship and lurking dengue fever.

We look around for orchids. Only a common flycatcher, filling up with water and soggy wings.

"...No less a favourite for its rank—some would claim—*waxy* sound. You folks couldn't know, unless you already knew, this was a poet reading from his opus."

"That must be the daffodil fellow. My rote recall's not what it was ...'I wandered lonely as a ... a sky?'"

"Lilac, madam. Though the scratchy derivation *is* difficult to attribute."

And so onward, forcing us to swim through steamy vapours, where ancient water boilers below expel mist from cast-iron floor vents. Calling ahead to him, removing her fogged-up lenses: "You must recycle your dead branches! This Victorian palace uses one mother of a furnace!"

That, or dry ice, with a fan in the wings blowing fog our way.

He shushes us, pulling up.

We listen again, wiping brows, having lost alas the sound of any party. This time our memory responds, triumphantly, to a barely audible voice out of tangled undergrowth among ironwoods ...

"Even I remember that!"

"Once thought to be extinct," curator informs. "Oldest specimen extant, but a mere cutting. Its owner invented the phonograph."

She finishes the heard, unfinished rhyme: "'. . . And everywhere that Mary went, the wolf was sure to go . . .' You could probably make a case for its being a dirty rhyme. Not that one *would*, of course."

Intended to tickle husband—fineness of memory, little leap of wit—mind forever green and joined to memories we both like to exaggerate. Hermit, if also tickled, doesn't let on, trotting off again after his doggy nose.

"*The Nose*," she whispers. Hooting us on down the path, not wanting to lose him *or* our way to the party: "You're the man of a thousand voices!"

"They've been entrusted, madam."

"And to you! Better watch out for Kew headhunters!"

Ignoring the compliment, he unzips more knitted tie. "Our glass structure expands to fit the arrival of every new exotic like yourself, clamouring to be housed."

"Us, clamouring?" Shawling off bare arms and spotted lenses, leaning a little not to fall.

"In the best possible way, of course. Where other guests, too, are clamouring."

"I knew it! That's why we're here, isn't it? To share and be shared."

"Exactly, madam."

"*What's he talking about?*" Smoothing her wrap so it doesn't wrinkle, remounting eyeware, wondering where in the world we've landed to've reached this imbroglio.

Above us again, a glimpse of blue, lost in soaring crowns and weeping vapours. "No, I saw her too," she claims. "Wish we could clamour up ourselves for a stroll."

A flame-coloured tanager sifts down into a kapok tree. The gallery staircase vanishes in a shower. Shawl over hair she expresses hope of finding shelter in a nearby naga grove.

"Madam, the importance of our waterworks can't be over-estimated. A hydrated structure, properly ventilated, affords one the grand tour."

Mistily disappointed, she sighs. Rain clouds part briefly to reveal a rainbow seeding itself over the upper canopy—leading, she must hope, to a gin pot. Laughing girlishly she lifts a speckled butterfly docked to her Edenshaw wrist.

Shimmering moment before flight.

"But you haven't told us, not in so many words"—peering enviously at a hut protected by the nagas, where custodial ropes of liana dangle to the forest floor—"why you think all this heavy breathing's so healthy."

"If you breathe right, madam, you will hear right."

"Oh, my drums never let me down. We're used to rain-forests."

"Ah then." He expects we therefore know why orchids, especially orchids, approach the delicacy of larynxes. "A voice requires the emission of carbon dioxide. Our specimens flourish in consequence."

"You can say that again." Grinning waggishly, for a senior citizen on statins.

"Each orchid gets by in its own way. *Stanhopea*—you see up there, in that tree's crown?—breathes its fragrance into the air, competing for survival and pollination. Nothing unique in this, madam, except that Amazonian bees, attracted to *Stanhopea's* scent, couldn't otherwise attract female bees of their species to help them pollinate an unrelated plant—the Brazil nut."

"Go on with you. I don't believe it. Is that hut *dry* inside...?"

"The rainforest's a Babel of gossip. Steamy tales of seduction and betrayal spread by every orchid. These garrulous specimens come from the largest plant family on earth. Untold thousands of progeny migrating across continents bearing blossoms as fine as vocal folds."

He has begun to ramble. Fingering the smooth-throated bloom of an adjacent letter plant—tan-dotted trumpet of a less clambering member of the orchid Joneses—our man of a thousand voices stops to collect himself.

"Hut, you ask? No, it needs a roof."

"Really?"

Duty, as he sees it, is to the moistness enveloping our clothes and skins. Expects us to trudge on, a duet of deep-breathers, breasting in slow motion the wonders of loquacious species growing from leaf mould and fallen carcasses of aphids and beetles.

"Not an easy swim, sir, all this damp." Trying to protect her hair. "We ought to shroud ourselves in this monkey jacket of yours, Hal…"

Suspendered thus together we make the mistake of sighing too loud from our tuxy tent—provoking another arboreal utterance:

> I was interrupted in the hey-day of this soliloquy, with a voice which I took to be of a child, which complained "it could not get out." I look'd up and down the passage, and seeing neither man, woman, or child, I went out without further attention.

We peek through satin lapels and spongy carnation to listen. "I feel like a dummy with this one." An afina tree, splotched green and brown, bears no clue of origin. She tries staring him in the face.

> In my return back through the passage, I heard the same words repeated twice over; and looking up, I saw it was a starling hung in a little cage—"I can't get out—I can't get out," said the starling.

"The voice—voices," curator proudly proclaims, his silver hair now lank—"of the unknown soldier. What's notable about the specimen is its origin, from a cutting at Kew. Kew, surviving like St. Paul's in the eye of bombs, remains to this day a depository for all species, not to mention a memorable oasis for marriages and anniversaries."

"Just like here!"

"If you like, madam."

"Except here it's all words and no bodies."

I had the voice, Larry had the legs.

"Who's that?" Rubbernecking out our tent door, confronting a curtain of slender, elegant ebonies spiced with camwood. "...Very plummy pipes."

A loud whoop, followed by more whoops in the ascending scale, pierces our ears from somewhere above.

"I know that voice. It belongs to a siamang. Right?"

"My lady, your ear becomes you."

She smiles, beautifully. "We used to live in Sumatra. What a racket, really. Are they part of the carbon monoxide circle?"

"Dioxide. They are part of the cycle, yes."

"Gibbons go back to the ancestors. Grandmother Beverly howled like that. I'm probably next. Why can parrots talk and not monkeys? You'd think they'd have caught up by now."

Our guide nods. "Powerful vocal apparatus, certainly. Pulsating larynx, high palate."

"Maybe," says she, "rainforest gas gives them the big voices. I think it makes my own voice bigger. Just the opposite of my hair—." Patting her do to discourage mist from squashing it. "Silver and lice, everything nice . . ." Cut this morning, not well, by a village girl at the Lake Palace Hotel, angled off-centre to look western, but—well, *who cares if you look Greek,* said the cuttee, after a satisfying lunch of mango and yogurt, *when that's how everybody else in Rome looks!*

Bedraggled hermit, sniffing pleasurably the munificent air, encourages our mobile teepee to follow him smartly. Then halts. This time his inspiration, long and luxurious, pauses a beat short of infinity, before a just-as-long arc of mellow exhalation meets it coming down.

Hospitable to rainy air, his lungs fill to the size of rooms.

She whispers, side-mouth: "*Doesn't sound like we're out of the woods yet.*"

Her own sniff occasions a faint cry ahead. Followed by a distinct gabbling for breath from some murky specimen, growing louder as nearby light brightens to crescendo . . . before its intensity causes us to stop breathing. Silence. Followed by a long audible expiration, bringing light back down to shade, our ears grazed by another small cry.

Again, silence.

"My goodness." She feels it judicious to ask, "What was that?"

This specimen has cost him more than he wishes to let on. Pausing, to catch his breath. "Tiniest performance of the last century." Voice, less reedy now, has acquired a certain Irish inflection. "Rarely glimpsed in its natural state."

"Well, I can see why. Plot sounded a bit limp." She'd like him to know we're not halibut when it comes to rising action. We enjoy a good yarn when there *is* one. Like a good party. "Oh, look!"

Re-spotting the rare owls like ourselves, emergent among treetops, she points: "That same couple—woman in a blue gown—mile up on the balcony? Are they imbibing, can you see?" Yearning to be among revellers, once our expedition's over and civilization achieved. "Put your jacket back on, Harold. Your pleats are losing their flounce."

Riotous jungle still teasing, it bemuses us now with exhibits in among what he takes to calling "the wets": where an egret, loyal to pond life, is afoot in lotus blossoms:

H—h—h—h—h—ello?   M—m—m—m—m—ay   I p—p—p—p—lease s—s—s speak to . . .

"I bet that's hard to say," she says kindly, "without giving yourself away?"

He looks chapfallen, her kind of remark having no place on safari. A trouper, though, he gets on with it. Promises we'll soon be through the dripping tree ferns, directing our ears to a dense cluster of them beside the teak-staved boardwalk, stopping near a swampy banyan to take in a bullhornish voice:

So ... did you hear about the new Supremacist slogan?
"Two Wongs don't make a White." A sick semantic sand-
wich, if you ask me, but the skinhead diet always throws
up slogans. "A turd in the hand is worth two in the bush."

"These stand-ups grow wild, we're always pruning."

"I don't see why you can't weed them out along with the stutterers." Looking around for hibiscus blossoms, something sweeter. "Haven't you anything better trained? My husband's an opera buff. I used to like the ones with tunes."

He glances at me, raising an eyebrow.

"Well," he says. I'm sure your husband can be counted on to have your interest at heart this evening."

"Really? He promised a surprise. You're not it, are you?"

"Not me, madam. But Rachel, about a kilometre in that direction—can you see someone up a ladder over there in subtropical, against a lemon tree? She might be. I sometimes hear her singing as she works."

We follow his arm to the far side of the universe, seeking a dark-haired young woman with a pruning pole. We listen, too, hoping for the conductivity of watery air to work its magic over time and distance. Breathing from the diaphragm, light-headedly, aiming to encourage this pruner into Italian, say.

Instead, from our own ecosystem, a raspish Englishman's voice out of a mangrove tree—not unpleasant, if you don't mind cigarettes on the breath:

*You seduced a woman in order to be able to finish your
talks with her. You could not do that without living with
her . . . for the intimate conversation that means the final
communion of your souls.*

She's quiet now, toeing a stave. Cast into gloomy thought
about growing silence between mates, maybe, communion of
aging souls . . . but it could be corns.

No such brooding for Hush-Puppied curator, staring into
the aquatic wetlands. Balanced to invoke more specimens, he
seems about to step full-weight onto the wide pie plate of an
Amazonian water lily.

Instead, pops a breath mint. And voices deluge us from
right and left, an inspiring display of vocal horticulture in the
drippy air.

Pilot announcements, jubilant World Cuppers, a barking
frog.

In ensuing silence, the rainbow reseeds its stripes above.

"*He's winded, I think. Praise the Lord.*"

". . . Acclimatized, madam, these hyacinths require moistness and air. *Maintenance.* Visitors, in other words, are crucial."

"Without us, they'd wither on the vine."

"Born to sound unheard, you are perfectly correct. Stray-
ing like unsniffed perfume. Tragic, really."

"It sounds like your mother was right."

"About my nose, you mean. She died so young I wandered
without a home for years. But she imparted her love of blossoms. I learned by listening. I attribute this evening's celebration to her influence."

"There *is* a celebration! My husband has been mute on the
subject."

Found!

A single note, almost missed. From someplace above us.

A handbag?

He points. "Voice of an old crow. In the fig leaves?"
We stare through steam of a small waterfall emerging from lava rock and another rain shower. "I didn't see any gibbons either," she says.

> *I would strongly advise you, Mr. Worthing, to try and acquire some relations as soon as possible, and to make a definite effort to produce at any rate one parent, of either sex, before the season is quite over.*

"Nothing limp about that specimen," says she. "We recognize a story when we hear one." Hoists her wrist lovingly, having attracted more burnished wings to her silver bracelet or else to her Shalamar.

> *I float like a butterfly, sting like a bee!*

"Oh, dear. Survival-of-the-fittest confuses me. That's a pretty-faced puncher, isn't it?"
Then, from direction of a strychnine tree, neither insect nor crow. What?

> *If it were only the other way! If it were I who was to be always young, and the picture that was to grow old!*

"Guessing now... A pin-up? You know, some husky-voicer the playboy rabbit man goes on to divorce, circa end-of-century?"

> *... For that—for that—I would give everything! Yes, there is nothing in the whole world I would not give! I would give my soul for that!*

"Listen," says wife, "would she give her brain? What's a body going to pot when her brain's down the dumper? I don't give a toot about my thirty-eight-inch waist when I can't remember the pizza number. I don't give a toot about it when I can, of course. *His* memory feasts on age. There's no compensation in nature. Not fair, is it?"

Vive, le Quebec Libre!

"Ah ha! A nose I finally recognize! Those French squits lording it over us—"

Ask not . . .

"*Hair* this time—I remember his Boston mop's what seduced the women, squared-off and parted nicely by water. *We* were all Brecking and spray-gunning. I looked as natural as a soufflé."

Smiling now, happy to be on a roll. Wondering though about the gap since mirthful buzz was last heard. "*What's happened to the party?*" We listen for chirruping cicadas.

Bear it, partner. Bear it.

"Quit it, Harold! Hard enough keeping him happy, without you starting up."

I have a dream that one day on the red hills of Georgia.

"Cripes, it's getting sticky! How much farther?"

Curator, in full flight now, tiptoes us from the boardwalk into towering mahoganies. Innumerable vines, with aerial ambitions, sucker to boles in these still sultry tropics. She, staring at the hot and humid muddle, picks at her uncomfortable hips, certain the "oak-a-noggin" was never this "unbrookable."

"My gown's a clinger, Harold."

Panting, as he's taught us, we've reached plants with leaves like pterodactyl wings, their growth abetted by diaphanous drizzle. Soundless, however. An untrammelled jungle of silent forebears. No birdsong. Not so much as a burp. We've arrived at the rainforest's gloomy heart.

"I don't hear anything."

She sounds relieved. "*Is it possible he's bushed?*" In the very midst of heavy air and conductivity.

"I must tell you, sir, your conservatory has been a virtual education, even for a dummy like me."

"Madam." Respectfully inclining his head. "Inside this city, as it sometimes feels, on the banks of barrenness, my job is to cultivate greenness and keep the desert out."

"You cultivate respect," she says. "Living here makes you listen and not cast stones. Do you ever read the Bible?" Surprising me a little, as she hasn't read it herself since hair was wheaten and genesis the recurrent goal.

O-M-M-M-M-M-M-M-M-M-M-M . . .

From somewhere nearby, a peepul tree.

"Breakfast chef," she guesses happily, "at a Shriners' convention. Are we almost there?"

He quickens the pace now, leading us from wetlands through a slowly drying forest into another region. Butterflies again, orioles and hoopoes, moving in the same vague direction as if gentled by breeze down a glass tunnel whirring with cicadas. Not a rat or driver ant in sight. Atmospheric changes grow more promising with every step.

"It's all so hos— . . . may I *please* have this word? Comes from the Latin. Akkadian, I mean. Pretty please, Harold?"

DAMAGES

Cheered by prospect of lighter air, not to mention a dry martini down the road, she's again looking forward to her "surprise."

Sun, meanwhile, has come out, tipping shadows eastward, making punga logs steam and epiphytic ferns unfurl. She stares at his tan nape, scarred by adolescent acne, silently daring him to share his whole blooming catalogue of acquisitions. Nothing can deter her now. Passing us by are mangoes and tamarinds, bread and jackfruit trees, a panoply of spoken sound. The fraud of it all has made us both better listeners. Huffing from the diaphragm, we're the beneficiaries of enlarged nasal membranes and retightened eardrums. We could swear the path has grown narrow to resemble a throat.

Pressed in by monkeypod and wattle, sasswoods and obeches, his flourishing tour has come to sound like the pilgrims' test of forbearance. *And the whole earth was of one language, and of one speech. And it came to pass, as they journeyed from the east . . .*

"What's he muttering now?"

Anyone's guess, this babble from Shem's incessant son: plantation chatter among tea pickers in Badulla (*or so he tells us*); a soapbox tee-totaller in Hyde Park (*not an omen, I pray*); underground gold miners talking Xhosa to a leafy surface; a Beverly Hills tour guide during the war years (*ask him about Dick Powell. No, Mortimer Snerd*) . . . a gibberish Irish woman on her last croak; some sermonizing missionary priest in vocal crack-up (*look at him, chortling*); voices of surgeons (*fatherly*), umpires (*hunnish*); a chef on cable cooking fowl; Pee Wee hockey players in a locker room discussing cups (*is he moonwalking?*); a snippet of vocal DNA from a dead parrot (*oh, come off it!*); a sidewalk barker complaining of tight straps on his sandwich boards; baby talk in Japanese from the south island of Shikoku . . .

"Stop! I'm out of breath!" *He's sung for his supper, now let's get on with my surprise.*

As if on cue a flock of grey parrots scatters ahead of us in welcome relief many opalescent butterflies to bewitch her. It makes us willing to go on.

The farther we trek the more our way opens up—its spaces between plants growing wide in building light—this prospect encouraging in us relaxed, ever deeper breathing to match expanding views. Never have we breathed so boundlessly, an anesthetist's dream.

Climate zones change. Curator asks us to set our watches back an hour.

"Your tour's gone faster than we could skin a rabbit."

"If we had all night, madam, we would arrive in the arid zone where specimens of sisal and prickly pear would test your ear with a nimbus of elocution . . ."

"Oh, I think you've tested it with a big crop already." *Show us the bar stools, Arnold, enough bull toot.* "We never realized the botanic voice was such a going concern. You're amazing. The life of the party—you do take time out for parties. . . ?" *What if he's just an elbow-grabber after all?*

"Our shed for transplanted seedlings has grown into quite a palace. The whole range, from steamy carnivores to shrinking violets, you could spend a lifetime here giving equal time. A world without furious photosynthesis would be a flat *inaudible* world."

She groans, listing a little in her high-heeled sandals, survivors of mud and bat goop. "That's easy for you to say. Isn't it hard on the back, though, if you're not used to huffing? I'm trying, like you showed us, only . . . *My,* wherever that breeze is from it's awfully welcome." Clasping my arm. "Like good company."

Little does she expect so much company.

Along the widening way, three abreast with room for twenty here, we begin to overhear more and more bodiless voices, emerging in clumps then interconnected clusters, till the cicada drone, where the sparse landscape unfolds under intense, shadowless light, creates a vast rainbow of sound.

"What a lark!"

Materializing before us, guests like ourselves in gowns and tuxedos, cropping up in knots then streaming crowds, thousands under the glass sky, where a gigantic cloud of rotating butterflies has settled high above into a lit dome, joined by ever more of these iridescent migrants, kept buoyant by orchestral music rising from below.

"Good night!"

Into this gaping mouth of space we've entered a kind of savannah without horizons, having left behind the forest's rank humidity and rain. It's like coming upon a New Year's Eve party inside St. Peter's. We can't understand all the cicada languages. Couples and singles of every age, men in Japanese robes, blond children escorted by Asian nannies, teenagers with parents who look American. . . And in the middle distance, on a raised stage under the dome, a plump man in a white tuxedo is conducting an orchestra, consoling with his other hand a humming chorus of kimonoed women.

She's stunned. Momentarily mute. Forgetting to remove her glasses in order to put on the dog.

"Is this my surprise? Can't be! I don't know anybody. Where did they all *come* from?"

"Sir, your driver dropped you at the tradesman's entrance. Had you arrived at the main nave, our resident conductor and his wife would have received you rather more grandly, leading you into our rotunda of free speech, instead of on safari through the rambling jungle."

"And we thought you were doing all these voices yourself."

"Our common language is voice, madam. It has its own music, which everyone here can appreciate, given the non-speaking role they have in common."

"I'm not going to ask, in case I'm supposed to remember. What role, Harold?"

Indulgent guide clarifies: "Every gentleman here was once a mute child. Now he can talk, is encouraged to talk, as much as he pleases."

"I wonder sometimes, with this one. Makes *me* carry the ball. I'm a bit lo— ... what's the word?"

"—quacious."

"Read his lips! Thank you, motormouth." Delighted at the same time to be set upon by a flapping waiter, Indian male in a silk-sleeved kimono, bowing Japanese-like from a slender, sash-wrapped waist.

"So," she says, helping to lighten his tray, "it can only follow that drinks must be free too."

"Anything to loosen the tongue, madam." And no abstainer after all, reaches for a glass himself, having brought us safely through jungle to civilization.

"Touché! Champagne, too. Prosit!"

"Prosit!"

"Parrot, isn't he? Regular belly talker." Happily, nosing her bubbles. "What's grief if it can't be soothed by a little give-and-take with your long-time squeeze? My memory blossoms with a drink. Just watch."

"May I guide you to your table, sir? I'm sure I could pick it out for you from among the many."

"Dinner too! I could eat a poached fox." Hoisting her glass again. "Prosit!"

Drops his head, thinks of shaking it perhaps, willing to accept us for what we appear to be, however worn out from responding in kind.

Table en famille turns out to be far into the savannah, an add-on safari, over little Japanese bridges and goldfish ponds, past crowds of newcomers grazing on California rolls and crackered antipasto, through potted larch and flowering cherry—acres of low-rise tables—till eventually we arrive ringside at music playing softly onstage.

Waiting for us, kneeling on a pillow, a blue-gowned woman, possibly she of the floating world earlier in the rainforest. My wife's surprise.

"*Richard!*" Stops, cannot believe it. "What are *you* doing here?"

Kisses, elation, hugs. General commotion of a mother long lost to son, before bumping into him on the world's other side. Much arm-patting, -pawing, -clutching—the overtures of reunited limbs—plus scalp-sniffing.

"I can't stop croodling! You've grown your father's dimple!"

It's true. Richard, forty-something, because of an involuntary migration of flesh from jowls, has ripened his chin—rearrangement of wisdom in face of divorce and whatever decision to uproot himself on behalf of good works, a Doctor Without Borders, all the way from some tent city in Africa. He, like father, eligible for this evening's grand celebration, at which we've quietly conspired to combine anniversary and anniversary.

Introduction of his young companion, strapped in blue shoestrings, confirms another stateless physician from the city of tents. Asian, beautiful. Beautiful smile. "Hello." Beautiful voice, too, impressing curator, who should be needed elsewhere though so far hasn't been.

Our wife and mother, now in heaven, clings to Richard before consenting to admire her rival's muff, a furry thing evidently uncovered from a prolific barrow in Portobello Road. "This brings back 'parley-voos', my dear, you couldn't imagine."

Could *she?* Confused by swelling voices, having expected no bigger surprise than a sedate evening, she prattles on. "Really, who *are* all these thousands? This isn't one of those Reverend Moon, Yankee Stadium all-in-ones—is it—you know, for wedding anniversaries?"

Curator, showing no inclination to excuse himself, bows like a very mindful hermit. "Not for a moment, madam, would we tolerate the mass voice of uniformity."

"Very noble of you, but what about the chopsticks?"

Ruefully, opening his arms, smiles. "You will have to judge our meal for yourselves. We have an optional menu, and an additional choice of knives and forks."

"Really, I'm fine with sticks. Don't trouble on my account."

Someone already has. Our table, set with teacups as well as wineglasses, rice bowls alongside flatware, sits like these numberless other tables among potted pear, andromeda, ornamental maple hedges. Have not dined in such deciduous variety since retirement from tropics, reposing ever since inside glass and cedar, gazing out at broom and salal, our coniferous west coast city given to luring early daffodils from the ground to delay its older citizens' burial beneath it. Curator (*Isn't he going to dress for dinner?*) claims to have heard of our capital, known for botanical wonders in abandoned quarries and imported crystal gardens. Nothing, mind you, like his own garden with this inflationary grandeur of an emperor's court.

Once everyone settles in to dine, a geisha-costumed diva appears onstage, stands, and peers to the horizon, patiently awaiting the brooding orchestra to catch up with her soul. And these many thousand guests their stomachs.

Waiters in kimonos, formerly adrift with champagne and canapés, have turned into geishas on wooden clogs bringing chopped scallop sushi, tempura udon, sashimi and green tea. Buddhist priests in saffron gowns serve an alternate menu of rigatoni con asparagi, veal parmigiana, vine-ripened tomatoes and red wine. The third choice of grainfed T-bone beefsteak, mashed Idaho potatoes, corn-on-the-cob and dark Lamb's rum, is borne by officers in white naval uniforms with brass buttons. Each menu offers a commemorative thread, leading to no rhyme or reason *she* can unravel, happy enough to eat Japanese along with family.

"I wonder if this place grows its own chopsticks? What kind of kindling would they need, Harold, balsa?"

We catch up on each other's far-off lives, grand feast passing like a dream under the halo of butterflies revolving to intermezzo music ... *forlorn Mozambique nomads ... they won't build without good feng shui and an eight in their street number—or is it a four, Harold? ... internally displaced and vaccinated for cholera under plastic sheeting ... who couldn't have bought a tool shed in Hong Kong for the same price ... trenchburied in gunny sacks and lye ... bringing bones with them in their suitcases, if you can imagine it, but who's complaining?*

Politely, once our hunger's satisfied for news of home and travel, career and grief, we petition our table guest, the curator, for his own perspective on life divided from loved ones. And he consents after scribbling an inky note handed to teapouring geisha—on a page torn from tiny gardening almanac—to share his story.

"... Travelled when I was younger, back and forth from New Zealand. During the war got interested in my past. Prison camp in Singapore cured that. Japanese were a deep shock, though not unknown to me from childhood. Recruited like you gentlemen for that stage of things ..." His voice, having grown younger, now ages gracefully with legato: "Long and short of it is I wandered to Ceylon and learned to plant tea, still listening for the voice of apology. Can't say I ever understood their code of silence. The warrior tradition included suicide, once they understood there was no future. I could never imagine no future. No voice ..."

Lifts his porcelain cup, sniffing a delicately painted cherry bough, before pressing the warm ceramic to his cheek.

"Anyway, after selling my plantation and expecting to retire in salty Hambantota, I ended up here, where an opening for a hermit-in-residence turned into chief cook and bottle washer."

"Listen," she says. "You should be thrilled. Your future's your past. Not me. Last night at the Lake Palace in U— ... Harold?"

"—daipur."

". . . I was standing in my nightin, what's the satin word, gale?"

"gown."

"...*nightingown.* Thank you, swivel lips. Last night, dressed for conquest, I was listening for a song my mother taught me. I'd come down to sing it in competition at the Empress, on Hastings, in the thirties. Well, to save my whistle I couldn't remember a bar. *The Maiden's Prayer*—was that a vocal or a keyboard...?"

Still canoodling his teacup, curator seems cheered by the boost its scent gives an old planter's nose. Says to her: "Here our business is *not* to forget. I imagine that's why you came this evening..."

"Really? Well, at least I haven't forgotten my son." Smiling, snuggling up to our prodigal, caressing his cheek. "I won't forget his nice companion, either." Caressing *her* cheek too, lost for a name. Young woman can't figure us out, but beams like she has her world without borders on a string, Richard dangling off her shoulder.

"...Nor have I forgotten Harold's and my anniversary. Isn't that really why we're here? To commemorate our wedding, sweetheart?"

Curator ponders me, his curiosity scarcely gratified. He sets down his cup. "Well, madam, it isn't *quite* why you are here."

"No? I knew that, I'm sure. Must have something to do with your big-band orchestra then. It's lowering my BP numbers, just listening to it purr."

"Rohan's certainly a charmer. He followed me up from Sri Lanka."

"Mother," says Richard, in the smooth manner doctors have of delivering news without sounding knowy, the way he might talk to a child. "Pops and I were invited for an anniversary he and I *also* share—with all these other men."

"Really? I'm all ears. See?" Pulling back cloud-grey hair, on the longer off-centred side, giving her the vulnerable look of a small girl. Pouting, in case she's supposed to remember what she can't now recall. "Are you two in cohesion?"

"Collusion, no." Squeezing his companion's hand. "But he and I once played the same role, separated by forty years. I was on stage in Brazil, where we lived once, do you remember?"

"I remember the jungle. We had a parrot."

"My father," says Richard, to his companion Ternynka. "They put him on stage in diapers. In Helsinki, Pops?" Richard's words cause his mother to frown—either at his airing them in company, or at her trying to remember if she already knows this tale of her husband's indiscretion long before she knew him.

She brightens. "Is dinner done, or can we expect a dish of apple betty à la Nipponese?"

Intermezzo waning, our regal conductor now turns to the vast babbling convocation. To encourage silence he folds brown hands over crimson cummerbund, bows his dark head and awaits stillness. Then lifts it slowly like the sun.

Good evening, boys and gentleman. In a few recent cases—from North America—girls. And of course ladies, parents, guardians. Welcome to you all . . .

So fine are acoustics under glass, his mikeless baritone floats effortlessly over tables, bridges, small wandering streams. Curator, sotto voce, is charmed by his maestro: "He came of age in New York. I used to see him in the Bronx Botanical Garden, and at midnight on Broadway, waiting for his reviews. His wife is the jewel in his crown."

"She's so young," says wife, of geisha onstage still waiting to sing.

"No, that's Rachel, our apprentice gardener. Remember?"
We recognize the lemon-tree pruner we couldn't manage to
locate earlier.

> ... We are gathered here, as you know, to celebrate the
> centenary this evening of the opera, Madama Butterfly,
> performed for the very first time one hundred years ago
> tonight in Milan, on February 17, 1904. We have invited
> all of you—every individual still living who ever played
> Butterfly's little boy, in a performance anywhere in the
> world since that first one—to travel here from the four
> hemispheres for a reunion of "Sorrows".

"Good night, there must be twenty thousand of you. By
the look of some of them, they're back *in* diapers. Richard, did
I let you out in diapers? In Brazil, you say ..."
Treasuring another in-the-flesh moment, Richard smiles
at Ternynka, a pair of borderless doctors unused to mothers-
in-law—for that matter sushi—in Rajasthan.

> ... From white hair to blond ringlets, your reunion
> appears a success beyond our curator's wildest dreams.
> Ours is now a richer world for knowing it possible to
> accommodate so many voices and languages under one
> soaring sky!

"This is *your* doing," she says to curator. "You've gone far
beyond the call of duty."

> ... The irony is you were all mutes once. On stage, you
> never said a word. Sang not a note. And from that
> unfortunate climax of your lives, after wandering the
> world ever since in search of a dead mother's voice,
> you've finally found yours.

"Not him. *I* do the talking. He writes the cheques."

Pressing old mate's forearm with a fondness for past wanderings, which she'd willingly recall for Richard, "if I weren't stuck in my stay-at-home facility where they dress me for bingo. *Harold, get me out of here! I can't get out!*"

"Madam, please, shush …"

This evening, you've come to remember. For indeed Madama Butterfly *is the great opera of remembering. And yet, well, what do any of you remember of your mother, Cio-Cio-San, or your brief childhood with her? Your stage age was supposed to be two years, seven months—though most of you were no doubt nearer five. At best, your memories are sketchy. Some of you might remember a large woman with bad breath and a black wig. Many will remember only what you were later told, or have imagined in the decades since. Perhaps you have a photograph of yourself dressed in a little kimono…*

515

"I still have yours, Richard. I must have. Unless it mouldered away in the damp. The monsoons we put up with—in Guyana, they gave us ponchos for the pigs."

… Let me remind you of life before voice, before your lives had really begun. Your American father, Pinkerton, purchases your fifteen-year-old mother from a marriage broker in Nagasaki. Butterfly changes her religion to please your father. Her relatives disapprove and so do the Buddhist priests. After your father seduces and abandons her, poor Butterfly lives in poverty, forsaking faith and family, stubbornly loyal to your father and her belief in his return, turning down a proposal of marriage from the prince who loves her. She's alone now,

except for Suzuki. You might remember Suzuki, your mother's maid . . . some of you in infant confusion may have thought she was your mother.

"We had a maid some place—name of Putter. Richard, you remember me, don't you?"

Son smiles at father. Remembering as she'd like him to, helping her "putt-putt" a wagon around a well-sprinkled patio, transplanting orchids into fatter pots, then going off with her in his sailor suit to a baroque opera house in a provincial town of endless forests along the Amazon.

"A few years after Genesis, Richard, before the lungs of Brazil were officially designated leaky balloons, your tree-cutter father and I were doing our level best to make the world a better place for emphysema."

Your childhoods were traumatic. You were born nine months after your navy-officer father married and deserted your mother. Three years after absconding, he returns to Nagasaki with his American wife. Your mother is devastated. She's eighteen now. She actually agrees to give you up to this stranger. She says goodbye, blindfolds you as if to play a game, and disappears behind a screen. Your father rushes in. You've never seen him before in your life . . .

"Her scream is important," says curator. "It has to be right."

"There is no scream," says Richard. "That's Tosca."

"Sisters in distress," suggests wife. "I've helped women in similar straits. I'm hoping to launch a hairdressing project. Hair's a renewable resource so they wouldn't have to replant it in the desert."

Curator is now confused about the scream. "You may be right. I'm glad Rohan's on top of it."

Maestro, having fasted before his address, has canted forward against railing, pinching either end of his baton like a chopstick. He continues:

> . . . It now looks like your father and Mrs. Pinkerton will take you away. You'll never see your mother again. Already, you are confused about your mother, though she sang to you once expressing the hope you would remember her. But why remember what you couldn't then imagine? Her death. As Sorrow, all you remember is being up past your bedtime, except at matinees. So you recall feeling sleepy. You remember a cup of cold cocoa offstage. Maybe a sharp pin in your sailor suit. But there's something else. Something joyous. I am certain all of you remember the powerful voices that enfolded you, not least your mother's voice. You may have been mute, but you weren't deaf. You may not have spoken a word, nor sung a note, but your childhood as Butterfly's son was the beginning of your vocal education.

517

"Was it, Richard? You can confess about your oral education, you know. Your friend won't mind."

Raised eyebrow from Ternynka, hinting Richard's relative's beyond the pale if she's heard the intimation right. Coarse old stooge.

> . . . Some of you might have sung like little angels, looked like little angels to win Sorrow's role but you'd never heard voices quite like those voices coming from grown-ups decked out in uniforms and kimonos. You learned, without knowing it, your language was the language of voice. And that of course is why we're gathered here in celebration tonight. To honour the voice you cannot remember losing. Your mother's voice. Your own voice of

innocence. You've come to remember Butterfly, to recall your childhood with her. And then, suddenly, without her. To do this, you've spent your lives waiting . . .

He turns onstage now and raises his baton. Butterfly, Rachel, girl from the lemon tree, accompanied by instrumental forces, launches "Un bel dí" in a translucent voice as resistant to gravity as the glass dome above.

We are overcome, and some weep like children for the past, knowing what's to follow. We remember now. He has reminded us.

. . . Yours is the story of the divided family. Half-Asian, half-American. Your mother calls you Sorrow, but if your father returns she promises to call you Joy. He returns a bigamist. No wonder your tragic name has fallowed you ever since. Only later, in adolescence, did you learn that after your mother blindfolded you, on the day you never saw her again, she killed herself. This changed you. As a teenager you began to know humiliation. Especially hers. Which is why, according to her culture of shame—half your own culture, of course— she needed to die an honourable death. Yet she abandoned you. Your grandfather also died an honourable death. Yet he abandoned his daughter. According to American culture—your other legacy—these deaths amounted to suicide. Not honour. Your mother used the same Samurai sword as your grandfather had used, to impale herself . . . in some cases, to cut her throat. That original sword, used in Milan, we have here this evening . . .

Murmurs of amazement, unbridled curiosity. Even the musicians appear interested, craning for a better look over horns and cellos.

Presented to him on a red pillow now, by one of the Indian waiters dressed as the bonze, maestro raises this thespian Excalibur for his whole audience to see it glint in the limelight. A great moment of recognition, even if we were all blindfolded when it plunged, playing marbles with ourselves on the floor of our mother's house, never seeing it at all.

"How do we know it isn't a fake?"

"That's the point, Mother, isn't it? It *is* a fake. It was probably made in Milan."

"So then it's the real one. You would have to admit...?"

Richard regards me reprovingly for a moment, refilling his friend's teacup from the white, blossom-painted pot. He's conscious in his doctorly way of boundaries beyond which family matters grow tiresome, even crackers.

And so, divided by suicide, separated from your proud but self-butchering family, you were adapted into the household of an American two-timer. In a manner of speaking, of course, for the opera closes on poor Butterfly's loss of voice. Yet it is this "manner of speaking" that has tracked you all ever since. The shame and sorrow of it. Raised by a tone-deaf stepmother, you grew up as outcast navy children with your father at sea, no doubt collecting Butterflies in other ports. Late to talk, delayed by shock, you forgot your mother tongue—Italian pretending to be Japanese. Italian pretending to be American. What was your mother tongue? ... Japanese? Italian? American? Left divided in your loyalties, confused in voice, it was easy to forget. You could be silent. You could babble. Fostered into adolescence by a tuneless woman, you refused after your father's retirement to move with them to Rhode Island...

"See what I'm finding out about you, Richard? You *were* always an independent little boy. You aren't married, are you dear? These days conscription's not necessary—not when you're abroad, anyway."

"Pops . . ." Warning, pleading, to curb this mother without manners."

. . . You set out to find your voice in the world. Cursed with forgetting you wandered widely, listening for the voice of a mother you'd loved, for a country's language you'd forgotten. It wasn't an easy journey. You had come from the east, yet grown up in the west. Rootless and divided, you lacked the assurance of native speakers. You seemed to have nothing in common with native speakers. You were alone in your travels and shy in quest. You seldom felt at home, anywhere. And so it was important for you to come here tonight, from all over the world, if only to meet siblings and compare voices. I know you've been listening to other Sorrows . . . for every single one of you has a story to tell. From the same role, same mother, same sadness, you branched off ten thousand different ways . . .

"But isn't that true of everybody? Dol- . . .orous or not, dear Richard, wouldn't you still have become a doctor without a country? Following in your father's footsteps, in too *many* countries. . . ? He and I wandered from Belize to the Cameroons scouting rainforests. Timber up and down the ying-yang. I'll never forget the shots. Stabbing ourselves over and over for the sake of the tsetse fly—festering to this day in our hippocampus. I confess, Harold, I'd rather have risked pine beetles in the Okanagan. Peaches and ponderosa opened me up to doh-ray-mees, and I miss all those songs my mother taught me."

. . . No matter if you grew up to become shoe salesmen or monks, plumbers or race-car drivers, bankers or rock

*hounds—you were travellers. No matter if you succeeded
in raising families, determined not to repeat the tragic
separation of your birth family—at heart you were travellers. Without a native tongue, dispersed like nomads,
tonight you've finally reached a common language . . .*

She turns to curator. "I can see why your retirement abode
was a good choice. The talky decor—and I love it, don't get me
wrong . . . Still, when's he going to stop waving that sword so we
can have some dessert?"

Silence everywhere now. Except for humming chorus—a
slow flow of fanny pack kimonos and folding fans, red sashes
and strewn cherry blossoms—in memory of all Sorrows who
couldn't come this evening because of death after long lives,
or else who, unable to face troubled futures after their mother's suicide, died young themselves, following shaky reloca-
tions in America.

Finally (white-tuxed maestro swerves upstage, level-
ling his sword like a graceful scythe), *we have a surprise for you. The Sorrow from whom you each descend,
the root of your many branches . . . is here this evening!
No, not Giacomo Puccini. Yet he might remember Puccini. He is the little boy who played Sorrow in that very
first performance of the opera, one hundred years ago
tonight . . .*

A fervent swelling of voices across space. Wood from the
true cross.

"No one's going to buy into this whopper."

"You should talk, Harold. I thought we were driving to Jaipur for the weekend. You know how I love tawny hills."

*Ironically, the child you are about to meet performed
in the only production of* Madama Butterfly *that ever*

failed. A complete flop. And hence doubly difficult for any Sorrow, his mother freshly dead, to have borne so much. All the more remarkable for him to have borne his legacy for a hundred years! Sr. Zambrotta is one hundred and four years old. He has flown all the way from Milan to be with us for tonight's reunion. Will you please welcome him, and with him his mother... Butterfly, who remains the age you remember her, while Sr. Zambrotta is of an age most of us can barely imagine...

From behind a bamboo screen, to soft-shoe bars from orchestra, wide-browed Rachel wheels onstage a bent-over figure in a wicker chair, possibly a dummy, dressed in an Edwardian tux and wing collar, a straw boater, patent boots blindingly polished. Across the savannah, applause builds to a crescendo, followed by a standing O for our lost, unexpected relative. The figure, after a word in the ear from Butterfly, lifts a wasted hand. She's holding it up. The applause dies.

...He's the "you" you all come from! He's the "you" you'll all become...

Enthralled, squinting a little to adjust her frames: "He's grotesque."

...Sadly, ladies and gentlemen, Sr. Zambrotta is now as silent as he was as little Sorrow. His great-grandson tells us the old man has lost his voice with age. So he cannot apprise us this evening of the ringworm he suffered while playing Sorrow, or of his large family he hoped to help through the opera's long run, before his production at La Scala closed after one performance, got retuned without him, and disappeared to Brescia. His story must remain untold.

"Thank Rome for small mercies." Stopping herself, just in time, from clapping.

. . . Instead Cio-Cio-San, Madama Butterfly, your mother, will sing to our guest of honour, and to you all, "Che tua madre dovrà prenderti in braccio". . . She hopes ardently that some day you will remember her, after she is gone. . . A touching Pietà for our reunion, his mortal body borne up by your mother's immortal voice . . .

During tableau aria, sung to decrepit son, response of all sons under heaven is various: dabbing of eyes, muttering of jokes, distracted talking from those too old or else too young to appreciate Babylonian sentiment of wholeness and song. Concentration by others, including Richard, to recall everything since lost to ancestral senility. Followed by another thunderous ovation.

Ur-Sorrow himself is unmoved, stunned senseless, conceivably dead.

"Your soprano sounds a little like I used to," she tells curator. "I had not a bad voice. I sang in competitions at The Empress, did I tell you?"

"I seem to remember you did, indeed yes . . ." Vernacular of a forbearing hermit, under siege from a rambler out of Nevada ersatz.

. . . So tonight, then, in conclusion, all your names are Joy!

"Isn't that reassuring? I have a son who is perfectly happy without me. Richard, can that be true?"

Summoning himself, out of family loyalty, to respond one more time: "Not for a second, Mother. Look how far I came for our reunion!"

523

Dark chords and brassy block of sound, orchestral flourish and abrupt end of opera. Sad to hear again, its resonance decaying in our ears in the after-image of euphonious suicide. Wayward affirmation, we suppose, of the life cycle. Somehow expected, though never appearing, forest animals migrating across the savannah in eternal rhythm. Not that our maestro notices, he's studying his now swordless hand.

> ... On that note, and by way of concluding my remarks, I have a memo here from our curator—to whom, incidentally, we owe a large debt for convening this splendid, multitudinous evening—asking me to mention that among you in attendance tonight there is a unique father-son team of Sorrows, a generational duet. He points out how Sorrow senior, now retired, has joined us from a part of the world where the same man who wrote the play upon which our composer based his opera, Mr. David Belasco, lived for much of his childhood ...

Wide buzz of satisfaction at closing out the happy evening with mention of one, two, three more relatives.

"Harold, speaking of teamwork, what the blinkity-blank would be the matter with having *my* ashes—yours too, if you liked—sprinkled from Mt. Douglas to the music of one of these lovely songs we've heard here tonight?"

> ... On his centenary as Sorrow, moreover, the father is celebrating his sixtieth wedding anniversary. This deserves an ovation. For both of them ...

Maestro, notwithstanding his baritone, here sounds like the TV weather person saluting some cake-stuffed survivor in the local nursing home surrounded by crones and descendant babes.

Ovation is impossible to ignore.

"I get it now!" Standing up, along with her son, to acknowledge the echoing acknowledgement.

We take in the savannah rippling away from us, its thumbs-up sound loosed like monsoon rain by many hands, same engulfing sound Richard and I knew onstage as pampered infants, when this wake-up call brought home to us how late at night it really was.

> ... Sadly, while their ailing wife and mother could not be with them this evening, we are assured, as with Sr. Zambrotta, she is here in spirit. She is—she was, I note here—a lively and vivacious woman, once devoted to the improvement of poor women's lives as her husband's career moved them from country to country with a timber company. A woman whose voice for those without a voice is destined not to be forgotten ...

"What's he talking about?" he asks. They look at me quite tenderly.

"This is *your* doing," she says to curator. "You've gone far beyond the call of duty."

Curator raises his cup to salute us.

> ... A toast, gentlemen and ladies and youngsters, to our family of Sorrows!

"Prosit!"
They look at me. "Prosit!"
"Well, I must say, this *has* been a surprise."

My lips do not move, drinking from a cup of green tea to demonstrate what has been earned or not. My love cannot hold its tongue. Above us in the towering dome, rainbow galaxy turns, no longer staccato as with each butterfly alone and to itself, but joined in this slow-moving swirl of spheres to accompany the full-throated, undying voices of the dead.

ETHICAL INVESTING
FOR THE BLIND

A Plenary Session with The Tabernacle Choir

ALLOW me to thank the Institute of the Blind for its invitation to address your weekend conference—and to apologize for my absence because of a to-do in the city. When I speak in public it isn't true as Howe Street says that everybody listens. And I wonder this evening how many here will welcome a speech read aloud for me by a stand-in? Listen, don't let this voice-over of his distract you. He's still me, so trust what he has to say about investing with integrity. We hope to supplement your weekend by coalescing the options ahead of anyone interested in stocks. Who knows when a casual remark from the podium will afford a gainful opportunity? I've sailed to your island in the past and recall its restorative powers. Did you know there used to be oysters in the bay?

A housekeeping note. Please, no voice recorders, otherwise I'll have to set the dogs on you. A free recording will follow to benefit blind folks like yourselves who aren't present this evening but stuck in libraries. Or possibly not blind and driving to work. Sighted, maybe you have an unsighted friend who slipped you the CD—or some bootlegger knows your land line. Frankly, the problem is undue exploitation. I try to protect Hathaway Cascadia by reserving my quarterly gems for clients in non-shareable software. I'm told a Braille transcription will also be available—no worries about that one on e-bay.

Housekeeping aside I am happy to declare this evening's talk a willing donation of my notes on ethical investing. Prior to specific picks, we'll need to talk larger picture, which brings out the Pepsi in me. I promise a list of stocks before the room regroups for more strategizing. But first let me ask if this bay window doesn't make a tempting backdrop for plotting retirement. I'm winging it here. Who isn't a fan of yachts at anchor? Of a brassy sunset? Not that any of you is ready yet for retirement. Still, speculation in the leisure trade is sometimes worthwhile. It is *always* worthwhile for the shrewd investor itching to become a director.

Incidentally, as an occasional Buffet-hyped speaker I'm not against needy pirates selling copies of my talk. I would only encourage them to issue tax receipts as part of the swap. Dream on, I know. Warren Buffet, by the way—Warren Buffay, as he's affectionately known in the industry—while this oracle of Wahoo offers his shareholders pretty much standard rations, I hear he also spends time at the Wigwam Café talking to the humblest of them. No airs of entitlement. No upmarket tasting menu leaving his clients unsatisfied and feeling cheated. That old square with his appetite for ketchup and hash browns sits on a bigger fortune than he ever dreamed, yet he's free with it and with himself. Folks listen when he talks, pondering choices for the future.

Next to dying with dignity I'd suggest your hardest job is choosing investments. It's tempting to guess wrong. Not to get sanctimonious about filthy lucre but the sad tale of divided capitalism usually sprouts from a lack of self-control. From the prospect of our fellow Canadian Bernie Ebbers, now in an American prison, acquisition in the absence of accountability is what some whiz guys understand by a triple-A rating, it shreds their credibility.

I haven't forgotten lip-readers, by the way. To any deaf folks here undercover, *G-o-o-d-e-v-e-n-i-n-g* . . . as Alfred Hitchcock used to say, stepping into his plump shadow on screen. Forgive a geezer. Most of you are too young to remember the old gobbler in black and white, but I'm said to resemble him a little in my chins—which is why I've hired a slender understudy to make me look less. . . But, listen, to anyone reading my lips in Braille, so to speak. . . *D-o-n-'t-r-u-b-m-e-t-h-e w-r-o-n-g-w-a-y.*

I hear your groans. Excellent. This tells me you won't hold back at some annual shareholders' meeting should the Chairman and CEO think himself a clever fellow treating your shares as his. Diversify your portfolio, certainly, but guard your integrity. Vote your *own* shares because proxies always vote in concert with management and barely one director in two will earn your trust. A corporation headed up by a Silver Spoon is often blind to the real price of its earnings—and it profits at the expense of small investors. In fact benefiting at someone else's expense is typical of the inbred celebration our financial community reserves as its highest accolade for successful members.

Can I be blunt? A roast is the reason for my absence this evening. True. The stock market gang is roasting me downtown, and forced to choose between your conference and a fundraiser for kidneys I felt obliged to choose the fundraiser. At the moment I'm being served up like a leg of mutton for the after-dinner amusement of ticket-holders. The custom at these events is for self-satisfied roasters to witter on before it's the roastee's turn. Most of their fat-jokes I've heard before. No, my investment legacy *isn't* in yoga or the one-block diet . . . and it isn't in horror shows like derivatives or insider-trading a lot of them swear by. Or in pump-and-dump moose pasture.

In our profession, to say creative accounting has been a sewer is an insult to sewage.

At Hathaway Cascadia we put our cards on the table. None of this vest-holding rife in boardrooms of the nation, or bet-hedging familiar to financial media forecasters in pink ties who love to be loved. Listen to *them* crowing at the podium, their accountability to shareholders zero, weather vanes who're never wrong since no one remembers the last way they pointed, swinging in four directions at once, telling you what you want to hear and nothing you don't already know.

At HC we call their bluff. Our own conduct at the table—and be warned, friends, even ethical investing can sometimes feel like a game—is responsible to a fault. The fault we're responsible to, by trying to avoid it, is the absence of transparency. The twin towers of results-based capitalism are still secrecy and dishonesty. Apples on Wall and Bay Streets go just as bad as our apples regularly do on Howe. Trumped-up figures will deceive us when we fail to examine our windfall profits. Nothing not earned comes sorted or untainted and it's an illusion to think you can divide up derivatives to hide a poor performance. Any forensic review of your books will eventually sort out the fiddle.

I notice you've slotted me into this evening's agenda under *Ethical Investing for the Blind*. I wonder if this doesn't sound patronizing—you know, principled investing made to seem a niche interest? I'm not sure my recommendations would differ for deaf drummers or even jockeys of female persuasion. I love sharing good news with anyone open to an honest hallelujah. My inflated label, by the way, The Tabernacle Choir, is a stage name I've made no attempt to acquire the domain for . . . it'd be like trying to buy up Vera Lynn or The Ode to Joy.

It popped up twenty-five years ago when I made the mistake of enthusiastically quoting a line to support a modest and unorthodox stock I was touting. *Mine eyes*, I wrote, a bar or two over the top, *have seen the glory of the coming of the Lord*. Youthful hyperbole though honestly meant. A financial columnist on a slow day happened to pick up on my prophecy, in hope of ridiculing my earnestness, and advised his readers that if they enjoyed listening to warhorses like "The Battle Hymn of the Republic" they should subscribe to the newsletter of a young blowhard who apparently entertained aspirations to sing with The Tabernacle Choir.

The name stuck. In fact, I helped it stick when my recommendation transformed itself into a pillar of gold and helped grow a small Brazilian firm into what one later weather vane called "portfolio paradise." For more than two decades Hathaway Cascadia has enjoyed an annual return on investments of 15.2%. With our emphasis on ethical profits we've managed to attract loyalty unmatched by other funds—where, as you might know, a one-time yield of 12% is considered the cat's pyjamas. I trust I have this last figure right. I don't want to undervalue those in striped suits. Managing any fund is tricky, including ours, though I seldom scratch more than numbers on an envelope. I then make sure to sing my choices loudly. At HC you won't find some shadowy CEO hiding backstage in Reno or the Cayman Islands.

Are there any questions before I go on?

None? Then let me ask you one. How is the weekend going so far? Any canoodling?

They used to call it canoodling. Some of you might remember it as "copping a feel." I guess I shouldn't talk incorrectly but don't the blind have an enviable reputation for sensitive touch? The dream once of a nerdy adolescent like me was to be felt up by a blind girl.

Let the volume of groans be noted. Good, excellent.

Just bear in mind Slim here has no choice but to read these asides without comment. The point worth making, I think, is it's well-known how the lopsided development of other senses in the blind compensates for your lack of visual stimulation. And you know how to *suffer* these asides because you're instinctively deferential.

Excellent . . . I think I even heard *shame on you!*

Hold on though. Chubby isn't finished.

I mouth off like this to challenge you, because in my world you'll hear a lot of so-called expert advice. Money is "blind," you'll hear, but not investors. The fact is you *are* blind and have no choice in the matter. Experts will impart all sorts of gibberish. If I go on to tell you, let's say, visually challenged people have a distinct talent for Braille because they actually "see" what they touch . . . you know, the way they—you— instinctively know a five-dollar bill from a fifty— . . .

Splendid. Your groans have gained choral status.

But wait, be patient. It's patience that lets us snub old capitalist thinking with its own chestnuts to find gems worth . . . worthy of your investment pursuit. If you're easily offended and expect to be a victim, maybe look forward to becoming a victim, you'll suffer moral exhaustion and even penury. Victimization in the stock market should be avoided—self-evidently so—but is it also self-evident down there where the sun don't shine? What's the origin of those gems? The truth is companies victimize underground miners every day. Full disclosure is associated more often with oncologists than with publicly traded companies.

Never buy shares in companies with "Resources" or "Capital" in their names. Also avoid businesses named "Fund," "Mining," or "Dynasty." Similarly, corporations calling themselves "Associates," "Products"—and especially "Systems." Ditto "Minerals," "Pharmaceuticals," "International," "Corp.," "Energy," "Income," "Communications," "Entertainment," "Drilling," "Cable," "Service" or "Petroleum." You don't want "Equity" or "Advantage" in your portfolios either. And tread warily in the generic indexes of "Limited," "Inc.," and "Group."

You can rest easy though with Hathaway Cascadia. We're an old-fashioned fund—marrying your money to lifelong stock instead of shacking it up with fly-by-night subsidiaries.

But I mock our earnestness. By naming names I hope to recommend whistle-blowing as the approved noise of ethical capitalism. I believe most of you appreciate the importance of having an alarm system in place—I see lots of guide dogs at their ease ready to warn you off a bad fall... *W-o-o-f!*

As unsuspecting investors you'll need to keep your ears perked. You require the foresight of skeptics with your inner eye fixed on something more than a graph of glitzy returns. I call it the broader spreadsheet, warning us against profiting offshore without due caution. Profiting anywhere, really, where regulations don't work because the regulators have no principles.

Consider this. You took the ferry across to profit from this weekend. To stroll in the sea- and forest-air and perhaps be taken for a speedboat ride. And while this lodge might be a splendid place for a conference on financial planning, for welcoming our panel of experts to lead your breakout sessions, you're just as interested in listening to what guests who share your disability have to say about waterskiing. Am I wrong? I wonder if some of you might be a little *too* fascinated by risk? You actually hope to get rich fast and wonder if the experts up here will be undue fuss-budgets. You're already wondering how long this speaker with the funny name, who hasn't even bothered to show up, is going to drone on from his pulpit.

You're on the right path. Skepticism, as the rabbi said to the rabbit, is your rehearsal for the fox.

But hold on, I've forgotten to welcome the foxes. I probably know some of you. Experts in your fields, wizards, last-word people of remarkable persuasiveness. Naturally, this isn't for you, you're sexual intellectuals, awaiting the breakout sessions to have the final say after Yours Truly finally shuts up. Top-of-your-class planners, you guys and gals, CFPs, PFPs,

RFPs, CLUs, FMAs, CFAs, CIMs, not to forget the FCSIs and the Chartered Professional Strategic Wealth specialists. All excellent pension persons, reputable financial advisers, eminent analysts, and chartered investors of hard-earned money who, of course, know where to put it. Bon appetit! Vive le retirement! We're all sexual intellectuals, aren't we? Fucking know-it-alls?

Pardon my French. You didn't hear that. Blame my impromptu mouth. I confess wanting to put some distance between myself and fellow foxes. Otherwise don't all of us end up vocalizing from the same zoo? Where the feeding frenzies of vultures and other corporate predators are de rigueur—bulls up, bears down, pork bellies soaring and Trojan horses lurking? It's no wonder, when Bernie Madoff spoke, he sounded like a zookeeper with a shovel. It *is* a zoo, the market, not to mention an aquarium with Bottom Feeders and Loan Sharks.

By the way, the Two Bernies? Our CEO poster faces for False Financial Reporting? They make you wonder if it doesn't seem more than copy-cattish how often capitalism ends up in mating pairs: Coke and Pepsi, Simon and Garfunkel, Shock and Awe. For what it's worth, and at HC we're always interested in value, I think of myself as *outside* the consorting zoo. Not quite a fox—maybe a guide dog. These Labs and golden retrievers I see at your feet ... I have a sneaking sense of kinship with the retrievers. For their colour, you understand, the both of us worth our weight in ... *patience*. Well-trained, unrattled in crisis, and we get you safely home. In a word, incorruptible. Am I allowed to go on? I avoid options, decline bonuses, have no faith in free shares or preferred dividends—and, you'll hear it whispered, I am notorious among CEOs for considering my salary a toxic asset.

I exaggerate only a tad. If my idiosyncrasies help to convince folks of Hathaway Cascadia's self-discipline, they also keep me at my desk fifteen hours a day. Poring over figures

DAMAGES

and eating potato chips. I won't invest in tech stocks. I live in the same Burnaby bungalow I have for thirty years. I'm accountable for every recommendation I make—even when markets go south.

And they will again.

For any of you interested in fiscal integrity, for those who can tell the difference between junk bonds and fair-trade coffee beans, full disclosure avoids fabrication. Maybe jail-time. As a fund manager I'm open only to opportunities I can live with and talk about. I could no more invest in a black hole than talk to an empty chair. My ethical investor is characterized as a regular guy or gal attuned to profits flowing in two directions at one time. You can't be an unfair trader in Guatemala and a good citizen at home.

I'm sometimes quoted as saying how I talk to myself as an analyst is the way I perform as trader. It sounds like something I might say and now wish I had. My line is still that I take satisfaction in the dutiful doing of my job. Sniffing out realistic price-earnings ratios, flushing out over-performing stocks, detecting high-pitched warnings no one else seems to hear or care about over at the zoo, and—to toot my whistle a little more—taking pride in my bland way when it comes to getting clients in and out of tight spots.

Shall I go on—ad-libbing for your possible profit?

I enjoy the leeway granted a guru-fogey like myself. Dogged in my enthusiasm for good securities and sustainable profit margins—hackles up at Ponzi schemes, glossy brochures, penny pitches . . . growling when my investors need to be warned off a misstep into hedges . . . also known as bubbles, credit default swaps . . . yes, in fact, all that widespread doo-doo lying around in the Promised Land of independent wealth, luxury cruises, marble bathrooms, three-star eateries, Rolex watches, encrusted slingbacks, Range Rovers, five-star bonking inns, Botox and pussy waxes, highlights-lowlights-crimping-and-extensions, hot tubs, arugula, side-by-side baby-carriages, tummy tucks, charter schools not to mention graduation breasts, fuck buddies, green roofs, 'erbs, designer gowns, warming and cooling drawers, "it" handbags, bamboo cabinets, *moss-coloured braces*, for heaven's sake, tasting menus, pedicures, Boston Whalers and foie gras, sipper and gulper wines, condo kings—hey, let's not forget fertility yoga...

Listen, you didn't hear this outburst from me. It's *him* now, freelancing. Just because theatre folk include improv in their subsidized agenda doesn't mean we have to listen to its self-satisfied preening. A non-socialist knows better than to upset himself with shopping lists. *My* address to your conference applauds balance and fair play, not wilfulness. In fact I stand on the side of civil citizens—we used to call ourselves good burghers—at arm's length from big government and minor moaners both. Isn't this still the definition of a non-socialist? Self-reliance? Self-determination?

Not hijacking the agenda by spouting off-the-cuff.

Be assured I know enough to know a stand-in isn't likely to read word-for-word what I've given him. Feel free at any time to vote him off your island.

Mind you, capitalism can be just as excessive as off-Broadway. Take a roast. A roast means you're finally important enough to be fair game for other burghers in the guise of a fundraiser. Getting roasted, the highest aspiration of my own bunch of players, has never been a goal of mine. Most of the time it's a license to get drunk and slag the guest of honour. The saving feature of a roast, aside from helping out dialysis, CAT scans or homeless horses, is you can write it off. It's part of the professional gravy train. Capitalists are entitled to their entitlements. But a successful roast is a rare occasion. You'll find most roastees make the mistake, as the banquet for them draws to a climax—as mine is doing right now—of choosing to roast the roasters. This is current roaster-practice and a stubborn strand in thinking you've finally made it—hard to resist, frankly, when you're sorely tempted to return insults. Like some office party gone bad, it's the chance to say up front what's usually reserved for behind the scenes.

You'll want to avoid this self-indulgence at your own roasts.

There's a higher calling. Let me confess to you what I'm about to tell them, since it's my turn to respond to all their cheap shots and bad aims, the ethical investor, me, who supposedly saw the light of the Lord only after seeing the shine of copper in a South American nation—where, of course, miners came cheap. At last I have a chance to respond to fairytales like this one from that triumphant CEO who knows all about cheap labour in South American mines—i.e. no matter how much of his gigantic income he now turns over to Mother Teresa and Brother Bubba, no matter how often he gilds his legend—

But I'll begin by telling them something else. Listen to me turn the other cheek:

> *My friends, I have a problem standing here before you this evening: after so long in business, decades longer than most of you, to play* myself *this evening the truth is I'd have to audition. So instead of trying to act responsibly I've decided to* roast *myself. I'm going to stand here and make a bigger fool of me than you have.*
>
> *Housekeeping aside let me say to the doubters among you how much I've long revelled in the coincidence of my reputation as The Tabernacle Choir . . . because, as I recall, at the time of my first investing in our hugely successful credit union for poor women in Brazil, which made HC what it is today, I was already on to my third, or possibly fourth wife, and the Mormon angle was one I could successfully brand. A good fit for sure. Unfortunately, as you can appreciate, such serendipity is no longer rampant at my age. Nowadays, I'm*

looking into opportunities to invest in a business called
Feels on Wheels. . . It's proving an ethical nightmare for
an opportunist like me.

This little turn earns me guffaws of recognition—and possibly it's true they think, the serial wives . . . I see it in their nudgy winks to one another over tiramisus. Just as they've accepted the sleazy copper mine in my legendary portfolio, so too the myth of a young Lothario.

. . . Yes, along with Mild Mining Myles—and who can't
wait to roast Myles with a peck of pickled peppers—I'm
so happy to be with you tonight supping on rack of lamb
and Mouton Cadet.

I pronounce it "cadet" as in sailor. Say no more. All these head honchos and social nabobs are instantly reminded of The Tab's daily diet—long rumoured to be Wendy fare and diet Pepsis in a cluttered Dunsmuir office of overworked interns called Ricky and Prudence. And listen to them chuckle at The Tab checking off his milestones. They love a cult figure to play up his milestones, in my case the ethical smarty pants who's collected more milestones than he once did bottle caps. These seem to round out our young players' notions of old promoters' progress on their Road to Riches! *Those guys?* Martini lunches at The Georgia! Cigar-chomping up The Roof! Oh, so outdated now, the Tab's lichen-covered markers—his high-stake putts—no, his salmon-trolling with Bob Hope . . . *yes.* The Tabernacle Yacht!

You folks take my point. Most of my milestones are smoke and mirrors. They sum up some parallel career that never was. Roasting needs markers to create the bawdy character everyone can agree is worth everyone's good-bad opinion. "Oh, that Tabernacle Choir, he's quite a character!" Who *doesn't* like to be remembered as a rascal? Don't all of us hope to

become a legend of our own some day, the freedom to be in two places at one time, the space—outside the rigged game of market fundamentalism—to be ourselves? A somebody in the needle's eye and a somebody in the public eye . . . loaded and philanthropic both?

But this isn't what they want to hear from a cult figure. They want more milestones. They're enjoying themselves. *Read my lips*, I want to tell them, *look at the big picture. Is the path you're on leading in the right direction? You know, to self-possession instead of a selfish choice of ethics . . . ?*

Listen, my weekend friends. Your own milestones will come soon enough, and whether your dog relieves himself on them, or you do, is a lot less important than whether you'll look back in discredit or with satisfaction at your progress. Who was in charge of who? Unsure of ourselves, it's hard to know how far any of us has come, or to what lengths we'll go, until the fat man sings. I'm speaking here for anyone who has ever clipped or ever will clip a coupon and neglects to read between the lines of their Annual Report. How do we know the numbers published in a financial statement are what they seem if we forget to test them against real-life figures? CEOs go to jail for turning a blind eye to accounts cooked by their sous chefs. Yet *not* to jail for plotting their own half-baked returns from strip mining, clear-cutting, sweatshops, dollar stores, gem exploitation, contracting out, Walmart, child labour, globalization, teak logging, bulletin board companies, selling short, salting assay certificates, illegal trading, leaky condos and under-researched drugs, over-subscribed options, bonus-pimping—yes ma'am, pretty much everything now known as the free market—no disclosure, no oversight—

I have a feeling Loose Lips is blowing me off-course again. I myself prefer to caution seed shareholders in non-categorical fashion against conniving in malfeasance. It's easy to call a spade a spade . . . I prefer instead the bay window. Is this tranquil view not less off-putting than a self-important checklist? You needn't reach my age to discover figures in the landscape will sometimes alert us—better than figures on balance sheets, on milestones, even backs of envelopes—*to a storybook opportunity.*

Let me appraise for you the transparency of such an option. Behind us a large fieldstone fireplace, then through the window and across the goose-down lawn I find myself looking past drooping cedars to a swimming beach and sailboats at anchor. Lifting above these are waterfront cottages and a mountain forest . . . oh, and right in front here, at the end of the long dock? . . . the lodge's speedboat.

I know it's the boat that interests you.

But the scenery, you ask. What's all this worth to someone who can't see any of it? Well, I'm just saying that if we wanted to make a judgement call on the scene *as an investment*—in this lodge, say, as a practicable prospect, should it happen to incorporate some day and go public—then the ethical return on investing in this green world, with its resort pedigree and notable charms, *would appear to be sound.* Yes?

Ah, but how can we know without closer scrutiny whether this seductive view of things is what it seems? Investing offshore is frequently a risk for investors seeking ethical security. Offshore is notorious for the absence of rules and regulations. Which not surprisingly is why infamous Mild Myles Mining—as we all know and love him for the integrity of his drill-core samples—*loves* offshore. Offshore is bound up in successes we've mined for decades, centuries, on behalf of colonial burghers like MMM.

You could throw the book at Myles and he'd still come up a promoter. Of ballparks, food parks, graveyards—you name it, any fable to enhance his local reputation as a purveyor of honest value. Of profit to himself, certainly, despite its penny issue.

Be skeptical of milestones recollected fondly. This island, for example, the destination in our parents' and grandparents' days of dance cruises out of Coal Harbour...thousands disembarking each summer and waltzing across spillway between lagoon and bay, to a hotel over there, its ballroom and croquet pitches now vanished, together with lawns and honeysuckle sweeping down to a flooding tide, picnics in the sand...

Spare us, Twinkle Toes. Besides all that, what else aren't we seeing in this wider frame? Besides the poached oysters and delinquent orchestra? The kaput resort? The salmon no longer swishing home—

...Yes, Mr. Fleck?...Did you all hear that? "How many accountants does it take to cook the books?" *Okaaay*...and repeating Mr. Fleck's punchline for the aurally challenged like myself. . . "One-to-fudge-the-crab-cakes—three-to-waylay-Gordon-Ramsay!"

541

Uh, thank you, Mr. Fleck. Very good, yes. You experts better be on your toes here for Mr. Fleck!

But first let me ask everybody to take a closer look at those boats at anchor. Those ones, yes. Some of the yachts are mastless and have trees growing out of oil drums on deck. What's up with that? Can your investment adviser be counted on to talk to you about scenes like this one? About the craft at anchor? About what's going on behind those tacked-up curtains?

Listen, my friends, what's going on out there is squatting. Uh huh. Squatting is going on. My sources tell me boats kicked out of free moorage in False Creek have recently dropped anchor here. Their tampon applicators and plastic bags are floating ashore. Beer cans, Styrofoam cups, water bottles and condom wrappers, shotgun casings, vegetable peels. Onboard toilets have lifted fecal counts in the bay. Hypodermic needles are washing up on the beach. *Hallelujah!* These city squatters are landing and demanding fresh water from cottage hoses to wash down their hulls. They're peeing against garbage cans and threatening now-grumpy residents. Should one of these boats start to sink, who exactly mucks up the leaking oil? The owner's vamoosed. We're left with floating, filthy ...

Honestly, this craven logging of malfeasance isn't my intention. The interest of a responsible fund director is not in speculation and hearsay, prattle off the top of his head. He could wish! It's in a thoughtfully composed prospectus clients need to assess before deciding whether or not to invest in an offshore company. Who is in charge of regulating the foreshore? Are there laws in place? Could the squatters be counted on to regulate themselves?

I hope you're starting to get the balanced view ethical investing demands. Rehearse your options, check out the terrain. Exactly what sort of dividends would you be banking?

We'd also need to know if there are any responsible boat people or only pirates. Potential taxpayers or just polluters. Would any of them volunteer to cut the lodge's lawn in exchange for fresh water? Or does this bay remain a paradise beyond island bylaws, a federal jurisdiction with no enforcement?

In other words, maybe the facts behind this idyllic scene are less forlorn than they appear and offer you an opportunity after all. The lodge is a charitable institution—yet the setting makes it potentially profitable as a resort incorporated as a public company. What are its chances of making money in the future? Who's in charge of subsidiary rights? What effect would degradation in the bay have on syndicating holidays or marketing adjunct condos? On marketing water sports, a green lifestyle, oyster regeneration? Or the locale for a film option ...

These are questions any good financial adviser would ask on your behalf. But the ethically inclined agent might go further.

He or she would recommend investment here *only if the following conditions were met*. If the staff received more pay. If culinary choices in the cafeteria dramatically improved through the hire of an executive chef. If the deterioration of rooms and outbuildings could be turned around and made the model of an island lifestyle. Similarly, I hear, the spotty catering for weddings—if the desire of couples to marry in this beautiful setting could be more widely exploited and profited from. Why not? Outstanding issues would then begin to fall into place, like a decision to restructure management in order to assure a decent return on investment, regardless of any future spinoffs including time-shares.

Well-paying guests could finally be counted on to tip the balance.

This sounds like a corporate plot, but it's really about the character of accountability. I would venture to say the bottom line is no more and no less than the kind of conduct acceptable to Mr. Fleck's master chef Mr. Ramsay.

Blunt but right.

Should such an opportunity open up, Hathaway Cascadia would welcome it warmly into our portfolio, notwithstanding the potential risk of uncertain moorage rights and the blind losing weekend subsidies and midweek subventions. There's always a downside. But likely you'd all be eager to participate as investors, confident in the integrity of this new, vetted company with the strong upside potential you've just learned about. We're not talking some penny dreadful hustled up via word-of-mouth by a downtown shell company. No sir, it would sell itself because you trusted the prospectus and valued our product.

Wait though. I refuse to bite any hand that extends itself. Which is why I declined to accept a fee this evening—leaving me free to look into our host's estate and talk openly about it as a case study on your behalf. Believe me, nothing more. My intention is simply to make clear how nothing in ethical investing is black and white—frustratingly, it's often quite grey. We all make mistakes. I alone am responsible for my share, more often than not made in a collaboration with convenience. No matter the good will and living wages all around for plantation workers, carpet weavers, denim stitchers—trust me, any security can go bad. The world of stocks, like the world of oil, balances on a spade edge of faith, while innocuous-seeming profits turn out to be the wrong kind.

There are known knowns, things we know that we know, like embezzlers and weather vanes. We also know there are known unknowns. Like milestones down the road. Which is to say there are things we know we don't know. We count on these no more than to give us a little panache. And finally there are unknown unknowns—the ones we don't know we don't know … beloved of evangelical funds, I suppose, though not ours … *those despicable self-righteous death merchants unfit to—*

Forgive me.

The risk I run in turning over the platform to an actor is his impulsive mouth. For sure our CD will need a good edit before donating it to the Crane Library. You can be confident, however, the buck stops with me. I alone am—

> *… coming like the glory of morning on the wave,*
> *Wisdom to the mighty… Succour to the brave…*

I used to have a voice. This one sounds like Wheels on Wheels.

> *Mine eyes have seen the glory—*

Oh, my understudy, spare us the musical rendition. Let us get down to a few success stories, shall we?

Keath Fraser won the Chapters / Books in Canada First Novel Award for his 1995 novel *Popular Anatomy*. His stories and novellas have been published in many anthologies in Canada and abroad. Collections of his short fiction include *Taking Cover* and *Telling My Love Lies*. The volume *Foreign Affairs* was short-listed for a Governor General's Award and won the Ethel Wilson Fiction Prize. His novella *Charity* recently launched a new genre series from Biblioasis. He is the author of *As For Me and My Body*, a memoir of his friend Sinclair Ross; and of *The Voice Gallery*, a narrative of his far-flung travels among broken voices. The royalties from his international best-selling anthologies *Bad Trips* and *Worst Journeys: The Picador Book of Travel* were given to Canada India Village Aid (CIVA), the late NGO founded by George Woodcock. Keath Fraser lives in Vancouver and his papers are held in the Thomas Fisher Library at the University of Toronto.

MIX
Paper from
responsible sources
FSC® C100212

Printed by Imprimerie Gauvin
Gatineau, Québec